Emily

Eva *Ellen*

Under the Almond Trees

Linda Ulleseit

San Jose, California

2014

Also by Linda Ulleseit:

Wings Over Tremeirchson (a flying horse novella)

On a Wing and a Dare

In the Winds of Danger

Under a Wild and Darkening Sky (coming 2014)

ISBN-13: 978-1499252200
ISBN-10: 149925220X

Flying Horse Books
San Jose, California

Email: flyinghorsebooks@gmail.com
Website: http://Ulleseit.wordpress.com

Cover design by Tirzah Goodwin
http://acleverwhatever.blogspot.com

For my father

Chapter 1: New York 1848-1849
Ellen Rand Perkins

I commit my first overt act of rebellion at the age of twenty-one when I insist to my mother that I must marry my cousin, Jacob Perkins.

"Mama, I have loved him my entire life." I stand square in front of her, shoulders back, feet in a wide stance instead of knees demurely together. My chin juts firmly. I'm sure she sees it as unattractive.

The late summer sunlight lances in through the window, a spear to her chest. She perches in her usual spot on the settee, as always prepared to leap to my father's beck and call. It's a hard habit to break even after seven years of widowhood. Her shoulders slump, and for a moment it seems the shaft of sunlight has wounded her. She purses her lips and sets her embroidery hoop beside her, eyes drooping with sadness and disappointment when she looks up at me. It's not the sunlight that's hurt her. A good mother must try once more, so of course she does. "There is a fine son of a friend…"

"I want only Jacob."

"He is your cousin," she begins, twisting her hands in her lap.

But I've heard it all before and rattle off the litany of rebuttals before she can voice her tired objections. "He's the son and heir of Papa's favorite brother, the Congressman. Jacob will have no trouble finding work. And I love him."

Mama drops her gaze to her lap, where she stills her hands. I know she is thinking of successful bankers, successful merchants, successful anybodies rather than my cousin. I also know she misses my father most when one of us, usually me, taxes her. Papa left her with four children: a student, an heir, a delight, and a rebel. I've always known my role among my siblings, but this is the first time I've held my ground. Then Mama sighs, and I know I have her.

Jacob and I marry in November of 1848, but after two blissful months together, the world intrudes. Word of gold discovered in California reaches New York. Cholera rages through our city. Everyone seems to be rushing about in a dither, either panicking or packing. People predict 1849 will change the face of the country forever. Maybe I am selfish to care only about my beloved and our life together.

Just before five o'clock on a frigid January day, my husband arrives home from the office. The solid front door clicks shut on a howling wind that rattles the windowpanes in our small flat, closing out the world of New York's Lower East Side, where increasing numbers of immigrants are spreading cholera to us all. I know Jacob isn't terribly happy working for my Uncle Moses at his newspaper, but the *New York Sun* is becoming quite popular and I pray Jacob will find an aspect of the business he enjoys.

The stove has been burning all day, and the oxtail soup smells delicious. I wipe my hands on my apron and peek at the boiled leg of mutton, which is almost done. I look over my kitchen, my domain, with satisfaction. Untying the apron, I wipe my hands and quickly smooth my skirt. In the hall, I pause by the mirror to tuck a few strands of light brown hair back into place before hurrying into the front room to greet my husband properly, with a smile and a kiss.

His expression halts me. He stands with his back against the closed front door, face filled with dread. He wears his suit like one unaccustomed to business. His slicked dark brown hair is neat and his mustache combed, but his expression is grim as he puts his hat on the rack. Why would he fear coming home?

"Jacob?"

"Ellen." He says my name softly, his eyes warm with love even as his mouth tightens into a line. He walks to his big chair, perching on the red velvet cushion as if it were a hard bench. "Come, sit. We must talk."

Clasping my hands to avoid wringing them, I sit in one of the carved Victorian chairs my mother presented to us upon our marriage. The ornate table clock strikes five, its stentorian tones echoing importantly before fading to silence.

"I have come across an amazing opportunity, my love," he says without directly looking at me. "The *Apollo* leaves New York for California in two weeks, and Lucian and I plan to be aboard her."

"Lucian? He's talked you into this?" My sister must be having a similar conversation with her husband at this very moment. I'm sure she would have told me had she known sooner.

"Cousin Joseph's going, too. He set up the whole thing."

Our cousin has a taste for adventure. That's what Mama says, anyway. I always think of Joseph as reckless. His father has the money and the ship to make this adventure happen. Suddenly I realize he means to go alone. Stricken, I ask, "Jacob, why?"

He finally looks at me, face etched with misery. "Ellen, I want to give you everything, but I want to earn it. This is my chance to make a future for us, independent of the family. I would bring you with me, my love, but California is a wild place. Let me go first and I shall send for you once we are settled."

I nod, but my mind whirls. What will I do without him? Jacob's been part of my world since we were small. My sister, Coelia, has her children to keep her busy, but I'll be alone.

"It's not so bad," he says. "Mama Perkins will relish your company. I can see you placed with her before I leave if you wish. Or with Coelia if you prefer. I'm sure she'd appreciate help with the children."

I shudder at the idea of living with Coelia and my three small nieces and nephew. My sister, the graduate from Rutgers Female Institute, who studied to no purpose other than to marry and have children. No, moving back with Mama and my younger sister, L'Amie, is the better choice. They have lived with my Uncle Benjamin since the death of my father. Uncle Benjamin's household with his wife and three children will reabsorb me as if I had never left to get married.

"Jacob, must you?" I ask, trying to keep the pleading tone out of my voice. "I will miss you so!"

I love him even more when he doesn't remind me that his word is law, like Lucian does to Coelia. Instead, he folds me in his arms. I cling to him, memorizing the smell of his cologne and the feel of his wool coat against my cheek. He murmurs in my ear, "As will I, my love. I will send for you the moment we have secured appropriate lodging in San Francisco."

In the next two weeks I object quietly, then vociferously, then with tears. But come sailing day Jacob walks up the plank to board the *Apollo*, my cousin Joseph and brother-in-law Lucian striding with him, handsome and confident. The three brash young men turn more than one head in the crowd with their smiles and camaraderie. The wind teases their coat flaps and hair, and I want to run to Jacob and button his coat and smooth his hair. I resist. Coelia can't bear to witness the sailing, and has stayed home with the children, but Mama and I watch the tugboat pull the *Apollo* away from the dock, and wave madly, hoping our men folk can see. The bitter bite of January drives us indoors before the ship is out of sight, but I will never forget the image of *Apollo's* belching stacks as she works up speed and diminishes with distance.

I spend the rest of January moping with my embroidery near a window in Uncle Benjamin's parlor but never picking up the needle. Instead I stare at raindrops smattering the glass. A small one quivers until another small drop joins it. Fused into one, it slowly moves down the pane, gathering drops and moving faster until it's hurtling down the outside wall. And my gaze returns to the top of the window to find another drop to watch.

A raucous clatter drags my attention away from the window. With a sigh, I prepare for the imminent intrusion of my two young cousins. My own children will never be so wild, running through their house as if it were a gymnasium! But it's Uncle Benjamin's house, and his sons. They run into the parlor, shirts awry and suspenders trailing, screeching as if being pursued by a demon. Today the demon is my sister, L'Amie. At fifteen she should know better, but she was Papa's delight and remains Mama's baby.

"L'Amie!" I snap. "They are wild enough without your encouragement!"

"Oh, Ellen, you are so stuffy," she complains. She scrunches up her pretty face, graced with a petite nose rather than my own hawked beak, and emits one more horrible roar that sends the boys scampering from the room. L'Amie doesn't follow. Turning to me, she says, "I shan't be an old stuffy married lady at twenty-one."

I tighten my lips into a disapproving line.

"I will be a doctor," she declares. She throws back her head, dark hair falling to the middle of her back. The ribbon that pulls it back off her face has come untied and straggles amidst the glossy waves. Her back straightens, and her chin juts out in an unattractive manner.

I allow my laugh to be loud and unladylike, caused no doubt by her earlier insult. "A lady physician? I don't think women will come that far in our lifetime, sister."

Rather than make her angry, my words seem to inspire her. Eyes alight with passion, she grabs my arm and says, "Oh, but we can make it happen! Did I tell you I met a girl the other day whose mother was at last summer's convention in Seneca Falls?"

"The women's convention?" My brow furrows. "Does Mama know you're consorting with those people?"

"It was fabulous, Ellen! Women from everywhere were there, and some men, too. They talked about women in professional careers, and even voting. A women's rights group meets at my friend's house. Will you come with me tomorrow night?"

My sister may be young and impetuous, but she's intelligent. She knows the immigrant women moving into the Lower East Side don't have the advantages our family connections give us. Women like our serving girl work long hours for our family then go home to toil for their own. "L'Amie," I say, laying a hand on her arm, "I appreciate the sentiment, but these women are not...respected. Do you understand?" At her blank stare, I try again. "Papa indulged you, maybe too much. You think everyone is wonderful, and that they all like you. I'm not sure these women are the right ones for you to follow."

"Stuffy," my sister huffs, but her eyes glitter and she won't look at me. Instead, she runs from the room roaring. Giggles and running feet tell me the boys have been waiting for her in the hall. At least she's taking their noise away from me.

I return to my contemplation of raindrops on the window, but my own reflection in the rain-streaked glass intrudes. I am a happily married woman. Yes, my husband is absent, but the state of matrimony contents me. Nonetheless I am interested in the politics of L'Amie's new friends, however reluctant I am to admit it. The notion of women voting for elected officials secretly thrills me. I fear I won't be able to keep my curiosity from my sister and thereby encourage her.

Two weeks linger as if they are months. I grow tired of the constant worry that is my companion. Besides, how long can I pine for word from Jacob? The *Apollo* will take months to get to San Francisco. I seek L'Amie in the parlor, where she is stabbing some fabric with a needle. I think she's trying to embroider.

"So isn't your women's meeting tonight?" I ask her.

She looks up with joyous stars in her eyes. "Will you finally come with me?"

"Yes," I tell her. "Someone needs to keep an eye on you."

By the time a weak spring sun spreads across New York, L'Amie and I have attended a handful of meetings and openly declared our support for women's rights. Mama remains silent on the matter, only giving us an occasional pained smile when we speak of voting someday. At these meetings I have met a handful of married women, two whose husbands are ardent supporters of women's rights. I am sure my Jacob will agree that women should have a voice in the running of the country, especially in as wild a place as California.

As the first heat of summer begins to bake the city, Mama's pained smiles turn to frowns as she realizes the cause is no passing fancy for L'Amie and I. It is a family dinner that brings the matter to open discussion.

Uncle Benjamin sits at the head of the long cherry wood table with my aunt at the foot. Mama's place is on one side, flanked by L'Amie and me. The boys usually sit on the opposite side, but tonight my brother Joey and Cousin Henry are visiting from college. Coelia and her three are here, too. The younger children have been banished to the kitchen. I face Cousin Henry across the bowl of turnips. Coelia is in the middle, and our brother across from L'Amie.

At eighteen and nineteen, Henry and Joey think they are old enough to bestow their opinions upon us, and have been doing so throughout the first few courses. The conversation slows for a moment when Aunt Eveline rings for the sixth course and the serving girl brings in a platter of fish. That's when L'Amie speaks.

"Ellen and I have been attending meetings for women's rights," she begins. Mama's fork clatters to her plate, and I can see her hand shake. "We are working with a temperance union." L'Amie's eyes are bright as an evangelist.

"Temperance!" laughs my brother. "You'll find no supporters at our school!"

Henry laughs too, but has the grace to stifle it. "Not many men at that meeting, I'll wager," he says to L'Amie.

"There are some," she insists.

"Men who value their partnership with a woman do not need to drink to gain power over them," I say.

Mama gasps. "Girls," she protests, with a glance at her brother.

Uncle Benjamin leans forward and pins me with the steely

eyes that make him a good businessman. "Are you saying, Ellen, that a man should never take a drink?"

"Some men cannot hold their liquor, Uncle," L'Amie says. Even to me she sounds too prim.

"Times are difficult for women," I say, warming to the topic. I intend a scholarly discussion that will end with the men in my family staunchly behind the issue of women's rights, but I forget with whom I am dealing.

"I cannot have a household full of rebellious girls, Mary," Uncle Benjamin warns, his stern gaze now focused on my mother.

"I am sorry, Benjamin," my mother says, interrupting me. "I thought this would pass, so I allowed it."

"How long have they been going to meetings?" Coelia asks. I wonder where her alliance lies. Her face is carefully neutral. I notice her hands resting on her stomach, where Lucian's parting gift grows.

Mama puts both hands in her lap, where I can see her tormenting a linen napkin between them. Her glare silencing me as I start to answer Coelia, she murmurs, "I shall speak with them after dinner."

The men talk among themselves for the remainder of the meal, discussing politics, prospects for gold in California, the cholera epidemic, anything that does not involve a woman.

As soon the serving girl clears the last dinner plate, Uncle Benjamin rises and leads his son and his nephew into the den, a world without womanly influence. There they will smoke cigars, sip cursed brandy, and discuss their flighty women.

My sisters and I follow Mama into the parlor. I settle into the seat by the window, where my embroidery has lain, largely forgotten, since January. Coelia sits near me, dropping heavily onto the settee, arranging her skirts neatly, and accepting a tiny cup of tea when Mama pours. I sip mine, but L'Amie leaves hers to get cold. She paces the room, waiting for Mama to speak. It's Coelia who speaks first, however.

"What were you thinking, L'Amie, to bring that up at dinner?" she demands.

"You don't support our cause, sister?" L'Amie turns on our eldest sister.

Coelia shakes her head, as if talking to a child. "I am busy with my household and my family, and worrying for my husband every day. I have no time for lost causes."

I bristle at her insinuation that I'm not worried for Jacob. "And does your worrying help, then?" I ask in as chill a tone as I can manage.

"What will Jacob think when he hears of your activities, Ellen?" Mama asks in a low tone. One of the grey strands in her hair has come loose from its knot and strays along her cheek. Her eyes are sad as they contemplate me.

"He loves me," I begin.

"Jacob is of our generation, Mama," L'Amie interrupts. "He will support his wife to build a better future for women."

I appreciate her effort to support me, but I'm tired of being interrupted. "I believe it is time to stand up for better conditions for women. Jacob and I will discuss this when we are reunited. Then, as now, it is our affair and no other's."

Mama looks at me, her eyes brimming with emotion. "I, too, know what it is like to lose a father young, and to be alone in a marriage. I am not unsympathetic to your ideas, but I ask you not to offend your uncle's hospitality by creating hostility at dinner?"

I nod, but L'Amie speaks first. "It is not worth my time to discuss reform with him. His views are a shame."

"What is a shame," Mama puts in, "is that Benjamin hurried away from the dinner table before cook had an opportunity to serve the almond cake."

Her eyes sparkle with humor and I know she has forgiven us as she always does. L'Amie and I rush to embrace her. I turn to my elder sister, curious. "Coelia, do you stand with us?"

"In spirit, I do. In actuality, my life is too busy to be running around attending meetings."

I'm content with this. She has her children, after all, to fill the lonely days, and one on the way to prepare for. I have only vivid terrors of storm swept ships lost at sea.

Summer fades to autumn, and Coelia gives birth to a baby girl. She has no way to send word to Lucian. As the days cool and the leaves turn, I spend more time watching for a letter or telegram than attending meetings. The *Apollo* is sailing around

Cape Horn, and Cousin Joseph is charged with setting her up in San Francisco as a floating store. Jacob and Lucian, of course, will head into the hills to look for gold. I hope they remember to send word first.

When it comes, late in October, I am both relieved and disappointed. The letter reads, *Have arrived. All well.* Four words after eight months?

I fret daily, waiting for the long letter with proclamations of undying love and a summons to reunite that I know will surely follow. Instead, in the middle of November I get a letter from Lucian. The courier places it in my hand and I close the front door. Still standing in the entry, I rip the envelope and let it drift to the floor. I am angry it's not from my husband. The single sheet flutters to join its envelope on the floor as I gasp in incomprehension at Lucian's terse words. I want more, but at the same time he's told me all.

Jacob killed in mining accident. My deepest condolences.

Chapter 2: New York 1851

Ellen Rand Perkins

Two and a half years after that telegram I find myself following L'Amie aboard the *Prometheus*, bound for California. I am clad head to toe in mourning black, and I cannot hold back memories of Jacob as he began his own trip to the gold fields. Having resisted this voyage as long as I could, and somewhat cheered by the brilliant autumn sun, I vow to try and make the best of it. Nonetheless, I cannot summon a smile to my face.

"Couldn't you have worn something more colorful?" my sister asks. She's dressed in a pretty frock of deep emerald green with an overcoat in a lighter shade. The sash and bow on her hat match her dress, of course, and she's a version of youthful anticipation.

"I am a widow," I say tersely. She knows of my love for

Jacob. I could not let my mourning go after the customary year. I may not ever let it go.

She sighs. "Do you think Mama will be waiting for us in San Francisco?"

"Mama and Lucian and Coelia will be there," I assure her over my doubts, "as will all the children, and Cousin Henry. It will be quite festive." We fall silent, I lost in gloom, she affected by my mood.

Steam hangs in the crisp October air as the departure whistle blows. Uncle Benjamin and Aunt Eveline have not come to see us off. I'm sure he is glad to be rid of us. A year after arriving in California, Lucian sent for Coelia and the children. I shudder to think I might have been awaiting Jacob's summons that long. My elder sister, eager to be reunited with her husband, did not delay. Mama went along to help with the four children, the littlest girl still a babe in arms. L'Amie, however, had not yet completed her schooling, so I stayed with her in New York, both of us ostensibly under Uncle Benjamin's watchful eye. In the year since, L'Amie and I have become rather outspoken on issues that plague our dear uncle. I fear we have quite worn out our welcome. Now we embark on the adventure of our lives, following the path of my greatest love.

I turn away from the ship's railing to follow L'Amie to our stateroom. A long hallway runs the length of the ship with twelve staterooms on either side. Ours adjoins that of a young married couple of our acquaintance, Mr. and Mrs. Brown. I'm sure Uncle Benjamin believes the Browns will be a stabilizing influence on L'Amie and me. I smile at the notion and busy myself unpacking as we get under way, engines rumbling gently below us.

The ship will take us to a new life, full of golden opportunities managed by Mama. At what point in a woman's life is she able to step out from under the reins of her mother and guide her own life? Mama would say when she marries. I've done that, and lost my husband. Mama crawled back to the bosom of her family when she lost Papa. She has always done what society expects. She's very proper and is determined that I learn to be.

"I won't waste this voyage in a stuffy stateroom," L'Amie declares, sailing forth with her luggage half-unpacked. "Let's take a turn on deck."

As the older sister, it's my duty to make sure our things are stowed properly, but I hesitate only a moment. "I'm coming," I call, and hurry after my sister.

Watching L'Amie greet strangers with ease, I'm very aware of my responsibility to fulfill Mama's role on this voyage, to keep L'Amie dependent on convention and family. I sigh deeply.

The glorious clear weather continues, and the moonlit evening is too pleasant to miss. The water before us ripples in a silver swath as one of the crew breaks out in a credible rendition of "Roll on Silver Moon." Mr. Brown surprises me with a deep baritone accompaniment, and before you know it the passengers are all singing. L'Amie has quite a good voice, but I sing softly so as not to scare people into diving overboard. When our self-styled song leader begins "Oh California," I wander to the far side of the ship. My past is in New York, and that includes Jacob. My future is in California without him, and my trepidation outshines my anticipation.

On the third day out, the ocean turns rough. L'Amie is almost immediately confined to her bunk with seasickness. While my stomach is queasy, I remain upright enough to help her sip the chicken broth that is suddenly quite in demand.

"Enough, Ellen," she fusses.

I attempt to distract her by discussing our favorite topic. "I wonder how Mrs. Anthony's lecture on abolition went last night?"

"And Mrs. Stanton on temperance the night before," L'Amie says, eyes bright with passion? Or with fever? "I'm so sorry we missed their talks! I was so looking forward to them!"

"Those women are so brave to take on the fight for women's rights as well as slaves' rights. I wish we could stay in New York and really do some good." I temper my tone so as not to overexcite my sister. Susan B. Anthony and Elizabeth Cady Stanton are working hard to ensure a better future for us, and we are shunted off to California where the news from New York will be months old by the time we hear it.

"No more broth, Ellen," she whines.

I ignore her and fill the spoon, lifting it to her mouth. "You must eat, dear heart. We have barely begun our adventure. You must get well!"

A sharp knock causes me to put down the bowl of soup. It's Mr. Brown.

"How is Miss Perkins?" he asks.

"Well enough to complain," I say with a smile. It's good of him to check in with us, since his own wife is also overcome by the ship's motion. "Has Mrs. Brown kept down the broth?"

"Only a bit," he admits, his eyes troubled.

"I'm sure the weather will be better in the morning," I assure him.

Thanking him for his concern, I shut the door and return to my sister. She has fallen into a fitful sleep, and I cover her broth with a towel so she can sup later.

The heaving seas stay with us for nearly ten days, which blend together in a haze of squeamishness. Proud of being able to rise from my bunk for at least part of every day, I force myself on deck when the weather, and the captain, allow. The captain is a kind man, and he usually has a pocket full of dried codfish strips that he gives to the lady passengers. He says it stimulates the appetite while calming the stomach. It does seem to work, although after seeing the turned up noses and labored chewing of passengers who eat it, I am grateful I do not need it.

I enjoy a brief conversation with the captain on a breezy morning. L'Amie is quite recovered, although pale and thin. She,

Mr. Brown, and I are taking a slow turn about the deck when the captain approaches. Mr. Brown asks him about our route.

"It is the Vanderbilt Line's route," the captain explains. "Mr. Vanderbilt has cut two days off the voyage by going through Nicaragua instead of Panama."

"The Panama route is the traditional one, is it not?" I ask.

"Yes, but this new route is safe and quite picturesque through the jungle," he assures us. "Much less enervating than the Panama route."

"We will be quite free with our opinions should we encounter you on a return voyage," L'Amie says.

He and Mr. Brown laugh, for we haven't yet arrived in San Francisco and she's already talking about returning! I, however, know that L'Amie wishes her sojourn in California to be a brief one. She's determined to attend medical school in New York as soon as she has reconnected with our mother and can make her wishes known. Ashamed of my selfishness, I can't help but hope my sister's insistence will take Mama's attention off finding me another spouse.

As we near Central America, the heat increases and Mrs. Brown recovers. We pack away our heavier dresses in favor of lighter fabrics. It's the warmest October we have ever experienced. Mrs. Brown walks the decks with us as we share impassioned discussions about temperance and abolition and even the notion of women voting. Mrs. Brown is quite alarmed at our views.

"You will not win yourselves husbands if you are so strident," she chides, and is surprised when we laugh.

"I have no desire to marry," L'Amie declares.

"And I have already done so," I tell her.

She looks me up and down, frowning at the black gown and black hat. "It's been two years since Jacob died. I am sure your mother plans husbands for you both." But her tone tells me she really doesn't care. I am glad, as I hold Jacob in my heart still.

We land at San Juan del Norte, recently renamed Greytown after its British governor, and disembark to find our land legs have quite deserted us. Almost immediately, though, we board a small stern-wheeled river steamer to head up the San Juan River. Although it should be exciting to be commencing another phase of our journey, the boat is very full. The river steamer scheduled to leave before ours has sunk in the river, and the passengers from the ill-fated boat have been added to ours. The idea of such danger, and the odor of so many people in close quarters, feeds my depression. Nonetheless I force a smile onto my face and wonder if the other passengers' high spirits are equally contrived.

On the *Prometheus*, Mr. Brown took up with a card player who was great fun. He has a wonderful deep singing voice, and together with Mr. Brown he serenades the jungle animals as we make our way up the narrow San Juan River.

"Look, Ellen!" my sister calls. "A howler monkey! The

captain was telling me about them just this morning!"

I frown, not wanting her to share pleasantries with the rough captain of our tiny river steamer. Before I can respond, however, she exclaims, "And the birds! Look at the beautiful colors!"

The monkeys and birds screech in a cacophony of noise. The deep green foliage reaches into the waterway, and natives in dugout canoes paddle past us. I stand near the ship's rail, clinging to the support post of the flimsy awning that provides a bit of shade from the ferocious tropical sun. A dugout approaches, pushed closer to our steamer by the straggling branches and roots of a large tree. A lone man paddles, kneeling in the center of the flimsy vessel. He is clad in naught but a cloth around his hips, and his darkly bronzed chest gleams with perspiration. A few ladies near me titter nervously and turn away, but my gaze is caught by his coal black eyes. He ceases paddling for a moment and drifts, his eyes locked on mine. I shiver, but cannot look away until he is past, paddling again, a long dark braid swinging down his back.

For a moment I wonder what my proper shipmates would think if I jumped overboard into this man's canoe and allowed him to take me away to his village. I would discard my heavy proper attire and go about dressed in very little, as do the natives. My heart free, I would laugh and love and raise little nut-brown children. The ridiculous notion makes me smile with genuine amusement for the first time in days, and the steel vise of despair clamped around my heart loosens just a bit. I resolve to think more positively about my future so as not to drive Mrs. Brown to distraction and L'Amie to gloom.

"Oh my, Ellen, alligators!" L'Amie's tone is one of excited horror and I turn to see the creatures. One sleeps in the sun, and another wallows in the shallow water. "Do you think they will follow us and upset the boat so they can try their jaws upon us?" my sister asks.

"Actually, they appear much too lazy to work that hard for a meal," I reassure her with a smile.

She smiles back, somehow catching exuberance from me. Her bright blue flowered dress enhances the mood of gaiety, and as the ship chugs upriver we laugh like carefree denizens of the jungle, for the moment impervious to the tropical sun.

Before long, however, the humidity saps our energy. By midmorning on the second day, we grow weary of the food, the sudden torrential rainstorms, the mosquitoes, and the crowded conditions. I notice a couple of industrious ladies who pull the steward aside and beg for some boon. They disappear below.

In due time, the result of their pleas appears on deck. They have made a pot of hasty pudding! In deep tin pie plates, holding as much corn meal mush swimming in molasses as they can carry, they distribute it to the crowd. Spoons are quickly employed to good use, and we soon hold our empty dishes up for more.

Finally, near the end of the second day, we complete our

125-mile journey to Lake Nicaragua. We walk a short distance around the Castilian Rapids to the lakeside town of San Carlos. It exists merely that we may transfer to a larger steamer. San Carlos boasts no visitor accommodations, so we are expected to sleep aboard ship. Even so, there is not enough room for all to sleep comfortably. L'Amie and I spend an uncomfortable night wrapped in our shawls lying atop our trunks.

"L'Amie," I whisper. "Do you ever wonder if the Panama route is truly worse than this?"

"It seems impossible, does it not?" she agrees. After a moment of silence broken only by the noises of the tropical night and the mechanical rumbles beneath us, she speaks again. "Ellen, what will we do when we reach California?"

"What do you mean?" I ask, but I know the answer. I am a childless widow, and she is a single young woman. We are expected to live with our mother or find a husband. Neither is acceptable to two young women who have lived as we have for the last year, making our own decisions. I suspected months ago, when Mama began pushing us to make this trip, that she already had a suitable match in mind for one if not both of us. Our dreams of independence will not matter at all when we return to the real world.

"I don't want to get married," L'Amie whispers. Her thoughts seem to be echoing mine. "Will I really be able to return to New York and attend medical school?"

"You finished your schooling with very good marks," I

compliment her, not wanting to be the one to dash her dreams. If Papa had lived, he might be surprised how good a student his delight turned out to be. More importantly, she thirsts for knowledge like a flower in the sun thirsts for water.

"Elizabeth Blackwell earned her medical degree two years ago at Geneva College. Do you think they'd accept me?"

"There should be nothing to prevent you." A split second of silence, then we say together, "Except Mama." Our giggles cause those curled next to us to mutter angrily.

I am grateful for my sister on this trip. Without her sunny disposition, I could easily have remained steeped in despair. Both of us have mosquito bites on top of mosquito bites, and the sun burns our complexion. Our hair resembles rain-drenched rat's nests. Even so, we are enjoying the adventure and each other.

Lake Nicaragua is more placid than the river, and the following day is spent crossing it. We disturb a huge flock of water birds that take our breath away with wonder as they rise from the water's surface crying outrage at our intrusion. A large island looms to the north of us, and L'Amie exclaims, "How beautiful it is!"

Mr. Brown hastens to dissuade her. "That is Ometepe Island. It means two mountains. Two very dangerous mountains."

"It is a wild and beautiful place," I tell him.

"That it is," he says. "But those two mountains are active

volcanoes. And to the north of the island, at the far end of the lake, is the city of Granada, home to some of the area's most active pirates."

"Pirates!"

I can't tell if L'Amie's squeal is delight or terror. It's as well we are staying to the south.

We dock at a rickety wooden piling and disembark. "Welcome to Rivas!" the captain shouts, as if we should celebrate.

Rivas holds more mud than people. The locals may call it a village, but it is nothing more than a few tents and some wooden walkways. It is here we prepare for the next leg of our journey, crossing eleven miles of land to the Pacific Ocean. Mr. Brown attempts to be helpful by telling us that Mr. Vanderbilt intends to install a stagecoach line to make the journey.

"He can afford it," he jokes. "Even though we each paid $200 less than those traveling around the Cape, Mr. Vanderbilt is a wealthy man. He plans to make the journey quite comfortable."

"It's hardly been comfortable up until now," I observe. "Why should he start here?"

Unbeknownst to me, my words are prophetic. There is no sign of Mr. Vanderbilt's stagecoaches, which apparently exist only in men's dreams at this point. We are to make the journey overland mounted on mules. The beasts are in such demand, however, that it is not certain we can all be supplied with one.

The lady passengers are directed to a huge blue tent to wait while the gentlemen complete the arrangements. I am much too bedraggled to object as I precede my sister inside.

We are assisted up a ladder to a loft that covers half the tent. We sit in groups on the wooden floor and listen to the rain hitting the canvas. Restless, I walk over to peek out the opening near the pointed roof. Water is everywhere: sky, river, lake, and street. I close the flap as well as I can, then look down into the tent proper. The scent of male sweat and damp canvas permeates the tent. A long counter below us is occupied by men playing cards, which they continue to do for the duration of our stay.

Delays plague us. I am tired of sleeping without undressing, and of listening to the quarrelsome talk of the natives in their foreign tongue. No better is the prattling conversation of shallow friendships forged by adversity. I'm afraid the close quarters, and the waiting, are beginning to affect us all.

My mind keeps circling back to that whispered conversation with L'Amie on the river steamer. I'm proud of her steadfast desire to become a doctor, and I vow to assist her however I can. My own political views are rather unattractive to most marriageable men, and I will not go backwards, forcing myself into a role that no longer fits. I must find a career or a forward-thinking man, neither of which seems easy on this mud-spattered journey. California, though, is a frontier, and frontiers are known for encouraging strong people to rise to the top. I will be one of those people.

Chapter 3: Rivas 1851
Ellen Rand Perkins

"Ellen, Ellen!" L'Amie rushes along the wooden walkway outside the blue tent that serves as the center of life in Rivas. The gray of early morning illuminates the rain-darkened trees surrounding this clearing that I refuse to call a village. The hem of L'Amie's skirt is so encrusted with mud that it will have to be burned once we arrive in San Francisco. Her shoes, once sturdy, are now muddy and worn. Neither of us wants to ruin another pair from our trunk, so we put on the dirty pair each day.

I sit on an upturned barrel where I have been contemplating life, until her shout breaks my reverie. Despite endless mud and the lack of progress on our journey, I am mostly content so I greet my sister with a smile.

"Ellen, today is the day! We are to be on our way this very day!"

Her news echoes across the camp, and behind me I feel the blue tent itself throb with life as everyone hurries to ready themselves. It's not raining, for a change, when we assemble in front of the tent. Eight of the lady passengers, including L'Amie and me, are to travel in one group. A string of mules is led up, saddled with men's saddles. A few of the women anxiously chatter to their husbands. Mr. Brown steps forward. "Sir," he addresses the guide, "the women are not prepared to ride astride. We were told ladies' saddles would be provided."

The guide strokes his wiry beard and squints at our dear friend and his bride. "Rain's made the roads slippery. Too dangerous."

"I hope you have an extra pair of trousers, dear," Mrs. Brown says to her husband with a nervous smile.

L'Amie grins at me and disappears into the blue tent. I follow, and we dig through our trunks for our bloomer suits, much ridiculed by Uncle Benjamin in New York. My sister and I acquired ours as soon as Amelia Bloomer began wearing them a few months ago. The suits cause consternation even in the fashion-conscious city. Who would have dreamed they would be so useful in the jungle of Nicaragua? We change quickly and return outside with smug smiles.

The women titter nervously at our attire, glancing at their husbands, but necessity erases the breath of scandal attached to these outfits. The men try not to glower at the ballooning pants pulled tight at the ankle, but outright laughter breaks out when each woman dons a pair of her husband's trousers. Some fit quite well, like Mrs. Brown's, since her husband is nearly the same size as she. On others, however, the misfit is quite comical. One woman is much taller than her husband, and the pant legs are much too short. She pulls on an extra pair of stockings, as if this will cover her ankles, and tries to squat to make the trousers reach her shoes. Another man is quite stout, and his wife swims in extra fabric.

We stop laughing very quickly as we mount the stubborn pungent animals and start out on the trail, which winds over steep territory. Rain pours down on us before long, and the low-hanging trees make the use of umbrellas impossible. My mood darkens as the mud grows deeper and I contemplate eleven miles of this. My mule slows, falling behind, and the guide returns for me. He ties the beast's head to his mule's tail.

"Use the whip lively, miss," he orders me.

I do as I am told since visions haunt me of his mule galloping on, leaving his tail behind him like Bo Peep's sheep, still tied to my rein. Down into deep gullies and up again on a dead run, I utter sharp little cries as the mule lurches, threatening to dump me into the mud. Never did I expect to encounter such a trying ordeal! I am slightly mollified when L'Amie's startled shrieks echo my own. If the single men in San Francisco could see us now, they would run for the hills faster than Mama could snare them!

Long past dark we arrive at an old adobe hut with a deep-roofed porch. Hammocks swing from the porch rafters in tight rows. The earthen floor is trodden to mud in this season. We dismount in relief, expecting to be shown to a room for the night. I almost crumple to the ground at the stiffness in my legs. My joints groan like those of an old grandmother, and my bottom feels like an angry father has thrashed it. L'Amie and I are further dismayed to discover that our accommodations consist of one hammock, here on the porch that we will share. At least we are offered supper.

A dipped candle fastened to the wall dimly lights the interior of the hut. Chicken is served, and coffee without milk. I'm so tired; I don't even care what I'm eating. Nor, I find out soon enough, do I have enough energy to protest the sleeping arrangements.

In the middle of the night I am disturbed by snortings and bumpings from below. I peek over the hammock and see some swine trying to get out of the rain. It's all I can do not to cry with frustration. L'Amie does begin to weep, and I hold her for the rest of the night. "Our future is bright," I whisper, "compared with tonight's darkness." Only the pigs respond, snorting. L'Amie has fallen into a restless sleep.

Gray morning and sore muscles find us once more aboard the stubbornest of creatures. I have nicknamed my mule Uncle, which cheers L'Amie. Another full day brings us at last to San Juan del Sur, on the Pacific Ocean. Uncle, being among the slowest beasts in the country, has caused us to be the last to arrive.

"Goodbye, Uncle," I say with an exaggerated bow to the wretched creature. "Yes, I will behave on the rest of our trip. No, I will not allow L'Amie to get into trouble." My silliness is rewarded with a tired laugh from my sister.

Those who arrived before us have taken what primitive rooms exist, and no lodging is available in the town. L'Amie and I are part of a small group that takes refuge aboard a vessel lying in the harbor. The steamer that is to take us north to San Francisco has not yet arrived.

It's a relief to lie on our bunks and give thanks that we are no longer on mule back. Bug bites itch and saddle sores ache, but we can close our eyes without falling off a beast into the mud. The air in the tiny cabin smells of sweaty sailors, but it's blissfully dry. We have completed another leg of our journey, and that's quite an accomplishment. The waters in the bay are restless, though, and the motion of the ship soon returns us to seaside distress.

L'Amie seems to have sunk into a perpetual state of weeping. Between sobs, she slaps at her arms. "Oh, Ellen, the mosquitoes are terrible!"

"But think of the stories we will tell to our family once we arrive in San Francisco!" She is not consoled by my attempt to cheer her. "Come on, sister, let's go up to the fresh air on deck." I help her up the ladder, and we are relieved when the breeze wafts away the pests. "Let's bring our mattresses up here so we have a chance of rest," I suggest.

L'Amie's mattress is stuffed with some very heavy plant material. I can barely budge it. Together, we manage to stand it up on its side. Our hair is in great disarray, and sweat beads on my forehead. The sweet night air beckons us onward, and we put our backs to the mattress. Shoving with our feet, we are able to get it into the narrow hallway. Tugging and grunting, with L'Amie going first and me pushing from behind, we manage to wrestle the mattress up the ladder. Breathing heavily, we flop it down on the deck and pat it to even out the lumps. We decide one mattress will do for the both of us since we are winded. L'Amie returns to the stuffy cabin for a couple of thin pillows.

Night-cooled skin makes even the mosquitoes more bearable. The sky stretches above us, filled with stars, washed clean and clear by the rain. A pristine crescent-shaped bay stretches from the beach out to sea. On shore, the gaiety from drinking and carousing makes us glad we are on the ship. This is our home for a couple of days, and we bask in the respite from traveling, discussing neither our past nor our future but living day by day.

Finally a steamer is spotted, and we are thankful to find it is our long-awaited transport. The large number of passengers creates considerable excitement getting all their belongings stowed on board. Captain Blethen welcomes us aboard the *North America*. He seems a most congenial host. His hugely pregnant wife is traveling with him, and I learn this is an arrangement that suits them. The captain tells us it is now just a two-week voyage up the coast to our destination. To be so close is exciting.

Compared to mules and mud, the *North America* is a luxury. L'Amie and I feel truly clean for the first time since we left the Caribbean to head up the San Juan River, even if we are only able to splash cool water on our faces and arms from a tiny sink. Early November may not be the most beautiful time to sail the Pacific Ocean, but today is magnificent. Everything is sunshine and blue sea; there is no rain and no mosquitoes. The thrum of the engines under my feet echoes the thrum of happiness in my heart. Journey's end will bring changes, but I am at peace with them. I have found more strength within myself on this trip than I even knew I had. After all, who can force me to marry when I've ridden a recalcitrant mule through a muddy jungle? Even Mama is tame compared to that.

Soon after leaving port, Captain Blethen's wife gives birth to a daughter. L'Amie is on hand to wipe Henrietta's brow as she labors, easing the pain of birth as best she can. Her bedside manner is natural and calming. I vow to help her convince Mama that medical school is her path. Baby Evelyn Georgina Blethen is the delight of crew and passengers. She is the cause of a grand celebratory feast. Mr. Brown begins singing, and we all join in to serenade the youngest member of our party.

L'Amie and I have a private ceremony of our own. One evening, as the sun slips beneath the horizon and turns the world orange and purple, we bring on deck the dresses we wore in Nicaragua. Her flowered blue and my black have been laundered, but are tattered from the abuse we subjected them to in the jungle. I need no rags to remind me of what I gained there. My shoulders are straighter, my chin higher, my smile wider with confidence. I see the same sort of changes in my sister. Together we lift the dresses over the rail and watch them float to the ocean's surface. The ship steams on into night. Somewhere in the blackness behind us, the symbols of our youth grow sodden with salt water and sink below the surface. L'Amie and I stand at the railing with our arms around each other's waists, content.

As if to test my newfound serenity, solemn occasions arise to dampen our spirits. Several people die, and we must carry out burials at sea. A young mother loses her infant daughter, whose father in San Francisco has never seen her. I think of Coelia, traveling with little Molly. I can imagine how joyfully Lucian greeted them in San Francisco, reaching for his new daughter for the first time. The father of this infant will be expecting such an arrival only to be met with empty arms. A woman in steerage is consigned to the waves, her two daughters wild with grief. I almost feel guilty worrying about Mama attempting to regain control of my life when they have lost their own mother. The ringing of the bells and reading of the service is sober and ceremonial, with the body sewn up in canvas lying ready to be placed upon the slide by a swarthy seaman. Seven such burials are conducted on this voyage.

L'Amie scurries about the ship with purpose. She is no

longer the flighty young girl who left New York with me. Passengers and crew alike seek her help with matters of the stomach, and even with no formal training my sister's able to help many of them. One of the crewmembers gives her a little book to record her cases, just like a professional doctor.

"Ellen, I feel as if I am already beginning my practice. I just wish there was more I could do for some of these people."

"My dear sister, I am impressed by your knowledge of herbal medicine. Have you been studying behind my back?"

She laughs then. "I learned a lot from Aunt Eveline, actually. It's a challenge to figure out what is wrong with a person and then decide what might help. I love it." Her eyes shine as she tells me all about her latest case, but at each of the deaths a shadow of regret clouds her features.

Acapulco is our final stop before San Francisco. The beautiful bay is enclosed on three sides by towering mountains that extend right up to the shoreline. It is another gem of sand and sea, but I am so anxious to reach our final destination I find myself longing for fog. I am not even tempted to disembark in the Mexican city, having heard plenty of the Spanish language in Nicaragua. L'Amie goes ashore with the Browns, and returns with tales of spicy food and hot-tempered natives. It only makes me long for my own country. However foreign San Francisco may seem compared to New York, it is still America.

I spend my last hours aboard the *North America* on deck, gazing over the railing at the wild beauty of the California coast as we move past it. In San Francisco at last, we dock at the foot of Market Street. Plain board shanties, used as stores, are arranged on either side of us, and crowds of men stand watching the latest arrivals. I spot the *Apollo*, doing a brisk business as the store it was intended to be. My heart twists, but my resolve does not. My focus is the future. The past must stay a memory.

It's November, but how different the air is from New York in this season! L'Amie becomes quite animated, waving her entire arm, and there on the dock are Mama and Cousin Henry. Tears well up as I wave and cry a greeting. Our journey has been a suspension of the real world, an opportunity to blend adventure and reflection. Now we return to family and society. I don't feel ready to think about the details of tomorrow, yet tomorrow looms.

"We are really in California," I tell my sister.

The ship Apollo *and the brig* Euphemia *were among the early vessels to be abandoned and used for other purposes needed by the rapidly growing city of San Francisco. By 1850, these vessels were used as store ships.*
Sacramento and Battery Streets, From the "Annals of San Francisco"

Chapter 4: California 1851-1853
Ellen Rand VanValkenburgh

Even though the bustle surrounding our arrival makes it seem longer, we stay in San Francisco only a week. This time when we board a river steamer Mama and Cousin Henry are with us. Our breath steams in the early morning chill as if to accompany the boilers. We are wearing new gowns, appropriate to the elegant *Senator*, one of the finest paddle wheelers anywhere. Mama is wearing a gown that was made here in San Francisco, modeled after New York fashion of last year. She has thickened about the waist in the year since I last saw her, and her hair is graying, but there is still steely determination in her eyes as she looks at L'Amie and me. Cousin Henry is the same as I remember, except for a luxuriant brown mustache that he is constantly smoothing with his fingers.

The fare from San Francisco to Sacramento is ten dollars for each of us, but the accommodations are more than adequate. It feels good to have the deck of a ship underfoot once more, but maybe it's just familiarity. That, and the certain knowledge it is a very short trip this time. L'Amie and I are looking forward to reuniting with Coelia and her family.

It is just after dark when the ship docks, but we hurry ashore. Coelia and Lucian live in a neat cottage, painted white, with green shutters. "Oh!" I exclaim. "How pretty!"

Mama looks at me quizzically. "What did you expect, Ellen?"

"I don't know." I bite my lip and feel my cheeks pinken. "I think I pictured unpainted shanties of used boards. This is quite luxurious."

Mama and Cousin Henry laugh. He says, "Ships arrive every day, all day, bringing furniture and household items from the East. California really is becoming quite civilized."

We tiptoe up the steps to the porch and wait impatiently for our knocks to be answered. Lucian opens the door, exclaims aloud, and immediately welcomes us inside. A sharp cry draws our attention to the stairs, where Coelia has come to see what the commotion is about. She immediately bursts into tears. "I am so relieved you are here! That horrible journey!"

In just a short time we are all crying, and handkerchiefs are brought out to wipe away the tears. Coelia relates some of her experiences of a year ago, and our own words scatter as we try to put all of our experiences into a few phrases.

"The jungle was so amazing," L'Amie says.

"But the mosquitoes...and the mules..." I share a glance

with her.

"Uncle!" L'Amie interrupts and we dissolve into laughter. I'm sure our family thinks we are quite mad.

"There's time for that later. Let's get you settled," Lucian says firmly.

The inside of the house is papered and painted, the floor covered with carpets from Brussels. The red plush easy chairs and sofa are quite modern. I say nothing, but I still marvel at how different the reality is from my ignorant imaginings. L'Amie and I share a bed in a tiny upstairs bedroom. We are too tired to stay awake talking, but too excited to sleep. She lies quietly with her thoughts and I with mine.

The next morning dawns with bright California sunshine, still a wonder to me as I am used to cold gray New York winters or the incessant rain of the jungle. Coelia makes quite a feast for breakfast, and her children are wide-eyed to see us.

"The boogeyman brought them in the night," seven-year-old Carlton tells his little sisters. His theatrical whisper causes Mary to gasp.

"Oh stop it," Leila says, frowning. "You're scaring her." Leila, a very mature five-year-old, puts a protective arm around three-year-old Mary. Molly, just a bundle in Coelia's arms when they left for California, is now just barely two. She sticks a thumb in her mouth.

"Molly, dear, big girls don't suck thumbs," Coelia tells her gently, to no avail.

L'Amie speaks in an undertone to Carlton. "The boogeyman is nothing compared to the vicious savages in the jungle. Your Aunt Ellen and I fought them off with just a glare." She glowers at him in illustration.

I smile, remembering her playing with Uncle Benjamin's boys in New York. Life in California will be an adjustment, but any way of life can be embraced if family is there to assist you.

Before long, Coelia has settled her children with Mama and leads L'Amie and me outdoors. "I need a few things at the store. Shall we walk about a bit then see to the purchase of bread and eggs?"

We agree and set off. Sacramento bustles around us, not unlike San Francisco. Men are going to the gold fields, returning from said fields, and making money on miners and mining. Most of them are under thirty years of age, and it seems odd to see a crowd of people with no gray or balding heads. Instead, everyone is energetic and bent on having a good time while making their fortune. One of the oddest customs is that of calling each other by their first name. The first time one of Mama's young men calls me Ellen instead of Mrs. Perkins I am rendered speechless.

Last year both rivers, the Sacramento and the American, flooded simultaneously, and the town is still recovering from the devastation. Men who had been unsuccessful in the gold fields returned after the flood to help rebuild. Some are making more money selling supplies, which are as essential as the gold required to buy them.

When we arrive at the general store, I am shocked by the enormous prices. Without batting an eye, Coelia pays twenty-five cents for a small loaf of bread and a dollar for a dozen eggs!

A man with a bristly overgrown beard and a dusty patched felt hat smiles at my obvious surprise. "Newly arrived?" he asks. Without waiting for my reply, he pulls something out of his pocket. "Picked this up before breakfast at the dry diggings. Ain't she a beauty?"

Gleaming in his hand is a fine gold nugget, the first one I've seen. "Yes, it is," I tell him. L'Amie exclaims over it, too, and we watch the man use it to pay for coffee, flour, and sugar. He winks at me as he leaves the store.

"You should be careful who you speak to," Coelia warns. "Many of the miners are mentally ill, or criminals. California is full of opportunity and all, but the gold fever brings out the worst elements, too."

"Oh, Coelia, we can take care of ourselves. We came all the way from New York with no problems, after all," L'Amie complains.

"Hopefully Mama will be careful," I say. They both look at me, heads tilted and eyebrows furrowed. "When she introduces us to prospective husbands." Coelia laughs, but L'Amie scowls.

Once back at Coelia's, Mama takes charge. Invitations have been piling up in anticipation of our arrival. Our dear mother spends the morning explaining which invitations she is accepting and why, giving us a quick lesson in Sacramento society. I cannot look directly at L'Amie, especially when I see the corners of her mouth twitch as if she is trying not to smile. Is she having the same problem I am reconciling Coelia's world of mentally ill criminals with Mama's world of gentle society?

We are thrust into the whirl of dinners and teas and dances and theatre, and it's not all horrible. In a few weeks, our piano arrives from New York. The expense of bringing it up to Sacramento from San Francisco is as much as the cost of its journey from the East Coast! But now Mama beams proudly when we give an occasional recital in Coelia's home.

At one of these gatherings, we meet a young woman from Downieville. L'Amie has just performed at the piano, and tea is being served as our new acquaintance explains that she cooks for the miners.

"The floor of the cookhouse is Mother Earth herself," she tells us. "One morning a miner came in, stamping his feet to rid them of extra mud. One of the nails in his boots disturbed the packed dirt, and there shone a bright glitter of gold where he stood."

"Oh my!" I exclaim, clasping my teacup. "Was it a nugget?"

She nods. "He picked it up and went for his pick. Several of the other men joined him, and the place was soon converted to a claim. The cooking implements had to be removed to other quarters."

We laugh and shake our heads, but stories like these abound. Equally prevalent are stories of marriages made in the most unusual of circumstances. In one of these, a merchant with a fine business in the interior of the state came to Sacramento to buy supplies. In crossing the street, he chanced to meet a girl of youthful appearance as she stepped out of the store where she was employed. No word passed between them, but he followed her with his eyes. After her return to the store he inquired about her and requested an introduction. Not long after, they married.

I, of course, do not have to resort to chance to find a husband. I have Mama. To her dismay I still dress in mourning black. I will not allow her to forget that I have already been married, however briefly. As days pass, her frowns and idle comments only harden my resolve to find something else. The piano only serves to point out how limited my musical ability is, and even little Leila draws better. The novelty of Sacramento begins to fade.

A month after arriving in California, a package comes for Mama from New York. Uncle Benjamin has sent one whole month's worth of the *New York Sun*. Mama and Coelia take the fashion sections, but L'Amie and I pore over the news. We skip past local election results and examine every tidbit about suffrage and temperance. It seems odd that we were on board ship when these events were actually occurring! The sense of being distanced from reality persists, and I have trouble sleeping that night.

In the morning, I rise early, tired of tossing and turning. L'Amie stirs, and I'm afraid I've woken her. "Shhh, go back to sleep," I whisper.

"Ellen? You didn't sleep." She sits up. "Are you all right?"

I ponder that question longer than the casual inquiry requires. "No," I finally say. She pats the bed next to her. Tucking my nightgown under me, I sit on her side of the bed. "I don't want to live with Mama and Coelia forever," I tell her.

"Are you thinking about getting married?" She raises an eyebrow.

My heart clenches at her words, but that's exactly what I've been thinking about. "I don't know. In New York, I thought I could do something wonderful to advance temperance or suffrage, but here the struggle for basic needs seems paramount. I'm sure California women would vote if they could, but no one has the time to bring about the needed change."

L'Amie closes her hand over mine. "You sound discouraged, Ellen."

"Is it so awful to be married? I mean, Coelia and Lucian do a good job of it. Couldn't a California woman be married and also help sway the power of women in the state?"

"Are you a California woman, then?" she asks me in surprise. "I think of myself as a New Yorker. I still want to go to medical school there."

"Yes, and Mama grinds her teeth every time you allude to it."

She grimaces. "Why don't you come with me, Ellen? We could live together, not with Uncle Benjamin. I could attend school and you could rally with Susan B. Anthony."

I smile at my sister. Her eyes are bright and her dark hair cascades in sleep-tumbled curls around her head. Reality is not so real at seventeen. "I am content in California, dear sister, but living here with Coelia or living in New York with you cannot be my only choices. I am not sure marriage is *the* answer, but it is *an* answer. It may well be the best shot at true freedom that I have."

We fall silent then, holding each other's hands like lifelines.

* * *

In March of 1852, the Sacramento and American Rivers once again rise together to flood stage. They acquire a velocity of current and strength of pressure that the levee cannot hold, and water pours into the city. All bridges are swept away and several people drown. To reach the capitol building, people must take a boat. Cousin Henry comes for us in a rowboat he's hired for an exorbitant fee. Tugging at his mustache with both hands, he and Lucian make several trips to move Mama, L'Amie, Coelia, myself, and the four children to solid land. There is no room for luggage, so we are a bit bedraggled. Molly and Mary fuss, wanting to be held. Carlton splashes in puddles until his legs are covered in mud. Leila draws in the wet dirt with a stick. The hotels are all full of displaced persons, and we have nowhere to go. Cousin Henry and Lucian talk in low tones.

"Vallejo is growing," Henry says. "The legislature moves there in May."

"I've heard there is land available," Lucian says, asking more than stating.

"General Vallejo is a friend of mine. He takes boarders at Rancho Petaluma. You could all live there while you built something in town."

Lucian nods, and it is settled, with no word to the women. Cousin Henry loads his wagon with women and children and basic supplies Lucian was able to retrieve in the rowboat. With nary a look back, we are off to Petaluma with squeaking wagon wheels, jangling horse harnesses, cranky children, and tired women.

Petaluma is certainly not New York, San Francisco, or Sacramento. The adobe ranch house sits on a rise overlooking the grassland that spreads in all directions like an ocean. Not too long ago this was a thriving cattle ranch, but legal issues have rendered it almost lifeless. Poor General Vallejo, born a Spaniard, served in the Mexican military, and lost it all to the American legal system.

Lucian is building a home in nearby Vallejo. The site was once Rancho Suscol, which merged with Rancho Petaluma into General Vallejo's gigantic holding, then separated out to sell off as times grew hard. At least the town is named for the general, who is something of a hero around here. Lucian successfully moves his engraving business to Vallejo, which is burgeoning in anticipation of the state capital moving here in May, and work progresses quickly on the house.

Meanwhile, L'Amie and I eagerly anticipate our monthly delivery of the *New York Sun,* Mama desperately tries to find single men in Petaluma, and Coelia tramps the ranch with her children. Occasionally we go for an outing in the wagon and visit the building site. It seems a perfect house for Lucian, Coelia, and the children. I suspect adding Mama, L'Amie, and myself will make it crowded.

Once we are all firmly settled in the new Vallejo house, though, my life changes forever. My brother comes from San Francisco to visit the new Lucian Curtis house. Joseph exclaims over each detail as Lucian proudly shows it off. Mama's much more interested in Joseph's companion.

Henry VanValkenburgh is an assayer for Wells Fargo. His brown hair and thick brown mustache are impeccably groomed. In appearance, he's not unlike hundreds of other men. Except for his eyes. Their intensity instantly sets Mr. VanValkenburgh apart, and as they fasten on me I fight the urge to squirm.

"Enchanted," he murmurs, holding my hand faintly longer than necessary. He doesn't even look at L'Amie.

"Lucian's house is nice," I say, and wonder if it's possible to sound any more stupid.

He is undeterred. "Yes, it is."

"Have you heard of Sojourner Truth's speech at the

Woman's Convention in Ohio?" L'Amie says.

I cringe at her verbal assault. Henry turns to her with an amused expression. "In December? I have, actually."

"A friend of mine attended the first Woman's Conference in Seneca Falls. Ellen and I are staunch advocates for women's rights."

Her tone is not as flighty as her words. If anything, she's challenging him to show he's good enough for us. For me.

"Are you now." Henry's eyes return to me.

"I'm sure there are better topics we can discuss," Mama offers, glaring at my sister.

We make our way into the dining room where Coelia rings for the first course as she surveys her table. Lucian clearly wants nothing to do with matchmaking. He and Joseph talk in low tones, heads close together.

"Women are intelligent and capable," I say quietly to Henry, across the table from me. "They deserve a voice."

"I don't mind women having a voice as long as they don't shriek from the rooftops."

"It's not necessary for a wife to suppress her convictions in order for a husband to support her," I say, striving to keep a neutral tone that won't draw Mama's attention.

"If a woman is permitted to think for herself she may disagree in her views with her husband, and family peace is destroyed."

"It doesn't need to be." Our eyes are locked. We are

sparring, feeling out the other's position to see how much common ground can be found.

"No, it doesn't need to be." He smiles, and the intensity in his eyes softens.

Suddenly I feel pretty, and the feeling shocks me. My beak of a nose chased all notions of conventional beauty out of my head long before adolescence. My black gown and severe hairstyle are not designed to enhance my appearance. Yet the way this man is looking at me I could be a queen. This should not please me, but it does. At the end of the table, Mama smiles.

After this dinner, any other would-be suitors fade away as Mama encourages Henry. I suppose I encourage him, too, if only by not refusing outright to see him. The idea of a life's companion is not unattractive. In September, San Francisco newspapers cover the women's convention in Syracuse, and the topic provides lively discussion between Henry and me. He's not in total support of temperance, although he supports abolition. On the issue of women voting, he is ambivalent.

"I realize women are educated on the issues," he tells me one evening, "but I am not sure I can trust them to vote with their brain and not their heart. I'm not saying I'm against women's rights, now, but some of the women in your movement have been slighted by men or married badly. As a result they hate all men."

"Some men support us, Henry."

He quirks an eyebrow at my use of 'us' but ignores it.

"They are mostly hen-pecked husbands who should be wearing petticoats themselves."

We're sitting in wicker chairs on Coelia's front porch on a lovely evening typical of California in October. I'm very conscious of my family in the room behind the window. "Men don't always vote with their brains," I say, trying not to sound sharp.

He takes a deep breath, momentarily at a loss for words. "I know, Ellen, I know. I'm sorry. A woman voting is just such a foreign idea. It's not something I've really considered."

It's odd to see this confident man, so powerful in his banking circle, fumbling for a position on this issue. I know better than to jump in and try to convince him, as L'Amie would've done. He'll come to his own mind over it, and in the meantime he won't prohibit me from attending meetings.

I find my marriage resistance weakening even further. I want to be in charge of my own house, not forever staying with Mama or Coelia. I want a family of daughters, and the company of a like-minded man. Henry might just do.

So in November of 1853, Henry and I are married. Mama is ecstatic, but distressed over my expressed desire to wear my customary black to the wedding.

"Oh Ellen, don't be silly. You cannot wear black to a wedding, much less to your own! It is time to put aside your mourning. You are marrying a new man and he deserves the opportunity to heal your heart." She's quite strict with me, more than she has been in years, so I acquiesce.

My new husband is from a prominent New York family, as am I, so we understand each other. He allows me an occasional suffragist meeting, and I allow him his drinking companions. I can probably grow fond of him, but he doesn't ignite the passion of my soul. He's no Jacob. I create a lovely home for us in San Francisco on Jones Street, near Lombard, and hire a serving girl. Mama and L'Amie come to live with us, allowing Coelia and Lucian to have their new home to themselves. My mother and sister say nothing when I return to wearing black.

Henry VanValkenburgh, painted by William S. Jewett

Chapter 5: San Francisco 1861
Ellen Rand VanValkenburgh

We have settled into a routine, my tiny daughters and I. After Henry leaves for the bank in the morning, and before Mama and L'Amie stir from bed, I bundle the girls against the damp fog and leave our house on Jones Street. Ellie's face is wrapped so only her round blue eyes are exposed. Marion jumps up and down with excitement, her blond ringlets bouncing.

"Don't jump so, Mary," I scold, but there is no heat in my words.

"Come on, Mama, the sun is pushing the fog away!"

"Come on, Mama," her little sister mimics.

Stepping out our front door, I look north and south along the street. Our white picket fence edges Jones Street, and our nearest neighbors are the Martins, just across Lombard. Three-year-old Ellie likes to look at the Martins' horses, so we head in that direction. I take one daughter by each hand, and we walk slowly toward Lombard, matching our pace to Ellie's stubby legs.

The sun momentarily loses its battle with the fog, and gray tendrils float above us. On the steep side of Lombard, some of the Italian immigrants are building new homes with fancy ornamental woodwork, but I prefer the formal lines of the stately homes that are already here, surrounded by their park-like gardens.

Five-year-old Marion lets go of my hand and hurries forward, not quite running because she knows I disapprove of running. I let her go, knowing how she loves the view from the corner. Looking down steep Lombard Street, the cold breeze blowing off the San Francisco Bay chills our faces. In the distance, the bay stretches to the east, a deeper shade of blue-gray than the fog above. Ellie burrows deeper into her wool coat. Marion throws her head back and laughs, the cold reddening her cheeks and nose. I shake my head and smile, refusing to dampen an independent spirit.

The view up Russian Hill, away from the ocean, is more fascinating to me. With my back to the ocean, I marvel at the steep road rising before us. No horse drawn conveyances are moving up Lombard Street this morning. Marion is disappointed, but manages to create drama nonetheless.

"Only brave horses try to go up the hill, Ellie," she tells her sister. "The hill is so steep that sometimes the carriage pulls the horse backwards all the way down!" Her hands swoop toward the bay, illustrating the path of a fateful carriage. Ellie's eyes widen to blue saucers.

"Mary, that's enough," I say. "You're scaring your sister."

It's a chilly enough morning that the girls are soon ready to return home. I send them to the kitchen for cocoa with the serving girl. Mama and L'Amie wander downstairs for breakfast, and we eat together.

"Coming to the meeting today?" L'Amie asks me.

I haven't been to a meeting of the local women's club since I overheard gossip that the president of Wells Fargo has warned my husband he may lose his job. I am too afraid to learn that it's true. "Not today. I have a lot to do." I can't meet my sister's eyes.

"You're missing more than you're attending," she complains.

"Now, L'Amie, your sister is a wife and mother. Her focus is different than yours," Mama chides.

L'Amie is not satisfied, but she subsides. And she goes to the meeting alone.

That evening, the girls play with their dolls on the floor of the parlor. Mama and L'Amie sit nearby, chatting. The fire blazes in the hearth, and I sit mending one of Marion's underskirts. L'Amie holds an official-looking envelope that arrived today for her. She is glowing. I raise an eyebrow at her, inquiring. She smiles at me, looks out the window, then fastens her gaze on Mama and takes a deep breath. It must be a letter from the medical school in New York that she has applied to. I hope she is accepted, but my heart pines already.

"Mama, I have something to tell you." My sister waves the envelope. "It's a letter of acceptance from New York."

Mama freezes. Recovering, she smiles at L'Amie. "I really am quite proud of you, sweetheart. When do you leave?"

L'Amie and I stare at each other in shock. Mama has resisted this moment for ten years.

"Oh come now, girls," Mama chides. "I am quite proud of your independence, you know. Besides, I like the idea of having a doctor in the house."

L'Amie's enthusiasm spills over then, and she fills us with her plans for the trip east, for her living and schooling arrangements, for the curriculum of this school brave enough to educate women in the field of medicine.

When Henry arrives home, we fall silent. I'm not sure if the temperature of the room is chilled more by the wind that sneaks in when he opens the door or by Henry's cold formality.

"Good evening, my dear," he says.

"Good evening," I respond, rising to take his coat and hat while he settles into his chair by the fire.

The serving girl scurries to pour him a drink, and I frown in spite of myself. His drinking has increased so that he almost always has a fresh one in his hand. Could that have anything to do with his job situation?

"Is everything well with you?" I ask.

He looks at me for a long moment, his handsome face sober. Although his brown hair is thin, he has a dashing thick mustache and lively dark eyes. He dresses well, as befits his position, and tends to draw a lady's eye. Tonight, however, he seems in no mood for frivolity. My stomach clenches as I remember a similar conversation with Jacob ten years earlier.

"Well enough, I suppose," he says in a tone that tells me it's not well at all. "If you call being dismissed for no cause *well.*"

"Dismissed? Oh, dear." So it's true. Mama and L'Amie quietly exit the room, taking the girls with them.

"The people at the bank are too concerned with image to do business the way it should be done. It will be all right, though. I have decided to develop our land in Santa Cruz. It's perfect for a logging operation and paper mill, and I seem to be free at the moment." He forces a laugh.

Panic threatens my composure. Will he dare suggest I stay here in the city with the girls? "When do we leave?" I ask, hoping to dissuade any idea of abandoning us.

Another long look nearly rattles my nerves to dust. I will my hands to sit calmly in my lap and not clench my skirts.

"Can you pack the household by the end of the week?"

Of course I can if it means not being left behind again.

* * *

By the time we are settled in our home on Union Street, it

is fall, the best time of year in Santa Cruz. The seaside fog disappears with the summer, and October is much nicer than July. Our yard contains an almond tree and an apple tree, both ready to harvest. I look forward to seeing them bare in winter, full of blossoms in spring and growing fruit in summer.

Henry thrives in the lumber business, disappearing every morning on horseback for the San Lorenzo Paper Mill, on the river of the same name. Every twenty-four hours the mill produces 150 reams of butcher paper, which is in great demand in San Francisco.

Henry brings me out to the mill almost at once, leaving the girls in the care of my mother, who came along from San Francisco to see us settled. The mill is a rough place, although the setting is tranquil. The forest crowds close, and the river rushes by. Henry's men have rigged a dam with tree trunks, constructed so that large trees and debris can flow over without breaking it. I congratulate him on his cleverness, both thrilled and cowed by the sheer ferocity of the operation.

That winter I am more content than at any time in my life. Mama has gone back to live with Coelia. L'Amie has finally gone east to medical school. Although I miss her dreadfully, I am very proud of her. I manage my own household, and do it well. I begin to teach Marion her letters, and I read to Ellie as she cuddles in my lap. Henry whistles a jaunty tune while he readies himself for work.

December brings a series of fierce Pacific storms that

batter the coast, trying to rip Santa Cruz off the Earth and drown it beneath the sea. The San Lorenzo River floods, bringing its banks to the very edge of Mission Hill, where we live, and damaging many businesses in the downtown area near the Lower Plaza. The *Sentinel* reports that a barn washed right out to sea, still in its upright position!

After tossing and turning to the accompaniment of nature's crescendo one January night, I am awakened by a kiss on my forehead, his luxurious mustache tickling my skin. Still dreaming, I murmur, "Jacob."

A sharp exclamation replaces the soft warmth of the kiss.

I force my eyes open and my brain to awareness. Henry paces the room, fully dressed. He checks his pocket watch without looking at me. "Ellen, I must go to the mill."

I wipe sleep remnants from my eyes and nod. He is desperate to assess the damage from the storm that has kept him home since before the New Year. Stiff and tired from a night disrupted by storms, I listen. The wind still howls outside our snug home, but the rain doesn't slam against the windows.

Henry stops before me, places his watch back in its pocket and puts his hands on his hips. The clock in the parlor strikes, but my husband's stern face captures my attention so I can't count the tolling bells.

"How many children must we have before you stop calling his name in your sleep?"

"I'm sorry." Normally I would rise and walk him to the

door, but I am so tired. When I close my eyes for a moment, the room tilts. "I think I'll sleep a little longer," I tell him without opening my eyes.

"Pleasant dreams," he snarls.

I hear the creak of the third stair, then the front door clicking shut. Now that I'm awake, guilt prevents me from falling back to sleep. Henry is a good man. He deserves my heart, but I gave it away long ago. I rise from bed and don a gown. I move slowly although I do not think I am ill.

Later I retire to the parlor, where I remove my knitting from a basket kept by the fire. I can knit and think about how to cheer Henry tonight. Maybe the cook can make his favorite vanilla almond cake for tonight's dessert. My guilt stabs me. It'll mean more if I make it. My knitting falls to my lap.

Our daughters play on the floor, quarreling quietly, moods matched to the weather. Moisture is in the air; the windowpanes are sweating. Another storm moves closer. Fresh rain pelts the windows as a sharp rap at the door draws me from my thoughts.

I rise and answer. On the stoop a mill worker has removed his hat and is shaking droplets to the boards below. Something about his expression... Dread descends on me and I feel the blood leave my face. Visions of a telegram ten years old haunt me. *Jacob killed in mining accident. My deepest condolences.*

"Mrs. VanValkenburgh?" the mill worker says, twisting the sodden bowler in his hands. He has trouble keeping his eyes to mine. Swallowing, he barrels on, "The mill sent me ma'am. There's been an accident—I'm so sorry."

"What are you saying!" I shout at him. If I have the courage to hear it, he should have the courage to say it.

"I'm so sorry. We was cuttin' a tree ma'am. It fell wrong ... A branch hit Mr. VanValkenburgh ... He's dead, ma'm..."

I am unable to respond, and he slinks away into the storm. For several minutes, I listen as the rain patters on the porch roof. Then I shut the door and lean my head against the painted wood.

Jacob and I were married a year—two months of bliss and ten months of waiting. Then the telegram. With Henry I had eight years and two daughters. In the eyes of some, the second marriage was more successful. To me, it makes no difference. I am once again widowed.

Gradually the sound of my daughters arguing over something trivial draws me back. I stagger to the parlor. For a moment I have no words. "Mary, Ellie." My soft voice silences them. "Darlings, your father will not be coming home tonight. We'll have our supper without him."

"Will he be home in time to kiss us goodnight, Mama?" Marion asks, scrunching her brow. Her father is never late.

"No, Mary, he won't." I don't want to have this conversation now. Three-year-old Ellie stares at me, her blue eyes as wide as the ocean. Marion is still trying to puzzle out my words.

The serving girl comes from the kitchen to see who was at the door. "It seems I am not meant to be a married woman," I tell her. She gasps and gathers the children, taking them off to the kitchen as I watch the rain pound the window. There will be no vanilla almond cake ever again for Henry.

Within days, Mama arrives and takes over the running of the house. I wander aimlessly from room to room, feeling sorry for myself. One morning Mama finds me in Henry's den, staring out the window.

"Ellen, you must busy yourself with something," she scolds. "Isn't there a meeting you can go to?"

She has taken upon herself everything that used to fill my time, but she means well. "Yes, Mama," I murmur.

Pursing her lips in frustration, she glares at me. "You look too imposing."

A small, pretty woman, Mama takes after her Day family relatives in New York. I have inherited the beaked nose of my father and the square build of a pioneer woman. Clad in black that is once again mourning, I suppose I am indeed imposing.

"Maybe Uncle Benjamin has room for you and the girls."

She can't be serious. Even so, I am jolted out of my self-pity into a course of action I have only begun to contemplate. "Mama, I need to run the mill. I will go in tomorrow and set it to rights."

Her face pales to the shade of the new moon. "Run the mill?" she says weakly.

The next morning I pin my black hat securely and don my coat and gloves. Kissing the girls goodbye, I wave to Mama and climb into the carriage. Having decided upon this course of action, I'm not even nervous. The mill cannot run itself, and there's no one else.

A bearded man in dirty pants, his suspenders hanging loose, occupies my husband's office. I sweep in and demand he vacate. He hurries to pull up the suspenders and leave Henry's chair, but he stands firm.

"What can I do for you, Mrs. VanValkenburgh?"

I remove my hat and gloves, placing them on the desk. I hang my coat on the rack and turn to face him. "I will need to meet with the mill foreman this morning." I seat myself at the desk and scan the open ledger atop it. I don't actually see any of the numbers written there as I wait for his response.

"Ma'am?" Clearly he's confused. "I'm the foreman."

I look up. "Then you are Samuel. Please gather the men. I wish to speak with them."

He still looks confused as I return my eyes to the ledger, and it's hard to hide a smile. Sixty men currently work for me. The plant is valued at $100,000, paper orders are strong, and production running well.

Samuel returns in an hour. He's doing a better job of masking his confusion. "The men are assembled, ma'am."

"Thank you, Samuel."

I sweep out of the room only to realize I don't know

where my workers are. Samuel hastens ahead of me. Outside in the January chill my mill workers stand in loose groups. Some are curious, but most are irritated they have been pulled away from their posts. I step up on the wooden walkway that rings the building. It's not a stage, but it puts me two steps above them.

"Good morning. I am Ellen VanValkenburgh, and I will be taking over my husband's duties here at the mill. I will relay my orders to you through Samuel." I nod to the foreman, whose face has gone as white as New York snow. "I expect the operation to continue to run smoothly. You may return to your posts."

No one moves for a long moment, and I expect rebellion. Instead, I get snorts of surprise, shaking heads, and bursts of decidedly negative conversation. The men do not look happy as they trudge back to work. I suppose I should be pleased I had no hoots of derision or outright defiance. Still looking after the last of the departing men, I address the foreman next to me.

"I want you to go over the books with me, Samuel."

"Yes, ma'am." His face and tone are carefully neutral. He's had time to adjust. The others will come around.

The rest of the day is spent in Henry's office, now mine, going over the operation with Samuel. At his suggestion, I call in the shift supervisors of each operation. I start with the end of the process and work backwards. The cocky man who runs the cutting and packaging of the paper rolls for shipment by rail to San Francisco and beyond clearly sees this meeting with me as an unnecessary delay. Samuel introduces him, but lets him describe his duties.

"It's as the title says. I cut and package the paper."

His tone is one I'd use with the girls. My eyes narrow. "I'm sure you'd like to get back to it. I appreciate your time." Conciliatory rather than confrontative. I need these men.

The next supervisor is garrulous, almost afraid to let me talk. He makes himself comfortable in the chair facing my desk as he goes on and on. "We take the pulp, ma'am and rinse it, then dilute it with good San Lorenzo river water, and then add some clay. Pump all that into the headbox of the paper machine where the water is drained away..."

I nod and smile, but I can't follow all he says. I find I'm not interested in the minute details of making paper.

When Samuel brings in the next man, my eyes water at the chlorine smell. He's our pulp bleacher, and I'm glad he is reticent. I can't maintain my dignity when my nose is twitching.

By comparison, the supervisor of pulping is practically mute. I sneak a glance at Samuel, wondering if he's done this on purpose, and catch a smile twitching on his face.

"We remove lignin."

"You do. And what is lignin?"

"Glue. Holds wood together."

"Why don't we want it?"

"Discolors paper."

My questions are clearly torture, but I extract the information before sending him on his way. While Samuel's fetching the last of the supervisors, I allow myself a wide grin. I'm smiling when I hear voices outside the office, but the smile evaporates when the men enter. Samuel has brought the man who notified me of Henry's death. He stands much as did on my front porch, but this time he does not have his hat in his hand.

"Good afternoon," I say softly.

He's determined to say his piece and get out. "I am in charge of logging. We cut the pines and take them by wagon to the mill. Crew takes off the bark and runs 'em through the chipper."

I don't really hear his words. I'm fixated on the image of this man watching as a falling tree branch kills my husband.

I'm unaccountably tired when I return home.

Mama greets me with disapproval. "Are you finished playing the man of the house?"

"The mill is our livelihood, Mama."

"Maybe so, but a good foreman can run it. Your place is here."

I move through the entry into the parlor, where Marion and Ellie greet me with hugs and kisses, saving me from having to answer. Mama's right. My place is here with my daughters. It's now my responsibility, however, to provide for them. That means my place is also at the mill.

By the end of the week, exhaustion is my constant companion. I hide it from the men at the mill, who must see me as competent, and I hide it from my mother, who must see me as coping, and I hide it from the girls, who must see me as loving. I attribute my fatigue to managing the mill. One morning, though, I am unable to keep down my breakfast and realization dawns. I am with child.

San Lorenzo Paper Mill, Santa Cruz, California, circa 1861
Photograph from the Lawrence & Houseworth Collection,
Bancroft Library, UC Berkeley

Chapter 6: Santa Cruz 1862
Ellen Rand VanValkenburgh

An almond tree may blossom in the spring of its life, but the value of its fruit is not known until fall. Can thirty-four be considered the fall of one's life? I'm not as excited by my condition as I would have been a few weeks ago. I lean against the rough bark of the almond tree, counting on the physical sensation to ground me and keep me from panic. The thought of running the mill while pregnant overwhelms me. The ocean roars and crashes, then roars and crashes again. It never stops for the problems of people, and I envy its strength and the stability of its future.

Mama joins me in the yard, sitting on a chair that has seen many sunny afternoons. Now the sky is gray and the wind laughs at us. Mama supports me in silence.

"The foreman at the mill has no passion for paper production, Mama. He cannot lead the men, just supervise them." I realize my hand is cupping my belly as a woman in my condition does, already protective of the tiny life inside. I move my hand to my leg.

"And *you* have passion for paper making?" Her eyebrow rises.

"I know very little about it, but it's where our money comes from. I will carry on, but I need your help. And please, Mama, not a lecture."

I give her credit for the hesitation that follows. She tries. Someday maybe I'll know what it is like to talk to a headstrong daughter who won't listen to advice.

"I do know about strong wills like yours," she begins. "I bore six children and had two die at a year old. Coelia got her college education then married, had four children, then moved out here to California and had a fifth. L'Amie came out here, then went back East to become a doctor. Who does she think will hire a female doctor?" She shook her head. "Your brother Joseph came out here dazzled by gold and is living in San Francisco. You've had two husbands die, Ellen, but you are not crumpled in a heap. You continue to live. So you go manage your mill, darling, and I will begin looking for your next husband."

"Mama," I begin, intending to protest that I know all the family history, and that I don't need a husband, but I'm not able to find the energy. Instead, we sit as we have all fall while the girls played in the yard.

Mama covers my hand with hers. "Now you know you

cannot manage a mill with an infant. You will need a man to handle your affairs so you can be a mother."

She does have a point. I'll need more help than only she can provide, and I can hardly hire a husband.

We break the news of their impending sibling to the girls at dinner that day. It's a blustery Sunday in late January, and their cheeks are flushed pink with wind kisses. Listening to them report to us about the level of the river, which has finally begun to recede, I think about Mama's earlier words and wonder what is ahead for these two. Marion is very independent, a thrill seeker, while Ellie is sweet and shy.

I wait until they finish their story, then I say, "In September you will have a new baby brother or sister." I pat my stomach, but they do not realize babies come from inside their mother.

"You don't know if it will be a brother or sister?" Marion asks, frowning. "Can we have a brother? I already have a sister."

"Me too," Ellie says.

Coelia was about Marion's age when I was born, and I wonder if she ordered a brother. "I'm sorry, darlings, but I don't get to choose."

"Do babies come from heaven, Mama?" Marion asks.

I know she's learned that her father is with God in heaven, and I decide that is the best way around complicated explanations. "Yes, they do. So we will be happy with whatever God and your father send us, won't we?"

"I still want a brother, but I guess a sister would be all right." Marion looks at Ellie with a frown.

Ellie, of course, has gravy smeared all over her face. "Brother, brother, brother," she chants.

I give Mama an imploring look. She laughs, but comes to my rescue. "You girls must be very helpful to your mother now." Conversation shifts to a discussion of what chores the girls can help with, and I'm free of uncomfortable questions about babies. I agree with them, though. I, too, hope it is a boy.

* * *

As my body swells, Mama is a blessing, helping with the girls and the grocery shopping. She even uses a portion of our savings to buy a laundry in nearby Brighton. Now we both leave the house to go to work each morning, leaving the girls in the care of our serving girl. I refrain from teasing her as our financial predicament is far from rosy.

My condition is easy to hide at the mill. I wear loose black gowns and depend upon the general lack of astuteness men have about such matters. I also wait until the morning sickness has passed before going in to work each day. Once or twice I hear an overloud mutter about the boss's hours, but I fix the culprit with a frosty glare and do not engage in conversation.

The San Lorenzo River runs down from the Santa Cruz Mountains to the Pacific Ocean through some beautiful country. Redwood trees reach for the sky amidst the softwoods we cut for our paper: fir, spruce, pine, hemlock, and larch. Birds sing in the forest, and the rushing water provides soothing background music until you near the mill.

In a raw dirt clearing, the paper mill is a vision of ugliness. The furnaces roar and belch smoke and steam all day and night. Trains answer with their own steam and smoke as they come and go, the locomotive whistles emptying the area of birdsong. Dirty unshaven men heave logs into the water so the bark can be stripped, then the wood is ground to remove pulp. In an adjacent building, the pulp is cooked to soften it. The men who work here cover their noses with kerchiefs, but it doesn't help since the horrible odor permeates the air and clings to clothing. The pulp is then dried and shaped, using steam-powered heavy machinery that deafens its operators and covers them with sweat as the endless sheet of paper winds up and down over countless cylinders. The finished paper is rolled and shipped by rail over the Santa Cruz Mountains to San Francisco in boxcars.

It's noisy, dirty, smelly, and full of men. The work is physically hard, but not particularly demanding mentally. The paper mill is never going to be a place to discuss national politics, or bring up issues like votes for women. My day is spent making sure the orders I receive balance the checks I write to pay invoices and salaries. I learn how to make paper, but I never learn to love it.

On an otherwise pleasant spring morning, I am sifting through my growing pile of unpaid invoices when Mrs. Lockner pokes her head into my office. She's my secretary and another female face, although not always a friendly one.

"Mr. Sime for you, ma'am."

I don't know Mr. Sime. I rise to greet him as he enters my office. He's a tall man, his hands too smooth to be those of a laborer, with small eyes and a weak chin. Leaning across my desk, I offer my right hand like a colleague. He looks a bit taken aback, but rallies and shakes my hand.

"Please, Mr. Sime, take a seat and tell me how I might assist you." I indicate the chair I use for visitors, and he sits, holding his hat in his hand.

"It's a pleasure to make your acquaintance, Mrs. VanValkenburgh. I am sorry I have not been by sooner to offer my condolences." He pauses, but I say nothing. "I am the banker supervising construction for the California Powder Works, building upriver from here." I nod, aware of the project. "I'm afraid your dam is backing up water into our facility, ma'am. I've come to ask you to remove it."

Before I reply, I take a moment to wonder why they have sent a banker instead of a foreman. "Remove it, Mr. Sime? Since it was there first, why do you not build your facility on higher ground?"

He turns his hat between his hands, a nervous gesture. Clearly he hasn't expected me to question him.

"I'm afraid that is impossible at this late date, ma'am."

"I rely on that dam to provide water power for some of the machinery, Mr. Sime. I'm sure you understand." I use the sweet-but-steely voice required to deal with men in this industry.

"I do understand, Mrs. VanValkenburgh, but I am afraid the dam must go. I am prepared to offer an arrangement, however." He pauses, but I merely wait. "Our engineer has determined that he can run a flume from our operation to provide water for your machinery."

I reach behind me for a rolled map, which I unroll over my desk. "Show me where you will build this flume," I say, ignoring his discomfort at having to move closer to me.

"Um...er...let me see." It is almost comical how carefully he moves to the side of the desk, as if he is in danger of catching some disease. He points out the proposed flume location on the map.

I have no idea if it will work for us or not, but my foreman will. "I see. I will take this under advisement, and my foreman, Samuel, will get back to you in a few days."

Mr. Sime stutters a goodbye and stumbles over himself to leave. I can't abide weak men. As I follow the banker to the door, I smile at Mrs. Lockner, hoping to share the experience with her, but she's carefully focused on the correspondence. I seem to have more in common with Samuel than with her.

Samuel believes the powder mill's flume will serve us adequately and is dispatched to tell Mr. Sime so. Unfortunately, not all my interactions with the local business people go as well.

Late in January, I put on my best black dress and hat,

heading for the bank. I know it chafed at Henry to have a loan outstanding with Wells Fargo, but there's no other bank with which to do business. Now I must persuade them to increase our loan so I may repair what remains of damage to the mill from the great storm that killed my husband. I've been called into the bank to hear the verdict of the loan specialist who is, of course, a man.

"Mrs. VanValkenburgh, thank you for coming."

He sits behind an ornate carved desk, polished to a wealthy gleam. The carpets are so thick I fear my feet will disappear. I need his good will too much to be snide about his gratitude for my compliance with his summons. He stares at me as if I'm some sort of exotic beast he's purchasing for a zoo. I stare back, impassive, as my heart beats erratically. "My pleasure, sir."

He shuffles the papers in his hand, as if he doesn't already know what they say. "I see here a Henry VanValkenburgh currently has a loan outstanding with us?"

"My deceased husband."

"I see. I am quite sorry that we are unable to extend any credit to you at this time. In fact, in light of the current situation, we are going to have to call in your husband's loan."

"He's been paying that off for a year." My despair echoes hollowly behind my words.

"Not regularly, I'm afraid. And with him gone..." He shrugs his shoulders in an exaggerated gesture. "Your financial acuity is untried, Mrs. VanValkenburgh. Please do not take offense. It's merely business."

He turns down a new loan and demands payment for the existing one, yet he doesn't expect me to take it personally? My anger cracks through the composure I have struggled to maintain. "I shall never bank with Wells Fargo again." We both know the threat is empty. It's the only bank in town and I have less money every day. Nonetheless, I lift my chin and sweep from his office.

That same day President Lincoln authorizes the Union to take aggressive action against the Confederacy. General McClellan ignores the president's order as the banker has ignored my request for a loan. By March, President Lincoln has relieved McClellan of command, but I'm still going to the mill each day.

I am two months pregnant, but it's still a private matter. No one can see the changes in my body, but I can feel new life in my heart and soul. This seed of a child means more to me than war in the East, more even than the paper mill. I take comfort in this child I don't yet know when suppliers refuse to ship orders scheduled by Henry or to take new orders from me.

"Are ya sure that ya need all these chemicals, little lady?" One man tells me as he stands before me. He has my order in front of him, and it's no different than Henry's regular orders. "These be pretty scary serious chemicals. I don't know as I can send them out without knowing you can handle them."

"It's the same place you've been sending them for a year," I protest sharply.

"But now a *woman's* in charge? Everyone knows women are too emotional to deal with the delicate nature of chemicals. I don't think I can fill this order. I'm sorry."

He's not sorry. And I'm too emotional to deal rationally with him—I want to kill him. He'd no doubt blame my emotional state on my condition if he knew of it.

In April, the Battle of Shiloh is a shallow victory for General Grant. The Confederate forces almost overcome the Union, and casualties are heavy. I read about it in the newspaper, but the ever-present struggle of running the mill is much more real and pressing.

I look up from the paper at a knock on my door. Samuel waits for me to bid him enter, which I do.

"Ma'am? I'm sorry to interrupt..."

Samuel has been a rock. I really don't know if he approves of me as his boss, but he's very conscious of his duty and does his job well. "Come in, Samuel."

He does, but stands nervously before me. "Five more men have left, ma'am."

"Reason?"

He rubs his neck. "I believe they are going east to enlist."

I fold the paper and set it on my desk. These are not the first men to leave, but at least they haven't disappeared in the night. "What have they said?"

He fidgets and looks at the floor. "One says his minister tells him he must not work for a woman. Another claims his increased drinking is due to the instability of the mill. Three admit they are going to war."

The reasons are ludicrous, but no more so than the excuses of others who have left, and I've had a lot of trouble hiring more men. "Thank you, Samuel."

He escapes with relief and the day goes on as they all do. Exhausted and frustrated, I battle my way to work each morning and home each night.

In the house on Union Street I can let down my guard. Here I can laugh and be silly with my daughters and gossip with my mother, and cry into my pillow at night with worry about my baby's future. It's not just the baby. Marion and Ellie are growing and need new clothes. Food must be on the table every day, and the serving girl must be paid. Cash reserves accumulated in San Francisco have gone long ago to pay for constructing the paper mill, and our income is drying up like the paper in the sheds.

In May, General Stonewall Jackson defeats Union forces in the Shenandoah Valley. Union troops retreat across the Potomac to protect Washington D.C. In news so local it doesn't reach the paper, Samuel defeats me. He comes into my office at quitting time and quits. To his credit, he looks miserable.

"I'm sorry, ma'am, but I have a family. The army offers advancement and good pay. It's not that I want to leave, or that I want to be a soldier. It's all about my family."

Since my chair was sized for Henry, it is the most uncomfortable one I own. I lean back and stretch, trying to control emotions that are too close to the surface these days. My body, with this third child, has remembered how to expand with a baby and my belly is beginning to round. Samuel has four children. His eyes pop.

"Mrs. VanValkenburgh?"

He is too polite to come right out and ask.

"Yes, Samuel, I am with child." I intend to be professional, to tell him I understand why he is leaving and to wish him well. But I can't. My mood has swung too far toward despair.

"Oh. Is it Henry's?" he asks, and then colors at his cheekiness.

Despair swings instantly to anger, and it has nothing to do with my condition. "That does not dignify a response, sir. Suffice it to say that I am five months along. You may collect your final pay from Mrs. Lockner. Good day."

He scampers from my office like a dog with a stolen treat.

My shape rounds further, and it's harder to get to the mill every day. Samuel must have spread the news of my condition before leaving the grounds, because soon even the most obtuse of my men are aware of it. It's physically difficult to move around the facility. Despite my condition, or maybe because of it, the men who are left slack off. Some have expressed their shock that I'm leaving home so pregnant, that I'm running the mill, that I make decisions. Others just shake their head and mutter. I'm unpopular and uncomfortable.

June brings the Battle of Seven Pines, and I wonder if any of my former workers take part. The Union is saved only by last-minute reinforcements, and I pray for some last-minute reinforcements to save the mill.

But it is not to be. I arrive one morning to be greeted by an eerie stillness. No steam hangs in the air; the factory is silent and empty of workers. A Notice of Foreclosure is nailed to the door of the main building. I stand and stare at it, crumpling inside. Then I turn, slowly waddle back to the carriage, and direct the driver to take me home.

Marion and Ellie are still at the breakfast table when I surprise them with my return. Mama looks up, instantly worried.

"Today is too nice a day to work, darlings," I say. "Shall we go to the beach?"

Amidst the delighted screams and excited chatter, I manage to tell Mama what has happened. "I will not worry about it today," I tell her in a low voice. "I cannot. Today we keep a light heart, and tomorrow we worry for the future."

She nods and gives my hand a quick squeeze. "I have the Brighton laundry. It's an income."

In no time, we four females set off, walking along Mission Street and through town to the beach near the wharf. I take Ellie with me into a changing cabana, and Mama takes Marion. We emerge in our fashionable beachwear, purchased last year on our arrival in this seaside town. Mama and I are clad in blousy pants reminiscent of the bloomers I wore aboard ship on my trip from New York. Our blouses are also loose fitting and long-sleeved. Wide-brimmed hats shelter our faces from the sun, which is just now burning away the morning fog.

Marion and Ellie wear one-piece bathing dresses and are soon running to and fro on the wet sand with the waves lapping at their bare feet. They resemble the sandpipers that rush in to nibble sand crabs and rush out again when the waves return. Marion builds a tall mountain of wet sand and decorates it with bits of seashell. Ellie digs in the sand with a stick her sister finds for her. Our serving girl has packed a picnic lunch that we spread on a checkered cloth to eat. Although I dislike the grit blown into my food, I am content with the warm sand, crashing waves, and screeching gulls. Around us, other families are enjoying the sun and sand and ocean. The beach is Santa Cruz. It endures, and so will I. We trudge back up the hill, tired and sunburned.

Mama cables my sister Coelia. Lucian helps us financially until the mill is auctioned and Henry's affairs settled. I can't be dismayed about my failure to keep the mill. I gave it my best effort. Family will provide. We've always rallied to support each other and will continue to do so. I have no desire to marry again, although I don't say this to my mother. She's a strong woman, but strength in her generation differs from strength in mine.

July passes without incident in Santa Cruz, although the war rages. The battle of the *Monitor* and the *Merrimac* takes place, but Mama is not one to discuss ironclad ships.

My wonderful daughters are six and four in August, and our baby due in a month. Union forces are defeated at the Second Battle of Bull Run, but I'm completely focused on delivering a healthy child.

On September 13, world events pale to insignificance. Eight months to the day after his father's death, my son is born. I name him Henry, of course, and his sisters are delighted.

Ellen VanValkenburgh and her son, Henry

Chapter 7: Santa Cruz 1868
Ellen Rand VanValkenburgh

In the front yard of our snug house on Union Street, I examine the tight green buds on the almond tree and try to ignore the letter in my hand. Soon spring will leaf out the tree, and blossoms will burst forth to hide the new green. Every year, the tree's exuberance of new life cheers me. The letter in my hand, however, has weighted my soul. I don't need to read the words again. Their pain is imprinted on my heart.

Oh, Ellen, I am bereft. My dear George has been taken from me, mere months from the birth of our child.

My little sister should not have to mimic my own past pain. How then does L'Amie lose the love of her life while pregnant with his child?

I know you will want me to come to you in California, and

*maybe I will once the babe is born. Rest assured my doctor friends will
see to my health and well-being.*

"No, I need you here, dear sister," I whisper to the wind.
"If only for my own peace of mind." For a year and a half,
L'Amie's letters have been full of happy pride as she and her
doctor husband practiced medicine together in Minnesota, a
state unknown to me.

"Mama? Is everything all right?"

Marion has come to find me. At eleven, she has a
precocious sense of when something is amiss. I was never so
sensitive to those around me, and I don't want to burden her
with my problems. I force a smile. "Just some sad news, darling.
Your Uncle George passed away in December."

"Uncle George?" she frowns.

"My sister L'Amie's husband," I remind her. They are just
names to Marion. L'Amie left for medical school in New York
when Marion was a toddler and Ellie just a baby. "And guess
what? Aunt L'Amie is going to have a baby." I try to infuse
pleasure into my voice, but I should know better. Her face is still
frowning, and her eyebrow arches.

"How can she do that with no husband?"

"Oh, Mary," I chide her gently. "Your brother was born
after Papa died, remember?"

She nods, but I can see behind her eyes the gears of her
brain working. In an hour, or two, she will ask another question.
I hope I'll be able to answer it.

A roughly dressed man comes up the walk, whistling. He waves a cheery greeting. Richard, who works as a laborer in an apple orchard, has boarded at our house for a couple of years now. The income is necessary, and the company not unpleasant. He tips his hat to me and continues into the house, calling back to me, "I'll check on Mrs. Perkins."

I nod agreement with a sigh. The leaf buds on the tree and valiant sun trying to warm away the cold breeze of winter have conspired with L'Amie's letter to distract me from Mama's illness. I put my arm around Marion, who crinkles her nose but doesn't pull away. It won't be long before she thinks she's too grown up for a mother's hug. "Let's go see what the children are doing, shall we?"

All smiles now that I have elevated her above her eight-year-old sister and five-year-old brother, Marion skips ahead.

I continue upstairs to Mama's bedroom, where the curtains are closed tight against the day's brilliance. The room is dim and smells of age. Mama is 61, and certainly that is not as old as I once thought, even though at forty years old I sometimes feel like Methuselah. I don't know what ails her because I cannot conceive of anything strong enough to strike her down. I enter the room quietly so as not to disturb her, but she turns toward me at once.

Her brown hair lays in a tangle around her face with its sunken cheeks and hollow eyes. She smiles, though, and I smile back. "Hello, Mama. It's a pretty spring day. May I open the curtains a bit?"

"Not too far, Ellen. The sun hurts my eyes." I can barely hear her response, and that makes my heart skip a beat.

I open the draperies so that a slice of golden sun angles across the room, and I return to sit in the chair beside the bed. She reaches for me, and our hands lay clasped on the coverlet. Hers is covered in paper-thin skin too big for its bones, while mine is work-roughened and coarse.

L'Amie's letter is in my mind, but I mustn't share bad news with Mama. In her current state of mind, she would dwell on George's death until she achieved her own. I must answer L'Amie and tell her of Mama's illness. I hardly know what to say. Maybe Mama will be feeling better tomorrow and I can share that with my sister.

"Mama, I've had a letter from L'Amie. She's expecting a child."

"Oh? How nice." Mama perks up a bit, but closes her eyes.

"It will be born in August, I think," I say, counting up the months in my head. "Maybe she'll bring the little one out here for a visit."

"That would be nice." Her voice trails off and I disengage my hand, patting it as I pull away. She doesn't respond.

I close her bedroom door softly and go down to the kitchen to see if there's any more broth for her supper.

By the time the almond tree is carpeted in white blossoms with deep pink throats, Mama is well enough to sit on the porch with a blanket over her legs. Her papery skin hangs over bones that are too visible, but she smiles at Henry, who is chasing Ellie with a stick around the yard. Both are screaming.

"I think he is trying to rescue her," I say, laughing.

"He's a pretty scary knight. I think she'd rather not be rescued at all." Mama's voice is too soft, but her chuckle warms my heart.

"He'll be six in September, Mama. It's past time for him to start school."

She frowns. "Already? Can't he stay home a bit longer?"

"No. The best public school in the county is right here on Mission Hill." I gave in to her desire to keep her grandson close last year, but this year I must send him. I want the girls to go, too, but I am afraid Mama's health won't stand it. I don't know why she is against public school. It's the most modern way to achieve an education, and she has always supported education. My oldest sister, Coelia, graduated from Rutgers Female Institute in 1841, and L'Amie, of course, is a doctor. My brother Joseph and I have no formal college, but both of us went to school for our basic education. Mama's mind changes as she ages. Today, she sees no value in school.

"Most children don't go to school," she says.

"Actually, Mama, most do attend now. The superintendent of county schools teaches at Mission Hill, and the school is funded mostly by public subscription." I am warming to my topic, but my audience has fallen asleep.

In a decision that will haunt me forever, I allow her to nap in the too-chilly spring sunshine. She awakes hours later with a cough that persists even after I tuck her back into bed and draw the curtains, returning her to dimness. She refuses broth. She refuses company as her lungs fill with fluid.

Three days later I pause outside her door and realize I hear no rasping breath, no cough. I grip the doorknob, hoping for improvement but fearing decline. The sun leaks in around the curtains, lighting the room enough to silhouette my mother in her bed. Impossibly, she has shrunken further, as if collapsing in upon herself. I am certain, before I place my hand on her chest, that she is gone. I clasp her cold hand in my warm one.

"Oh, Mama, I shall miss you so," I whisper as my tears fall. Guilt over that afternoon in the yard strangles my breath, but I will treasure our last shared pleasure for all my days.

April showers water the earth as we prepare to bury my mother. Some of the society ladies arrive with casseroles and condolences, chattering and over-enthusiastic. Their children race about the garden with Ellie and Henry. I am detached emotionally, watching it all and doing what is expected. Nothing touches my heart but Marion, hovering in the shadows, watching me with worried eyes.

In the days that follow, I walk along Cliff Drive to Point Santa Cruz, where the city plans to build a lighthouse. The breakers far below me crash against the rocks, causing the foaming spray to spatter the cliffs. The tumult of the sea echoes in my heart. Once again, though, I must go on.

With a pang of guilt, I enroll all three children at Mission Hill School, and they start immediately. Marion will be in the upper grade, in the main room. Ellie and Henry will be with the younger children in the side room of the school. Only a month or so remains in the school term, but I want them to accustom themselves before beginning the new term in the fall. On their first day, the bright sun has overcome the fog and lingering winter chill. I walk them along Mission Street, chatting lightly to cover my own nervous butterflies.

Marion's eyes gleam with new zeal. I have taught her to read, but more than simple mathematics is beyond me. "Mama, what do you think I will learn today?"

"Today you will learn where to hang your hat and when to have lunch." I smile at her. "You do not have to conquer the world on your first day, Mary."

"Tomorrow, then?" she asks me, and we laugh together.

She walks on ahead, and I am so proud of her independence. Ellie walks next to me, clutching her satchel instead of my hand. I tried to take her hand as we left home, but she shook it off, wanting to be independent like her sister. Her forehead crinkles with anxiety, though, and I want to hug her.

"The school will have lots of new stories to read, Ellie." She loves to read, and luring her with books has been the only way she's come willingly. I hope her fear of the unknown doesn't keep her inside the walls of her own home forever.

"I know, Mama." She takes a deep breath and stands a little straighter. She still clutches her bag, but she's looking more determined than terrified.

Henry holds my hand, as befits the baby of the family. He scuffles his feet in the dirt to make dust clouds. "Henry, you must be clean for school. Pick up your feet, sweetheart," I tell him. He regards me with eyes that are deep brown like his father's. The girls are a blend of both of us, but I'm sure if I could see pictures of his father at five, he and his son would be alike.

Before I know it we have arrived outside the white-painted single-story building that will open my children's world. The bell in the tower calls the children to class, echoing the tolling of the bell at the mission up the street. I kiss Henry and Ellie, putting Henry's hand in Ellie's and giving them a gentle push toward the door. I have to catch hold of Marion's hand to hold her back so I can place a quick kiss on her cheek. "Watch out for them," I beg her. She rolls her eyes and hurries after her younger siblings.

One of the reasons I chose to start them today is that some of the mothers are gathering this morning to discuss school needs. Mrs. James Manor happened to be in the school office when I enrolled my three, and she invited me on the spot to today's affair. Her house is across from an apple orchard near the school. I am admitted quickly, and find half a dozen women already there. Mrs. Manor introduces me, and I realize this is the cream of Santa Cruz society.

Mrs. Hihn's husband is the county's first millionaire. Mrs. Blackburn's husband is an apple orchardist. My business sense did not die with the paper mill. I know the apple business is suffering now. A box of apples that once cost $2.50 is now worth only a quarter. Mrs. Waters is present, too. Her husband lost a thousand trees to a flood a few years back. We all are facing hard times financially although no one, of course, says so.

Mrs. Blackburn leans forward with a smile. "Welcome, Mrs. VanValkenburgh."

I take a seat in the elegantly furnished parlor and sip tea from a porcelain cup as fragile as an almond blossom. Mrs. Manor takes her place near the piano and turns to me. "Mrs. VanValkenburgh, currently we see three areas where our school can improve." She ticks them off on her fingers. "First, the school needs a library on campus for the use of the students. Secondly, the students need uniform textbooks. Most importantly, we must compel attendance."

Assuming my agreement, she turns to the group. They begin discussing ongoing efforts and quickly lose me. I'm not sure what they mean by uniform textbooks, but I agree that attendance should be required. I will catch on quickly. In the meantime, I bask in once more having a cause to rally around.

* * *

Summer fog rolls across the coastal towns, making July the dreariest month of the year. When the Fourteenth Amendment is ratified, though, I call on Mrs. Manor. It's been over a month since our last school meeting, and I am avidly writing letters to support compulsory attendance. Today, though, I want to discuss something else.

"Why, Mrs. VanValkenburgh, what a pleasant surprise!"

"Mrs. Manor, may we talk briefly? I am sorry to come by unannounced."

"Nonsense! Please come in."

Once settled in the parlor, I refuse her offer of tea. "Oh, no, I won't be here long. I just want to ask you to think about something. You've heard of the new amendment?"

Her face darkens. "Citizenship for freed slaves? Of course."

"It's more than that. It gives citizenship to all persons born in the United States."

She looks at me, brow furrowed, not making the connection.

"Weren't you and I born in the United States?" I ask softly. "And citizens can vote."

Her mouth rounds to an O. "Men believe that women are so different from them that they should never be considered in the same political discussions."

She is repeating common knowledge, not speaking gospel truth, so I say, "And we both know that is rubbish."

The consternation leaves her face and she laughs. "So true! We must discuss this further."

I take my leave, knowing that I have begun a conversation

among the women of Santa Cruz that will not be soon quenched.

The rest of the summer passes in a flurry of days at the beach with the children, letters to the city and county about textbooks and school attendance, and meetings. At this point we are merely discussing the idea of a suffrage society, but I am content that something is happening.

A letter arrives late in August that L'Amie has successfully delivered a son. I cry over the letter.

I rejoice and sorrow at the same time, as I know you will understand, she writes. *I can hardly wait to bring him West for a visit. I may very well relocate to Santa Cruz. I know it will please us both to be together again.*

"Oh yes, dear sister, I have missed you so," I tell the words on the page. "It would be wonderful to have you here. Santa Cruz needs a woman doctor, and I need my sister!"

School starts again in the fall, and all three of my children set off eagerly without me. Even Henry says, "Mama, I am too big to hold hands." My heart breaks with sorrow and pride.

In November, though, news strikes fear into every mother's heart. Smallpox has broken out in San Juan Bautista. It's far enough away that my children are not in immediate danger, but close enough to worry. Stagecoaches cancel their runs into the nearby town and the roads are barricaded to try and localize the outbreak. I read the paper every morning with increasing trepidation, but continue sending my children to school for now.

At one of our meetings, the women decide to collect money to assist the afflicted.

"We can protect our own children by inoculating theirs," Mrs. Blackburn says. We solemnly agree.

The town of Santa Cruz raises two hundred dollars that weekend. Two young Irishmen volunteer to brave the disease to deliver the serum. I hold Henry tight in my arms, as if a mother's love can battle smallpox, until we hear that they are safely returned.

Our prayers and our money do no good. In two days the plague has spread to Watsonville. Mr. Blackburn heads a group who rides along the Watsonville Road to demolish the bridge into town. I keep my children safe within the walls of our home. The rest of the school term is cancelled, probably because no one dares venture out. The *Sentinel* publishes daily remedies for preventing the spread of smallpox as well as treating it should that become necessary.

In November, it becomes difficult to put a dinner on the table. I have been unable to get to the market since the smallpox has reached Santa Cruz and the only thing barricading us from disaster is the front door. Henry is fussy and irritable, and I am tired with worry. I place our last chicken, roasted in onion gravy, on a platter.

"Ellen, you'd better look at this." Richard, our boarder, calls from the dining room. He stands beside Henry, who is slumped in his chair at the table. Richard waves at the boy's flushed face. I put down the platter of chicken and peer closer. Three red bumps glare from Henry's cheek.

The power of disease is truly amazing. It wipes from your mind any passion over school issues or voting in an election. All seems trivial compared to the illness of a child. I don't know whether to clutch him tightly or turn to check on my daughters, also seated at the table. My roasted chicken sits forgotten on its platter. I will always associate the smell of onion gravy and chicken with gut-wrenching fear.

"Ohhhh, Henry. Are you sick, sweetheart?" I feel his forehead. It's warm, but what is too warm for an active boy?

Richard, meanwhile, has examined the faces of my girls. "No spots here, Ellen."

"Take them into the parlor, please." My focus is all on Henry. I gather him in my arms and take him to his room. He twists and struggles to be free, but I have to hold him.

The next day, I peruse the *Sentinel* looking for remedies and symptoms and the list of those dead. I have not left Henry's room, where the curtains are closed against sunlight and pestilence both. The dimness reminds me of Mama's room just before she died. Henry tosses and turns in his bed. Only time will appease his discomfort and my anxiety, but waiting is torture. I make him curdled milk with lemon juice and pray it will work as the *Sentinel* promises.

Once a day I emerge from Henry's room to make sure Marion and Ellie are spot free. I am so proud of Marion as she helps Richard with meals for us all. Henry's spots linger, but do not fill with pus. Is it possible that this is not smallpox? I allow myself a speck of hope.

By the first week in December, the Sentinel reports fewer new cases and more recoveries. It also lists all four of the Blackburn children among the dead. Marion and Ellie both cry at the loss of school friends. I ache for their mother, but nothing can contain my own joy. Henry's spots are gone and he is demanding to get out of bed.

"Mama, I'm hungry and I don't want to be in bed any more." He kicks his feet under the covers for emphasis.

I throw back curtains and sunshine floods the room. "Darling, how about I make you a vanilla almond cake?"

Chapter 8: Santa Cruz 1871
Ellen Rand VanValkenburgh

Yellow has always been a color that is sunny, bright, and optimistic. No coincidence then that the suffrage movement has adopted it. This afternoon the hall we rent at the new Unity Church glows yellow. Early spring roses and daffodils, from the gardens of the ladies assembled here, fill tables covered in yellow cloth. The Women's Suffrage Association gathers in style, as they have for the past year.

Issues raise their heads and roar, each one clouding the main cause of the vote. I support temperance and abolition, but I long to vote. In Santa Cruz, my Women's Suffrage Association works with the churches and the other ladies' clubs to bring progress to each of our causes. There is a lot of work to do, but at least suffrage now has a face in our fair town.

"Good evening, Mrs. VanValkenburgh." The speaker is younger than I am, but a married woman. "So glad to be a part of this fine effort."

"Yes, Mrs. Hihn, thank you again for coming," I tell her with a polite smile.

"She says that every month," L'Amie, standing beside me, whispers.

"Yes, dear sister, but her husband is a member of the County Assembly and has real power to help us." For two years L'Amie has been back at my side where she belongs.

A few men, mostly husbands of the members, sit in a row of chairs along the back wall. I wish I could measure the depth of their devotion to the cause so as to determine if and when they are willing to act. I fear most are merely waiting for their wives.

Continuing to scan the room, I spot Marion pouring tea at the refreshment table. My oldest daughter has excellent posture, poise, and erudition, and her character is above reproach. Not bad for fifteen years old. When Mama passed three years ago, she left us money that keeps us housed and fed and pays for the simple but stylish dresses we wear. It is not enough, however, to fill the space she left in my heart or to attract a suitor for Marion. My political views are even more of a detriment, and now she has allied herself with the suffragists, possibly sealing her fate as a radical spinster. Her entire life has been molded by strong women with strong ideas, though, and I am proud of the young woman she is becoming.

The president's gavel brings the meeting to order, and I see Mrs. Hihn hurry to sit with Mrs. Kirby and Mrs. Blackburn and Mrs. Manor. They are the elite of Santa Cruz society, leaders of every civic group that supports the arts and the downtrodden. Their presence is a benediction, but I need warriors. They've not yet proven themselves as such.

"Hundreds of those freed negroes have arrived in Santa Cruz County," our president, Mrs. Howay, declares with just the right mix of pride and horror.

Having yielded my yearlong presidency to the pretty woman with more vision than action, I stifle a groan. Abolition of slavery is a victory, even if it means former slaves will be our neighbors. The women here don't all agree. Heads nod, but are accompanied by nervous titters. I am tired of nervous titters. I am tired of head nods, too. We must do something to make our struggle visible to the community.

"Actually, the group was not that large." Marion's interruption draws attention, and a roomful of skirts rustle as everyone turns toward her. "They joined a negro group already in Watsonville. That is not the issue."

"She's magnificent, Ellen," L'Amie whispers.

I agree. Marion is afire with youthful passion, idealism at its best, clad in one of her first grown-up floor-length skirts.

"What, pray tell, is the issue?" Mrs. Howay's tone is frostier than it should be. I frown in her direction. All other eyes are on my daughter, who reminds me of L'Amie at the same age.

"The Fifteenth Amendment has been ratified. Those negroes will be voting on our new trustee." Silence follows her words, and I know Marion has captured them. Everyone's face reflects outraged horror at the idea of Negro men being able to vote but not fine upstanding female citizens. The trustee election will put a new member on the board that runs our county and our town.

"Whatever will we do?" A theatrical gasp punctuates Mrs. Howay's words. It's a blatant attempt to retake control of the meeting. It doesn't work.

Marion is young. She has made her observation, but has no idea what to do now. She looks to me, panic starting to show on her face. Last year, when I started this organization, I was proud to serve as its first president. The ladies are eager to attend the meetings, but they dither about like a flock of chickens with a dog in the pen—lots of noise and motion, but no progress. They read the newspapers from New York and San Francisco. They held a grand party when Wyoming women won the vote in 1867, and they elected Mrs. Howay for our second president. Clearly they are lost. They need a leader. I step forward.

"The Fourteenth Amendment clearly states that all persons born in the United States are citizens. The Fifteenth Amendment prohibits the government from denying citizens the right to vote." At my words Marion smiles with relief, and the others are listening. "I think we should take advantage of that and register to vote in the next election."

A cacophony of clucking erupts.

"But those amendments were meant for the Negroes!"

"Can we do that?"

"The *Sentinel* would support us."

"The *Surf* would ridicule us!"

"My husband would not approve."

That last comment deadens the room. More than one of the ladies present agrees, or suspects it's true. I'm not sure how many will risk disapproval that will rock their homes, but I must continue. "We can sit here and sip tea, whining about what we want, or we can go get it. Some of our opponents say that women wouldn't vote if they had the right. We can refute that. The election is in April. That gives us a month."

Mrs. Howay proves she has worth. "An excellent idea, Mrs. VanValkenburgh. Shall we vote on the idea?"

A motion is quickly made and seconded. It passes. We'll be showing up to vote at the trustee election. Somber faces look at me.

"All of us?" I ask.

"I don't think that will happen," a reluctant voice near Marion says.

"Maybe we can elect a representative," suggests Mrs. Howay.

Everyone's already looking at me. They continue to do so as my name is suggested, a motion made and seconded, and the vote taken. Not long ago, L'Amie would have been included, but she is to be married later this week. She will be on her wedding trip during my attempt to register for the vote.

"Mrs. Ellen VanValkenburgh will be our representative. She will present herself to the registrar's office for the next election." I can't decide if Mrs. Howay is proud of me or relieved they didn't ask this of her.

A wail from the back corner announces that my younger children are bored with the proceedings and beginning to bicker. At nine, Henry's main source of amusement seems to be eliciting a shriek from his twelve-year-old sister, usually with a pinch. Ellie obliges, her blue eyes outraged. Marion hurries over to chastise her brother and soothe her sister, but the mood is broken and the meeting adjourns.

I gently receive congratulations and somber encouragement. Most of the ladies realize this is no frivolous matter, but they also seem to be realizing that they want no part of it. They will be openly supportive if I'm successful, this I know, but what will they say if I'm denied? L'Amie has left my side to join her fiancé, Simeon.

When L'Amie arrived two years ago, practically the first passenger on the new Transcontinental Railroad, she was ravaged with grief. It seems that as I celebrated Henry's deliverance from the threat of smallpox, L'Amie was burying her own small son. It still amazes me that such an important part of her life, a husband and a son, were gone before I could know them.

Simeon Herring, publisher of *The Independent Californian*, was the only person who managed to erase the dark circles under my sister's eyes. They are to be married this week. She still supports suffrage, but her husband comes first. I suppose that's as it should be.

"Mama?" Marion asks. "Are you pleased with the decision?"

Her hand firmly clenches her brother's. Ellie walks near, too old for holding hands. "Yes, I am," I tell them, my children, who will reap the seeds sown by my actions.

* * *

Two days later, we gather at Unity Church for my sister's second wedding. My girls are gowned in white and bedecked in fresh flowers. They look sweet and feminine. Amidst the bustle of preparations, I steal a moment alone with L'Amie.

For my second wedding, Mama refused to allow me to wear black. For hers, L'Amie has chosen a burgundy satin gown with tiny covered buttons up the front. The bodice and sleeves are tight fitting, and the front draped slightly to show the dark striped contrast fabric. Behind the dress billows more burgundy satin, as if the entire mass was bunched upon her behind, puddling in soft cloud about her feet. It is a very modern dress, appropriate for the occasion. She looks wonderful.

"Is it all right, Ellen?" she asks, straining to see her full reflection in some man's idea of a mirror.

"You're beautiful," I assure her, and she glows.

Fussing a bit with her veil, she meets my eye in the reflection of our faces. "So you will make history next week."

I nod. "The local officials have been cooperative. The county clerk has invited women to register. It's possible others will be there, too."

"Oh, Ellen, I know you believe in the vote, but you cannot make this your entire life. It's a lonely life, isn't it?" She turns to face me in person.

"I have my children," I say, staring into her face, wondering where her passion for suffrage has gone.

Her face darkens for a moment. "Not a substitute for another person who shares your heart and your dreams." The bride-glow returns to her face.

I try for a light tone. "Hasn't worked that way for me, but I truly hope it does for you."

"It's not too late, Ellen. You're only forty-four. Simeon completes me in ways I never thought possible again after George."

"Will you continue to practice medicine?"

She turns away. "My practice is here in Santa Cruz. We will be moving over the hill to Los Gatos, where Simeon has his newspaper."

My question lies between us, still, and grows heavy. Somewhere deep within, where I've tried to banish it, thoughts of betrayal try to escape. My sister got me involved in the movement, and now she is leaving it to become a wife and follow her husband's lead. I do hope she will be happy, but her choice only underscores how different we have become.

"You know, Ellen," she says softly, her thoughts clearly connected to mine, "married women also work for suffrage. Some are quite happy to share their lives, and many marriages are built on trust and teamwork."

Clearly I have nothing to offer her since I have never experienced the utopia she envisions. I kiss her on the cheek and smile my congratulations while squeezing her gloved hands for luck. Then I leave her to my daughters, who are her bridesmaids, and find my place in the church. The ceremony is a blur of family and friends, well-wishers all. If marriages are founded on good wishes, L'Amie and Simeon's will be blissful.

* * *

When I think ahead about presenting myself to the clerk at the county courthouse, it is always a faceless representative of The Government that greets me. On the day I head downtown to register for the vote, it is not like that at all. The sun has come out and I choose to see that as an omen. I leave the children at home with Marion, who wants to come, but I want to do this alone. I am in favor of results, not pomp. I pass people I know on the street and nod hello as I would on any normal day. Calm and confident, I near the courthouse. Walking toward me, no doubt coming from his office inside, Mr. Hihn recognizes me and tips his hat. I nod, wondering if his wife has told him what I am about. Of course, I have told no one but Marion that today is the day. Even so, the citizens of Santa Cruz are not daft. I hear a small group of people gathering behind me. Mr. Hihn turns on his heel and reenters the building without speaking.

The new courthouse is some eighty feet tall, topped with a soaring dome and trimmed with stone. Inside is a world of men. I pass offices of men whose wives I can categorize: suffragists, socialites, abolitionists, and milksops. The office of the County Clerk is devoid of visitors. I approach the desk of Captain Albert Brown, late of the U.S. Army, now clerk of our county as well as auditor and recorder. I wait in silence until he looks up from his ledger.

"Good morning, Captain Brown. I am here to register for the vote."

He carefully lays his fountain pen on its holder and removes his glasses from his face, folding them and putting them in his pocket. "I am afraid, Mrs. VanValkenburgh, that I cannot enter the name of a woman into the Great Register."

Anger flames inside me. This man has spoken well of women voting, has encouraged our registration, and now he denies me. "Why can you not enter my name?"

"It is not allowed, madam."

"Why is it not allowed?"

"You are not eligible, madam."

"Not eligible? I was born in New York, and as such am a citizen of this country. I have paid taxes in this county as sole supporter of three children for almost a decade. I demand that you do your duty and register my name."

"You are not eligible because of your gender, madam. You are a woman and therefore not eligible to vote."

"Then I will file suit."

He looks up at me, and my conviction is reflected in his eyes. Toughened by the battlefields of the Civil War, Captain Brown is no weakling. This is a man acting on strong beliefs, as I am. My anger dies, but not my resolve. Then he sighs and drops his gaze.

Pulling a sheaf of papers out of a desk drawer, he says, "I will initiate the paperwork for the lawsuit of VanValkenburgh v. Brown today."

I raise my chin and look down my prodigious nose at him. "Ellen R. VanValkenburgh."

His flint-black eyes are steady. "Versus Albert Brown."

Unity Church, built 1868

From Santa Cruz Public Library Photograph Collection

Chapter 9: Santa Cruz 1871-1872
Ellen Rand VanValkenburgh

The spring of 1871 is so busy with women's rights meetings that at first my noble action goes unnoticed. As days pass, I scan the pages of the *Sentinel* and skim articles about political conventions, party platforms, speeches and meetings, rallies and fundraisers, and nominations, all with names of men attached. Meanwhile, Judge Hagan of Santa Cruz County agrees to be my attorney. We petition the district court for a writ of mandamus to force Captain Brown to enroll my name in his precious Great Register. So this remains a local matter, submerged

by state and national furor.

Santa Cruz suffragists are likewise in a dither. Mrs. Susan

B. Anthony, our tireless national advocate, is coming to Santa Cruz! A relative of hers, Mr. Elihu Anthony, founded our town, and he has apparently informed her of our ardent support. I wonder if he has thought to relate the status of my lawsuit to the esteemed speaker? Her visit is set for August, and that is also when my case will come before the court.

L'Amie and Simeon return from a short wedding trip only to float off to Los Gatos on a cloud of wedded bliss. She thinks she will be happy opening a reading room, the first in San Jose, while her husband publishes his independent newspaper. He'll be in the thick of local and state events. She will be buried among dusty tomes and octogenarians with nothing better to do than read. Nonetheless, I wish her well.

Waiting is something I have long abhorred, and August is too far away. I dabble at needlework, letter writing, and lessons with the children, but my mind relentlessly returns to the lawsuit. On a blustery day in June, I leave Ellie and Marion at home and strike out on an adventure with Henry. My son and I spend too little time together, just the two of us, so these spontaneous days are precious.

He is a gentleman in miniature as he offers me his arm when we leave the house. I take it, nodding graciously and hiding my smile. Of average height for a nine year old, Henry takes to the clothes of a grown man well. His long trousers and Norfolk jacket are probably too old for him, but he is, after all, the man of our house. The salty wind blows at his brown hair, luring him to the ocean. It's not the vast sea itself that intrigues Henry, but the bustle of the wharf.

California Powder Works, the state's only source of gunpowder, sends its wares to the world from right here at Steamship Wharf. The company thrived during the Civil War due to overwhelming demand. I remember the flume that they installed upstream of the San Lorenzo Paper Mill, which was auctioned off and eventually came under the control of John Sime, the banker. Come to find out, he was also a partner of the California Powder Works. I am best out from under such political machinations as those Mr. Sime employed to gain control of the mill. Recently, his death has enabled the president of the California Powder Works to purchase my husband's mill. I am certain that will ensure the mill's demise.

My attention returns to the bustling wharves and my young son. The second wharf has railroad tracks running the length of it. Freight and passengers are loaded aboard trains for destinations all over the county. Henry loves the belching of the smokestacks on ship and train alike, the piercing whistles, and the shouts of men on the dock.

We walk partly up the wharf along the tracks. The fishing boats are beginning to come in with the day's catch, some of which will end up on local tables tonight. Raucous seabirds swoop overhead, calling to each other and scolding people on the wharf.

Henry points to a flash of silver on the scarred planks of

the wharf. "Mama, look!"

"What is it, Henry?"

He runs to the writhing shape and bends over it. "A fish fell from the sky, Mama," he says.

I look at the circling birds above us. "Dropped by a pelican, no doubt."

"I must save it," Henry declares, his brown eyes wide and solemn.

"Save it?" I ask weakly.

It takes a couple of attempts before my son is able to capture the slippery fish in his cupped hands. It is about four inches long, and not happy about its exposure to the air. I follow Henry as he runs for the edge of the wharf and tosses the fish toward the sea. It sails through the air and drops below the level of the wharf, directly into the mouth of a very surprised pelican, perched on a piling at the water's surface.

"Oh, Mama!" Henry cries, face twisted in horror.

I stifle a laugh, more at the pelican's expression than Henry's. A couple of weather-grizzled fishermen witness the event and burst into hearty guffaws. One pats my son on the shoulder with a gnarled hand. "You start out saving the fish and end up saving the pelican. That's life, kid."

"That's life, I guess," Henry echoes, clearly still unsure.

I thank the fisherman and take my son's hand. "Noble effort, Henry my dear, you did your best. Remember, the pelican has to eat, too."

He is diverted by a train whistle and we watch a locomotive arrive, steam hissing from either side in great billows, the brakes screeching louder than the gulls. Once fully stopped, the engine rumbles like a resting beast. Henry gets bored and we walk back toward town, fish forgotten.

I watch him as he walks, lost in his own imagination, face animated in contemplation of some other world. I think I see his father in the shape of Henry's head, and the way he sometimes holds it at a quizzical angle. Maybe there will be more as he grows older. In Marion, I see myself. In Ellie, the more feminine features of Mama's family. It's difficult to see my husband's imprint when none of his children has had the opportunity to imitate him.

On August second, the *Sentinel* announces Susan B. Anthony's address to be given on Saturday, the fifth. The settlement of my case is due the following week, and I wonder again if the famous suffragist is aware of my own contribution. Marion and I attend Mrs. Anthony's speech, of course, and are part of a large audience. I am expecting a woman of gigantic proportions to match her reputation. She is near my own height of five and a half feet, and she is stocky, almost matronly in appearance. Her dark hair is pulled back into a severe bun, and her downturned mouth shows an undemonstrative nature. Not everyone present is a supporter, but Mrs. Anthony is a powerful speaker. Her clear statements inspire me, give me courage to continue with my own battle. Her practical view of the suffrage issues moves even those who are not ardent supporters. My well of idealism overflows once again, even though my own case is not mentioned.

On Sunday, Mrs. Kirby entertains the speaker at her home and I have been invited. For two hours our small local group chats with this powerhouse of the suffrage movement and sips tea. Mrs. Kirby tells her of my lawsuit, and Mrs. Anthony grasps my hand in hers.

"My dear Mrs. VanValkenburgh, what a brave attempt! I dare say you must let me know of the outcome."

Her eyes are kind yet intense as I assure her I will write to her as soon as the matter is settled.

Mrs. Anthony moves on to speak in Watsonville on Monday, and our suffragist group's attention turns to Elizabeth Cady Stanton, also touring California. Her speaking engagement in San Francisco is well received, and she arrives in Santa Cruz for a series of three lectures. Marion and I attend all of them. Mrs. Stanton is slightly shorter than her protégée, Mrs. Anthony, but possesses a lively optimistic spirit that leads me to fancy I can see a twinkle in her blue eyes even from my seat. Her hands, as they wave to punctuate her words, are small, their motions graceful. Her gloriously coiffed curls are prematurely whitened, but not a one is out of place. She is well-dressed and confident, not at all hurried in manner. It is hard to believe she is the mother of six children!

During this time, my case comes before Judge McKee for a

decision. The courtroom is full of people: supporters, hecklers, newspapermen. I stand before the judge, my eyes on him. His wig and robes, and the solid mass of the bench he presides over, give additional weight to the moment. Judge McKee looks up only when my attorney and I are in place. Judge Hagan squeezes my arm, but I don't need the reassurance.

A particularly loud male voice calls out, "Jezebel!"

"Bailiff, please clear the courtroom," the judge says. His direction is carried out, and silence falls over the imposing room.

The courtroom is upstairs, above the office where I was denied registration. The room is large, with an eighteen foot ceiling designed to make those arraigned here feel small. In its current emptiness, the weight of judicial responsibility thickens the air.

"Judge Hagan, Mrs. VanValkenburgh." Judge McKee nods to each of us in turn. "The Fourteenth Amendment guarantees civil rights but not political rights to women, Indians, and male infants. The Fifteenth Amendment applies strictly to male Africans who have been slaves. It is the ruling of this court that women are persons physically, but not politically, and Mrs. VanValkenburgh has not acted within the meaning and intention of the law."

I remain facing forward, watching him as he reads the verdict, refusing to lower my gaze or tremble in rage as he continues speaking, but I hear nothing but the negative verdict. It is what I expected, but I am still astounded. I have been riding a wave of euphoria created by impassioned suffragist speeches whose ringing tones reverberate through crowded halls. Such passion fueled the belief that I had an opportunity to win. Now that false hope deflates like an old balloon.

The pounding of the gavel echoes off the walls as Judge Hagan leads me from the court. It seems the procedure has taken longer than I thought. Hecklers and newspapermen have disappeared. Marion is there to walk me home.

That night, at Unity Church, Mr. Kirby addresses a large indignant crowd. I am grateful for his support as he relates the judge's words. The crowd mutters angrily. He waits for their attention before continuing, "Our dear Mrs. VanValkenburgh became a widow in 1862, under the most painful circumstances, and for ten years she has been obliged to manage her own affairs, pay her own taxes, and struggle along to bring up her family. In spite of her personal trials, she takes a stand for the women of Santa Cruz, of California, and of our nation."

He waves his hand in my direction accompanied by thunderous applause. I stand, and as the cheers echo around me, make my way to the podium. Before me I see women strong and weak, unified in common cause. Some men, more than just husbands, support me. I am right, and they know it as I do.

"I am grateful for your support." My voice is calm and strong. Their respectful attention gives me confidence. "Santa Cruz is a most beautiful place to live, and I have enjoyed much of my time here. I continue to believe in the legitimacy of what we are doing. It is proper and womanly for your wives and daughters and sisters to have a voice in our government. We have made a good start, and I am confident we will be crowned with success in a short time."

I sit down amidst thunderous applause that revitalizes my resolve. Mr. Kirby resumes speaking, telling those gathered of my decision to take the case to the California Supreme Court. I bask in the approval of the crowd, for the moment feeling as important to the movement as Susan B. Anthony or Elizabeth Cady Stanton.

On August nineteenth, I am in the audience at Unity Church once more to hear Mrs. Stanton herself. She doesn't mince words as she opens her lecture with comments on my case.

"I feel somewhat depressed in appearing before you this evening. One of your judges in his decision this week has denied women the right to vote. He stated that in the eye of the civil law we are persons, but in representation we are not persons, and women have no political rights which men are bound to respect."

She goes on to reiterate that under the Fourteenth and Fifteenth amendments, women are citizens and cannot be denied. Public indignation seems to agree with her. For weeks, optimism runs high. Long after Mrs. Anthony and Mrs. Stanton board trains for the East, the citizens of Santa Cruz clamor for women's suffrage.

In the November election, the Independent party nominates Laura de Force Gordon to the office of state senator for San Joaquin County. The idea of a female senator is ridiculed, and her eligibility contested, but she receives about two hundred votes — all from men, of course. I cheer aloud as if she's won the presidency, and my teenaged daughters join me in a lively dance around the parlor.

In January, the Supreme Court upholds Judge McKee's decision in my case. The *Sentinel* states, "This settles the question of the right of suffrage being extended to the women, in the State of California, for the present. As they cannot vote directly themselves, let all single ones exercise their privileges this year, get married and vote by proxy."

"I don't understand," I tell Marion. "The *Sentinel* has always been our ally."

"I'm sure they still are, Mama. I read it as sarcasm. Don't let ignorance deter you."

"You're wise beyond your years, my daughter," I tell her with a smile.

Elsewhere, Mrs. Anthony embarks on a speaking tour that crosses the nation during 1872. Her lecture is titled "Is it a Crime for a Citizen of the United States to Vote?" and she includes the details of my case within. Inspired by her forthright stance, I give her a quote, asserting I will never pay another dollar of tax until I am allowed to vote.

Her lecture series is a success, but it never reaches

California. Here in Santa Cruz, the suffrage issue seems to have been swept under the carpet for a time. Mrs. Kirby has shifted her focus to temperance, and the townswomen follow. I work for temperance and dream about voting. I attend meetings, give my children their lessons, and refuse to pay taxes as long as I can. Of course tax collection is so spotty in Santa Cruz County it is doubtful anyone will notice.

Chapter 10: Santa Cruz 1879
Ellen Rand VanValkenburgh

Our suffragist meetings have become rather monotonous. The men have stopped attending, and the women would rather discuss the new ice rink in Madison Square Garden than the ratification of the state constitution. They are more intrigued by the new five and dime store, Woolworth's in New York, than the new bill allowing female attorneys to discuss cases before the U.S. Supreme Court. I am even more discouraged when I learn that a high number of citizens in our county don't pay taxes. I believe
in the basic strength of our government, so I quietly begin paying my taxes again.

Mrs. Manor, a sometimes suffragist, travels in loftier social circles than I do. Nonetheless, our paths cross from time to time. Often, her son, James Henry, accompanies her. For years we nod and comment on how the boys have grown, how nicely behaved they are, how polite. During meetings, James Henry Manor and Marion played together as children. As young adults, they sit demurely and discuss issues of vast importance to no one but them. I begin to wonder if Marion is falling in love.

But James Henry Manor has his eyes on another, and I notice before Marion does. When I see him at meetings now, his gaze follows Ellie, not Marion. He is more likely to be present if Ellie is also there. I watch Marion closely, but her face is neutral. After a meeting one evening, Marion and I walk home together. My son has stayed home to study, as he does more often than not these days. Ellie walks ahead with James Henry, her laugh floating back to us. I peek at Marion without turning my head toward her. She scowls.

"Why aren't you walking with Ellie and James Henry?" I ask. She knows I'm not stupid, but that comment doesn't prove it.

"He's in love with her." Her tone tells me nothing about her feelings.

"I don't know, Mary, I think he has feelings for you, too. He's spent a lot of time with you."

"I was there. He was there. It was easy. But this…" she motions toward her sister. "This is different. He's like a puppy begging for a ball to be thrown."

"Ellie seems happy," I venture. It's an understatement. My daughter comes alive when she catches a glimpse of young Mr. Manor.

"I suppose."

I can't stand this any more. I stop and face her. "Mary, do you love him?"

An incredulous look of shock spreads over her face. "Mama, I *introduced* them! How could you think I would love James Henry? He's as much a brother to me as Henry is. I wish Ellie well."

"Then why do you seem so morose?"

She laughs. "Is that what this is? You think I'm pining for my sister's beau? No, Mama, I merely miss time spent with a friend. I have no desire to marry."

We continue walking in silence. I am glad on many levels that my daughters will not be competing for a man. I cannot bear the thought of our days being taken up with the shallowness of such a competition, nor do I want to see either of my daughters hurt.

When eventually Ellie becomes engaged to James Henry Manor, I still find it difficult to reconcile the boy, seashells in his pockets and sand his hair, with the young man who makes my daughter's eyes glow. Marion is as pleased with their match as if she alone was responsible, even though she is not a proponent of the state of marriage.

At the wedding in January of 1879, I sit misty-eyed with memories of my own weddings and husbands--the hope and promise of dear Jacob, and the businesslike necessity of Henry.

Marion sits with me in the church pew, her face solemn. "She's beautiful and happy, but I can't help but think she's throwing her life away," she whispers.

"No, Mary, she is making a different choice than you are. That's all. Marriage is not for all of us, but maybe it is for Ellie."

"It will tie her down to her husband's wishes and the demands of her children," Marion insists.

I lay my hand on her leg in reassurance. "And that may be the life that pleases her, as it does many. It is her choice. Be happy for her. It is possible to work for a cause and be married. In fact, most of our leaders have husbands and families."

"If Papa hadn't died, would you be just a wife and mother?"

I pause to consider the tone of her words, the derision faint but present, and wonder what sort of memories my daughter has of her father. "A wife and mother can be a powerful position," I tell her.

Ellie floats down the aisle in a vision of white satin, white lace, and pearls. Her veil is a cloud on her blond hair, and her blue eyes shine like sapphires. I marvel that such a creature is my daughter. Henry is best man. He and James Henry are dashing in their fine clothes. The elite of Santa Cruz are here to witness this wedding and attend the reception afterwards where they will toast the newlyweds. L'Amie and Simeon come in from Los Gatos on the train. All is laughter and joy. My words to Marion are solid mothering, but in my deepest heart I wonder. And worry as only a mother can.

But Ellie blooms. James Henry sets off each morning to his produce store in town, and she cooks and cleans and flits about society as if she'd been trained for that and nothing more. The nation's economy is recovering from a post-war depression, and her future is bright. She draws me into her whirlwind for a time, first as the mother of the bride then as the grandmother-to-be. Ellie often sends a servant around to collect almond butter that I make from the tree in my yard. Her newly acquired social position as Mrs. Manor the younger requires her presence at a number of soirees where my almond butter is appreciated. Often I attend with her.

One day that summer, I assist Ellie in the kitchen. She is with child and preparing for a luncheon with five of her friends. She slices cucumbers paper-thin for sandwiches. My job is to remove the crusts from the white bread and spread the slices with butter.

"So how are you feeling, dear?" I ask. "Has the morning sickness passed?"

She nods. "Yes, Mama, I feel much better. I think of you going to Papa's mill every day in this condition and I cannot imagine how strong you must have been."

"It's truly a vindication of my effort to hear that," I say

with a smile.

An hour later, Ellie and her friends are nibbling sandwiches and sipping tea. I note only to myself that they are imitating a custom already grown cold in Britain. I am conscious of being older than them, and feel so wise.

"Oh but you simply must engage a nursemaid," one of the young ladies is saying. I think her mother attends my meetings.

"Raising your own baby is so exhausting," another affirms. She looks as if she has never changed a diaper in her life. Her nails are perfect, and not a hair on her head is out of place.

"James Henry's family has a nanny we will use," Ellie says. I am proud of her quiet confidence. She doesn't have to remind these young women that the Manor family could afford three nannies.

I am tired of nannies. "Have any of you heard that the Susan B. Anthony Amendment was defeated in Congress?"

They look at the wall, the floor, anywhere but me. They sip their tea. Ellie leans toward me and says gently, as you would to an old woman, "Mama, that was months ago. You know Senator Sargent will introduce it again."

They wait a long moment. Then the animation returns to their faces and they begin discussing fall fashion. It is all I can do to subside into silence, struggling to comprehend how this round of shallow interactions with women of no depth can fulfill one's soul.

Harder still is comprehending, three months later, the

miracle of my first grandchild, Harold, born a proper ten months after his parents' wedding. I thank God for vanquishing the diphtheria epidemic that took all four of Mrs. Hind's children just before this precious bundle arrived.

At the tender age of three weeks, I hold the tiny bundle in my arms. He is swaddled tightly in a blue blanket crocheted by his mother, his eyes squeezed shut. He yawns, his tiny mouth resembling a hungry bird's.

"Ah Harold," I murmur.

Ellie is as starstruck as I am. "We call him Hal, Mama."

"Hello, little Hal," I croon. I am smitten long before he smiles at me.

"Married life and motherhood agree with you, Ellie," I tell her as I hand the baby back to be fed.

She beams, but directs it at her son. "He's perfect, Mama. I want a dozen more!"

"That's a lot of babies, dear." I laugh with her. "And this fills you, Ellie?" She darts a quizzical look at me, and I remember the first months of motherhood. "Your time is filled, I know, and your heart, but your soul?"

"I don't know what you mean." Her brow furrows and her mouth frowns. The tone of her voice is sharp.

With her blond hair swept back and pinned up, and her starched apron, she is every bit the mother. Maybe the fire in her soul burns for this, is fueled by the day-to-day tasks of raising children. It is too early to tell. "Never mind, honey, he is beautiful."

"Mama, not everyone is brave like you," she tells me, with what appears to be sympathy in her eyes.

Now it's my turn to feign ignorance. "What do you mean?"

"Women's rights are important to you. While I was growing up you were always pushing for reform. Abolish slavery, temperance, the vote—always some wrong that needed to be put right." She tucks the blanket closer around Hal, then looks right at me. "Were you ever happy, Mama? If Papa hadn't died would you have had more children and stayed home more?"

Happy? A montage of past moments plays through my mind, of sandy children at the beach, of dolls and laughter and picnics in the yard. Yes, I was happy, but I am stung to waspishness. "Would you have rather had a mother like Mrs. Manor?"

Ellie grimaces, but polishes her features back to neutrality. I know she is not fond of her vapid mother-in-law. "Mama, your substance is not in question here. Maybe you should look at your motives. Who are you really striving to right the world for? Me? Or you? Did it ever occur to you that I might not want to vote?"

"I will never force you to vote against your will," I tell her. I cannot control the edge to my voice, and I know it won't help. I try for a smoother tone. "My efforts are all about giving you the choice."

Without smiling or responding, she takes Hal from me and escapes into the nursery to feed him, leaving me alone with my thoughts.

When Marion was born, I felt complete for a while. Then I became pregnant again, and Ellie's birth filled my time. Amusing a baby and a toddler chased notions of any other use of my time right out of my head. My husband's death threw me into the business world, and I hardly noticed my last pregnancy. That taste of the greater world ruined me as a full-time mother. Would I have been content had I not stepped up to run the mill? Or if Henry hadn't died? That is water under the bridge, as they say. My eyes, my heart, my soul, were opened and will not be shut. I am in a position to make a difference for those who are unable to help themselves, and so I must.

Later that evening at home, I am still pensive. Marion brings me a cup of tea and I smile my thanks.

"Hal is a cute little fellow," Marion says, taking a seat near me.

I am fully aware that she senses my mood and is testing to see where my thoughts are dwelling. "Yes, he is. Not for you, though?"

She shakes her head.

"My children are a great joy to me, Mary. I grieve that you choose not to know the same joy."

"I will share Ellie's children," she says, "and Henry's." There is no hint of loss in her tone or expression.

In fact, we both smile at the notion of Henry having children. Although he approaches adulthood, he is still a child himself in so many ways.

"I am content, Mama."

"As am I, my dear." I don't want my daughter to think I disapprove of her choice not to marry, and I am well aware that her decision could change with a simple introduction to the right man. I refuse to do as my own mother did and push every eligible man at her. But by doing so have I limited her choices? I can only do as I see fit.

My children are certainly capable, but only Marion shares my passion for women's rights. I consider the women I know in our little town. Many of them dabble in political causes to fill their social calendars. I don't think it matters to them if it is the vote for women or homes for stray kittens. Their world is limited to their family, focused on raising happy healthy children and creating a pleasant home. I cannot fault them for that any more than I personally can be content with that life. I only hope that someday Ellie sees value in a political cause, and Marion sees value in a family.

Daughters stay close to their mothers. My mother lived with me, or with my sister, until she passed away. Marion still lives with me. Hal is a son, though, and destined to leave. My brother left home at seventeen and made only quick visits after that. His home was never again with us. Even my son has gone to Hayward to work on his cousin's farm. Seventeen must be the age of separation for young men. They feel they are adults, but their mothers see only children striking out alone in the world. It is a lonely thing to watch your youngest child seek their future alone, and I am glad I have my politics to fill my heart. I wonder where Hal will be at seventeen.

Wedding photo of James Henry Manor and Ellie VanValkenburgh, J.R. Richard Photographer, Santa Cruz

Chapter 11: San Jose 1888
Ellen Rand VanValkenburgh

It's been quite a journey for my Henry from his boyhood in Santa Cruz through twenty-six years to this day in San Jose. A few years ago he took advantage of a government offer to ranch land in San Luis Obispo County that the United States had acquired from some of the old Spanish ranchos. So he is a cattle rancher now in Cholame. Apparently he has also been taking the train to San Jose, ostensibly to visit his Aunt L'Amie in nearby Los Gatos.

Nina Williams, a frequent visitor to L'Amie's reading room, is a thickset young woman with a stubborn jaw line. She is quiet, and reads voraciously. I have no idea how she caught my son's eye, much less how she held it. Nevertheless, they are to be wed. L'Amie says the Williams family is quite well respected in San Jose.

"Her father is the president of the San Jose Water Works," she tells me. "His ideas about supplying water to the city are quite innovative. His wife is not Nina's mother, but she is from a fine family back East."

"When have I ever cared about family, L'Amie?" I demand. I am sixty-one to her fifty-four, yet her memory is the one that's failing. "One afternoon with this young woman and I will have a sense of her mettle."

"But will it matter, Ellen? Henry has chosen her."

Yes, Henry has chosen her. But a mother must keep her children close, and for that to happen their spouses should be agreeable. Marion, now thirty-two, lives with me; Ellie and her family are next door. I prefer to keep Henry on our side of the mountains, rather than the Central Valley or the Bay Area. That may not be a wife's decision, but a smart woman can exert influence. I hope Nina proves to be smart.

Marion, L'Amie, and I join the Williams women for tea one crisp fall afternoon before the wedding. L'Amie and Marion greet Nina and her sisters warmly while I assess the stepmother. Nina must have been nine when Fannie Williams became her mother, the same age my grandson Hal is now. It's not a good age to replace a lost mother, as if any age could be so.

The Williams home on Third Street is large enough to accommodate the entire family easily, and is graciously appointed. The parlor doesn't seem crowded, even with the seven women seated in front of the fireplace on couches and chairs covered with embroidered pillows. A large mirror hangs over the marble mantle. Lace curtains hang on the windows; several pieces of heavy, old wooden furniture line the room.

"That chaise came with me on a covered wagon from Vermont during the Gold Rush," Fannie tells us, pointing to the seat L'Amie has chosen.

I harrumph. She is not the only one to have arrived in California prior to statehood. I will not allow her to put on airs.

"The girls were all born in mining towns with colorful names," Fannie continues. Her voice is pert and perky like a little bird. I hate pert and perky, being a more grounded sort of person myself. "Edith and Nina were born in You Bet, and Emily in Rough and Ready. Isn't that quaint?"

The three girls smile, but they are pained, frozen smiles. The oldest, Edith, is unmarried. She begins a side conversation with Marion. I wonder if they are discussing the evils of men or the ascendancy of women. At twenty-one, Emily is the youngest sister, also unmarried. Her eyes sparkle with a lively intelligence. I know she is a schoolteacher. Nina is the middle daughter. She is twenty-four to Henry's twenty-six. Fannie babbles on as I examine Nina. The girl politely listens to her stepmother, but fingers drum against the teacup and feet fidget. She is smart enough to know I am watching and to be nervous as a result.

"So I gathered the poor motherless lambs to my bosom," Fannie says.

I force myself not to roll my eyes, but Emily hides a smile behind her teacup. When Fannie stops to take a breath, I take the opportunity to ask a question. "Where are you teaching school now, Emily?"

"I teach for the Midway School District, in north San Jose. Nina taught for a year, too," she says, graciously gesturing to her sister.

"Is that so?" I ask, turning my attention to Henry's beloved.

She swallows and hesitates before meeting my gaze. "Yes, but only for a year. I have most recently been attending art school in San Francisco."

"Art school?" Could Nina be giving up dreams of a career to marry my son? Interest piques my brain.

Nina blushes and fumbles with pouring herself a cup of tea. Henry has apparently chosen the sister with the least social graces. I don't care if the girl is able to discuss politics with foreign diplomats, but it would be nice if she could avoid tripping over her tongue and pinkening her cheeks during afternoon tea.

"All three girls are artistic," their stepmother gushes. "Nina's still life paintings are praised by her teacher, and Emily draws beautifully."

I don't really care about the artistic merits of the Williams sisters. I am not interested in attempts at seascapes or vases of flowers. I want to know the mettle of their hearts and souls.

"It's merely a hobby," Nina demurs. I contemplate my tea in its fine porcelain cup and try not to appear disappointed that she hasn't revealed a passion for portraiture or the like.

"Actually, I draw buildings," Emily says. "Someday I want to be an architect."

An architect? Now there is a woman with character, with dreams and backbone! Fannie quickly shushes her, as if ashamed of her ambition, but I lean forward, intrigued. "And how does a woman go about doing that?"

"It's not easy, Mrs. VanValkenburgh," she says, and laughs with real joy. "But I will do it. There are mechanical arts schools in California that will accept women, and I am trying to secure a place. One step at a time."

"Well, good luck young lady," I tell her.

"Her father will never allow it," Fannie murmurs. I ignore her and smile at Emily.

"Do you know of Susan B. Anthony's latest efforts to unify the suffrage associations?" I ask.

She smiles apologetically. "I'm sorry, Mrs. VanValkenburgh. I am not really current on the tribulations of the various associations. I am, of course, a member of the American Equal Rights Association. Suffrage is an important issue, but I believe equal career opportunities are as important."

I am surprised, having expected any forward-thinking young woman to be driving for the vote. Shaking my head at the stupidity of my assumption, I am about to respond when Nina speaks up.

"For women to really achieve anything they set out to do, our leaders must be unified. Mrs. Stone and Mrs. Anthony must overcome their differences over support of the Fifteenth Amendment. After all, that is twenty years past. I support suffrage and am a member of National Woman's Suffrage Association."

Again, I am surprised and more than a little impressed. The mousy one is smart and current. "I, too, support Susan B. Anthony, and I agree that we need one unified voice for suffrage, temperance, and equal opportunities for all women."

For some reason, Fannie feels she needs to interject. "I hear from Nina that you are quite the local celebrity in Santa Cruz, Mrs. V. May I call you Mrs. V?"

"No, you may not. Please call me Ellen." I respond to Fannie, but my eyes are on the sisters, Nina and Emily.

Our afternoon draws to an end, leaving me desiring to know more about Emily Williams. Emily is the one with the fire to realize her full potential as a woman. Some day she will be an architect, marry and have children if she so chooses. Nina is quieter but no less intelligent. I admit I like her, but I am more drawn to Emily.

* * *

By the time Henry and Nina marry, in November, Nina has secured a place in the heart of the family. Ellie's son, Hal, is nine now and has a sister, Florence, now seven. They are dressed for the wedding in imitation of the adults, silk-embroidered black suede boots pinching Flo's feet and an ascot tie strangling Hal. Ellie clothes her daughter in the height of fashion, but I think the girl looks ridiculous in the bustled frock. I refuse to wear a bustle. My own rear end is prodigious enough for a sixty-one year-old woman. No one will be looking at me anyway. It's the bride's day, Nina's day.

In the months leading up to the wedding, Nina has persuaded me to love her. My ideal dream of a wife for Henry — the suffragist who would take her place at my side — vanishes with a poof. She is replaced with Nina, a gentle woman with a spine of steel. She wants Henry; she will have him. In her determination I hear an echo of my younger self declaring my love for Jacob. As I watch them together, I see that they are two halves of the same person. Apart, they are incomplete. They will be a good team. She will help him be the best cattle rancher he can be, and he will help with home and children. Someday, if she wants to fight for the vote, he will stand beside her. In truth, that is what I want for him. The vanished suffragist was for me.

They are to be married at Nina's home in a small ceremony that includes only family. The room where we had tea just a few months ago is elegantly decorated with choice blossoms, potted palms and tropical plants. The lace draperies are caught up with smilax and Duchess of Brabant roses. The large bay window that faces Third Street is wreathed in ivy and yellow chrysanthemums. A large wicker basket of the roses sits at the center of the mantles, and more chrysanthemums adorn either side of it. A tracery of smilax drapes over the mirror above the fireplace mantle, and the Rev. Dr. Wakefield, from Trinity Episcopal Church, stands ready to officiate.

Flo and Hal do the family proud as they appear in the doorway of the parlor. I sit next to Marion in the front row on the groom's side. Ellie and her Henry are on the aisle, ready to capture the children when they reach us. The room is full of cousins and family on both sides.

I fasten my eyes on my elegant son, standing next to the minister, his gaze locked on the doorway where his bride will soon appear. Today he is not a cattle rancher, but the scion of a well-to-do New York family. His father would be proud. Henry would be proud of Ellie and her family, too, I know. Marion would cause him consternation.

Although he wasn't opposed to women's rights, he wouldn't understand a daughter's desire to remain single. The most well-known leaders of our movement are all married or widowed, and some have children. It is not necessary to completely shun men, yet Marion has done so. I wonder if I have been a poor example in this regard. I was too busy for a beau when the children were small, then too set in my ways, then too old. Always content alone, I never missed the companionship of a man.

Again I wonder if I would have married a third time had Mama paraded enough men before me. If that is what Marion needs, she is right to be at ease with spinsterhood. I will not offer my daughter like a piece of meat to be sold to the highest bidder. Nonetheless guilt pricks me. Marriage is not evil; if I can change that image for her I must try, if only to make sure she has a fair opportunity to choose her path.

A giggle escapes my granddaughter as she spots her mother, and the concentration on her face gives way to smiles. Ellie hustles Flo and Hal into seats them between her and their father, all the time praising how grown up they looked as they walked in. I lean forward to nod and smile at my grandchildren before turning back to the front. My son's eyes are alight, so Nina must have entered. His smile stretches his face muscles. He loves her, and I love him.

All heads turn to Nina, as they should. She is a vision in yards of white satin complete with flounces and ruffles. A pearl collar and floor-length veil complete her ensemble. She glows, her eyes fixed on Henry.

My own eyes stray to the chairs on the bride's side. Fannie sits there like a porcelain doll, all decked out in her best finery. Her face is alight with joy. Seated next to her, Emily appears sober in raiment and expression. Two squirrels of young boys wriggling next to them must be Waldo and Paul, Nina's stepbrothers.

I watch Fannie closely. She and I could have much in common with our similar social status and children, but how could our attitudes be more different? Some might say she has realized all her dreams with her marriage and children. By keeping a neat home and entertaining often, she is happy. I know women like her, and they amaze me not for their industriousness but for their shallow vision. Of course, they look at me in horror because they perceive my choice is to toss away all they hold dear, marriage, keeping a home, and child raising. They don't bother to get to know me well enough to discover how much I love my children and enjoy the stability of my home. In watching Fannie, my fondest hope is that this woman and I can help Henry and Nina blend these families. I'm sure both of us want harmony for the newlyweds.

Williams family pictured left to right: Ed (Emily's twin), Edith, Lillian Palmer (in white), Paul, Emily, and Waldo

Chapter 12: San Jose 1888
Emily Williams

I sit quietly, basking in the rose-scented aura of the parlor. My stepmother outdid herself creating the feel of a floral paradise for my sister's wedding. My eyes gaze out the bay window, truly a window to the world for me. Out on Third Street and beyond, the world makes progress in transportation, politics, and fashion. Out there, women work to control their own destinies. Transcending the cares of daily life, I allow my mind to wander like a young girl's.

As a child, life swirled around me, boisterous and outdoors. Papa came to the California gold fields to make a fortune mining. Instead, he made it selling water to the miners. He married, had five children, lost one, then lost his wife, my dear mother. Even so, I remember those first six years of my life with fondness. We lived, surrounded by men, in towns with names like You Bet, Rough and Ready, and Red Bluff. The towns consisted of miners and those who supported the industry, like my father. My older sisters, Edith and Nina, bossed me horribly from the time I was born. My twin brother, Ed, was my champion.

Ed and I, named for our parents, Edward and Emily Williams, were tiny sprites when my father settled us in Nevada City, the largest mining town in California. Its brick buildings seemed quite civilized compared to the canvas tents and mud of the camps. Our mother constantly wiped mud off us after we scampered about the city. Once the wooden sidewalks of the town collapsed as miners bored under them in search of a gold vein, nearly toppling my brother into the depths of the Earth. He came home muddier than I that day.

As if summoned by my thoughts, Ed appears at the front of the room, taking his place beside the groom. Henry VanValkenburgh has no brothers of his own, so mine will have to do. As the bride's older sister, Edith precedes Nina through the glass doorways of the room. As the bride's younger sister, I sit in the front row with my stepmother and stepbrothers. Lovely and demure, the perfect bride, Nina's radiant face glows even more as she fixes her gaze on Henry, her soft brown curls escaping tightly coifed hair. His face echoes her happiness. I shift uncomfortably in my chair. I don't like such overt display of love since I am so unused to seeing it.

Papa escorts Nina down the aisle between the chairs set up for our guests. He is a study in grays; gray hair, gray eyes, gray suit. His sober countenance enhances the dignity of the event. As the president of San Jose Water Works, Papa remains one of the city's elite. Nina's wedding should be a Social Event, but Nina prefers to share this day with family only.

Next to me, Waldo fidgets. No boy of fourteen professes a fondness for weddings. He makes a face at my youngest stepbrother, Paul, only five years old. Waldo has been sickly and cosseted since his birth, but Paul makes up for it by being twice as active. Such bristling exuberance makes my twenty-one years feel ancient. Their mother hisses at them to behave and smiles serenely at me. I return the vapid smile. My mother should be here, not this woman my father married to care for his family while he built his career.

Miss Fannie Sibley simpered her way west from a family seat in Vermont to stay with her sister, who married into the Coleman family of San Francisco. Fannie brought with her a dowry from the East, a houseful of ponderous vintage furniture, intending to attract a man. My father, widowed almost three years, fell easily into her snare. Ed and I were six years old, Nina nine, and Edith eleven when they wed, but our affections were not so easy to capture.

Once she became Mrs. Fannie Williams, my stepmother pulled us up by the roots and moved us to San Jose. Assuring him she would mother his poor lambs, Fannie freed my father to establish his place among the wealthy and important. I have never felt like a poor lamb, even after Waldo and Paul were born and her mothering deserted me almost completely.

My wandering attention returns to my sister's wedding. Nina and Henry face the minister with straight backs, standing motionless before the gathering of relations. Edith's posture looks stiffer than Ed's, even though he takes his role quite seriously. I listen to the hum of the celebrant's voice rather than his words, and drift.

As little girls, my sisters and I played a variety of games. I built structures with blocks and twigs and rocks. Dress up and house were always Nina's favorites. Edith and I went along, but never summoned her enthusiasm. With sudden clarity, I realize my dreams have never included finding a Henry. I dream of a home built with my own hands, but never a husband and children. My sucked in breath brings a glare from my stepmother and giggles from Waldo and Paul.

Fannie pushes me to meet San Jose's eligible bachelors. Somewhere outside that bay window, I am sure there is a crowd of them, waiting only for Fannie's introduction. I picture them in a row, all clothed in conservative dark suits, hair slicked back and mustaches neat, their faces eager as a child in O'Brien's Candy Store. Smiling at the absurdity of that image, I watch my sister marry the man of her dreams and wonder why my dreams are so different.

Once again wandering, my mind travels the road out of San Jose toward Alviso, approaching Midway School, where I have begun my second year of teaching. At the front of the room my desk sits in a corner of the instructional platform. On this

November Saturday, the stove will be cold and the cloak room empty. I imagine my fingers opening my correspondence case. I can almost feel the crisp paper and hear it crinkle as the letter unfolds. The words are seared into my memory.

Dear Miss Williams,

While our school is still in the planning stages, we are, as your inquiry stated, accepting applications for the inaugural academic year. We anticipate opening the doors for the 1894-1895 school year. I hope that date fits well into your schooling plans.

Yours truly,

George Merrill, Director

California School of Mechanical Arts

San Francisco

I sigh aloud, drawing another disapproving frown from Fannie. I cannot imagine explaining to my stepmother's shocked disapproval and my father's implacable gray stare that I would rather design buildings than marry and have a family. The application enclosed with that letter will not be mailed any time soon. Still, the reality of the new school is years away. Something may yet happen to change my circumstances.

Meanwhile I teach. Another sigh, another frown. Teaching remains more difficult than it should be since my heart sings elsewhere. Nina taught as well, but her marriage is now her career. Ironic, since she loved instructing children. She set it aside, though, without a second thought. Someday she will probably school her own children at home. In the meantime she will make a home for Henry.

Watching Nina and Henry, surrounded by family and friends, join themselves together in holy matrimony, I imagine what their children will be like. Sturdy, I pray. They will be living on a ranch in Cholame, a town in remote San Luis Obispo County. Cattle, I think. I hope Nina stays so in love she won't miss life in town.

From across the aisle, Henry's mother catches my eye. Above the heads of our families, we nod and smile. I admire Ellen VanValkenburgh as much as I do any of the national leaders of the women's movement. She is fearless. Her eyes can be as hard as my father's when he learns of some ill-advised exploit of Ed's. Someday I'd like to see Ellen VanValkenburgh and my father face off. I envy Nina the inspiration this woman could be.

"Are you going to sit there all day, Em?" Waldo snipes as he pushes past me into the aisle, Paul on his heels.

The parlor comes alive with murmurs and rustling skirts as the wedding guests rise and file out behind the new Mr. and Mrs. VanValkenburgh. I fix a smile on my face, prepared for an onslaught of well-meaning wedding advice from the family. My oldest sister, Edith, also unmarried, shares their attention as we all adjourn to the dining room for the wedding repast.

At Nina and Henry's end of the table, conversation focuses on the honeymoon to Del Monte, on the coast near

Monterey. I hear Father commenting on Mr. Crocker's luxury hotel and how fitting that they will ride in one of Crocker's Southern Pacific trains to arrive at the resort.

At my end of the table, Fannie sits with Edith and me on either side of her. "On Sunday, a few important sons are expecting to meet you after church." Of course they are. She pats my arm, and I can feel her anxiety.

"Yes, Fannie. I will be gracious." I don't have to say this. She knows I am well trained. Her mouth slips into a momentary frown.

"As will I," Edith murmurs. Fannie's smile returns.

* * *

On Sunday, with Nina and Henry still in Del Monte, we arrive at Trinity Episcopal Church among a crowd of well-wishers. All the elite of San Jose who could not be present at the wedding congratulate Papa and Fannie on marrying off one of their daughters. They seem to recognize that it will be harder with Edith and me. I stiffen my spine and freeze a smile on my face. How many fawning young financiers will I have to endure?

"Your curls aren't fluffed," Fannie complains, reaching over to touch my hair.

I lean away with a frown. I am not five years old. My hair parts down the middle, combed straight on top with soft short curls gathered around my ears and the nape of my neck. I like it even more because Fannie doesn't.

Ignoring her, I sit quietly, basking in the embrace of wood

surrounding me from hard pew to warm walls. Built of redwood logged in the Santa Cruz Mountains, Trinity Episcopal Church is as close to a natural setting as one can get inside a building. The organ music ebbs and flows around me, vibrating through my body as it reaches crescendo. My eyes gaze upward to the top of the stained glass windows depicting the crucifixion of our Lord. Stained glass and organ music always foster reverence in my soul. The celebration of mass is an opportunity to escape, for an hour or so, a life that does not measure up to my expectations.

As soon as mass concludes and we manage to decorously remove ourselves from the church proper, they appear.

"Miss Williams?"

The hopeful son of an illustrious father peers at me and waits for Fannie to introduce us. I am petite, but he is short.

"Good afternoon, Mr. Field." Fannie blossoms into the epitome of social matron introducing her daughter to prospective suitors. But I'm not her daughter. I'm also more interested in the architecture of the church than the oily chatter of boring men. "This is my stepdaughter, Emily. Emily, this is Charles Field. His father is a business associate of your father's."

I almost let an incredulous snort escape. As president of the San Jose Water Works, anyone who uses water can be considered a business associate of my father! I flash a dutiful smile at Charles Field and hold out my gloved hand. He takes the hand and bows over it, but my eyes have lifted again to the church's tower.

"Did you know that the church didn't always face Second Street?" Charles says, trying to start a conversation.

Of course I know that. I watched avidly as the old church was torn asunder by a team of horses, then the wings added. Now shaped like our Lord's cross, the building sports a new bell tower. Four years ago they added a spire to the top of that tower. Anyone living in San Jose for the last fifteen years knows of Trinity Church's expansion! "I was confirmed here shortly after the completion," I tell him, my voice serene.

"I'm sorry, of course you were." He seems more delighted that I am speaking to him than apologetic for his ignorance. "That steep hipped roof is an interesting bit of design, isn't it?"

Design? My interest quickens. "Such a roof makes the inside space smaller," I venture, glancing at Fannie. She doesn't believe a lady should know anything about architecture. Although she pretends not to listen, I know she hears every word.

"Ah, but the soaring peak reaches toward heaven. It inspires the congregation."

I hear a note of sarcasm in his voice and am intrigued in spite of myself. Behind him, I can see my father talking with William Hart, son of the department store magnate. They look over at me, then away.

"Do you like architecture, Mr. Field?" I ask.

"I hope to begin my studies soon at the University of California in Berkeley," he says, his voice a shade too eager for the polite detachment one expects from society conversation.

My stomach flips, sending a wave of sick jealousy through me. I hope he appreciates his ability to attend this school. Although Berkeley does accept women, my father will not allow me to study a man's field. With great effort, I respond brightly, "Oh, how marvelous to see a man pursuing his dreams."

His eyes flicker. I don't know how else to describe the look that passes over his face and disappears. Is Charles, too, trying to hide his true feelings? He offers his elbow to me rather abruptly and I let my fingertips rest on the inside of his arm. We walk away from the lingering groups of churchgoers, almost to the edge of Second Street itself. Carriages pull away from the church, the horses' hooves clattering and harnesses jangling.

"You are interested in architecture?" he asks, his eyes suddenly too intense for proper conversation.

I meet his glare steadily. "It is my life's ambition to attend the California School for Mechanical Arts so I can design and build houses."

For an instant we are connected. Then he recalls himself to reality, shaking his head and smiling grimly. Very properly, and very detached, he says, "I wish you success at that."

"You think I'm ridiculous." I pull my hand away from his arm and step back.

He laughs. "Oh of course not. I meet women every day who desire to build buildings right alongside men."

Since society considers rage unfeminine, I rejoin my

family with no further words spoken between us. My father shakes Charles's hand, and produces the Hart son for an introduction the minute Charles turns away. I repaste the society smile on my face and pretend to be overcome with joy at the attentions of such an illustrious suitor.

From the corner of my eye I see Fannie gather Charles Field for an introduction to Edith, who responds with great propriety and grace, of course. I wonder what my sister truly thinks. Flights of fancy from my head put dreams into her head. I imagine us escaping together to a world of blueprints and sawdust. I laugh then at the absurdity, and Mr. Hart recoils. I laugh again, wondering what he was saying that I improperly think so funny.

Behind him, the spire of Trinity Church reflects the fading November sun, tantalizing me with dreams.

Left: Edith Williams and her little sister Nina; Bayley and Cramer Photography, San Francisco

Right: Twins Emily and Ed, Wright's Art and Portrait Gallery, San Jose, California

Chapter 13: Stanford 1893
Emily Williams

The June sun bakes the sandstone building as I exit on the last day of class at Leland Stanford University. The school year has ended, and maybe the university, too. Earlier this week, Leland Stanford himself passed away after being ill some months. My studies last year in the sciences, and this year in English, have passed the time but not fired my passion. I toss my book satchel over my shoulder as I head for the train station.

A couple of women, dressed entirely in black, pass me and head down the wide sandstone steps. I know they attended Mr. Fluegel's English composition class with me. They nod and I nod back. No one smiles. In light of recent events, a somber mood has fallen over all of us.

Sighing, I walk beneath the graceful arched entry for the last time, and descend the steps. Looking back at the building, I critically inspect the half-circle arches and rectangular stone building. The sandstone and red tiled roofs are classic Spanish colonial. It's a style becoming common in California because it complements the bright blue sky. I appreciate a design element that takes into account the environment. I wonder if I will ever be given the opportunity to create something so grand.

I turn away and stroll past a scattering of other women and the family members who have come to collect them, crossing the road to a grassy oval. As the late morning breeze plays with the ribbon on my somber hat, I recognize my three-year-old niece racing to greet me, her face shining. "Eva, what a surprise!" I kneel down to hug her sturdy body, looking over her shoulder for my sister. Sure enough, Nina and Papa are walking over in a proper sedate manner. I stand and take Eva's hand. She's quiet now, her exuberance replaced by the realization that she really doesn't know me well.

"Surprise!" Nina calls. "Henry, Eva and I came up to San Jose on the train to visit. Henry stayed at the house with Fannie and the boys, but Eva and I came on with Papa to collect you."

"I needed collecting?" I ask. "I've ridden the train home from university alone these two years!"

"Oh, don't get prickly, Emily!" Nina scolds. "It's an adventure for Eva. We had lunch at the Stanford Inn." Her eyes slide to Papa and her smile fades as she buries her face in her daughter's hair.

Papa's face is grim. "Are you ready to go, daughter?"

"Yes, Papa."

He nods and turns to walk at a brisk pace in the direction I was heading, toward the train station.

"We had lunch with Mr. Jordan," Nina reports in a low voice. "He asked Papa why you are not enrolled for next term."

David Starr Jordan, the president of Stanford, has been a friend of my father's since he arrived in California to take the helm of the new university. "Did they come to a decision about why I am leaving university?" I ask dryly.

Nina laughs. "Well, they couldn't ask *you*! Papa thinks the university can't survive without Mr. Stanford. He believes Mrs. Stanford will bankrupt it in a year, but it sounds like Mr. Jordan believes Papa is making you come home. Papa didn't let on he knew nothing of your decision, even though I think he supports it."

"At twenty-six years of age, I would hope I know my own mind." Our eyes meet and we laugh. As modern as my father thinks he is, he still believes a woman's place is in the home. "You say Papa supports me leaving Stanford? Then why is he angry?"

My sister shrugs. "He thinks the university is doomed and won't waste good money. He's angry because you didn't discuss it with him and let him guide you to a decision. I had to hear all about it on the train."

In Nina's eyes, I see questions I don't want to answer. I change the subject. "Eva is getting so big, Nina. I wish you could bring her to see me more often."

"I was surprised when she ran ahead. She's usually shy with people she doesn't know well." She flushed. "And she should know her aunt much better."

"She will," I reassured her." Kneeling once more to child height, I tell Eva, "It's wonderful to see you again, sweetheart."

At first I think she doesn't hear me, but then she glances at me and smiles. She pulls away, tucks her chin into her chest, and runs to Nina, but that brief smile thrills me.

I stand up and walk in the direction of University Avenue. "Papa will be impatient. And I need to talk to him about my schooling. I've left it too long as it is." Nina follows, holding Eva's hand, and I ask, "So how is the cattle ranching life?"

"Cholame is in the middle of nowhere, but it's home," my sister says. Her eyes light up as she continues, "Henry works hard but he's doing well. We have a snug house where the three of us are happy. I am beginning to teach Eva her letters. Eva, sweetie, can you tell Aunt Emily the alphabet?"

The little girl looks up and obediently says, "A. B. C. E. D."

I laugh. "That's very good for three."

"She'll be four in August. I think we'll bring her to San Jose to celebrate. Fannie will set out the croquet. Maybe Eva can kick the balls around." She smiles indulgently at her daughter.

My heart twists at the sight of my sister and her child. It's not jealousy, really. I love Eva and sometimes would like to have a child of my own, but I cannot imagine giving up my dreams to focus on building a home and family. Since Nina's wedding five years ago, I've dabbled in college at University of the Pacific and later at Stanford, studying English. It's not what I want to do. I don't want to teach, either. I want to attend California School for Mechanical Arts and learn to build houses. Papa supports education of his daughters as long as they study something he approves. He does not approve of women studying men's subjects. So I rant inside while my exterior remains calm, and I wait for some sort of divine intervention to offer me an opportunity.

Papa awaits his daughters and granddaughter before heading along University to the station. As I prepare to leave this campus for the last time, my eyes return to the building behind us. No, I will never design anything so grand and imposing. I want to build homes that are warm and inviting, that nurture the spirit of the family within them. But first I have to go to school. I'll never be able to get an architect's license without some training.

The biggest obstacle to my dreams walks beside me to the station. Nina walks behind, keeping Eva close by holding onto her hand. My young niece will not be repressed and chatters away. It relieves the need for me to talk to Papa, although I know I must. By the time we reach the Southern Pacific depot, my nerves are shattered.

I pretend an interest in the vast empty field that is Palo Alto. I read somewhere that less than 100 people live here. University students keep the railroad busy, though. The train station consists of a plain room, heated only in the winter. As we approach, the southbound train pulls up, steam hissing and rods clanking.

We board the train and take our seats on the polished wooden benches. I get the window seat, with Papa on the aisle. Eva is across from me, and Nina from Papa, whose grey eyes have darkened like storm clouds. It is three and half hours to San Jose. I know I will not be strong enough to stay quiet the entire time. I will have to talk to him or find a way to endure his implacable accusing gaze. And why should I? I am twenty-six years old and well able to run my own life. I do not need a man, husband or father, to decide if where and what I should study. I sit up straighter, infusing my backbone with courage.

The train pulls out of the station and settles into its ground-covering rhythm. Normally the rocking of the coach and clacking of the rails soothes me, but today I push serenity away. Nina softly sings the Alphabet Song to Eva, who chimes in for some of the letters. Normally I would be amused, but I am, in spite of myself, tense with anticipation of Papa's words. Will he ask me straight out what my plans are? I don't think he will disown me before I get a chance to speak. He has not done so to Ed, who also disappoints him. Poor Papa! His firstborn son died as an infant. Edith is yet unmarried and didn't even graduate school. Ed and I are disappointments. Waldo is sickly and Paul is young. Nina is the only one who has made a success of her life by marrying and having a family. That may not be my measure of success, but it is surely his.

The silence suffocates us as we steam through the summer-dry California hills. Papa must have the window open even though he sits on the aisle. The air is dusty from the fields and smoky from the locomotive. My chest tightens with the asthma that all four of Mama's children have. Nina looks at me, then at Papa, but focuses on Eva, who is too young to be affected. Finally I realize I must tell my father of my plans, not wait for him to ask.

"I am not returning to Stanford in the fall, Papa," I say in a clear, confident voice. I don't quite manage to hold his gaze.

Unsurprised, of course, he fixes steely eyes on me. "What are your plans, daughter?"

"I would like to attend the California School for Mechanical Arts in San Francisco."

He doesn't react for a minute, just looks into my eyes. Is he trying to see into my heart? I stiffen every muscle in my body to avoid twitching.

"Have you applied to that school?" he asks.

"No, sir. I waited to speak with you." Even I am not foolish enough to go ahead without his permission, even if it is not enthusiastically given.

"What course of study would you be pursuing?"

"I want to be an architect."

My father has not achieved his social position by letting a facial expression give away his thoughts. In business, he achieves success for the same reason. I strive to imitate his neutrality.

"An architect is it now? What happened to your dream of teaching? Weren't you going back to that?" he doesn't sound angry, just amused. That seems worse.

I shake my head and look down at my hands clasped in my lap. "That was Nina's dream, not mine." Out of the corner of my eye, I see my sister's lips clench into a thin line. Was she worried that Papa's scrutiny would now turn to her?

Eva squirms next to me, kicking her feet in the air and letting them thunk against the wooden seat when they come down. Nina makes no attempt to shush her as we wait for Papa's reply.

He nods and narrows his eyes. "An architect is rather a child's dream, Emily. You know, the kind that will never come true?" He turns to Eva and a bright smile lights his face. "Eva, sweetheart, what do you want to be when you grow up?"

The little girl beams back at him. "A ballerina and a teacher and a artist!" She dissolves into giggles.

Papa turns back to me. "Or architect," he hisses. "You are old enough to step out of the dream world, Emily. Your stepmother could use your help around the house with the boys if you no longer want to pursue your education. You and Edith can also assist with the entertaining. Or you can return to University of the Pacific and complete your studies of literature. There will be no further discussion about this school in San Francisco."

"Yes, Papa."

Can he hear my heart breaking? I turn my face as far away from him as I can, watching the landscape rush by and pretending interest in the sight while I focus on keeping my emotions from showing on my face.

I can see reflections in the window glass of people moving up and down the aisle. Some conversations, too low to be more than a buzz of voices, erupt into laughter or exclamation. These are people on their way somewhere. Many are probably Stanford students who plan to return in the fall, to continue their studies. Summer stretches ahead of them, a time to spend with family, to travel, to read for pleasure. For a college student, summer is a hiatus, a temporary ceasing of the bustle to move ahead. Summer is for recreation. During this season, a student's brain recharges and their soul flourishes, allowing them to return to school in the fall refreshed and ready to work hard again.

Odd, when I think of those I know in the business world, like my father, they seem to have lost that sense of summer. The job takes over their whole world as they strive to improve something, to make it bigger or better, to make more money or win more customers. Some work seven days a week and never take a vacation. Surely their souls wither and their brains tire. The entire country should declare Summer and require everyone to step back and assess their lives. I wonder how many of them would come to realize their heart lies in a different place than where their livelihood or society's expectations place them.

The silence among us three adults lengthens. Before long, Eva senses it and crawls on Nina's lap. She falls into the instant slumber of childhood, her rosy cheeks and soft eyelashes melting my heart.

When the train pulls into the San Jose station with a hiss of steam and screeching of brakes, it lurches enough to rouse Eva. Papa helps Nina into the aisle, Eva in her arms. He offers me his hand, but I ignore it and gracefully rise on my own. The passengers' conversations increase, laced with excitement that we have arrived. We disembark, and Papa goes off to see about the carriage.

Eva, now fully awake, fusses to get down. Nina holds her tight. I try to distract her.

"Eva, did you enjoy the train ride?" I ask her.

She makes a face. I don't know if this indicates confusion, disgust, or happiness. She nods. "It was noisy," she says.

"Yes, it was," I agree. "Trains seem like they are alive, don't they? They hiss and chatter and rumble."

"Trains are alive?" Now she looks frightened.

Nina breaks in. "No, sweetheart, trains are machines.

Aunt Emily is just teasing." She bounces the child on her hip, her eyes on me. "Speaking of just teasing, what were you thinking of, telling Papa you want to be an architect? Isn't he angry enough that you aren't going back to school?"

"Nina," I begin, but she's not ready to listen.

"You're twenty-six years old. Men have jobs and wives and families by that age. Yet you want a man's career. Men will block you because you are a woman, and because you are too old. What twenty-four year old architect will want an inexperienced apprentice that is a *woman* and older than he is? All you've done is anger Papa and push him away. Hasn't he been distanced enough from his girls?"

I wonder if Nina realized how odd her words sound in the child-calming cadence she uses to soothe Eva. At the end of the platform, I spot our carriage. Ed stands next to it, listening to Papa. "Nina, I don't want to argue about this. I know what I want. It has taken a long time for me to stand up and be firm about it, that's all. And how would you know about Papa's distance? You haven't lived at home for five years." My tone accuses even though I really don't intend it to.

"Edith writes letters," she says, rushing her words as Papa approaches. "You might try it sometime."

Stung, I turn to smile serenely at Papa. I accept Ed's warm hug, but my heart wraps itself around Nina's words. I assumed my sisters would support me. They should understand, but it seems not all women want to break the mold society has locked them into. I watch my sister pointing and exclaiming at the birds perched on the station roof for Eva's benefit. She is entirely caught up in her daughter and her husband. I always assumed that somewhere deep inside she longs for the teaching career that fired her passion. Could I be wrong? Or does my sister hide it even from herself?

"The carriage awaits," Papa says with his usual economy of words. Never have I heard him say 'Wonderful to see you' or 'Are you having a splendid day' like some of the men of my acquaintance, and I don't remember the last time he hugged me as my brother has just done.

We walk to the carriage. Ed picks up the crop and leaps into the driver's seat. Papa frowns, but apparently he's already had this conversation with his son. He and Nina, with Eva, get into the carriage. Impulsively, I gather my skirts and climb to the high driver's seat next to Ed. I can't face another minute enclosed with disapproval.

Ed laughs and tips his hat to me. "Home, milady?"

It feels good to laugh back at him. While my soft brown curls lay tight against my head, his are wild. They twist in every direction as if trying to leap from his head. His green eyes dance in reflection of my own, and my heart lightens.

The late afternoon sun smiles down on us as Ed calls to the horse and we begin the last part of our journey home. The carriage rocks and jangles, creating a breeze that teases the curls escaping from my hat. From the train station, it is not far to downtown proper, and to our home on Third and Reed Streets.

"So where's Carlo?" I ask Ed. Our usual driver should have picked us up.

Ed laughs. "Papa is so angry! Can I help it if I wanted to see my favorite twin a bit sooner?"

"Of course not!" He always makes me smile.

We approach the white Victorian that has been our home since Papa and Fannie moved to San Jose twenty years ago. Many hot summer evenings have been spent on this front porch, perching on a step with a glass of lemonade, reading a book or chatting with family and friends. My thoughts have been heavy, though, and my smile fades into a sigh.

"Em? What's wrong?"

"I told Papa I'm not going back to Stanford for the fall term."

Ed whistles. "And I show up with the carriage. Papa's not having a good day." He winks at me and I grin. No one keeps Ed's spirits down.

He pulls up in front of the house where Carlo hurries to take the horse. Ed dismounts and helps me down. Carlo pales even further when my father gets out of the carriage. I can't see Papa's face, but I empathize with the driver. Ed squeezes my arm and goes over to make it better.

"Papa, it's all my fault. I insisted," Ed says.

I leave the men and turn toward the house. Eva has already run up the steps and now jumps back down them. No doubt she'll race up and down again before Nina and I can ascend. The heavy front door opens, and Edith appears on the porch wreathed in welcoming smiles. She scoops up Eva and covers her face with kisses as the little girl giggles. Nina and I both smile as we hug our oldest sister. Fannie comes out then, her face smiling but her eyes searching for Papa. His heavy footsteps move faster as he approaches, and he enfolds Fannie in a very uncharacteristic hug. He even kisses her forehead. Ed and I have made this a very difficult day for Papa.

My family goes inside, but I linger on the porch at the top of the steps and enjoy the quiet. The heat of the day begins to dissipate from the air. In mid-June there is still a welcome coolness to the evening. As the sun sets, the relief of the dark spreads across the valley. A couple of hours of dusky daylight remain, but the families have gone inside.

"Emily? Are you coming inside?" Edith has come back outside to find me.

"In a minute."

She joins me at the porch railing. "You told Papa about not going back to school." I nod. "Did Nina tell you he knew already?" I nod again. "I'm glad you told him before he could ask. That showed courage."

Smiling, I say, "Thank you, Edith."

"He just told Fannie you want to be an architect." She pauses, possibly waiting for my admission I was joking.

"That's true."

"Oh, Emily, why would you choose such a difficult path? If by some miracle Papa allows it, and you manage to be admitted, the coursework will not be easy. Your classmates won't want to work with you. Even if you graduate, wherever do will you be able to work?"

I am too tired to defend myself to another family member. "You, too, Edith?"

"Don't mistake me, my sister. I completely support your choice. I just want to make sure you understand the obstacles."

She supports me. For the first time today, the anxiety clenching my heart eases. I feel tears choking my throat and building up behind my eyes. "Oh, Edith."

She enfolds me in her arms, and I bury my face in her shoulder. A sister's embrace supports me like the pillars of a tall building. Our shared strength gives me the courage to go inside and face my family again.

Edward Williams

Chapter 14: New York 1896
Ellen Rand VanValkenburgh

November is chilly in New York, but I sit with the window open and look down upon the Lower East Side, the air nipping at my cheeks. When I lived here almost fifty years ago with Mama and L'Amie, it was an older, respectable neighborhood. Now it is shabby and overcrowded and poor. The heat wave last summer killed hundreds of people in this city, many in this area. I have no idea why Uncle Benjamin didn't sell and move to a more appropriate home, but the poor old dear is gone now and beyond such things. I have put off this return to New York too long. Uncle Benjamin marks the last of my aunts and uncles to depart this earth, and his estate is large. I will return to California as a lady of substantial means.

The newspaper falls from my lap, rustling to the floor. Mr.

McKinley has been elected President of our fair country, and the nation celebrates. All summer while New Yorkers perspired and succumbed to the heat, the presidential battle raged. The Democrat, Mr. William Jennings Bryan, gave a fierce effort but in the end was defeated. In Wyoming, Colorado, and Utah, women cast their vote. In this same election, Idaho men voted to allow the women of their state to vote. Although my heart thrills with that small victory, California's measure did not pass.

Last summer, while New York sweltered, Susan B. Anthony spoke in Oakland at the Populist Convention that nominated Mr. Bryan's ticket. My heart thrummed with her words as I boarded the train for New York in September. My presence in California would not have changed the outcome. I have no vote, after all. Still, I feel so far away and so despondent. As I do when I am feeling this way, I miss those that are no longer with me.

My husbands, of course, are long gone. With Henry, I would discuss the election, but it would always be Jacob that loved away the despair of the night. Mama has been gone some thirty-seven years, and my sister Coelia passed six years ago, leaving a bereft Lucian and five grown children scattered across Northern California. L'Amie and Simeon are both sixty-two now, and rarely leave their home in Los Gatos. Their two sons are at college.

At least my children will outlive me. Marion still keeps me company at my Union Street home, a forty-year-old spinster.

Ellie and her family have moved to San Francisco. I am not needed there every day to assist now that Flo and Hal are practically grown. Henry and Nina still live on the ranch in Cholame. Their daughter, Eva, is seven, and so smart and independent. I never get to the ranch, and have to rely on Henry bringing his family to visit. I hear from Nina that her sister, Emily, studied English at Stanford for two years and wishes to be admitted into the California School of Mechanical Arts in San Francisco. It's not entry that creates the obstruction but her father. I wish I could box the stubborn man's ears.

So my family flourishes far away in body and spirit, and California has resoundingly defeated the vote for women. Santa Cruz County favored the measure, but the larger counties, like San Francisco, were strongly opposed. My dark mood cries that all is lost, my life has been for naught. But somewhere inside my heart beats strong. I have three healthy, happy children and three delightful grandchildren. The suffragist part of me shudders that I turn to such a feminine solace, but what am I if not a woman and a mother?

My sixty-ninth birthday passed in June, and I fear I shall never legally vote. Slavery has been abolished in my time, and the black man given the vote. All is progress, but progress is as slow as my bones on these cold New York mornings.

Maybe I should have been less forward for myself and encouraged my daughters to push themselves forward more. I was a role model, blazing the trail with torch held high. Maybe they would have preferred to be alongside. I made the mistake once of trying to explain to Ellie that my generation has striven for many advances so that her generation would have an easier life.

"You did none of this for me, Mama," she spat in my face. "This you did for you. Don't force me into wonderful new paths I never wanted. You work so women can have more choice, isn't that right? Then let me have my choice!"

Stunned by her vehemence, I snapped, "How can you choose when you never explored the options open to you?"

I chose marriage once, agreed to it once more. I suppose I was a good wife. If I never had to work while raising children, I would have spent more time with them. But were they lacking in their experiences with me? I think not. We had our lesson time, and bedtime stories, and trips to the beach, and ice cream. It was different from the families of their friends, but it worked for us. And I showed them passion for something important to the world, not just to themselves. I would never trade that.

Yet if I go home today it will be to a spinster daughter, destined to be alone like I am. This is not the progress I envisioned as a younger woman.

Below me on the street, a little girl skips along. Her bright red coat is a beacon to the gray in my soul. From this height, she looks to be around six years old, an age full of wonder and joy. An older woman I assume to be her mother follows, watching closely. The little one twirls, and her red coat spins wide. My heart lifts.

Turning away from the window, I find a precious photograph brought with me from California. Taken on occasion of my birthday this past June, the glowing faces of my three grandchildren smile at me. Flo and Hal stand behind, little Eva in front. They are the future of my family and my country. I have much to give them, and discouragement is not among those gifts. I will teach them independence, perseverance, and love. I will help them through the worst times, and celebrate the best. Someday, Flo and Eva will cast their vote.

Suddenly I am eager to return to California.

Chapter 15: San Jose 1899
Emily Williams

For almost my entire life, September meant a time of beginnings. A new school year brings great hope of achieving academic dreams, but over the last six years, September has meant nothing. Days stretch into months which linger endlessly before becoming years. I miss the challenge of classes and the discussions with schoolmates. This September marks the biggest change my life has yet experienced.

I sit on Fannie's stiff Victorian love seat, leaning against the uncomfortable carved armrest with my slippered feet tucked under me. This way I can look out on Third Street, newly paved past our house. Horse-drawn carriages still outnumber automobiles, but I see Mr. Holmes' Stanley Steamer chug by. Papa has a keen interest in the automobile, but now might never get the opportunity to own one. He lies near death in his bedroom upstairs, and I sit here full of guilty hope.

Since leaving Stanford six years ago, I have put on a good face and reluctantly become part of Fannie's social world, to her delight and my dismay. I share this term of exile from my dreams with Edith and we console each other. Meanwhile, Ed comes and goes on a schedule known only to himself with not a care in the world. Paul attends the new high school on Washington Square in town, and Waldo grows paler by the day, so frail I fancy I can see through his translucent skin. Fannie hovers over him, and he hasn't the strength to protest.

The only positive aspect of the social whirl has been meeting Lillian Palmer. The Palmers attend Trinity Episcopal Church with us. One Sunday last year, at a church social event, my gaze met Lil's. Instantly it seemed as though our hearts and souls locked with an audible click. Now we are inseparable. Her company would make today more bearable.

For the last five weeks, Papa's severe stomach trouble has hushed the conversations, quickened the footsteps, and elevated the concern of all who dwell here. Long past the point where the doctor claimed he should get better or surely die, the household waits as hope slips away.

Edith comes into the room. I look up. Our eyes meet for a moment before she quietly says, "He's gone."

And just like that, I am released. All the angst of the last few years exits my body with an audible whoosh, and my shoulders slump. My father, the strongest icon in my life, is gone.

Edith joins me on the love seat, sitting properly. "Fannie is with him. Waldo has gone to lie down. Will you go up?"

I gaze out the window, where the world continues normally. When San Jose learns that my father has died, the Freemasons will come, the mayor will come, the board of the San Jose Water Works will come. Fannie will hold court as the grieving widow. Edith and I will manage the food and drink. "Of course," I answer her. "Tell the servants, will you?"

She nods, but we both realize our two servants probably knew before we did. I rise, my skirts rustling as they fall into place around my ankles. Slowly I head upstairs to my duty. Each step brings a memory, the left leg happy ones, the right leg sad ones.

My earliest memories recall happy times with Ed, my sisters, my laughing Papa and Mama in Nevada City. Since Mama's death and Fannie entering our lives, the happy memories don't include Papa so much.

My most recent recollections are more about Fannie. She tried, under my father's watchful eye, to direct my life into proper channels. I dutifully joined the San Jose Woman's Club where we are working to save the Santa Cruz redwoods. I endure callers each afternoon and suitors in the evening.

Through all of it I have been going through the motions, tamping my passions deep within me.

Now they have been released.

The shades pulled down over the window dim Papa's bedroom. The heavily carved bed dominates the room, but Fannie's lacy curtains and bedspread give evidence of her decorating influence. The bed seems empty, my father has shrunk so. Fannie sits hunched over beside the bed. She, too, seems smaller. I put my hand on her shoulder, and she reaches up to cover it with her own.

The man in the bed seems serene, not the terror who has dominated my adult life, nor the beloved Papa of my youth. He is a stranger, deceased at seventy-four years of age, and my heart is numb.

Hours later, the expected mourners fill our home with flowers and condolences. Paul comes home from school and goes immediately to his departed father's side. At sixteen, Papa's youngest son holds vigil at his side. Edith and I greet neighbors and notables alike, and Fannie sits in the drawing room, an embroidered handkerchief held to her eyes. Waldo sits near her and holds her hand. Edith sends a telegram to Henry and Nina, who will be here tomorrow. Faces blur before me as I nod to each visitor, thanking them for coming and agreeing yes, our family has suffered a terrible loss.

Lil arrives with her parents, the brightest spot in my day. I hug her warmly and greet her parents, who love me as their own. They move on to speak to Fannie, and I pull Lil aside.

"I am so sorry, Em," she says, clasping my hand tightly in hers. Her black hair pulled back in its usual bun makes her nose jut severely from her face.

"I know, Lil, but I have mixed feelings." I look into her eyes and see understanding blossom there.

Lil, too, has dreams. Maybe what drew me to her is her role in a career long dominated by men. Currently a journalist for the San Jose Mercury News, she longs to work in copper, of all things. I tease that her dreams are as crazy as mine. She responds that we will be crazy together.

"I can apply to school now," I say, trying the words aloud for the first time.

"Before your father is even buried?" she chastises me.

Flustered, I stammer, "I will have to wait an appropriate amount of time, but yes, that is the plan."

"Oh, Em, I am happy for you, and so sad that this is what it took for you to pursue your dream."

I smile in relief, then ask, "And what of your dream, Lil?"

"I can be a journalist anywhere and learn about copper where I need to." Her eyes light with excitement that I know reflects in my own. Such a time seems far away, but for once it seems achievable. We whisper like little girls, talking over each other as our dreams take wing together.

Before long, however, reality breaks in. Lil's parents are ready to depart, and Edith comes to find us. She doesn't even scold me for disappearing. I fold grief back into my face and give Lil a secret smile as she leaves.

When the well-meaning mourners have all left, the mortuary next door comes to take charge of my father's body. As they leave, the owner has the nerve to ask Fannie if she will now sell the house. They would like to demolish it and build a parking lot. Fannie almost faints with offense. They wisely interpret that as a no.

Any discussion of applying to the drafting school is equally inappropriate. I bite my tongue and wait.

The next day Henry and Nina arrive with Eva, now ten and the light of my life. Unable to process the severity of her grandfather's death, she mingles sober behavior with laughter and dancing through the house. I adore her. She reads avidly, and I share some of my own childhood books with her. I find spending time with Eva easier than being with grieving adults. Many years have been spent putting off my life, and I am eager to get past death and live.

The next few days bustle with reporters wanting stories of the life of San Jose Water Works' first president, with funeral plans, with cards and plants and food arriving from friends, and with the stress of too much family living under the same roof. Ed must be feeling the same way I am as he announces plans to find his own living arrangements. He is currently employed, and as we are now thirty-two years old, my twin must make his own way. Fannie seems relieved.

We bury my father on a clear September day cool with impending autumn. Oak Hill Memorial Park provides a tranquil setting for the well-attended funeral and eternal rest of the Williams family patriarch.

The same day, I send off my application for admission to the California School for Mechanical Arts in San Francisco. My hand trembles as I drop the letter in the mail.

Lil and I spend most afternoons together, deep in plans both practical and silly. I will need a place to live in San Francisco, of course, but it will not be one I design. Not yet, anyway.

When the letter comes from the school, Fannie sees it before I do. She holds the letter as if it was poisonous.

"What is this?" she asks. If she has half a brain, she knows the answer.

"Hopefully my acceptance for next term."

"You applied without checking with me first?" She mimics the very picture of an outraged parent.

"You are not my mother. My father has left me enough money to pay for the schooling I want. You have no say at all." I try to be firm without sounding belligerent.

She deflates before my eyes. "I have tried to be a good mother to you."

"I had a good mother. I never needed another." Now I am just being mean, and I am instantly contrite. This woman achieved her life's dream of a home and family. I cannot disparage her for that dream any more than she should disabuse me of mine. "I'm sorry, Fannie. I know you have done your best. It's just that I have wanted this for so long."

She hands me the letter, her eyes brimming with tears.

I open it and scan the contents. A buzzing sound surrounds me, cutting me off from all reality. Nothing exists but the words on the page, *We regret to inform you...*

Now what will I do?

I slump onto the bench in the hallway, and the letter flutters to the floor. I lift a shaking hand to my eyes as Fannie retrieves the letter, reads it, and gasps. "Oh, I am so sorry, Emily."

"I was so sure..." I begin. "I must call Lil."

Leaving Fannie in the hallway, I enter Papa's study. The bookcases loom, lending a solid air to the room. The empty leather chair near the fireplace looks odd. Imagining my father sitting there with the evening paper reassures me. The telephone hangs on the wall near the door. Most of my acquaintances installed this device in the hallway or kitchen. Fannie had no interest in it, so Papa put it here. I pick up the receiver and turn the crank. When the operator comes on, I ask her to ring Lillian Palmer. Years ago, Papa worked tirelessly to bring the telephone to San Jose. He loved progress. My hand tightens on the receiver.

"Your party is on the line," the operator says in a singsong voice.

"Thank you. Lil?"

"Em, hello! Did the mail come?"

For a moment I can't speak. If I had been accepted, how could I leave Lil in San Jose? "I didn't get in."

"Oh, Em." But I detect a note of relief in her voice.

I laugh, pleased that she wants me to stay in San Jose. By the time I ring off, Lil has encouraged me to reapply for the fall term of 1901. In the new century, surely women will be able to secure a place in a mechanical arts school.

I enter the parlor, humming softly. Edith sits stiffly on one of Fannie's old sofas from Vermont. It came overland during the Gold Rush along with some other hideously heavy pieces. I prefer the airier carvings and gilt of modern pieces.

"You seem happy?" Edith frowns, looking puzzled.

I laugh. "No, I am not exactly happy, dear sister. I am hopeful for the future, however. I will try again next year. In the meantime, I go on as I have been."

Edith nods. "Fannie has invited the sons of an investment banker to dinner tomorrow evening. They are newly arrived in San Jose and need the respectability of marriage."

Not even this can dampen my spirits. Lil and I have a future, and it does not include husbands. "We can handle them, Edith." I smile widely, but she does not. I wonder if she intends to marry. She has never stated a desire for a forbidden career, nor does she pine for a husband. "Are you considering these bankers?"

She looks startled, her eyes wide. "No. I have no desire to

marry. Nina's mother-in-law has the right of it. Marriage strips a woman of everything she is. She has to give up her very self in order to become what her husband wants her to be. I don't want that."

I muse over her words, seeing passion I didn't know existed within Edith. "Ellen VanValkenburgh is an amazing woman," I admit, "but she has been married twice. She has three children. Won't you miss not having children?"

"That's what society has taught, isn't it? That a woman's life is not complete without children? I see them as more work, more stripping of what is essentially me. Now if I could find an enlightened man who would be my partner in all things, I might reconsider."

"A partner in all things? If that were the foundation for marriage, Lil and I would marry!"

She laughs at me, shaking her head. "I am happy you have found your soul mate," she teases. "I suppose I will have to be nice to these bankers. Now we'd better find Fannie. She no doubt has our afternoon planned."

The dinner with the Thomas brothers, Thomas and Terrence, almost entertains me. But really, Thomas Thomas? It would only be worse if one of my brothers were William Williams! Edith and I, the very picture of gracious unmarried daughters, welcome these young men to San Jose and nod encouragingly as they effuse about high finance in our fine city.

Edith sits at her usual place at the foot of the table, and she has pressed Waldo to sit at Papa's place. Twenty-five years old and still pale as milk, Waldo walks with a cane as if every step is agony. Fannie celebrates each day of his frail health as a miracle. Waldo does his best to engage our guests in conversation, but his life has been spent fighting illness, not learning how to operate in the world of finance.

Emily and I sit beside each other, facing the brothers across the table. Curly dark hair on their heads and beards gives them the illusion of bears, and I can hardly wait to tell Lil I have supped with ursus. Thomas quite animatedly speaks with hands flying. "I tell you, San Jose has the potential to be the gem of Western finance!" Terrence ducks a waving hand and takes a bite of Fannie's excellent roast. "San Francisco will be hampered by the influx of foreigners! San Jose, run by good solid Americans, can easily triumph!"

"Fascinating," Fannie murmurs. "Would you like another slice of meat?" She offers the tray to Terrence, who helps himself to two more thick slices of roast while still chewing his last.

Talk of finance makes me twist my napkin in my lap, stifle a yawn, and tap my feet. I cannot resist turning the talk to architecture. "So Mr. Thomas, as part of this financial superiority, do you see San Jose leading California in architecture, also? I mean, the Queen Anne detailing of Victorian homes is quite beautiful, but it really doesn't take into consideration the ample light available in our fair climate. Something simpler, maybe a single story, to allow for light and air to circulate within the home, might be appropriate. Do you agree?"

The light fades from his eyes as I'm sure mine did the minute he began talking finance. "Um, er, sure," he stammers.

Next to me, Edith raises her napkin to her lips. I am sure she smiles behind it. The serving girl brings in the dessert, and I silently congratulate myself on a tiny conversational victory.

Terrence fixes intelligent eyes on me. Pointing with his empty fork, he says, "You know, a California woman currently studies architecture in Paris, at the Beaux-Arts school. Do you know of Julia Morgan?"

I stare at him. I realize an odd amount of time has passed, and I hasten to say, "The Beaux-Arts has never accepted women."

"They have now, miss, a California girl, schooled at the university in Berkeley. When she returns, we hope she will consider settling in San Jose. We might be willing to fund such innovative work." Terrence resumes eating.

I pick at my own meal, my thoughts lost in dreams. I will have to write to Julia Morgan, or enroll at Berkeley. I can hardly wait to call Lil. Edith apparently wishes these men to think her a mute, for she nods and smiles like an imbecile and says nothing. Fannie maintains conversation through the apple pie and coffee. Her glares show her disapproval over my attempt at conversation. She must be too afraid of what I might say in rebuttal to reprove me openly.

When finally the banker brothers depart, Fannie stalks off to her sitting room without a word to us. I could have told her it would be no use, but she must parade eligible men before us like confections, hoping one will tempt us. I don't know whether she does so because she wishes us gone from her home, or whether she truly believes marriage will make us happy.

I sit beside the front window and gaze into the night. Although still relatively early, the streets are empty. The new electric streetlights give a harsher light than the old gas ones did, but they illuminate the streets better than that folly of a light tower downtown, modeled on one in Paris where Julia Morgan is studying to be an architect.

I wonder about studying in beautiful Paris. It must be somewhat easier, as a woman studying a man's subject, to overcome obstacles with family around you. Even if they don't agree with you, family supports you. The most disappointing stepdaughter always triumphs over a neighbor in one's affections. I know Fannie won't ever understand my desire to design homes, but she won't forbid it.

Dreaming has filled too many of my days in recent years. I go upstairs to my bedroom. There I have a small correspondence desk. I search through the drawers until I find a letter from a family friend studying at Berkeley. Copying the address onto a new sheet of stationery, I pen a letter to the engineering department, addressing it merely to 'Julia Morgan's mentor.'

The following day, I drop my letter into the post and

forget about it since some male student will probably throw it away. I am pleasantly surprised by a response scant weeks later.

Fannie brings me the letter, a cloud on her face. "You've now applied to Berkeley without even telling me?"

"No, no," I hasten to assure her. "I want to attend the mechanical arts school in San Francisco, as you know." I take the letter from her. "Thank you for bringing this to me."

I take the letter upstairs to my room and slide the opener into the envelope eagerly. It is a short note, written on university stationary in an elegant hand.

Dear Miss Williams,

I am Bernard Maybeck, on the engineering faculty at the University of California, Berkeley. I am also an architect, and Julia Morgan was one of my students. Therefore, I have taken it upon myself to answer your letter. I applaud your interest in architecture and encourage you to keep trying for the schooling you need. California needs more architects with a vision to the future, and I believe women will be a big part of that future. I wish you the best of luck, and if you wish to continue correspondence, I would be delighted to hear from you again.

Sincerely,

Bernard Maybeck

A warm glow begins in the hand that holds the letter and spreads to my heart and very soul. A professional architect, a professor of engineering, encourages me in my dream. I know I have firmly stated that I want to be an architect, but for the first time it truly feels possible.

Emily Williams and her niece, Eva VanValkenburgh (12 years old in this picture)

Chapter 16: Santa Cruz 1901
Eva VanValkenburgh

My family's home burned to the ground in a dramatic burst of terrible flame. Although the blaze caught us unaware, all three of us exited the house safely. I remember watching my parents standing close enough to be one person, my mother clutching the single china plate she managed to save. Everything else was lost—my few precious books, my dresses, wildflowers gathered that morning—with no never mind about importance to a lonely twelve-year-old girl. After the fire, we left the ranch in Cholame, among the warm rolling grasslands dotted with cattle, and moved to Santa Cruz, surrounding ourselves with family. My mother's plate sits on our mantel in a place of honor.

I don't mind our relocation to the city where my

grandmother lives with Aunt Mary, who taught me how to whistle with a blade of grass when I was younger. Grandma Van loves to share wonderful stories, and I love listening, so we will get on just fine. She intimidates, though, with her hawk-beak nose, piercing eyes, and penchant for dressing head to toe in black. Father says she still mourns her first husband, dead in the gold fields some fifty years.

Today, Grandma Van's stiff black skirts rustle as she walks along Union Street with a very businesslike stride. I hurry to match her pace, amusing myself by stepping in shadows, or dancing around them, or skipping over them. Anything to keep my mind off the next few hours. All summer the mornings have been dulled by fog. Now the sun shines and the dusky shadow of Grandma Van's parasol tempts me. Resisting, I clutch the pail that holds my lunch and lift my chin, mimicking what I believe to be dignity.

Shortly after my family arrived in Santa Cruz and settled ourselves at 18 Union Street, next door to Grandma Van and Aunt Mary at number 16, my mother announced the planned arrival of a baby brother or sister for me. My parents profess to love me, but I often feel left out of their closeness. An only child has no one else, but at twelve years younger, a new sibling will never be a confidante. He or she will only be a distraction to my parents' affections and an annoyance in mine.

My grandmother pauses before an imposing white building stretching three stories into the air. Impersonal windows seem to glare down at me, as if the building wonders why a simple country girl dares breach its doors. Grandma Van straightens my hat and reties the sash at the hip of my dress, pulling it so tight I can barely breathe. She thinks I am too fat, but Mama says I am just thickly built. Smoothing my wavy dark hair into a single fall to the middle of my back, she frowns at the dust collected on the toes of my black shoes. Thankfully, she does not attempt to wipe them clean before we climb the steps of Mission Hill School.

In Cholame, no school sat close enough to the ranch to make attendance a reality. My mother instructed me at home in reading, writing, and arithmetic, and I saw no other children except on very rare occasions when we went into town. Alone with my books and dreams I was happy, but now I am to be among children of my own age on a daily basis. The idea fills me with delighted terror.

"Go on then," my grandmother says without smiling, giving me a gentle push toward the classroom door.

I nod and force my legs to carry my body inside the school that educated my father. Peals of the morning bell have long since died away, and rows of hooks near the door are filled with hats. I remove mine and twirl it in my hand before finding an empty hook, and put my lunch pail on a shelf with those of the other children. Rows and rows of children turn their heads to stare at me without blinking. Surely somewhere in that room awaits a knight in shining armor who will save me from disgrace.

"Children, this is Eva VanValkenburgh, our new student. Eva, I am Miss Cooper."

The teacher pronounces my name *Ay-va*, as if I am the child of a Mexican laborer, instead of *EE-va*, the descendant of colonial founding fathers. She wears a plain gray dress, and her hair is rolled tight up on her head.

"It's Eva," I murmur as I sink into the vacant seat she indicates.

Next to me a mousy brown-haired girl winks, suffusing me with a welcome warmer than any shining knight could offer. A titter somewhere behind me chills the spark of welcome from my near neighbor. The boy in back of me shoves his book hard against the back of my chair, ensuring his place in the dungeon of my regard.

At some signal I miss entirely, four boys and a girl rise from their seats and join the teacher at the front of the room. They sit along a wooden bench, backs stiff and proper, holding small books. I lean into the aisle, just a bit, to see the title of their book. I fancy myself well read, and wonder if I have read this one. They take turns reading stiffly in voices too low for me to catch. I think again of three new books, sent by my Aunt Emily from San Jose, reduced to ashes in our home fire.

I shake my head in frustration. Miss Cooper looks up, her eye caught by the motion of my head. "Eva, you will recite with the next group. Please memorize the poem at the end of lesson six."

A quick glance confirms that the mousy girl is indeed reading poetry. "Yes, ma'am," I mumble, panicking for an instant. By sheer luck a student across the room opens his desk, and I realize the majority of the scarred wooden top lifts, leaving behind a flat solid space that holds a white china ink well and a pen. Inside, three books and a slate await me. I snatch the reader and close the lid too hard, accidentally creating a sound loud enough to draw a few giggles and gasps.

Opening the second McGuffey's reader and leaning forward, I hide my reddening face and locate lesson six. Mama had been teaching me from the fourth reader, but that book perished in the fire. Now I regress to the second reader, boring in its simplicity. I silently read the little poem.

Beautiful faces are they that wear
The light of a pleasant spirit there;
Beautiful hands are they that do
Deeds that are noble, good, and true;
  Beautiful feet are they that go
Swiftly to lighten another's woe.

I wonder when a classmate will swiftly lighten my woe or show me the light of a pleasant spirit.

The bustle of students returning to their seats breaks my concentration. I gather the reader into my hands, swallow hard, and follow Mousy Girl, Book Shoving Boy, and one other girl to the recitation bench at the front of the room. They dutifully take turns reciting the poetry in tones of drudgery that banish all life from the words. When it comes my turn, I stand and speak the lines with passion, great self-pity rising within me.

The teacher closes her book on her lap and leans toward me. She tilts her head slightly, brow furrowed, as if I am some puzzle to be solved, then opens her mouth to speak. She closes it, as if reconsidering, then rushes on. "Eva, in this school we recite the poet's words. You will not presume to interpret those words until you attain enough life experience to fully understand what the poet intends. Children, please return to your seats and write out the poem on your slates."

At least she pronounces my name correctly.

Without another word, the other three students in my group follow her direction, and I hasten to do the same.

In Cholame, Mama and I played with poetry. We shouted it, laughed it, growled it, or cried it, as the words demanded. Our front room looked out over pastures dotted with cattle and wildflowers; a place designed for poetry. Here the crash of the ocean prevents even a moment of reflective silence, and the dampness in the salty air frizzes hair.

I write the first line of the poem, chalk gritching on my slate. An itch on my leg distracts me, and my left hand reaches for the half-healed scratch, just below the knee but above my stocking. I rub it, feeling the scab give way. Pushing the top of my stocking lower in case the scratch decides to bleed, I remember the nail on the fence that wounded me. This injury remains the last vestige of home, the last tangible reminder of my early childhood that is not trusted to memory. I scratch, and hope it forms a new scab so it will stay with me a bit longer.

After the longest two hours of my life, Miss Cooper leads the class outside to give our laboring minds a respite. The grounds of the school seem pleasant enough, with benches to rest on, a few trees and some shrubbery. We are near the sea, however, and the raucous call of gulls grates on gentle nerves.

"Welcome, Ayyy-va," a girl sneers. She sticks her nose in the air and flips her long blond curls over her shoulder as she turns her back. Her friends laugh. Clearly, she does not intend to befriend me, so I do not answer.

"Don't pay attention to her, Eva," Mousy Girl tells me.

She pronounces my name correctly, so I smile.

"I'm Annie," she says. "Annie Hollingsworth."

"Eva," I say. But of course she knows that.

"Could your grandmother be the Mrs. Ellen VanValkenburgh who lives in town?"

Annie's awestruck tone is not new. Half of Santa Cruz admires my grandmother, and half disdain her. The latter seem to be mostly men. "Yes," I answer her, and dare to lift my head with pride.

"Are you new to Santa Cruz?"

"Yes. We moved here from Cholame." Annie's information will no doubt be shared with others, but I do not begrudge her that. Her nose wrinkles. Apparently she is unfamiliar with rural San Luis Obispo County. I add, "My father took up government land south of here. He is a cattle rancher."

"Oh."

How can so much disapproval be thrust into one word? Annie pats my hand. "If I can help you with anything, just ask," she says with a bright smile. Then she walks away.

Left alone, but without the need to impress anyone or excuse my origins, I am somewhat relieved.

Near me, three girls younger than I are playing catch with a ball made of string. On the far side of the yard, a mixed-age group of boys plays a rough game that involves shouting and lurching through clasped arms. Annie joins two other girls on a bench near the doorway, and Blond Curls and her friends stand aloof from everyone. I have never seen so many children all in one place. Before I can muster enough courage to approach anyone, the teacher comes out and rings a small handbell. We all shuffle inside.

On the blackboard, a different arithmetic problem has been written for each age group of students. I must concentrate to read the fifth-form problem since arithmetic confounds me. *A farmer killed 3 pigs and 2 sheep, and had 9 pigs and 4 sheep left. How many of both had he at first?* I rub the side of my chalk with my thumb. Next to me, Annie is writing. My mind blanks.

Miss Cooper calls another group. As they assemble, her eyes scan the class and settle on me, on my blank slate. She frowns. I drop my head. They will all think I am stupid, but I am not. If it weren't for the newness of the whole situation, I am sure I could complete the problem. I look at it again and manage to scribble *26* before the teacher calls my group.

Of course, I am shamed by an incorrect answer. I erase it with my sleeve and endure a shocked gasp from Annie. My face reddens again, and I feel a tear trying to break loose and race down my cheek. I nod when Miss Cooper asks if I now understand, even though I don't even glance at what she has written on the board. I return to my desk where the mysteries of the arithmetic textbook continue to degrade me.

Twenty to forty tons of alfalfa, squash, and corn are grown in San Luis Obispo County. The ranch in Cholame has 150 cattle that roam 1000 acres. One Holstein cow, milked twice a day, gives 17,720 pounds of milk in one year. One pound of butter can be made from 17.76 pounds of milk, and 8 3/8 pounds of milk can make one pound of good solid cheese from the press. I *can* do arithmetic. I am *not* stupid.

My stomach begins an unladylike rumble just about the time Miss Cooper stands up and dismisses us for lunch. In the yard, I find a bench and sit squarely in the middle, hoping to deter others from joining me. I am used to being alone, but I frankly fear the motives of classmates who might brave the displeasure of their peers to speak with me.

Opening the pail Mama packed for me, I select a ham and cheese sandwich and eat, enjoying it without worrying about who might see me drop a crumb. I focus my eyes on my food and my thoughts inward, where they are so often happy.

When Miss Cooper rings her bell to begin class once more, I am refreshed. I even manage to smile at Annie as we take our seats. She looks startled, but she returns the smile. Confidence builds within me, only to be dashed by Miss Cooper.

"Poor penmanship gives a poor impression of the writer to whomever reads your work," she says in a tone that tells me she often repeats these words. "Write neatly. Be proud of your penmanship and proud of your work."

I quail, gripping the chalk tightly, hearing Mama's words echo behind my teacher's. "Eva, you must slow down. Form the letters more carefully so I can read what you are attempting to write."

I've never possessed patience, especially since my ideas come far too rapidly for my hands to manage. Words and phrases tumble over themselves in their dash to exit my fingertips. I often smear or scribble words, afraid they will vanish from my mind before I can capture them with my quill or chalk.

Annie, however, begins to copy the day's spelling words in a precise hand, three times each, on her slate. There are too many words, the slate too small. The fat chalk fills in the centers of my a's and e's. I slump my shoulders and a frustrated sigh pushes its way out of my mouth. The younger boy in front of me looks back and laughs. Miss Cooper frowns.

"Ernie, is there a problem?" she asks.

He shakes his head from side to side and answers in a sing song voice of innocence. "No, Miss Cooper."

I want to scream.

The teacher sets us to copying a passage from McGuffey's reader. We use the inkwell and a fountain pen for this because it challenges our ability to maintain cleanliness while scribing letters. It makes a difficult task near impossible. My words straggle across the page punctuated with inkblots and frustration. The teacher walks around the classroom. She pauses by me, murmurs, "Oh, dear," and continues up the row as I smear another carefully crafted capital.

The teacher calls me to the front of the room and attempts to make my hand flow across the page leaving behind beautifully looped letters. My hand cramps, and she gives up. I start back to my seat and a younger classmate giggles. I refuse to blush again. Surely the quality of the composition outweighs the occasional smudge! I lift my chin and stomp toward my desk.

With my nose in that position, I can't tell if Ernie's foot juts into the aisle on purpose to trip me. Nonetheless, I stumble over it and grasp at my desk to keep from falling flat on my face. The class erupts in laughter and once again I blush with shame and embarrassment.

Would this day never end?

Then Annie speaks, her voice timid but sure. "Miss Cooper, Ernie did that on purpose."

My eyes fasten on Annie and I smile. I don't hear what Miss Cooper says to Ernie, and I don't even glance his way. Just maybe I have made a friend. She smiles back.

The afternoon passes swiftly. I am a strong speller, and I have a tenuous friendship. Miss Cooper does not allow me to participate in the day's spelling bee since I have not had the opportunity to study the words. Even so, I know them all, and I bask in that knowledge. Tomorrow I will win the top award.

Finally, the school day ends. I force myself to use the ladylike walk Grandma Van will approve of, instead of the undignified gait of a cattle rancher's daughter. It takes all my concentration to manage it, then my grandmother is there. She greets the teacher and asks after my day. Miss Cooper responds with more pleasantries, but I am overwhelmed with desire to be gone.

We exit the school and descend the steps in placid companionship. I think of Annie's welcoming smile, but dislike and failure shadows the memory. My lip starts to quiver. I bite it. "Public school isn't so bad," I tell my grandmother. I have never lied to her before.

As we leave Mission Hill School behind us, the salty tang of Santa Cruz's sea air tickles my nose. We've hardly exited the grounds when a bustling woman, rounded by thick skirts and short stature, hails my grandmother. Annie, my almost-friend, hovers almost hidden behind her. I offer a smile, but she lowers her eyes.

"Mrs. VanValkenburgh! Delighted to run into you, just delighted." Round Woman clasps her hands together and leans forward to punctuate her delight.

"Mrs. Hollingsworth." My grandmother nods, acknowledging her.

It must be Annie's mother. My heart skips a beat. Has Annie already told some tale of a horrible indiscretion on my part?

"Will you be attending the Union meeting tomorrow evening?" Annie's mother sounds anxious.

"Of course. Plans are coming along for the Convention next year, but we have a lot of work to do yet. I will be there." Grandma Van actually smiles at Annie's mother.

I remember my grandmother talking with my mother this morning about the meeting of the Women's Christian Temperance Union. Mama showed very little interest. While Mrs. Hollingsworth seems a trifle overeager, I suspect Grandma Van might like to see some of her enthusiasm in my mother.

"Excellent! I will see you then," Mrs. Hollingsworth beams. "Say goodbye, Annie."

Annie blushes as she looks up. "Bye, Eva."

"Goodbye, Annie. It was a pleasure to meet you," I say, secretly hoping my formal manners will impress my grandmother.

They head off down Mission Street while we continue in the opposite direction toward Union. I ponder telling my mother about Annie. The hard-packed dirt road is easier walking than the grassy verge, but we must be vigilant and watch for carriages.

Sure enough, before we reach our corner a black carriage drawn by matched bays clatters up. I scamper for the edge of the road, but Grandma Van stands firm. The carriage swerves to miss her, and the driver pulls up the horses to shout at her, "Stay out of the road, lady!"

My grandmother pulls herself up straighter, seeming to grow taller with rage. Her eyes fasten like hooks on the driver and she stares. He shakes his head and stifles a chuckle, but backs down.

"Pardon me, Mrs. VanValkenburgh. I thought I was dealing with a lady."

He drives off at full speed before she actually speaks. I rejoin her on the road.

"Why is he so rude, Grandma Van?"

She shakes her head. "Some men are very foolish, Eva. That man, and others like him, think I am determined to give their wives and daughters the wrong ideas about how to live their lives. Listening to what a woman says, allowing her to speak her mind, remains a foreign idea to men like those. But mark my words, someday women will vote."

"Yes, Grandmother." If Grandma Van feels that strongly, I must agree. At home we don't discuss votes for women unless Papa is telling Mama something about what Grandma Van has done.

During the remainder of the walk, I plan the words I will use to tell Mama about Miss Cooper, and even Ernie.

Upon reaching home, I open the white picket gate and hold it for my grandmother.

"Look, Eva, the almond tree is full of green nuts. In another month or so I will show you how to pick them."

But I have noticed a carriage tied outside, and I am curious to see our visitor. On the porch that runs the length of the house my mother sits in one of the large wicker chairs. In the other her sister Emily, my favorite aunt, waves. I run to greet her.

"Aunt Emily! When did you get here?"

"Hello, Eva! I came to visit you and Nina before I left."

"Left?" I look at my mother, then back to my aunt.

My mother asks if we would like some iced tea, and the three adults exchange a few polite grown-up words while I sit carefully on the top porch step to await an answer. Finally, Aunt Emily turns to me.

"I am moving to San Francisco, Eva. I've been offered a place at Wheeler and Wilson Manufacturing Company. I'll be teaching clients to use their sewing machines. It's not the work I am anticipating, though, but the nearness to the California School for Mechanical Arts. If I'm practically on their doorstep, I am sure to be admitted."

I know she loves to draw, and her enthusiasm echoes

within me, but traveling from San Francisco will be harder than traveling from San Jose, so I shall not see her as often as I hoped when we moved to this town.

"Really, Emily, I don't know why you insist on that school," my mother says, gently reproving, as she returns with the iced tea.

"Ah, Nina, I must get away." She shares a long glance with Mama that I fail to comprehend. "With Father gone, the house became Fannie's. Waldo remains there so she can look after him, and Paul stays in school."

Mama reaches over to pat her hand, no doubt thinking of my grandfather, who died last year. I think of my Uncle Paul, six years older than I but closer to my age than any of my cousins. The adults share more pointless chatter as they sip. Mama has brought me a lemonade, and I sip properly like a lady, wondering if maybe Aunt Emily would like to hear about my day.

Mama tries again. "You aren't living at home anyway, right? You've moved in with the Palmers. If you leave San Jose, Fannie will most certainly miss you. "

"I know, I know. But Fannie is not Mama. She keeps poking me to find a husband and start a family like you. I just want to design things."

"You have your asthma to consider," my mother points out. "Will San Francisco's dampness help or hinder it?"

"You have the same problem," my aunt says. "Does Santa

Cruz bother you?"

Mama frowns. "Emily," she begins.

"Emily will do as she sees best," my grandmother declares, "whether it's marriage or school." She nods to my aunt. "Good luck to you."

"Thank you, Mrs. VanValkenburgh, your good wishes mean a lot."

I am more proud of my grandmother's grace than I am of my mother's whining. "Write and tell me about your school," I tell my aunt, striving for the grown-up tone my grandmother used.

"Of course I will, my precious darling!" She hugs me, enveloping me in a scent more spicy than floral. I hug her back and scrunch my eyes to hold back tears. It has been a long day.

The late afternoon begins to cool as fog drifts in from the Pacific Ocean. The ladies stand up and make their farewells. Aunt Emily prepares to depart, taking the carriage to the depot to catch the train home to San Jose. Grandma Van walks next door. I can see, over the hedge separating the houses, that Aunt Mary has already lit the lamp in the front room. The sun drops low enough in the sky so that the orange clouds peek through the windswept branches of the cypress trees. Mama goes inside to light our lamps, draw the curtains, and begin supper. I stand on the porch and watch Aunt Emily's carriage take her away. After the day's discouragement, it seems as if I will never see her again.

And no one has asked about my day. I vow to tell Father about it at supper whether he asks or not.

Ellen VanValkenburgh, Santa Cruz Beach Boardwalk, circa 1901

Chapter 17: San Francisco 1901-1902

Emily Williams

San Francisco, the largest city on the Pacific Coast, simply bustles with life. With the biggest port, it has become the most important financial center despite the Charles brothers' assertion that San Jose would eclipse its northern neighbor. San Francisco has been called the Paris of the West, and it houses the California School for Mechanical Arts. In my wildest dreams I study in Paris with Julia Morgan, but in reality I love being in San Francisco where I can be near a school I might actually attend.

To my overjoyed astonishment, Lil agrees to come to the city with me, asserting she can be a journalist anywhere. I am humbled by her generosity and that of her parents. Unable to stomach Fannie's pressure to marry, I moved in with the

Palmers shortly after Papa's death. They are my wonderful second family, supportive and encouraging. I had no idea parents could be so. Lil and I, with her parents' help, find a place in the city on 14th Street, just off Van Ness. It's not Russian Hill, but still a respectable neighborhood in the Mission District. This will be our home as we work our daily jobs and encourage each other to pursue our dreams. An added benefit is that the perpetual cool fog seems to calm my asthma. Hopefully it won't worsen over time from the damp.

At first, we glory in being residents of the most exciting city in the world. We ride the cable cars, sip steam beer on the wharf, and watch the ferries arrive at the Ferry Building. Alive and connected to every country on Earth, San Francisco's people, food, fashion, and most importantly the architecture, blend many cultures. San Francisco is an industrial port city, very dirty and yet, so beautiful. Lil and I temporarily set aside the fight for our future and just enjoy the present.

I continue to write to Bernard Maybeck, and we quickly become pen pals. I have read about his work in magazines while we have been corresponding, and when he invites Lil and me to visit him at the Berkeley campus I am thrilled.

"He's known for his eclectic designs," I whisper to Lil as we approach Maybeck's office.

"We should be eclectic enough to appeal to him," she says, smiling indulgently. Her arm rests comfortably around my waist, and her thumb traces circles on my back. Dear Lil never shows impatience with me even though I fill her head with tidbits about this great man all the way from our Mission District home.

The man himself appears eccentric. His grizzled beard, white and unkempt, is still fuller than the wispy strands on his head. He wears the sort of knickers I've seen on young boys, with colorful argyle socks. He grins when he sees us, and ushers us into an office crowded with books and papers.

"Lovely of you to come, ladies! Miss Williams, you are interested in architecture?"

He knows I am from our correspondence. I am relieved he is so eager to get to the point of our visit since I don't have much patience with half an hour of social niceties. I am here to discuss my passion, not flitter about the weather. Yet the first words out of my mouth are vapid. "Was Paris a wonderful place to study, Mr. Maybeck?" Of course it was. I make a face. Lil takes my hand and squeezes reassuringly.

He laughs heartily. "You might say so. All that lovely architecture is inspiring, but no less so than California's regional forms and construction. Every place has its own style."

I nod, barely able to contain myself. Hadn't I said something similar to Terrence Charles years ago? "Your Mission work is eminently suitable for California, but I love the Arts and Crafts style."

"Remember, young lady," he cautions, "do not fall in love with one style. Each architectural problem requires an original solution. To be an excellent architect requires solid training and a good eye."

"Yes, well, that solid training has been a problem," I say.

He waves away my words. "I know you've applied again to your school. If you don't get in, please consider Berkeley. I would love to have a passionate student such as yourself."

"Thank you, sir." His words surprise me. I have never considered Berkeley. The course is rigorous there, many years instead of a few months at the San Francisco school. It is also much more expensive.

He turns to Lil. "And what is the nature of your passion, Lillian?"

"I am inspired by California's sunshine," she responds. "As a journalist I have traveled the state a bit. There's a quality to the natural light that I wish to capture and bring inside."

"What is your medium?"

"I would like to learn more about working in copper. There's so much I don't know about its temperament. I just know that copper lamps will be stunning." Frustration echoes in her words.

"Lil is a gifted copper artist," I tell him. The pride shines from my words, and Lil smiles at me.

"The role of an educator is to take passion such as yours and channel it so you can reach your full potential. It saddens me that in this enlightened age students capable of great things, such as yourselves, are not even being allowed entrance to our finest schools."

I don't dare to disagree with him. It's not the entrance to a good school that's the issue, but the course of study allowed once you are enrolled. I have, after all, attended fine schools such as University of the Pacific as well as Stanford. The California School for the Mechanical Arts is not a university, nor is it an educational institution of the caliber of the others, but it offers the training I want in a concise program. I believe Berkeley would accept me if I applied, and Mr. Maybeck would support my choice of coursework, but I doubt my father's money will cover a four-year program.

We discuss specifics of different architectural styles, and he includes Lil easily. We take our leave and chatter excitedly all the way home. Mr. Maybeck has relit the fire that propels us. We await only a direction.

Late in 1901, I receive a letter from the California School of Mechanical Arts.

Dear Miss Williams,

It is with great pleasure that I am able to offer you a position at our school for the term beginning in January, 1902. I hope you will be able to take advantage of this offer and are still interested in attending our school.

Yours truly,

George Merrill, Director

California School of Mechanical Arts

San Francisco

All strength leaks from my body, and I sink onto the sofa. With shaking hands I hand the letter to Lil. My opportunity has arrived.

She scans the note and looks at me with shining eyes. "Oh Em! This is too wonderful for words! We must have dinner tonight at the Palace Hotel to celebrate!"

She knows the Palace Hotel's Beaux Arts style reminds me of Julia Morgan and the Paris school.

"But, Lil, what about your dreams?" The idea of her sacrificing her career to be in San Francisco with me is overwhelming. I burst into tears.

She takes me in her arms and strokes my hair. "Em, my darling, you *must* be pleased. I am so happy for you, I couldn't bear it if you were sad. At the worst, I will continue as I have been. I'll work as a journalist until my path reveals itself." Gently, she kisses me. "Hush now. This is cause for celebration. Just think—when I get my break, we can celebrate again."

She continues holding and reassuring me until I can stop crying. I know our strength together will see us both through the next months.

Just after the new year dawns, I present myself at the California School of Mechanical Arts as a student. Impeccably dressed in properly conservative dark clothing, the male students sweep wide of me like a river with a boulder in its midst. They are too polite to stare with their eyes, but they stare instead with their stiff backs and too-carefully averted faces. I don't need their approval or their regard. I square my shoulders and find a seat in Chemistry.

My first ray of hope that first day begins to shine when my Chemistry teacher introduces herself. Miss Bridgman's eyes locate me immediately, and she acknowledges her only female student with a smile and a nod. Part of her introduction to us is a statement that she has designed her own house in Berkeley. To the other students that may merely establish her credentials, but to me she's a mentor. I cannot wait for class to be over so I can approach her privately.

That night, Lil is treated to a barrage of words about my day, most of them about Miss Bridgman. "Lil, she designed her own house! She's not actually an architect, certainly not licensed, but she has the skills I need. When I talked to her, she was very encouraging, like Mr. Maybeck. The house she designed is in Berkeley, and she knows Mr. Maybeck. He helped her with the concept!"

Lil is smart enough to know that the parts of the day that I gloss over are the ones that are difficult, but she doesn't speak of them. "I'm so proud of you, Em!"

After a couple of weeks of hearing about the wonderful Miss Bridgman, though, Lil grows impatient. "Surely you are taking classes other than Chemistry?" she snaps.

I recoil, shocked. "Well, yes." My mind recalls drafting class, where no one sits at my table because I am the only woman, where I scramble inelegantly atop the stool designed for men in pants, where I consistently outscore the men who spend their time staring and sniggering instead of drawing. "I have drafting," I say, my voice dead.

"I'm sorry, Em," she says, contrite. "It's just all you have spoken about for weeks. I know every little detail of the amazing Miss Bridgman's life. Oh, what did she have for breakfast this morning? You omitted that tidbit in today's recitation."

I take in her flashing eyes and heightened color. "Why Lillian Palmer! Are you *jealous*?"

She flushes, immediately denying it, and I forebear teasing. Instead, I ask her about her work. She has been working part time as a journalist, which she enjoys as a hobby, while looking for a coppersmith to take her as an apprentice. Lil is confident she can teach herself to work with the copper, but it's an expensive hobby. She wants to get on with an established shop.

By the end of February, my male classmates accustom themselves to ignoring me and don't have to work so studiously at it. I am content to avoid the need to be polite while still not encouraging suitors. Occasionally a professor requires students to work together on a project, but I am always alone. Some professors mark me down for not working as a member of a team, but Miss Bridgman never does. She continues to encourage me, and I ravenously consume every bit of information that comes my way in my classes.

Lil waits. She never complains and seems content to run

our tiny house, leaving me to concentrate on my studies. Her time will come, though. We both believe that.

In May, I receive a letter from my niece, Eva.

Dear Aunt Emily,

> *I hope you are enjoying San Francisco because I miss you and wish you were closer to Santa Cruz. I am writing to tell you that I have been presented with a baby brother. His name is Carl. My parents are over the moon, but I have yet to render a verdict. He cries a lot.*

> *Study hard at your drafting school and visit soon.*

Yours truly,

Eva VanValkenburgh

I show the letter to Lil and we chuckle over it. Independent little Eva has been too long alone. Carl will be good for her. My niece is already tough and has the potential to be a very strong woman. She clearly has the backbone of her grandmother, Ellen VanValkenburgh. I adore Eva and hasten to respond.

My darling Eva,

> *Having a brother can be a wonderful thing. I should know, I have three. I was fifteen when your Uncle Paul was born, and to my regret we are not as close as I am to my twin, your Uncle Ed. That is to be expected, I suppose. Nonetheless, take good care of Carl and help your mother care for him. You will come to love him, I am sure.*

> *When I am next in Santa Cruz, I have so much to tell*

you about San Francisco. It is an amazing place to live and
go to school.

With all my love,

Emily Williams

Just a few days after I send off the letter to Eva, my school term ends. I have completed the classes I need to become a junior architect, but I hesitate to apply for a license.

"Why did you bother with school if you weren't going to try for a license?" Lil asks.

"I have the knowledge I need now, Lil. What I need is experience."

"No one will hire you without a license."

I laugh. License or no, I won't be welcome in many architectural firms. To my knowledge no women work in any such firms in California, not in any capacity. Julia Morgan, the great female hope, is still in Europe. I must blaze my own trail. "I will send off the license application tomorrow, Lil. And as soon as I put it in the post, I will begin looking for a place as a draftsman." The words make my head swim with trepidation, but I have wanted this too long.

Lil throws her arms around me. "Good for you!"

I pull back, and nose to nose I glare at her. "And now it's your turn. No more delays."

She laughs and demurs, but I am firm. If there is an architectural firm in San Francisco that will hire a woman, surely there is a coppersmith who will do the same.

It soon becomes clear that there is no place in San Francisco for either of us. The architectural firms' names blend together into an amalgamate of men's initials and surnames.

At one such firm I am ushered into the inner sanctum by a male secretary. The name on the door says C. Field, and I wonder if it is Charles Field, son of Mr. Field who was an associate of my father, the same Charles Field that Fannie once thought was husband material. I recognize him immediately as he enters the room full of apologies for being late for our appointment. Thirteen years have added a bit of distinguished gray to his hair even though he is probably not yet forty. His face registers shock, and I am unsure if it is because he recognizes me or because I am a woman. I have put E. Williams on the application.

"I was expecting Ed," he tells me in consternation.

"My brother is no architect," I tell him primly.

He drops into the chair behind the desk. "And you are?"

I have managed to remain unflustered by much harsher interviewers. "I hope to secure a position as draftsman and eventually earn my license."

He leans forward and puts his elbows on the desk. "You do realize you are a woman?"

"Yes, Mr. Field, I do. I believe a woman's perspective will change the face of architecture in this new century."

He is already shaking his head. "I respect your family, Miss Williams, but this firm does not hire women and is not likely to ever do so."

"Do you lack vision, Mr. Field?" I have maintained my equilibrium, but he quickly loses his.

"Now look here. It is not my vision that is in question. I completed my schooling and have worked hard to establish myself here. As a junior partner, I am tasked with bringing aboard employees who will work hard and garner prestige for our firm."

I say nothing, waiting for him to hear his own words.

"No, Miss Williams, I do not believe you fit the bill. You will bring unwelcome attention, gossip and speculation, not respect. If you are serious about becoming an architect, go build something to show you can do it. Maybe then someone will take you seriously." He turns away, dismissing me.

"Give my regard to your parents," I jab at him on the way out.

I trudge up the steps into the house with a particularly heavy heart. I stand at the kitchen door and watch Lil for a moment. She stands at the stove, stirring a pot of something that will be supper. A few tendrils of fuzzy black escape from the pile of thick dark hair on her head. An apron covers her finely made dress, but it's not the clothes I admire so. The tilt of her head and the curve of her back are beloved both for their familiarity and their steel. She is no less a woman because of her strength of character. I see the same trait in myself. Apart we are strong, but together we are invincible.

She sees me then and smiles, her entire face lighting up with welcome. The smile fades when my eyes don't respond. "Em? Everything all right?"

"I am tired, Lil." I enter the room and take the spoon from her hand. "Today I was told that if I were a man, I wouldn't beg for a job I'd just go build a house to show what I could do." I dip the spoon into the pot and blow on it, tasting the red sauce that will no doubt top the meat in the oven whose odor permeates the kitchen and makes my stomach rumble.

Lil retrieves the spoon and stirs the pot. "That's really not a bad idea."

"Really? And where would I get the property and the materials to build a house?"

"First, do you have a design idea to work up?" She begins to be excited by the idea, but I have not yet embraced it.

"Of course. I have been thinking of nothing else for months." My tone dismisses her, but Lil persists.

"Where would be the best place for this venture? Not San Francisco. We need a smaller community, one that appreciates art. Maybe Santa Cruz?"

"I would love to work in Santa Cruz. I'll write Nina after our meal." In spite of my many misgivings, I warm to the idea.

Lil says nothing more on the subject, wisely allowing the idea to simmer. We sit down to supper and discuss the day's events, avoiding any talk of my future or hers. Around our careful words, my thoughts zoom at an amazing speed. In my mind I can see my first house, a small cottage really, with windows to let in light. Maybe I could push the windows out a bit. They'd stick out from the side of the house, but it would give the illusion of more interior space. I'll have to use natural materials, to blend the house into the landscape. Oh, I hope the site we find has rocks for a natural rock chimney. That would make the place quite charming.

I look up to find Lil smiling knowingly at me from across the table. She's been reading my thoughts again. I grin, guilty. "I think we can do this if we do it together," I tell her.

She whoops with delight. As she clears up the supper dishes, I pen a letter to Nina. The rest of the evening, and late into the night, Lil and I spin dreams of snug cottages tucked among the redwoods, all cheerily illuminated with stunning copper light fixtures.

We are unable to wait for Nina's response. Our excitement over the idea of building our own house together takes over, and the very next day we are on a train to Santa Cruz. Feeling guilty that we do not plan to stop and visit Nina and her family, I urge Lil to continue past Santa Cruz. I can't bear Eva learning I am in town and I don't visit her. But we have a task before us, and it is paramount.

The Southern Pacific locomotive steams its way south along the coast. Ocean spray leaves salty crystals on the windows, and puffy clouds of steam hang in the air. July on the coast is cold. The fog blankets everything, coming down to the ground in the early morning and rising barely high enough to improve visibility during the day. Today is truly spectacular, one of the rare days when the sun has broken through the fog and the coast looks like a picture postcard.

When the train pulls into Pacific Grove, I know we have found what we seek. "Lil, this is perfect," I tell her, peering out the windows at the wild natural beauty of Lover's Point. The artist community, small enough to support our efforts, sits on a gorgeous rocky point covered in cypress and pine trees.

Lil nods and stands up. We leave the train and stand on the ocean side of the tracks. Lover's Point juts out into the Pacific Ocean. Mighty waves crash against gray boulders. A handful of the ever-present artists sit with easel and paints trying to capture the image on canvas from every possible angle. Across the tracks and Ocean View Boulevard a row of bath houses offer heated salt water pools. The ocean itself, as I know from personal experience, is shockingly chilly year round.

The stiff breeze grabs my hat and threatens to tear it from my head. The sun shines bravely, but the ocean's cold wins today. The majestic vista glitters in the sun, but the temperature does not invite lingering outdoors.

Lil rubs her cold arms. We ran out of the house without coats like children, even though we know all about the coastal weather. I laugh at the red roses on her cheeks, knowing mine are the same. Our exhilaration overflows, and we stand in the wind on Lover's Point laughing like lunatics.

California School of the Mechanical Arts, circa 1910
From the Lick-Wilmerding High School website, 2011

Chapter 18: Pacific Grove 1902-1904
Emily Williams

Convinced that we belong in Pacific Grove, Lil and I rent a small place to live as we scour the neighborhoods for a suitable property. Late in 1902, we buy a small lot on Chestnut Street among the pine trees. The address of our first home will be 246 Chestnut Street, Pacific Grove. We must save every penny for the construction, so we plan to live in a tent on an adjoining lot. Living there we will be able to do all the work ourselves. We are not crazy enough to begin tent living in winter, however.

I labor over the plans, attempting to put down every idea in my head the proper way. The board and batten cottage will have six rooms: two bedrooms, a bathroom, kitchen, dining room, and parlor. We must show the world what we can do, so it will be small. We cannot afford to spend ten years building it.

The final plan is 834 square feet.

Lil and I busy ourselves with purchasing the property, filing plans to build, and locating suppliers. There are two building suppliers in Pacific Grove. At the first, T.A. Works All Builders Supply, I find the owner pompous and arrogant. He clearly doesn't want to deal with a female builder, so I take my business to Union Supply Company. I receive no further resistance. Apparently in Pacific Grove it is not unusual to be unusual. We will thrive here.

In mid-January, a letter arrives from San Jose. It already seems as if my life and family there are distant memories.

Dear Emily,

It is my duty to inform you that your brother, Waldo, passed away on January 4. He had been ill some time, but we had no idea the pain he was in. His appendix was troubling him, but he passed away during the surgery. The entire family, excepting yourself, was there. It is not necessary to trouble yourself with attending a funeral, as services have been held.

Frances Sibley Williams

"I had no idea," I murmur, handing the letter to Lil.

She reads it and hands it back, her hand lingering on my arm. "He was ill his entire life, Em. They could have let you know."

I really didn't know my stepbrother well, but passing at twenty-eight years old is a tragedy. I weep for his potential as Lil holds me. Maybe guilt clouds the tears, too, that I haven't tried harder to stay in touch or make nice with my stepmother, but I have no time for regrets.

When spring arrives, we move into our tent with relish. Now we are motivated to complete the project and live in a house built completely with our own four hands before winter. The tent covers seven square feet, with an extra flap of canvas called a fly that gives us a bit of a porch. Lil and I dig a v-shaped moat, about three inches deep, around the outside to let rainwater drain away from our new home. The interior boasts two camp beds along adjacent canvas walls. The heads of the bed come together in the corner. Lil thinks we will whisper together late at night, but I think we will probably be so exhausted we will fall asleep at dusk. We place our trunks of clothes along the other walls. Outside we have a folding table with matching folding chairs, four of them in case we have company. Near the table we clear our fire pit, stack wood ready to burn, and set up a wooden box full of camp utensils for cooking. For lighting at night, we have ordered a Ham's Cold Blast Tubular Lantern from Sears Roebuck.

Our venture officially begins when the Pacific Grove Review runs this article on July 4:

> *Young Ladies Doing Carpenter Work by Erecting a*
> *Cottage Which They Will Occupy: Miss Williams and Miss*
> *Palmer of San Jose are building with their own fair hands on*
> *Chestnut Street a cottage 20 x 25 feet in size. Miss Williams*

is studying with the idea of taking up architecture as a profession and is by her present efforts gaining practical knowledge of the construction of buildings. The young ladies are employing no carpenters to assist them. They laid the sills a few days since and the work of construction is now well under way. While building their cottage they are occupying a tent which they pitched on an adjoining lot.

The article will likely draw the attention of residents and visitors alike as the paper places it prominently next to a program announcement of the annual Chautauqua Assembly. Someone must really want to help us, to put us on the front page!

Sitting at the small table outside our tent, Lil ruefully surveys the cracked blisters. "Our own fair hands are no more," she observes, "and we employ no carpenters because none of them will work for women."

My spirits are running too high to be downcast. "But we have begun! You know we can do this, Lil. We *are* doing it! And our community notices. I don't need a license to design small houses such as our masterpiece," I wave my hand in the direction of the raw building rising beyond our canvas walls, "but if I plan to do anything grander, I will need it."

Her face lights up. "As always, my dear, I am so proud of you!"

We are beaming at each other when a woman calls to us from outside. We lift the tent flap and emerge. A well-dressed woman stands there with a covered dish.

"Good morning, ladies. I presume you are Miss Williams and Miss Palmer?" We nod. "I am Mrs. Lucy Pray. My daughter and I spend summers here in Pacific Grove. You are wonderful role models for her, and I'd like you to have this casserole."

"Why thank you and welcome to our humble home," I say, stepping forward to take the dish. It is still warm and smells of succulent beef and onion.

Lil and I do a bit of camp cooking, but we too often are so weary that we dine at a local restaurant. We welcome Mrs. Pray's home cooking. Other visitors begin to come by. It seems Pacific Grove is home to many summer residents from elsewhere in California. They enjoy the ocean view, the artist community, and the air of slightly scandalous progress. Lil and I definitely fill the bill for that latter category. Over the next few days we meet many well-wishers and receive many casseroles and invitations to dine. Our hearts are light and our souls complete.

Once we finish the exterior and are working on the inside of our house, we begin to dismantle the tent and officially move into the cottage. That very afternoon Edith arrives on the afternoon train and surprises us when she comes walking up the street. The sight of her nearly brings me to tears as I am already nostalgic for our days in the tent.

"I thought I'd come see how you were making out," she says.

"Welcome, Edith, welcome dear sister." I lead her past the

pile of wood scraps and through the sawdust layering the ground. Facing the street, two newly installed windows flank the chimney of round river stones I initially dreamed about. The windows jut out of the wall, looking a bit odd from the outside. Inside, though, the extra light gives the illusion of more space — exactly what I hoped they would do.

I lead Edith down the side of the house to the front door, calling to Lil. "Look who has come to visit us!"

Lil appears from the side yard, wiping hands on her carpenter's apron. "Edith, what a pleasant surprise. Are you alone?"

I frown. Clearly no one accompanies my sister. Did Lil think Fannie would come?

"Yes, I am. It's a pleasant day for a train ride, so I thought I'd surprise you." She grins and sweeps her hands wide. "This is an amazing accomplishment for both of you. It's a wonderful place."

"Thank you," I say, smiling. "Wait until Lil outfits it with her copper lamps."

"Copper? I had no idea you were a metal artist, Lil." Edith turns to my partner in surprise. I frown. Have I said nothing to Edith of Lil's talent?

"It's a hobby, really," Lil demurs.

"It's more than that," I respond. "She's developing quite a talent, and her work is remarkable."

Lil just smiles. I wish her confidence would grow as

quickly as her skill.

I take Edith inside for a detailed tour of our tiny abode, filling in the unfinished parts with glowing descriptions of our plans. Looking out one of the parlor windows facing the back of the house, Edith surveys the tall pines that dwarf our cottage.

"This is a beautiful setting, Emily," she tells me.

"The ocean and the pines are spectacular," I agree. "The cypress trees twisted by the wind are works of art themselves."

In the yard, Lil returns to painting the interior doors. They are laid flat across a couple of stands she built out of scrap wood. I watch the play of light on her face, intent on her task.

I must be smiling, for Edith notices. "I'm happy for the two of you. Fannie would make your lives miserable if you tried to do this in San Jose."

"You should stay for a vacation, Edith," I say impulsively.

She considers for a moment and smiles. "Why not? I can rent a summer cottage nearby."

Having both Lil and Edith nearby becomes even more important when I receive my official-looking letter from the state of California. With shaking hands, I tear it open. They refuse to grant me an architect's license because I am a woman. I rage, I cry, I protest, I howl, but it changes nothing. I can still build residences, even small apartment buildings. The state's refusal has not blocked me. Instead, it shapes my career.

Edith has been holding onto the money she inherited from Papa, and she now uses it to buy four vacant lots in Pacific

Grove. She commissions me to build cottages on all of them, planning to live in one and rent out the others. Meanwhile, she mixes with the elite of Pacific Grove, both summer and year-round residents. With Edith's help, we begin to make quite a stir in this beautiful seaside community.

In 1904, Julia Morgan returns to California and promptly receives an architect's license. I am astounded, but I follow her career because she inspires me. Denied entry to Beaux Arts not once but twice before she was finally accepted, she had to complete her course of study before she turned 30 in 1902. It seems the school prohibits older students. That amuses me. I am 36 years old and still learning every day. I read in *American Architect* magazine that Miss Morgan submitted an outstanding design for a palatial theatre to win her certificate in architecture. An American woman engaged Miss Morgan, for her first project, to build a grand salon at her residence in Fontainebleau.

The wonderfully grand statement pieces she designs will sear her name into the souls of Americans forever. My creations will not. Four years younger than me, Miss Morgan has a better education as well as better opportunities. If somehow I'd been able to go to Berkeley, maybe I'd be competing head to head with Morgan for commissions. As it stands, she shines while I toil.

Now that my career begins to grow, I need to share my success. Lil and Edith are extensions of myself, and our friends in Pacific Grove are potential clients. I want to inspire someone as Julia Morgan has inspired me, so I hire a carriage and set off for Santa Cruz early one morning in June of 1904.

Nina, Henry, and their children live on Union Street next door to Ellen VanValkenburgh and Marion, Henry's maiden sister. I visit briefly with the women, but I plan to spirit Eva away for a day in Pacific Grove. Nina pre-approves and helps me get away gracefully with my fifteen-year-old niece. Carl is walking and getting into her things, so Eva seems thrilled to escape her two-year-old brother.

She tells me about her school in Santa Cruz, where she thrives now that she is settled in. Santa Cruz, like Pacific Grove, teems with women's rights supporters who can be marvelous inspiration for young women. Eva speaks glowingly of her Grandmother Van, whom I know as Ellen. I am glad such a strong woman influences my niece's life.

I have kept for a surprise my invitation to tea at the Point Pinos Lighthouse. Mrs. Emily Fish took on the position of lighthouse keeper after her husband died. She lives there quite comfortably with a Chinese servant. Mrs. Fish has created lovely grounds surrounding the lighthouse, planting grass, hedges, and trees. I have attended functions at the lighthouse before and know her to be a wonderfully gracious hostess. I know Eva will enjoy the French poodles, Holstein cows, and thoroughbred horses Mrs. Fish keeps.

The hired carriage rolls down Lighthouse Road, and Eva's eyes grow wide. She has lived in Santa Cruz only two years, so the ocean still amazes her. The lighthouse's headland protects Santa Cruz, so possibly my niece has never encountered such thunderous crashing waves.

Mrs. Fish greets us as we disembark. A small group of women I recognize from various Pacific Grove functions stroll through the lighthouse grounds. Lil has come over from the house on Chestnut and greets us both with a discreet hug as the other women approach. I nod to them as our hostess welcomes Eva.

"Why you must be Emily's niece! What a young lady you are. Welcome, my dear, welcome." She ushers us into the main room of the lighthouse. Far above us, an incandescent vapor lamp propels its beacon out to sea where ship's captains can see it and know the rocky headland is here. Inside, all is cozy and comfortable.

The servant brings in a silver tray laden with tiny frosted cakes and petite scones. Mrs. Fish pours tea from a lovely porcelain teapot painted with English roses. I am proud of Eva's manners and her polite speech as she thanks our hostess.

"So are you planning an illustrious career like your aunt, Eva?" one of the women asks.

"I love seeing the houses she designs," Eva responds, "but I don't think it's for me."

"Eva has a talent for seeing light," Lil says. "She's more artistic than she knows. I think she just needs to find her medium." She looks at Eva with love and pride.

"I suppose you're right," Eva says graciously, helping herself to a pink cake.

"And will you marry someday?" a well-meaning busybody asks.

Eva looks at me, then at Lil, before turning her attention to the speaker. "If it is right for me, I will."

Mrs. Fish laughs and refills my teacup. "What a politician! Maybe women will win the right to vote and Eva here will someday be our president!"

The women titter at the absurdity, but Eva remains silent. I smile. Her Grandma Van's influence has taught her that all things are possible, even for women.

Lil says quietly, "Eva's grandmother is Ellen VanValkenburgh." Before she can say more, a few of the ladies gasp in recognition.

"Oh, she is such a *brave* soul. Imagine raising three children alone and still working for the vote." Nods show that all are in agreement.

"Ellen believes strongly in a woman's right to cast her own vote," Lil says to more affirmative nods.

Eva turns to me. "Don't you believe so, Aunt Emily?" Her eyes are innocent and trusting. My words are for her alone although everyone hears them.

"Eva, sweetheart, I have been working so hard to establish my career that I haven't given a single thought to voting. I would vote, of course, if given the option, but for me, women's rights mean being able to choose whatever career inspires you." Nods all around again. I wonder if I say the sky is purple they will all nod and agree.

Lil is quick to support me. "Women are oppressed in many areas, and it will take years of striving for individual progress before we see a marked change in attitudes."

"My husband oppresses me," one lady says, her eyes wide. "He insists I make him dinner every night and keep a clean house!"

She is clearly joking, but no one laughs. A few nervous titters escape, but it seems they support Ellen and me. Before I can say anything, Mrs. Fish speaks.

"We are so proud of you and others in our community that strive to make their way in an unconventional manner," she says. Others nod. "Pacific Grove is a hotbed of equality." She smiles and changes the subject. "Has anyone tried the lemon tea cakes? Are they too dry?"

I nibble a tea cake, but let Lil and the others assure our hostess of their perfection. I have never really considered myself a women's rights activist, and the mantle sits tight on my shoulders. It's never been about every woman in America being an architect, but about me. Now that feels selfish. Nonetheless, Eva's eyes are shining with pride, and that is good enough.

After a nice visit, some tea and treats, Lil and I walk Eva back to our house on Chestnut. She examines every inch of it with a great deal of excitement and comes to rest staring out one of the windows toward the street. She peers at the pushed-out construction carefully.

"This is really inspired, Aunt Emily. It changes how the light comes into the room. It's so bright in here, and the room seems much bigger."

Lil laughs. "You've just made her day, Eva. That's exactly what she hoped for when she envisioned these windows."

"I wish I could paint a picture of the view from this window," Eva says, "but my painting skills are just not good enough. The light never looks right."

"Don't fret, sweetheart. Everyone is born with a muse that speaks to them. You will find your way to communicate that passion, and it may well be something entirely new, something no man has yet thought of!" Her face lights up.

In late afternoon Eva and I embark by train back to Santa Cruz. The fog rolls in, and the mournful foghorn blends with the locomotive whistle.

"I had a wonderful day, Aunt Emily." Eva smiles widely, but her eyes and shoulders droop.

"I'm so glad, dear. You know I love to spoil you." I hug her close.

Henry meets us at the station and invites me back to the house for supper. I decline, eager to return to Pacific Grove. The return train is due soon. I insist to Henry that I can wait alone. Clearly eager to seek his own supper, he loads Eva into the carriage.

I board the train and let the clackety clack of the rails lull me into dreams. I have Edith's houses to build, and my mind reviews details as the train steams through the foggy dusk. At home, Lil and light and warmth wait. It doesn't matter if you are a world traveler or a day tripper, coming home should always be a good feeling. The homes I design will always be cozy and inviting, not cold and elaborate like some of the Victorian mansions I have visited. They will appeal to women, who will appeal to their men to buy them. By the time I arrive home, I am Architect of the Year in my own head.

Williams-Palmer house, Pacific Grove
Courtesy of Inge Horton, *Early Women Architects of the San Francisco Bay Area*

Chapter 19: Pacific Grove 1904-1906

Emily Williams

As the lovely town of Pacific Grove expands, I revel in the architectural styles that appear. San Francisco and even San Jose's wealthy elite feel compelled to build mansions in their cities of elegance and grandeur, but in Pacific Grove the residents are working people and the residences simpler. When Lil and I moved here, the town consisted mostly of later Victorian homes and some Gothic Revival. The lacy fripperies of the Queen Anne style appeared infrequently. The attractiveness of the town and the multitude of cultural events held each summer draw visitors who want vacation homes here. Now buildings go up in a Colonial Revival style, and some Mission. My forte is the Craftsman cottage, and it seems to be catching on as well.

I have completed four houses near my own for Edith. She occupies one and rents the others to summer visitors, just as she planned. Last year the widow Mrs. Lucy Pray, who brought us our first welcoming casserole, commissioned me to design a home for her and her daughter, also named Lucy. It seems Lucy the younger wishes to attend Berkeley, and her mother wishes her to live at home. I built a home in Berkeley where they now reside.

Lil and I join the local Chautauqua Literary and Scientific Circle. This group provides entertainment and culture for the whole community, with speakers, teachers, musicians, entertainers, preachers and specialists. President Roosevelt says that Chautauqua is "the most American thing in America." General participation in these events, however, diminishes. Lil says too many things are happening in town and people distracted with other things. The Circle decides to hold a large ceremony to recapture public attention.

The Feast of Lanterns, updated for Pacific Grove, comes from an old Chinese legend. In the story, a wealthy Mandarin's daughter falls in love with her father's humble accounting assistant. He, of course, is outraged and builds a high fence around his house to keep the lovers apart. He arranges for her to marry a powerful duke, but the accountant disguises himself and gains entrance to the palace. The lovers escape to a secluded island where they live blissfully for years. The duke eventually learns where they are and sends soldiers to capture the lovers and put them to death. In the original, the gods transform the lovers into doves, but here in Pacific Grove we use Monarch butterflies. These butterflies are like tiny stained-glass windows. They drift gently down shafts of sunlight to rest in the trees of Pacific Grove during their migration each October. It's inspired us to use this symbol of the town in the festival.

Through the society Lil and I meet Etta Belle Lloyd, a prominent businesswoman in town. The three of us bond instantly. One afternoon in late January, at tea in our little cottage, I realize that the three of us are alike on the outside. We all wear dark conservative clothing, long skirts of good fabric. With our hair upswept and our hats proper, we look like every woman our age in California. Inside each of us, however, burns a fire that cannot be seen but somehow recognizes itself in others.

We finish discussing plans for the festival, which will be held this summer, and conversation has ceased. We sip our tea in contentment.

"Em has just agreed to design a home in San Jose for my parents," Lil tells Etta.

"I hope you won't be too busy with that," Etta says with a twinkle in her eye. "I have an acquaintance who is interested in your skills."

I lean forward eagerly. "Truly? Here in Pacific Grove?"

Etta nods. "A summer resident. During the winter she lives in New York, or on her farm in Pennsylvania. She is still locating property, but I can introduce you."

I nod. "At the next meeting?" She agrees that a suitable introduction can be arranged in that time.

The following month, Etta introduces me to Anna Lukens and her companion Miss Mary Conrad. Mary's arm easily rests around Anna's waist, and Anna leans into the embrace. Lil and I have stood thus, and the recognition resonates. I am impressed that Anna is a physician with a stable practice in New York. She seems impressed that I am an architect with five homes completed and another commission in the works. We verbally dance around each other for the socially acceptable time before we propose business. Etta and Mary content themselves in soft conversation so as not to interrupt.

"I am hunting a piece of property for a larger winter residence," Anna tells me, "and I would like to discuss another design once I find the right location."

"Our fair town offers no shortage of beautiful sites, Dr. Lukens. Would you like me to suggest some?" I have not yet finished the design for the Palmer house in San Jose, so I hope the timing for this one does not interfere.

That spring, though, the world is shaken to its core. What the Great Earthquake doesn't level, the subsequent fire destroys. A great deal of the San Francisco I love crumbles to dust, and I mourn the little house in the Mission where Lil and I lived such a short time. In Monterey, the quake destroys the Hotel Del Monte. A collapsing chimney there kills a bridal couple from

Arizona in their bed. The wharf at Moss Landing is lost, as well as the courthouse and twelve other buildings in Santa Cruz. Monstrous waves near Santa Cruz beach carry away three buildings.

In Pacific Grove our unshakable faith in the solid construction of our homes suffers. So many beautiful buildings have proved unable to withstand the violent movement of the earth, and it breaks my heart to lose such wonderful architectural examples. What remains becomes even more of a treasure. I look at my design for Lil's parents' house and hunt for ways to brace its beams.

Human nature remains essentially optimistic, and later in April Dr. Lukens pays the exorbitant sum of $7,000 for a property on Ocean View Boulevard between Forest and Fountain Avenues. She hires me as supervising architect. I find it a relief to direct others in building my vision rather than wielding the hammer myself. This house is the biggest one I've designed to date, and beyond me to construct. As it nears completion, I select the furnishings together with Anna's neighbors, T.J. and Flora Richardson. The Richardsons are artists in their own right, and I enjoy working with them.

That summer Lil and I return to San Jose to build a home for her parents. Living with them as I did after Papa died, I am overcome with guilt that I have not stayed in touch with my stepmother. Edith moved to Pacific Grove with me, and Papa and Waldo are gone. At twenty-three, Paul studies banking in school. He must be her entire world. I have written to Paul as I write to Eva, but he says very little about his mother.

The Palmer home overflows with warmth and love. Lil's mother has news for her. "Your Uncle James passed away and has left you some money."

Lil nods. She apparently knew of his passing but not of the money. "Uncle James?" I ask.

"Uncle James Whistler." She smiles wryly. "Yes, the painter. My name for his painting *Whistler's Mother* used to drive him crazy. I called it *Lil's Aunt Anna*."

I laugh, and the Palmers join in even though they must have heard this many times before. Lil puts the money in the bank for our future together, and once again I am warmed by her generosity and her faith in me.

I design a home for her parents on South Priest Street, and I design one for Reverend Foote, minister at Trinity Church, too. Mrs. Gertrude Austin, widow of former San Jose Mayor Paul Austin, commissions a house in San Francisco, but first I need to get back to Anna Lukens' project in Pacific Grove.

I am so busy, I am afraid Lil may feel neglected. She has been so supportive of my career. I never would have done this well without her encouragement. To fill her days here in San Jose, she sets up a metalworking studio in the basement of the home on South Priest and creates wonderful copper lighting fixtures. What time constraints limit our conversation, our souls make up for. Words are unnecessary between us. This is proven again when my darling Lil writes an article about me for the *San Jose Mercury and Herald* in mid November.

The headline reads, "Women as Architects, With a Special Application to Miss Emily Williams, San Jose's Successful Woman Architect." It is quite lengthy. In part, it reads:

> *There was a time when men planned and built houses, and when the family moved in, lo, there wasn't a closet larger than two by four where woman might store her possessions. And even those little two by fours were scarce. Men learned the closet lesson some time ago. The humblest carpenter now understands that houses must have generous closets. But a woman architect with less training than a man will prove his superior in the nice adjustment of inside arrangements. She will not only plan a place for the bookcase, but she will plan the place for it that will best balance the room. She will not only plan a place for the dresser, but she will plan a place where there is a good light on the dresser.*

At a lavish Sunday dinner with Mr. and Mrs. Palmer, I toast Lil's article with a glass of wine. She believes the dinner to be a send off as we head back to Pacific Grove, but her mother and I have planned this as a tribute to Lil. She smiles, surprised. Her byline was not on the piece, but who else could have written it?

"How did you know?" she asks, her eyes shining.

"How could I not?" I respond, clasping her hand in mine.

She leans toward me, squeezing my hand.

We return to Pacific Grove expecting to put the finishing touches on Sequoia Lodge for Dr. Lukens. While we were gone, the Richardsons have nearly finished furnishing it. Dr. Lukens has sent ahead china to be set on shelves in the closet, and I hasten to put flowers in vases. My favorite room is the parlor with its broad fireplace and handsome wood mantle. Deep built-in seats take advantage of the spectacular view through the windows that frame the rocky shoreline. The Dutch architecture is new for me, but the clean lines of the house are stunning in their simplicity.

Dr. Lukens and Miss Conrad are so enamored of Sequoia Lodge that they plan to spend every winter in Pacific Grove. This thrills Etta, as Anna's weekly study groups for the Chautauqua Literary and Scientific Circle remain very popular. I am excited that my design works so well for them, and they tell everyone they know who built it.

As 1906 draws to a close, I find the shock and despair that hit me after the Great Earthquake heals a bit. I'm sure it helps that no one I know was injured, killed, or left homeless. Also, my success as an architect continues to grow. With Lil at my side, 1907 will be even better.

Chapter 20: Pacific Grove 1907
Emily Williams

The year begins with a rush. Mr. W. S. Richards, president of Security State Bank in San Jose, desires a two story vacation house in Pacific Grove. He knew my father and seems to be taking an interest in Paul, so I am pleased to do his design. He buys property at 119 Grand Avenue, and I envision a shingled home with a large ground-floor bay window and a gabled bedroom window above the entry. Mr. Richards engages Chivers Brothers to build the home. Although I have learned to be a capable carpenter, I find that I rather enjoy supervising the construction of my designs rather than building them myself. Wielding pen and ink fulfills me more than the blisters and racket of hammering nails.

The *Pacific Grove Review* describes the house on Grand Avenue as a "handsome, $4,000 home." I wink at Lil, but she disavows any credit for the small item. I'm pretty sure she's written it and I'm confused why she doesn't want to take credit. Maybe it's too small an item for her journalistic soul to take pride in. Even so, I trust Lil not to keep secrets from me, and I begin to wonder who else might want to write such items.

Before I have quite finished the Richards' vacation home, I get a letter from Mrs. Jesse Jordan. Her husband, David Starr Jordan, is still president of Stanford. She would like a vacation cottage in Carmel and will allow no one but me to design it.

Lil hesitates when I share Mrs. Jordan's letter. "Em, it's wonderful that you are becoming so successful, but I think you need to build something more for us. We could use some income property. Your bungalows do very well for Edith."

"A house nearby? So it's easy to oversee?"

"We need steady income. Can you build a couple more houses like ours?"

So I design two houses similar to ours to be built on Chestnut and Alder, respectively. In March, The *Pacific Grove Review* reports, *Among other smaller buildings going up in that locality is a four room bungalow on Chestnut which Miss Williams and Miss Palmer are building.*

I tease Lil about not using a byline. She reacts with irritation. "I am a journalist by profession, Em. Why would I not take credit, even for a small item?"

"You didn't sign the piece in the San Jose paper, Lil. And if you aren't writing them, who is?"

"I suspect it's Etta," Lil replies. "She's well known enough that they will print her pieces, and they're too short for a professional journalist to write."

"Well, I certainly didn't mean to insult your professional pride," I snark at her.

She walks away. I am left to choose between anger and worry over something she might be hiding.

Another article appears in May, this one in the *Monterey Daily Cypress*. It notes:

> *Mrs. David Starr Jordan came over from Carmel-by-the-Sea yesterday and registered at the Hotel Del Mar. She will return to Carmel this afternoon. Mrs. Jordan's handsome home in the Carmel bay town, which has been in the process of erection under the supervising architect Miss Emily Williams during the past two months, is nearly ready for occupancy.*

Lil just shakes her head when I lift an inquiring eyebrow. I shall have to thank Etta when next I see her and ascertain by her response if she is indeed the writer. These items appear frequently in the local newspapers, often just a line or two. It doesn't truly matter who pens these items since the wonderful advertising costs me nothing, but it piques my curiosity.

Before I can talk with Etta, I receive a letter from Elizabeth Austin, living with her mother in the San Francisco house I designed for them. She pens that she wants to be an architect. Her youthful passion reminds me of Eva. How wonderful it would be to mentor my niece in an artistic career! After answering Elizabeth's letter, I sit down to write one to Eva, telling her all about my current projects.

So revitalized, I attend a meeting of the Woman's Civic Club. Lil, of course, accompanies me. As expected, Etta also comes. This group of women meets to socialize but also to find ways to beautify Pacific Grove. Over the last few years they have removed a lot of garbage on empty lots and accomplished some street improvements. I sit next to Etta, but before I can ask her about the tiny articles, she rises to speak.

"I have an idea for a convenient and artistic lookout at Lover's Point, a place where one can sit out of the weather and admire the view. I believe our esteemed Miss Emily Williams could come up with a suitable design."

A buzz of excited approving conversation erupts before I, too, stand to speak. "I would be happy to donate the design free of charge as a service to this fine organization." I sit down. Etta beams.

They immediately call for the vote and approve the commission. I hope to gain some paid commissions from the donation of this design. As I smile and nod to acknowledge their well wishes, I picture the rocky promontory swept by wind and salt spray. The Lookout will need to be solid, so stone, and have access to the view, so glass. Encasing the whole structure in natural redwood will make it warmer, blending it into the natural surroundings.

Lil and I walk out to the point to survey the site in person. Across from the Japanese Tea House and a row of bath houses for summer tourists, a windmill spins in the breeze. As I share my ideas with Lil, tendrils of hair escape firmly tied hats and whip around our laughing faces.

"My ears are too frozen to hear you!" Lil complains good-naturedly.

I cup my hand over her ear and try to blow warm air over it, but my laughter makes this impossible. I grip her icy hands in my slightly warmer ones. We head for the warmth of the tea house, hoping to thaw our chilled fingers against a warm cup. Here we can discuss ideas for Lookout as well as the two houses I am working on for us.

"We should each put one of the new homes on Chestnut in our name," Lil says.

I frown. "Whatever for?"

"For our future, Em. You own the cottage we live in. I'd like something of my own."

"So you are free to leave?" My voice trembles between incredulous and nervous.

"Of course not, silly. You know I care not what society thinks, but it makes better financial sense to split our assets between us."

"It makes sense," I agree reluctantly. "After all, if we were married we could jointly own the property. As housemates, we cannot."

"I love you no less," she promises, caressing me with her eyes.

I laugh and sip my tea, unsure how to answer with words.

Over the next couple of days I step lightly around Lil, afraid of giving offense yet not sure why I believe I might. Several times I catch odd looks on her face that seem to indicate she feels as I do. We are strangely unable to discuss this with each other, maybe because I am not quite sure what 'this' is.

During this time I receive a letter with an impressive logo on the envelope, the entwined letters so embellished I cannot make out the initials. It does appear to be an architectural firm, however, in San Francisco. The letter makes me laugh.

Dear Miss Williams,

I regret that I was unable to offer you a position with the firm when last you inquired. Although it has been over five years since you queried us, I am pleased to say that a position has become available as a junior draftsman. We would be honored if you considered employment with us.

Sincerely,

Charles Field

So now that I finally have some successes, Mr. Field can find a position for me? The notion is ludicrous. I hand the letter to Lil, still smiling. The pompous man's note has lightened my mood.

Lil's smile, however, is tight. "Isn't this the man you almost married?"

"Married?" I frown. "Hardly. Fannie had high hopes for a marriage with any unmarried man at church, Lil." I shrug. "This one wasn't any nearer the altar than any other."

"But you interviewed with him." Her tone perplexes me. Anger? Jealousy? She should know better.

"Since when is interviewing a courtship ritual? The interview was a strange coincidence, that's all. Now his firm wants a woman to show how progressive they are. Junior draftsman? Ha! I have designed and built homes and he wants me to go backwards!"

Lil folds the letter carefully. "It might be good for your career to work for such a prestigious firm."

"I don't want to draw up someone else's visions. I want to design what's in *my* head. Come on, Lil, you know this. What's wrong?"

"Wrong?" She looks at me with a smile, but her eyes are clearly pained. What isn't she telling me?

Frustration twists my lips as I snap, "Something's wrong, and it's not Mr. Field. What are you keeping from me?"

"It's all about you as usual?"

"What?" I'm stunned. "What are you talking about?"

"I'm hardly talking. Talking requires listening, and that's something you don't do well."

"Oh no? I haven't had much to listen to!" Fury thrums through my body. A rational thought cools my temper, though. I cannot even put into words what we are fighting about. We subside into individual pools of simmering emotion.

By the end of 1907 two bungalows begin to arise on Chestnut, one owned by Miss Lillian Palmer, and one owned by Miss Emily Williams. Designed almost exactly the same as the others I have done for Edith and for our first home, the building comes along well. With Lil at my side to share sawdust in our hair and blisters on our hands, the physical labor of carpentry, plumbing, and masonry once more becomes an adventure. Part of me dreads completion because deep down inside I worry that Lillian Palmer will want to live in the house she owns while I live alone in mine.

My career shoots forward in 1907, and the first months of 1908 find us exhausted, me from overwork and over worry, and Lil from dealing with my crankiness and her secret angst. Property in Pacific Grove gets more expensive. I like to believe it might be partly due to the increasing number of my designs that have been built here. But Lil and I cannot come up with the last payment for our new properties on Chestnut, and I have no commissions at the moment.

"We'll have to ask Etta for a loan," Lil says with a deep sigh.

"Why Etta?" I am resistant, since asking for a loan makes it appear my business is not successful.

"Look, Em. Etta is a friend. She will keep it private that we have asked for the loan. You know she can afford it. She runs an insurance agency and manages her late father's commercial property. She has income and good business sense."

"And she's a friend," I repeat, reluctantly nodding.

Etta loans us $300 without question. When I pick up the bank draft from her office, I take the opportunity to ask her a question that has been nagging me. "Etta, have you been writing those marvelous bits for the local papers about me?"

"Me?" She looks startled. "Honey, I value any opportunity to put my name into the business community. No, I didn't write them."

"Thank you for the loan, dear friend." I take my leave, convinced that Lil has written the articles and deliberately hides the fact from me. Something needs to be done to clear the air between us, but my feeble head has no idea what.

One evening as dusk is settling over the town, I walk home from a meeting of the Woman's Civic Club deep in thought. The fog lingers offshore like a mountain of cotton painted orange and purple by the setting sun. The spectacular display distracts me for a moment, then the sun dips lower and the light fades to gray. I continue walking.

Lil declined to join me tonight at the meeting. She didn't say why, although she did say she isn't ill. Our cottages are finished. Soon we must move in, together or separately. Whatever weighs on her must soon explode. I eagerly anticipate this event so we can move past it and on with our lives.

The house is dark. By now, Lil usually lights the kerosene lamp in the front window to welcome me home with its soft glow. No smoke billows from the chimney. Has she let the fire go out?

"Hello, Lil?" I call as I come in the door. No sound comes from the kitchen, and no smells of a scrumptious dinner greet me as they usually do when Lil arrives home before me.

I find her sitting in the front room in the gathering dark, naught but a darker shadow against the dusk-grayed walls and furniture. She faces the window, showing no sign that she knows I am there.

"Lil?" I ask softly. I cross to her, the swishing of my skirts suddenly loud. I stand beside her chair and place my left hand on her left shoulder, sliding my right hand behind her to squeeze her right shoulder. Laying my cheek on her head, I whisper, "What is it, my dear? Please let me help you."

She rouses then and a lightning-quick smile flashes. "Sorry, Em, I was lost in a bit of a daydream. My, it's gotten quite dark. Let me light a few lamps, tend the fire..."

She begins to get up, but I hold her in the chair. "Lil, talk to me." I look her straight in the eyes. Beneath my hands, her shoulders slump.

"Oh, Em, I feel so foolish."

I wait, rubbing her shoulder in a gentle circular pattern. In the half-dark it is easier to bare your soul. Somehow even lamplight inhibits a person from divulging the contents of their heart. With a deep sigh, Lil begins to talk.

"It's not that I'm unhappy with you, my dear Em. Please

don't think that! I just feel so useless. I know you value my assistance with your building projects, but lately it's not been enough. I was so happy last summer with the studio at home in San Jose. Could it be time for me to learn more about metalworking?" Her tone is one of discovery, of wonder.

"Lil, copper has always held your heart. If you want to go to school, of course you should. Where would you study?" I hold my breath. Our conversations have been so fragile lately, I hate to shatter this one.

She holds up a much-folded paper, a brochure, vaunting the wonders of Vienna. I sink to my knees beside her chair. "Vienna?" I say weakly.

"Europe would be amazing, Em," she says. I can hear the lilt in her voice and know her eyes are alight with passion. "Vienna has wonderful schools for metal crafting and electrical design. It would be heaven to study in a place so rich with history! Think of the architecture in Rome and the Far East— maybe we could even see some pagodas in Japan!"

Relief washes over me, draining every ounce of energy and leaving my hands shaking. "We?" I confirm weakly.

"Of course, you silly goose! Why would I want to embark on such an adventure alone?" She sweeps to her feet and lights the lamp to show me the brochure.

She has other brochures, too, from points all across Europe. How long has she been thinking about this? "Lil, why haven't you said anything?"

"Your business flourished last year. How could I pull you away when you were finally seeing success? I was content to wait."

"For a time you were," I tease. "You've been pretty sad for awhile now."

"I was afraid to say I wanted this trip so badly," she admits, her hands clasping mine like lifelines.

"You have done so much for me that I would love to give you this. Let's take the year off and discover Europe together. We could even go to Paris!"

We pore over the brochures, giddy with relief that secrets have been shared. I ignore a pang of worry about leaving just as my business is thriving. We have enough put away to make this trip happen, and Lil's parents will lend us more if we need it. This will be good for her, so we will do it.

Chapter 21: Inverness 1908
Eva VanValkenburgh

By the time my family leaves Santa Cruz in 1905, I have acquired a brother, a friend, and an appreciation of the seashore. My father hates the town of his birth and eagerly accepts an offer to work for one of the Howard-Shafter dairies in Inverness. Coming from Santa Cruz in a horse-drawn buggy laden with family and worldly goods, we cross the tree-covered Inverness Ridge and leave the forest behind. The grassland stretches before dotted with cattle and scattered ranches, and the air holds the tang of the sea which surrounds the point on three sides. The area reminds me both of Cholame and Santa Cruz, and I instantly feel at home. We settle in the tiny town of Inverness, near Tomales Bay, where my father builds us a house and begins work as a superintendent of farms, responsible for collecting rent from the tenant farmers.

The trio of gnarled almond trees in back of the house remind me of Grandma Van's tree. I love the almond trees in all seasons, but spring is my favorite. The trees are covered in new leaves and tight buds that will open to masses of white blossoms that later fall like a warm snowstorm. The soft shirring of the breeze plays with the leaves and my hair. It is the perfect place to read and to dream. Today, as usual, I am flat on my stomach on the ground, my face in magazine, *The Dial*, sent by Aunt Emily from Pacific Grove. It has enough literary bits to keep Mama happy and enough stories to entertain me. The ground under my stomach is lumpy, and I shift position.

"Eva! Eva! A letter for you!"

If I didn't know better, I would think a herd of horses gallops down the back steps of the house, but no, it's just my brother, Carl. I hunch my shoulders and drop my head into the pages of my magazine, closing my eyes for good measure.

"Eva!" he bellows, leaning over to push me on the shoulder.

Whatever restraint was born into me as a lady of quality goes completely missing when I must deal with my six-year-old sibling. "What?" I snap at him.

"The postman brought a letter for you." He bends in half as he speaks, his face inches from mine. His too-big overalls, already worn thin at the knee, show layers of dirt. His hair is the color of wet straw, and his hat is missing.

"I'm coming," I tell him. Slipping *The Dial* into a pocket, I stand up and brush the apron that tries so valiantly to keep my dress clean.

Carl races back to the house, shouting for Mama and slamming the door behind him. The boy never learned to walk. He went straight from crawling to running. I follow at a more sedate pace.

Although I am not unhappy, I feel a certain disquiet that prevents true happiness. Mama blames the novels I love. She says they give me dreams of unattainable adventure and romance, and I should put them away and focus on things a grown up young lady needs to know. Father dreams more himself, and while he doesn't encourage me, he doesn't scold either. Entranced by the visions of the future held by Aunt Emily and Grandma Van, I still don't see myself spending my life alone. And that's where the dreams of romance come in.

I enter the house through the back door, finding Mama in the kitchen. Her asthma makes her breath raspy and her eyes puffy with spring allergies. "I've sent Carl to get his books. Open your letter, then we will start the afternoon lessons," she tells me as she wipes the kitchen table.

"Yes, Mama." She has resumed schooling me at home and started Carl on his letters. So far it seems an impossible task to teach the boy anything and at nineteen I have mastered what she can teach me. I spend my lesson time reading and discuss what I've read with Mama later.

I take my letter and examine the address. Pacific Grove. That means Aunt Emily! I hurry into the parlor to savor the letter alone. I slit the envelope. A newspaper clipping falls out, and I retrieve it as I read the letter.

My darling Eva,

I hope this letter finds you and your family well. Lil and I have been busy building wonderful homes in San Jose, Santa Cruz, and Pacific Grove, where we've just finished a tiny Lookout shelter for the Women's Civic Club. I have enclosed an article cut from the San Jose Mercury and Herald. It is about me, written by my dear Lil! How I delight at her description of our work!

I scan the article. It is an editorial titled "Women as Architects." Aunt Emily has circled a passage that reads: *Miss Williams's houses have won her an enviable reputation...They are not only beautiful and artistic, but convenient, livable and planned to save steps and with places to put things.* I smile and return to my letter.

I am writing to tell you that we are coming to Inverness to see you. Lil and I will arrive on the train next Tuesday. We are looking forward to spending a few days with your family before returning to San Francisco and boarding ship for a year abroad. I will share the itinerary with you when we arrive. Such wonderful sights we will see!

Looking forward to our visit,

Emily Williams

The idea of a visit from Aunt Emily and Aunt Lil thrills

me and promises to enliven days of redundant activity. Inverness consists mostly of summer homes for those who live in San Francisco or Oakland. The nearby town of Point Reyes includes a schoolhouse, a train station, and little else of interest to me. Two years ago the Great Earthquake created such excitement that local people still exclaim over how it knocked the schoolhouse completely off its foundation, tipped a locomotive at the station over on its side, and shifted the land so straight fences curved across pastures. It was a terribly scary time, but over and gone, and the days stretch on like the grass on the peninsula or the ocean to the horizon.

I know my unease means I am nearing the time in my life when I must make a decision about my future. Children can dream, but women must act. Mama waits for me to tell her which of the local ranchers' sons I fancy. My mind knows that is a practical option, but my heart is not ready to wither from practicality. I still want a knight to sweep me off my feet and carry me away. In the distant future, I see myself raising a family and working alongside a husband I love to create a home. I have not yet met that man.

Mama, too, receives a letter from Aunt Emily and the next few days bustle with preparations for the visit. I do laundry until my hands wrinkle and seem permanently damp. I trim the garden, and Mama fills the pantry with delectable food. Carl runs from Mama to me and back, shrieking. I don't know if he makes noise because he is excited, or because he is Carl.

On Tuesday, the four of us stand at the Point Reyes train station and listen for the far-off whistle of an approaching train. Actually, three of us stand. Carl runs the length of the platform and back, his feet thundering on the wooden planks. Mama and I have nearly identical hats and light traveling coats. It is spring, so the sun warms through a chilly breeze.

The train arrives with screeching brakes, puffs of steam, and a shrill whistle. It crouches on the tracks, hissing and growling like a caged animal. Searching the passengers, I spot Aunt Emily and wave madly until she waves back and walks toward us, followed by Aunt Lil.

Aunt Emily is slightly built like Mama, which means my solid frame is most likely from my father's side of the family. My aunt's conservative dark hat and coat most likely hide a dress of vibrant color or pattern that will make Mama's head hurt. Aunt Lil, too, is conservative only on the outside. She takes my aunt's arm and they arrive together in front of us.

Aunt Emily's green eyes sparkle as she reaches to hug me. "Eva, it seems like forever since I've seen you!"

Mama embraces her sister and nods to Lil. "Welcome, Emily, Lil. I hope your trip up from the city was uneventful."

Lil nods. "It was fine, Nina, thank you."

Aunt Emily grins with delight and produces two Hershey bars from her bag. "Look! They make them with almonds now!" She hands one to Carl and one to me.

I slip the bar into my pocket to savor on the way home.

My father greets the two women, then collects their luggage while Carl runs around and between us all. I am relegated to the role of child, forced to sit in the wagon with Carl while the four adults sit on the benches behind the horses. It is not far to our house, but I am unable to hear any of the adults' conversation, and unable to entice Carl to silence until I unwrap his chocolate bar. I crunch my nut-filled chocolate and watch my brother smear his all over his face and hands.

Once home, the travelers collapse in weary relief while Mama sets out dinner, including vermicelli soup and a stew of radishes, pickles, pork, and parsnip. I know there is almond cake for dessert, so I save room and listen to our visitors talk with my parents.

"We leave from San Francisco later this month," my aunt says of the trip, "heading for the Far East and Europe, anywhere we can study art and relax." She smiles and puts her hand lightly on Lil's arm.

"When will you come home?" Mama asks.

"We plan to be gone a year," Lil says.

"A year?" In my dismay, the words slip out. They don't visit often, but knowing I absolutely won't see my favorite aunt for a year stuns me.

Aunt Emily hugs me. "I will write, my darling. Time will pass quickly, I promise."

Maybe if you are traveling around Europe. At my house, time crawls like a garden snail. I hug her back and keep my thoughts to myself.

After dinner, Mama serves coffee in the parlor, banishing Carl, and Father leaves the women alone. Aunt Emily turns the topic of conversation to me.

"Eva is nineteen now, Nina. Have you thought about her college?"

Mama frowns. "Eva does not need to attend college."

"I really wouldn't know what to do at one," I put in quickly. It's true. I have no desire to be an architect like my aunt, or a doctor like great-aunt L'Amie was. I suppose I could teach. My dreams have always been about loving a man and raising his children. Aunt Emily and Aunt Lil don't understand that, however. Grandma Van does, I think. I know that should a career suggest itself I would be able to pursue it with their support, but the world needs mothers as well as architects and activists and teachers. I would love to be a mother like Mama, married to a man who mirrors my soul.

"You've always been artistic," Lil suggests.

I frown at the same time Mama does. "I guess so," I say, not at all sure, "but my paintings never turn out well and I haven't the patience to sketch details."

Aunt Lil and Aunt Emily share a smile. My aunt says, "Maybe you will enjoy the present we brought, then." She pauses, her eyes sparkling. "Since we will be abroad in August, it is an early birthday present."

"Oh, how wonderful!" I exclaim, ignoring Mama's glare.

There's no putting it off then; they must retrieve the present from their traveling case. Laughing, Aunt Emily places it on my lap. I turn it every which way, overcome. It's a Kodak camera. The leather case opens to reveal a Brownie Box. I've seen pictures of them in magazines.

"That's to record impressions that move your soul," Aunt Emily tells me. "You can take portraits of your brother and your parents if you want, but photography is becoming an art form. Be creative and experiment! And be ready to show me every one of your photographs when we return!"

"Oh, Aunt Emily, thank you! Thank you, Aunt Lil! This will be an amazing summer!" I jump up and rush to kiss each of them on the cheek.

"Make sure you take care of it, Eva," my mother says. She knows nothing about art.

"Women photographers are gaining a name for themselves, too," Lil says. "A few years ago, American women put on an exhibition of photographs in Europe. I hope we can still see some of it when we get there."

"Women are making great strides everywhere," Aunt Emily says.

"When can we vote? Grandma Van says I'm old enough now," I tease my aunt, knowing she cares more for career than the vote. I'm sure she'd be excited about voting if an election was held that helped women pursue their desired career.

"There is more to life than college and voting," my mother

says. "Lots of women have full lives with husbands and children."

Lil and Aunt Emily stare at her for a moment. Mama seems to be defending herself, which embarrasses me, even though she is right. Then she continues, and humiliates me, too.

"Eva might marry a dairy rancher. A lot of eligible young men live around here, and she knows her way around a ranch."

The idea dashes romantic dreams from my head like a winter storm off the Pacific whips across the grass. I'm not a child any more, but I do still dream of a knight in shining armor riding up to take me away. I'm practical enough to realize he won't be wearing armor or serving a king, but surely he'll have more romance in his soul than a dairy rancher. I clasp my hands in my lap to prevent a shudder.

"Nina," my aunt begins.

"Em, she's Nina's daughter," Lil says softly.

"She's my niece," Aunt Emily declares. "I don't suggest she attend rallies or become a suffragist, I just offer her the choice. It's a new century, and she should be able to choose."

My mother retreats into the guise of perfect hostess. "That's very true, Emily. Would you like another cup of coffee? More almond cake?"

I excuse myself and leave the room, moving through the back door and down the steps. Dusk softens the line between shadow and sunlight, and the almond trees blur together. I lean on a sturdy trunk, the rough bark against my back. Behind me, the screen door squeaks and a light tread descends the steps. Aunt Emily puts her arm around me.

"The world is open to you," she says. She's told me this before, so I wait. "You know my sister Edith, then your mother, then my twin brother Ed and I were all born in different mining towns as my father moved around selling drinking water to the miners." She pauses, but I say nothing. I know her history, but I sense there is more she wants to say tonight.

"My mother died when Ed and I were three years old. Fannie was a good enough stepmother. It wasn't until I was older that she couldn't mother me any more. She was completely unable to envision the life I wanted to live, so I left. Eva, you have a lot of people who love you and will support whatever you decide to do. Promise me that you will keep your mind open to all possibilities."

All possibilities includes growing old alone, marrying a rancher, going to college, pushing for women's rights as well as being swept into the arms of a handsome knight. "I promise, Aunt Emily."

Eva VanValkenburgh, reading under the almond trees

Chapter 22: Paris 1908

Emily Williams

We depart from San Francisco in May 1908 with plans to see the Far East and Europe and return in January 1909. Fog, of course, chills the air. Lil and I laugh at the weather because our exuberance makes everything amusing. The ship steams out past Alcatraz Island, which used to be a Civil War fort protecting our fair city without ever firing a gun. The same buildings have taken on a more sinister air now that they will soon house military prisoners. The fog wisps past the Citadel, perched high atop the rock. I shudder and turn away, not willing to think of war and prisoners at the beginning of my grand adventure.

The San Francisco Bay is choppy, but the Pacific Ocean itself is worse. We have chosen to travel with the Pacific Mail Steamship Company. Their ships may not be as fast as those of Cunard or White Star, but they are the largest and steadiest ships that travel from San Francisco to the East. Our ship, the *Siberia*, is one of the line's finest. Our staterooms are quite comfortable. They are paneled in white, with cherry trim, with a white enameled iron bedstead trimmed in brass. The sofa converts to another bed, and the folding lavatory stand boasts porcelain and cut-glass fittings. The room even has an electric light and fan.

A Filipino band plays as we steam away from California, as if to encourage us to look forward to adventure, not behind to miss our homes. Lil and I play golf on deck and eat our fair share of wonderful food, made even more luscious by the brisk sea air. This morning I eat strawberries and oatmeal for breakfast, with maple syrup. Lil has grilled ham and fried eggs. We both consume toast with marmalade and our usual tea. I may gain more than a few pounds on this trip!

We first stop in the Hawaiian islands. We have a day to sight-see in Honolulu, which is a vision of sun and flowers, before we once again are steaming east.

Ten days out, we enter Yokohama harbor. Snow-topped Mt. Fujiyama towers above us in stark contrast to Honolulu's sun and sand. In Japan, I study the medieval shrines and temples. The Japanese culture seems free of the industrialism that has ruined modern design in Europe. On the surface, Japanese art is full of birds, flowers, landscapes, and seasons. The underlying design strategy appeals to me, however. Everything balances, with good geometry and modularity. Many pieces resonate within me, but Lil refuses to let me hire a ship to haul furniture home.

When we are on land, Lil and I are euphoric but exhausted as we try to see it all. Aboard ship I write to those at home, to Eva about the color and light, to Paul with reassurances about money, to Etta about the sightseeing, and to Bernard Maybeck about the architecture.

We continue on through China, leaving our Pacific Mail Steamship in Shanghai. When we agree that we have exhausted ourselves in Asia, we board a Blue Funnel Line ship for London. The trip takes five weeks and we relax, reading, writing letters, walking along the promenade deck, eating delicious food, and napping right in the middle of the day.

Meandering through Europe with Vienna as our goal is delightful. My favorite non-architectural time is spent in Palestrina, Italy. Lil comes alive when she sees the magnificent local copper urns. The craftsmen stare while she pores over them as they work. Once they realize she has knowledge and skill, though, they are thrilled to show off how they roll the big sheets of copper in two directions resulting in a large flat urn that looks like an hourglass. With handles, the village women balance the urns on their heads to carry water. Overheated in the Italian sun, we stop for refreshment at a cave-like wine cellar.

"Those urns were amazing!" Lil says, as if we haven't been discussing the urns since we left the shop.

"Do you want me to leave you here?" I tease. "It seems we don't need to go to Vienna?"

She looks shocked, then realizes I am teasing. We double over laughing, gasping for breath. Onlookers look away as we giggle uncontrollably like schoolgirls.

Once in Vienna, though, Lil's entire demeanor changes. Before this trip, she was my helpmate, assisting me to build houses of my design. Now she comes into her own. She studies the hammered metal crafting, and I can see her mind awhirl, designing lamps with this sort of shade. She learns about electrical design, power-efficient lighting, and placement of lighting to reduce eyestrain.

During this time I am content to dream in cathedrals and read about the Arts and Crafts movement in Europe, where designs are returning to simple, almost medieval forms with romantic folk art decoration. I am consumed by the anti-industrialist statement this type of design makes. I doubt if an art movement can advocate economic and social reform, yet when I look at a beautiful Arts and Crafts piece, it speaks to me in that vein.

As Lil's skill with metal and lighting grows, so does her confidence. She no longer hangs back in my shadow. It is her turn to shine. Making the most of every minute in Vienna, she attracts quite a following and meets some fellow artists she no doubt will continue to correspond with once we return to California. I nod and beam my pride of her to these new colleagues as she has done over and over again for me. I fully realize I am biding my time, content with Lil's happiness, until we reach Paris.

One of our favorite places in Vienna is the Prater. It used to be imperial hunting grounds, and hunters still are active in a good part of it. Lil and I love the area where the world exhibition took place in 1873. Here we can listen to barrel organs and Heurigen singers and ladies' orchestras. One day a children's puppet show catches our attention and a young girl reminds me so strongly of Eva at that age I have the strongest pang of homesickness I have yet endured.

We stroll past the terrifying Riesenrad, a two hundred twelve foot tall wheel that in the United States is called a Ferris Wheel. This is the tallest one in the world. Neither Lil nor I have any desire to ride in its thirty swinging gondolas, but we can sit at the Schweizerhaus, have tea, and watch others tempt death.

Lil's face relaxes into a smile. She loosely piles her hair into a more modern European style that becomes her, and she adopts a more slender, more fashionable gown. Today she wears one in pale lavender, a good hue for her dark hair. It fits snugly enough to show her shape but bells out at sleeves and hemline. Lil is the image of a modern artist, and my heart flutters.

"This is an amazing city, Em. The art and ideas fly thicker than the butterflies in Pacific Grove. The inspiration is overwhelming."

"You are happy here, Lil, I can see that. I'm glad." A young woman on the big wheel with her beau catches my attention. She screams daintily, and I shake my head in disgust.

Lil grins. "The art world in Vienna offers enough to keep me studying for decades. The celebratory air in the city is pleasant, too."

"Yes," Lil nods. "Vienna is home to so many different people. It has a greater variety of cultures than San Francisco. I'm sure that is why there's so much great art here."

"But it's not all smooth," I say, looking over to the wheel, where the operator turns away a man in the yarmulke of the Jewish. He looks angry. I have attended the Episcopal church since we moved to San Jose, but I have never understood why the Jews are so vilified. Here in Hapsburg Vienna it is particularly blatant.

Lil follows my gaze and grimaces. "It's too bad politics have to mar this artistic perfection."

"The Bourgeousie are growing in wealth and numbers daily here," I tell her as I watch the Jewish man argue a bit then give up and stalk off. "But none of them are really gaining any power. That is going to be a problem for the Kaiser some day."

"Well, look at you," Lil says with a smile. "I've never heard so much politics come from your mouth! Maybe I'll make a true fighter for women's rights out of you yet."

"No," I demur, "I'm willing to work for my right to a career and let others do the rest."

"You don't want to vote?"

"I'll vote as soon as I'm able, but I don't have time to carry signs and write letters and give speeches about it. I'll leave that to Ellen

VanValkenburgh." We laugh together.

"This is our last day here. How do you feel about leaving Vienna?" I ask.

She turns a radiant smile on me that melts my heart. I will do anything for this woman. "I am at peace with it. I have scores of new ideas I am eager to try at home. It is time to move on." A teasing lilt enters her voice as she echoes my words from earlier in the trip. "Shall we take ship from here to the States? Do we really need to go to Paris?"

"We're going to Paris!" I growl in mock outrage. We have laughed together more in the course of this adventure than we have in the entire year prior to our trip. For that alone, I am thankful.

We arrive in Paris late in November, eager to see what the city has to offer, eager for new adventure. This is the last stop on our European tour. After our time here, we return to San Francisco, but for Lil the trip finished in Vienna. She comes to Paris because I want to be here. For me the trip has culminated in the jewel of the Continent. Like Vienna, Paris teems with artists, writers, publishers, patrons and art dealers from all disciplines and many countries.

Our place of residence in this fair city is the Hotel du Louvre. Its brochure says it *has always had a reputation as a hotel of character, and attracts discerning guests of social, political, and artistic importance.* Lil and I raise our chins, point our noses to the sky, and play the role of guests of artistic importance.

On our first morning in Paris, I am so full of anticipation that I go downstairs before Lil is ready. While I wait for her, I shop at Les Galeries du Louvre, a fashion store on the ground floor. I am not really one to return to San Francisco with an entire French wardrobe, but surely a few new gowns would be appropriate. An artificial Christmas tree festoons the store. I have never seen one before, and I peer closely at it. Constructed of feathers dyed green, probably swan feathers, the overall effect stuns, but it doesn't smell like a fresh cut pine from the Santa Cruz mountains. Homesickness washes over me again and I firmly turn my attention to the lighting on the tree. In San Francisco people are beginning to put electric lights on their Christmas trees, but this tree still has tiny lanterns and delicate glass balls with candles inside. I realize Lil and I will be at sea on Christmas Day, on the first leg of our journey home.

Lil arrives with a cheery wave, and I put off shopping for another time. We explore the delights of Paris, including the fabulous Eiffel Tower. The city is full of machines, speed, noise, and confusion. I love it. Everything new and popular inspires me; film, vaudeville, the circus, jazz music. A quality to this place speaks to the soul of the artist, and I know I am not the only one to feel it.

We discover the Chat Noir, a cafe in the Montmarte neighborhood, and spend many nights there. The bohemian atmosphere fills our spirits and our stomachs with good food and debates about art trends. We meet high spirited and literary people—the Chat Noir even has its own newspaper.

The incredible natural light surrounding Paris overlays the whirl of the city. I think of Eva and her camera, and long to share this place with her. I write letters describing with inadequate words the specialness of this place.

When we tour the Beaux Arts School, I expect the heavens to open and angels to sing. It is, however, a quite ordinary school. I have presented myself as a prospective architecture student. I don't know if my femininity or my forty-one years is more off-putting. The male bastion that leads the school has perfected the art of looking down their respective noses with a sniff of disapproval. I cannot imagine anyone finding the teaching here more inspirational than the streets of Paris or supping at the Chat Noir. Lil and I take our leave, looking down our noses and saying we might consider their school.

We giggle like school girls until we are once more among our own people in the Montmarte.

All good things must come to an end, or so the old proverb says. By the time we leave Paris I am ready to go home.

We take a train to London and embark on a Blue Funnel Line ship to retrace our route to Shanghai. Christmas Day dawns while we are somewhere off the coast of Hong Kong. The weather is warmer than any Christmas I've experienced, and there is none of the tradition that usually surrounds the day.

At home, when I was a child, we would have a candlelit tree with gaily wrapped presents piled beneath it. Papa and Fannie and all of us children would eat a sumptuous meal with holiday music and special treats. I remember it as only a child can, a happy family time. Adult Christmases never quite live up to those magical early years, and this one is the oddest.

The steamship line prepares a holiday dinner and sings some carols next to a tiny tree festooned with candles, and that helps put me in the spirit a bit. Later, in my stateroom, Lil and I exchange gifts. Mine is clearly a painting, and I am dumbfounded that she was able to buy and secure it aboard ship without my knowledge. I uncrate it and nearly weep. It is an Impressionist painting of the street in front of our Paris hotel, probably painted from one of the rooms above the one where we actually stayed. The scene is recognizable, but most impressive is the light. I peer at the signature. "Pissaro?"

"Camille Pissaro recently died," she tells me. "He lived in our hotel and painted this there. I thought you'd like it."

"Oh, Lil, I love it. Thank you so much." And I can hardly wait to show it to Eva.

I lean it against the wall for now and hand Lil a tiny box. She is overcome with the silver bracelet I bought. It has two charms, one of the Riesenrad and one of the Eiffel Tower. Each charm has its own tiny diamond set into the design. "It's our light," I tell her.

"You and I together forever," she whispers. Then she turns to me with tears of joy in her eyes, her arms wide and inviting.

Chapter 23: Inverness 1908-1909
Eva VanValkenburgh

The camera has a mind of its own. My first roll of film produces blurry images of Carl, who won't sit still for anything, and indistinct shots of uniformly gray pasture under flat gray skies. I teach myself about contrast and lighting and composition, and pore over books my father brings me to learn about aperture and shutter speed and focus.

I walk for miles through Point Reyes and Inverness, photographing birds and cattle and people and fences. I love the vistas over Tomales Bay, and take pictures of boats and water and docks. Mama says my father will provide rolls of film as long as I take some pictures of people, too, so I oblige her with an occasional almost-focused picture of Carl.

My father fixes a darkroom for me in a corner of the barn.

There I explore the mysteries of negatives, emulsions, and chemical processes, learning to develop my own film and gradually getting used to the stench of chemicals. My father admonishes me to be careful, and not to tell Mama how quickly the nitrocellulose film bursts into flame if heated incorrectly. I pledge to exercise the utmost care.

Gradually, my skill improves and I begin to glimpse what Aunt Emily meant when she said to record impressions that move my soul. A photograph I snap of a seabird sitting atop an overturned rowboat makes me laugh. The quirky tilt of the bird's head seems to be listening to something trapped under the boat. I print a copy of the image for everyone I know.

Miss Annie Hollingsworth

3396 East 14th Street

Fruitvale, California

June 15, 1908

Dearest Annie,

Enclosed please find a photograph of a silly bird on a boat. I hope it makes you laugh. I continue to take pictures of everything around me, and photography seems to be filling a void in the artistic part of my soul.

Aunt Emily sends postcards and letters from exotic locations in Europe. Maybe I will make a postcard of Tomales Bay and send it to her! Speaking of exotic locations, how are you enjoying life amongst the apricots? I remember you as a city girl in Santa Cruz. Has the orchard life yet grown on you? And what of the fight for women's rights in your area? I know Alameda County helped defeat the vote for women when last it was posed. Please write soon!

Love from

Eva

Miss Eva VanValkenburgh

160 Inverness Road

Point Reyes, California

June 29, 1908

Dearest Eva,

I am quite stunned to admit that I enjoy the country life very much. My father's orchard is very beautiful year round. Since Alameda County voted against women in 1896, much has changed. The Great Earthquake drove so many people out of San Francisco that the population of Alameda County grew hugely. There has been much discussion in the churches about giving women the vote, and I believe support is growing since the march in Oakland on your birthday last summer. I have even joined the California Equal Suffrage Association! Your grandmother is still quite active in Santa Cruz, I know, but they have always been more liberal in their thinking there. We must win in Alameda and San Francisco next time around.

I very much enjoyed your picture of Silly Bird, as I have named him. Please continue to send your pictures, as I enjoy them very much.

Love from

Annie

Miss Eva VanValkenburgh

160 Inverness Road

Point Reyes, California

July 1, 1908

My darling Eva,

Lil and I are having such fun in Europe! The architecture here is amazing. Lil says to tell you that she will make sure I do not come home with any ideas about building a cathedral in California. I agree that would be out of place, but they are truly a wonder to behold. Not too many women scramble around looking at joists and buttresses and puzzle over soaring arches. As usual, we are quite unusual!

I hope you are making use of the camera we gave you, and developing some skill. I look forward to seeing a portfolio of your photographs upon our return. I've heard of quite a few well-known women photographers over here, a number of them from the States. I will try to purchase magazines with their work, as books are much too heavy to carry home.

Your loving aunt,

Emily Williams

Miss Annie Hollingsworth

3396 East 14th Street

Fruitvale, California

July 21, 1908

Dearest Annie,

Today I completed the next set of photographs for my series entitled 'Year of Almonds.' I plan to have pictures of the almond trees in my yard during all four seasons. I love the one of Carl pretending to doze in the shade of a fully leafed summer tree. I spend my days taking photographs or developing them, reading The Dial, *and writing letters. Aunt Emily is due home from abroad in January, where she will find a year's worth of letters and photographs waiting for her! When are you going to come visit? Spring is beautiful in Inverness, and summer is nice on Tomales Bay. With love,*

Eva

Miss Emily Williams

246 Chestnut Street

Pacific Grove, California

August 25, 1908

Dear Aunt Emily,

I am so glad you are enjoying your trip. I laugh to imagine a Gothic cathedral in Pacific Grove! Your cozy cottage is much more appropriate to the area. I hope you know how much I appreciate your letters of encouragement.

My photography gets better each day, as you will see from the mountain of letters that must be piling up at your home, all containing copies of my efforts. I wish I could afford to mail them to you in Europe, but you'll have to wait. I hope all my letters and photographs are a nice surprise on your return!

Sentiments are heating up here over allowing women to vote. Inverness may be tiny, but Marin County supports suffrage efforts. After all, Julia Ward Howe's sister lives in Marin! You will be pleased to hear that I have joined both the California Equal Suffrage Association and the International Photographic Association. I plan to achieve much with both groups.

Your niece,

Eva VanValkenburgh

Late in October, I once again walk to Point Reyes to mail a letter to Annie. As I stroll along Sir Francis Drake Boulevard, birds sing. I peer into the bay trees and Bishop pines for a glimpse of the shy ones. Occasionally a car clatters by; more often a horse drawn conveyance clops along. Usually, though, it's just me.

I love the flowers around Inverness. The red Indian paintbrush, Douglas irises, and orange monkey-flowers with their funny faces cheerfully reach for the sun and I snap pictures to preserve their beauty. By the time I return home, I have mailed my letter to Aunt Emily and taken two rolls of film that I must develop. I hum to myself as I head to my darkroom.

"Eva!" Mama sticks her head out the kitchen door.

"Mama?"

"Don't you think you should come inside and dress? Surely you remember the Whitneys are coming to dinner?"

I am in too content a mood to have remembered. George Whitney, the esteemed only son of the ranch family, is Mama's latest enticement into the world of matrimony. My flower photographs will have to wait.

Later, when Mr. and Mrs. Whitney arrive with their oh-so-eligible son George, I am demure and respectable in shiny button-top shoes and clean green dress that highlights my eyes. Mama attempts to tighten the corset to give me the illusion of a waistline, but I am too short and square of figure, and I prefer to breathe.

Mama also dislikes how badly I want to cut my hair. The dark waves that hang to the middle of my back constantly need to be braided to keep the breeze off the bay from covering my eyes. I just know if I cut off the braid my hair will curl nicely. I tell Mama if George Whitney is going to like me, he'd better like me in short curls like Aunt Emily's.

In fact, George looks as uncomfortable to be there as I am. Mr. Whitney and my father speak about the ranches, and I am surprised how much my father knows about the local grass. They laud the native purple needle grass, the fescue, and the oat grass. Mr. Whitney claims his cattle like the Italian rye grass and clover that he's planted. They both dislike the newer velvet grass and Harding grass that kill off the native grasses. It's all I can do not to roll my eyes in a blatant display of unladylike boredom.

Mama and Mrs. Whitney and I will adjourn to the parlor after dinner while the men have cigars and drinks. I know I will undergo interrogation at that time, couched as an interview by a mother on behalf of a young woman ostensibly interested in her son.

George has weathered skin, blue eyes, and straight brown hair. His eyes lack the intelligence I require in a friend, although he is clearly no stranger to hard work. At first he is shy, then his father brings up the vote.

"So Henry, I hear your mother is quite infamous in Santa Cruz with this whole vote thing." He laughs, as if expecting my father to agree with him.

My mother has just laid the food on the table: a great tureen of split pea soup, pot roast that has been cooking since I got home from mailing my letter, browned potatoes, peas, and lettuce with French dressing. It is a filling meal. I know Mama wishes she could tell George I cooked it, but I am much better in the darkroom than the kitchen. Perusing the food cannot keep my mind from attaching itself to my father's response, however.

"She is working very hard for the women's vote," my father says in a neutral voice.

"Why, George," I say sweetly as my mother cringes, "how do you feel about the vote? Do you think women are smart enough to vote?"

"Well," he stops to clear his throat. I think it is the first time he has spoken. "It's true politics is no place for women."

Is that my father groaning softly? "That's interesting, George," I say, leaning forward, "but more women than men are among our college graduates in this country. Surely they deserve representation?"

My mother stares at us, frozen in horror. My father hides a smile. Carl continues to stuff potatoes in his mouth and hide his peas under his lettuce. George, however, isn't at all uncomfortable. In fact, he's starting to show signs of life. He continues, "Women belong in the home, learning modesty, patience, and gentleness. They can influence our nation most by providing an exceptional home and raising sons with a conscience."

I lay my fork alongside my plate and smile at him. "So you agree that a woman, a mother, is an important part of the family." He nods. "Isn't our great nation just a bigger family? Shouldn't a woman be able to assist in governing the state as she assists in governing her household?"

George shakes his head, but before he can reply my father steps in. "You'd best curtail this discussion, George. I am afraid this is one subject that Eva is adamant about."

The fact that he doesn't try to pass off my political views as a testament to my intelligence impresses me. Mama keeps silent. She cares more for my views than she may realize.

Mr. Whitney says, "Most women don't want to vote anyway. It's only the mannish political females who are pushing for this foolish amendment. Most women realize their men will take care of them. After all our women are very dear to us." He pats his wife's hand while I stare at him.

My father rescues us. "Yes, they are dear to us. And that's why we allow them their dreams, isn't that right?" He heartily claps Mr. Whitney on the shoulder.

Before anyone can respond, Carl looks at Mama and asks, "Do we have Fig Newtons to go with our milk?"

Everyone laughs in relief, eager to discuss cookies or milk or seven-year-old brothers. George darts quizzical glances at me throughout dinner, and shows no desire to speak with me further. I relax and spend the rest of the evening listening to conversation about ranching in Inverness. Later, with the women, the conversation circles around families that ranch in Inverness. I smile and nod graciously until boredom threatens to topple me from my chair.

Much later, in the privacy of my own room, I lay on my bed and stare at the ceiling. The soft green paneling and white shutters on the window soothe my sense of disquiet. George is a dolt, and I have no qualms about admitting it, but it is troubling that there seem to be no men my age, anywhere in my life, who take women seriously. Beneath me, the quilt Mama sewed for me reminds me of my family's loving support. I do not have to settle for backward ranchers' sons.

Rolling over on my stomach, I pick up the latest issue of *The Dial*. No matter what my mood, I can always find escape or intellectual challenge within its pages. Tonight I'm distracted and flip pages without reading more than a sentence or two of a story or an article. The showy ads catch my eye, and I read all of them. A small section of personal ads is headed 'Pen Pals.' One notice jumps out at me.

E.J. Walters, 21 years old, freshly arrived from Scotland, wishes to correspond with intelligent woman of modern ideas. I am currently living in the Los Angeles area picking oranges, but plan a far more illustrious future.

I am intelligent and have modern ideas. Before I can second guess myself, I pull out a piece of stationery and begin to write to the magazine. I will never know if knights in shining armor come from Scotland unless I send this letter.

An early Eva VanValkenburgh photograph postcard of Tomales
Bay, California

Chapter 24: San Francisco 1910-1912

Emily Williams

We return to California floating in a dream world but reality soon creates a nightmare. Moving in with Lil's parents in San Francisco, we can continue to rent out all three cottages in Pacific Grove. My contacts remain in Pacific Grove, however, and commissions just about dry up for me. I design a house in Alameda for Mrs. Alice Wright, then my pen and ink gather cobwebs on my desk.

Lil, on the other hand, burns with the fire of Vienna. She opens The Palmer Shop to focus on art metal and pays every man and woman at the shop is equally in a profit-sharing arrangement that benefits all. Her copper lamps succeed hugely, and she ships orders all over the world. Now small articles appear in San

Francisco newspapers praising her work. A story circulates that her interest in metalwork came from her father. I read this and look at her quizzically. "Your father knows about metal?"

She laughs and shakes her head. "He was a miner, as was yours in the early years. Apparently he had some interactions with blacksmiths and that supposedly gave rise to my interest in copper."

I let that muddle of reasoning sink into my brain before I laugh. "You could have made up something better than that, Lil." I continue reading the article. "Well, you are quite the celebrity. It is an honor to know you."

She laughs and waves away my silliness with her hand. I smile, pleased to see her happy.

Although the time before our European adventure seems a lifetime ago, I easily recall the restlessness Lil felt in the months leading up to the trip. She felt less than she could be, less than I was, and it grated on her. I feel myself heading down that same slippery path to melancholy, and I do what she did — try to hide it. I must busy myself with designing, so I find a beautiful site in the Santa Cruz mountains and build a private retreat for us. We call it Wake Robin and spend whatever time we can there.

Meanwhile, Julia Morgan's name crops up everywhere. While I was out of the country, other women have been licensed as architects. I see mention of Grace Jewett, Elizabeth Austin, Ida McCain, Dorothy Wormser, Grace Weeks, Florence Hinks. By the end of the year, however, these women, too, are struggling to find clients. I hear that Ella Castlehun gives up practicing architecture altogether.

The time I spend building Wake Robin puts me back in Etta Belle Lloyd's circle in Pacific Grove. She negotiates the lease for the land where she wants the Women's Civic Improvement Club to build a clubhouse, and the ladies exclaim with enthusiasm. Of course, she sponsors me as architect. I am embarrassed that Lil and I have not yet been able to repay in its entirety the loan Etta gave us before we went to Europe, so I insist on doing the clubhouse plans for free.

I don't skimp on the design even though I am donating the plans. The assembly room will be fifty feet by twelve feet, with a porch running the length of it. I plan to shingle the exterior of the bungalow, and border it with geranium boxes. The windows and interior finish will be colonial. I expect this piece to revitalize my contacts in Pacific Grove and get my business going again.

The local papers don't mention the project. At the well-attended opening ceremonies, I expect gratitude or at least acknowledgement of my design. Is it uncharitable of me to be irritated when my name is not mentioned? I am unable to smile as if it doesn't matter, so I stop attending social events. The club ladies send Etta to talk with me.

"I'm sorry, Etta, if I seem out of sorts over this, but times have been hard." I pour lemonade and offer her a cookie from a plate I've hastily arranged. She accepts both.

"I know, Emily, but these women feel you should be grateful that they gave you the commission."

She sits in my house, sipping my lemonade, and has the nerve to suggest I should be gushing thanks for a free design? I lean forward in my chair. "Grateful for the commission? I don't even care if they neglect to mention the design was donated. For my future business, however, it should be noted *somewhere* that Emily Williams designed that building!" My frustration causes my tone to be snappy and Etta's face closes like a book.

Nonetheless, a small article appears in the local paper.

Miss Emily Williams, the architect, donated the plans for the new clubhouse to the Civic Club, and the ladies feel very grateful to her. They feel that to her is very largely due the handsome home that they are now enjoying. In their resolutions they did not forget her generosity.

I snort in derision when I read it. Shortly afterward, the club president, Julia Pratt, builds a house and does not even consider me as architect. I rejoin Lil in San Francisco and suspect I will never build another house in Pacific Grove.

Conversely, Lil's importance grows. 1911 brings a whirlwind year to California, and she jumps into the fray with both feet. After losing momentum, it seems that women's suffrage may actually have a chance to pass in our golden state. Speakers, organizers, automobile tours and press material reach out to distant voters in the remote corners of the great state. Women in every county organize clubs and associations to win the support of prominent men, newspaper editors, business and clergymen as well as individual voters. I hear women spout the mantra spreading throughout the state, "I appeal to you as a mother, a grandmother, as a garment worker, a school teacher, a trained nurse."

Lil drags me along to meeting after meeting after meeting where women declare it is time to take charge. I long to take charge of my career, not waste time discussing what-ifs with people who cannot yet vote their wishes into action. I know even as I think them that I must not speak those words to Lil. She might interpret my frustration with my declining career as jealousy since her career takes off, and I cannot have that. I don't want to return to the relationship we had before our voyage.

In October, the San Francisco Bay Area soundly defeats votes for women. In Los Angeles, it barely passes. It takes five days for the count to come in from rural counties. Equal Suffrage passes in the state of California by just 3,587 votes. I will vote in next year's presidential election. Women with much more political savvy than me organize a massive voter registration campaign in Los Angeles so that women can vote for the first time in the local elections on December 5. I am pleased that I help elect people to push for women's rights. Someday women will choose their profession and actually be hired, even respected, by their peers. First, we must elect the right people.

Over breakfast on a cold, gray San Francisco morning, Mr. Palmer reads the paper to us. "65,000 women voted in Los

Angeles. That's only a few thousand votes less than the number of men. You women will rule the world one day." He grins at his wife, and Lil and I smile.

"Next year we vote for president," Lil says, her eyes dreaming.

Mr. Palmer rolls his eyes. "Whatever is the world coming to?" he teases.

"Oh don't worry, dear," his wife says, "of course all three of us will vote exactly how you tell us to." She bats her eyelashes and infuses such a sugary sweet tone to her words that Mr. Palmer groans as Lil and I laugh.

It may be a presidential election year, but 1912 shows no promise for me whatsoever. The months crawl by, filled with events that superficially interest me. Lil and her artsy friends work in politics, supporting Mr. Roosevelt. He is the candidate for the Progressive Party, which sprung from the Republican Party and endorses women's suffrage. He's also been president before, so no one questions his experience. President Taft runs for reelection, and Mr. Wilson challenges him as a Democrat. Of the three, Mr. Roosevelt is the only one to speak in favor of women's suffrage, so he has my vote. There is much suffrage yet to be achieved in our nation since California is only the sixth state to allow women to vote.While Lil pushes for suffrage, I dare to dream of equal career opportunities.

A letter from Mr. Maybeck reminds me I am an architect.

Dear Miss Williams,

Under the Almond Trees

I read with interest your letters detailing your fabulous experiences in Europe and the Far East. You must be brimming over with design innovation. I hope the right project comes your way, and you are able to use what you have learned. I have learned of Miss Palmer's efforts with copper lamps and lighting effects, and I am proud of the two of you. You are creating an enterprise that will outlast both of you.

Surely you recall Miss Bridgman, who taught chemistry at the California School for Mechanical Arts? She has left said position to enroll at Berkeley to learn architecture. She has some talent, and I hope she will follow your successful lead.

Sincerely,

Bernard Maybeck

I hand the letter to Lil without a word.

"Oh, the famous Miss Bridgman," she says, smiling at me.

I smile back, recalling how jealous Lil was of the time I spent with the teacher, and of how much I admired her. "I wish her well, but sure don't relish the competition," I say.

"You're just on a prolonged vacation," Lil reassures me.

Her words seem to have the opposite effect, as nothing turns up. San Francisco still recovers from the devastating earthquake and fire of 1906. Everywhere the sounds of rebuilding remind me that architects are in great demand in this place at this time.

I write letters to everyone I have designed homes for and ask if they know anyone who might need my services. I tramp through job sites talking to foremen, and I visit Mr. Maybeck to let him know I am now in San Francisco. I refuse to resort to begging, but my head fills with unbuilt designs. How can a state full of women's clubs not support female architects? Here in the city, the downtown women's clubs have all heard of Julia Morgan's work for the Oakland and San Jose YWCA, and of her buildings on the campus of Mills College. Yet they consistently choose male architectural firms. They all live a lie, working for women's rights yet hiring men. I have wanted this career too long, and I have fought too hard to get this far. There is something out there for me. I just need to find it.

Chapter 25: Santa Cruz 1912
Ellen VanValkenburgh

The turn of the century came and went in a blaze of promise. I'm sure anyone who reaches my esteemed eighty-five years can claim to have seen much progress. There's something special about living in two centuries, though. When a new century begins, mankind seems bent upon leaving a mark, and this century has not disappointed.

I am mostly sedentary these days, sitting by my window and watching the world pass by. Battles for women's rights rage in my head, and I follow the meetings and debates through newspapers and letters. My passion beats strong, but my body weakens. Outside that window, the Santa Cruz fog rolls in to an ever more popular resort town. Mr. Swanton's marvelous seaside casino burned downed in 1904 and was replaced with an entire boardwalk of amusements. There's a bandstand where Marion hears the Lou Williams Santa Cruz Beach Band play. Visitors drive in their horse and buggies right onto the beach to visit the opulent Neptune Casino. My favorite part of the boardwalk is the Plunge, where they bring salt water in from Monterey Bay and heat it to a respectable swimming temperature. I manage to attend a Water Carnival held there, which is resplendent with swimming races and fire dives.

"Mama, are you ready to go?" Marion breaks my reverie as she does most days, dispersing my glorious memories with the intrusion of the present. Today, though, I don't mind.

"I've been ready for decades," I say. I smile, and I know she understands. Marion has been friend, confidant, and daughter these many years.

"Come on then, your adoring fans await." She assists me to my feet, and I take her arm.

Outside, she helps me into the carriage and we drive downtown. Butterflies tickle my stomach, unexpected since I have fought the better part of my life for this day. Every November of my adult life I stewed and sputtered as men went to the polls. Today I will vote for the next president of the United States.

Marion and I avidly followed the campaign. President Taft never once mentioned women, so he will never receive my vote. Six states have women going to the polls today, and I predict Mr. Taft will win none of them. Former President

Roosevelt formed a new party this year, the Progressive Party. He campaigned vigorously for the female vote and secured mine because of it. He did a fine job as president before and will again. The Democrat, Mr. Woodrow Wilson, campaigned strongly and cannot be counted out. At this point, all I can do is cast my vote.

"Do you think Mr. Roosevelt is strong enough to lead?" Marion asks me anxiously. "It's only been three weeks since he was shot."

"He's a bull moose," I reply, referring to the nickname of the Progressive Party. Marion laughs.

"Well, it is amazing that the bullet was slowed by his glasses case and the text of his speech. If it were a shorter speech that bullet may have killed him!"

We fall silent as the import of what we are about to do sobers us. I swell with pride to share this moment with her. The jangle of harness and clop of hooves lull me into a reverie where I imagine I can feel the other women of my family.

My other daughter, Ellie, lives in San Francisco. She vows she will never vote, a petulant rebellion against me. Florence, my granddaughter, is old enough to accompany her mother to the polls. If Ellie doesn't vote, no doubt Florence won't either. Florence is artistic, but in an odd way. She never seems happy, always hiding behind her glasses.

My daughter-in-law, Nina, will vote with Henry in Marin County. My granddaughter Eva sends pictures of Tomales Bay and Inverness. She, too, will vote for Mr. Roosevelt as she told me in her letters. I hope she takes a picture of her mother voting!

Nina's family is as divided as mine. Her sister Emily, with her companion Lillian, will vote in San Francisco. Miss Palmer will ensure it! Nina's older sister, Edith, lives apart from the family in Pacific Grove. I am confident she, too, will cast a vote. That insipid stepmother of theirs, however, probably is not even aware an election is taking place.

Mrs. Fannie Williams remains the epitome of all I despise. She clings to her youngest son, Paul, as if without him she will just perish from the Earth. She must have more strength than that. After all, she married a widowed man, uprooted him from the gold fields and moved them all to San Jose. She raised his four children and gave him two more, kept his house and entertained for him as he became quite prominent. These are not tasks for a simpering woman, yet she simpers. I have no patience for her. Just as well she probably won't vote, since she would probably throw away her vote on Taft.

We arrive at the courthouse at midmorning. Both men and women step back to watch as they recognize our carriage. I sit for a moment and contemplate the courthouse. Forty years ago I tried to vote here and Captain Brown turned me away. Forty years ago I sued for my right to vote and the men laughed at me. Now my vote will help turn the tide of the nation and elect a new president.

"It's time, Mama." Marion smiles proudly. A gray tendril escapes from her upswept hair, and I realize with a shock that she is now fifty-six years old. When I was her age, I'd lost two husbands and had three children on the brink of adulthood. Yet here she stands, with an aging mother instead of a brood of children.

"I am ready," I say in the strongest voice I can manage.

She helps me from the carriage. I put out my cane with one hand, and tuck the other in the crook of Marion's arm. Slowly we make our way to the registrar's desk. Of course a young man replaced Captain Brown. It used to be I knew everyone in Santa Cruz, but this one is a stranger.

"Ellen Rand Perkins VanValkenburgh," I say loudly. My declaration now is every bit as important as the signing of the Declaration of Independence, and I want my voice to be the John Hancock signature of this election.

"Welcome," the clerk says, smiling. He shakes my hand and gives me the ballot.

With only my cane, I move toward the voting booth. Behind me, I hear Marion give the clerk her name. Tucking the ballot into my cane hand, I struggle a bit with the flimsy door of the small booth. Then I am inside and it clatters shut behind me. I lean against the shelf where I place my ballot and hang my cane on the edge. With a shaking hand, I smooth the official ballot. This moment is no longer for all the women who come after me. It's no longer a Historical Moment. This moment is the culmination of my life's ambition, of more than forty years of struggle. At this very instant, I am overcome with emotion. I am proud, and I am elated.

As I mark my ballot, I imagine women all across the state doing the same.

Taking one more minute to savor the experience, I gather my very first marked ballot and return to the registrar's desk to place it in the locked box. I vote, and the world changes.

To most of the people gathered here, I am just one more old woman voting for the first time. I am not the first woman to vote in the county, nor will I be the last. There is no political milestone here, only a personal one. Marion senses some of this, and insists on taking me out to lunch to celebrate.

In the next days, it becomes clear that President Taft will not be reelected. His Republican slate did not even make the ballot in California, although I'm sure some people wrote in his name. In our state, former president Mr. Roosevelt wins by a narrow margin, and I am jubilant. In the final tally, though, Mr. Woodrow Wilson wins the presidency. It hardly matters. I voted in a major election, and I will do so again.

The first letter to arrive after the election is from Eva.

Dear Grandma Van,

I voted! Mama and I were the very first women to vote in our precinct. We walked right up there with Papa and cast our votes like we'd been doing it all along. Carl wanted to vote, too, but he is only ten. He was quite distraught until Papa promised him a treat on the way home. He is such a child! I thought about you as I put my ballot in the box, and knew you would be as proud of me as I am of you.

Love,

Eva

I write back and assure her she is the jewel of my heart, and her future is bright. A day or so later, I am astonished to receive a letter from Emily Williams. I have not heard from her in ages.

Dear Mrs. VanValkenburgh,

As did many women in our fair state, I voted today. There were long lines of women at our precinct in San Francisco, and a very festive air. Lil and I blended into the crowd and marked our ballots. It is such a turning point for our country. I hope other states follow suit soon. I know I have not been as tireless an advocate for suffrage as you have, but I wanted to let you know that I gladly participated in my new right. Thank you for all you have done over the years to further women's causes.

Sincerely,

Emily Williams

"She must think I am the grand dame of suffrage," I tell Marion.

"Oh, Mama, for each letter like this you receive, there are ten others who feel the same but never write." She pats my hand and fetches my tea.

When you are young, you hop on life's train and take off,

with no destination in mind. Have you ever seen a child on a train? They fasten themselves to the window and marvel over the speed of the train and the black smoke as the locomotive works a grade. They live in the moment. A child has no control over who her parents are or how she is raised any more than she can control the destination of that train.

In the middle years, idealism charts a path and a young woman, or man I suppose, charges forth to drive the train. For me, it was about achieving the vote. Emily Williams wanted to be able to pursue her chosen career. For Ellie and Nina, it has always been about raising a strong family. The middle years are all about taking charge and steaming into the future with a full tender of coal. We've all done that admirably.

In old age, however, life wins again. It rushes by like a steam locomotive and pushes the old souls aside to sit in the station and watch, the thrill now gone. I have done many things I'm proud of, and I've loved many people who have loved me, too. In the grandest scheme, isn't that the most beautiful epitaph?

I'm a tough old girl, though. I don't curl up and die just because I'm no longer in charge. I bask in the reverence my family showers on me. I will be here to mentor my children and my grandchildren for a while yet. It's my turn to give sage advice and watch youth ignore it. I laugh with them and cry with them, knowing they will find their own way when all is said and done.

Marion returns with the tea and a plate of almond cookies, my favorite. The almond tree in the yard is old now, too. It still showers us with magnificent pale blossoms each spring, but the birds get most of the almonds before we can pick them. Marion must have bought these, a sacrilege in her youth. I smile, remembering.

She pats my hand. "Mama, I so enjoy having tea with you by this window. It's like the entire world is laid out before us."

"Yes, my dear, it is." I bite into my almond cookie and marvel in the flavors of the present.

Ellen VanValkenburgh, on the right, with her daughter Marion. Marion is holding her sister Ellie's granddaughter, also Marion.

Chapter 26: San Francisco 1913-1917

Emily Williams

In 1913 I build a house at 1137 Broadway in San Francisco, and one in San Jose for Mr. Walter McIntire, an engineer. Lil and I move out of her parents' home and into the Broadway house, but one paying job in a year satisfies neither my financial obligations nor my artistic zeal. Lil's shop continues to prosper. What kind of world allows only one of us at a time to be successful?

The same year, Julia Morgan builds Asilomar Conference Center in Pacific Grove. Lauded for its shingled exterior and exposed stone fireplaces, the design mirrors similar bungalows in the area— bungalows built by me.

"Why did they hire Julia Morgan?" I complain to Lil, pacing our parlor, so new the scent of wood shavings lingers in the air.

"You didn't invent the Arts and Crafts style, dear heart," she tells me.

Logic tells me I could never have built Asilomar without an architect's license, but I am in no mood to listen to logic.

"Be proud that a woman thought of it, a woman designed it, and a woman named it," Lil advises. "I like the name. *Asilo*, a refuge, *mar*, the sea. Refuge by the sea."

I allow her to console me, but my heart hardens toward Julia Morgan and Pacific Grove. I focus on San Francisco and the future. Women now command more political power as civic clubs become organizations with real voting clout. I love the intimate bungalows I created in Pacific Grove, but draw plans for anything a paying customer wants. Part of me feels it sells out my art, and my soul craves expression.

All such petty personal thoughts are obliterated from my brain when, in July, Lil returns home after closing the shop with a face pale as milk. She trembles as she sinks onto the couch.

I rush to her side. "Lil? Are you sick?" I don't know whether I hope for physical illness or bad news. Lil mingles in the business world every day and most often hears of world events before I do.

"Oh, Em, the most horrible news..."

I rush to fetch a glass of water. I don't know how it helps, but it is what is done at these times. Lil takes one shaky sip. I quiver, waiting for her words.

She looks into my eyes, hers full of tragedy. "Em, they've assassinated Archduke Ferdinand."

Shock claims me as I recall our blissful days in Vienna. In hindsight, of course, everything seems idyllic. The concept of such underlying tensions that would lead to this staggers my mind. The implications for the world are not lost on me. "If Austria-Hungary declares war, than all of Europe..."

She nods, already ahead of me. "War. Can the United States stay out of it?"

"Oh, Lil the U.S. cannot get involved in a European war! It's hardly any of our business."

"No, you're wrong. Too many issues are simmering. America might well become involved."

"Oh, I hope not." My mind immediately fastens on my brothers. Ed is now 47 and surely too old to serve, but Paul is 31.

Lil grasps my hand, already becoming the stronger one. "We will take each day as it comes."

Good advice since a month later San Francisco erupts in jubilation over the opening of the Panama Canal. Traveling and sending freight to and from New York immediately becomes simple. I never thought it would really happen. They've been working on this canal for fifty years! My thoughts turn to Ellen VanValkenburgh's stories of her harrowing journey from New York. So many people made the journey when it was difficult. Now that it is easier, California will be inundated!

For once, though, I am able to give Lil news that I hear at a club meeting. "The city is going ahead with the Exposition," I announce over dinner.

She sets her fork down. "The Pan Pacific?"

"It will be held next year and commemorate the opening of the Panama Canal. Surely six hundred acres of buildings will need an architect of my skill."

"They would be foolish if they didn't hire you!"

We finish our meal with a more celebratory air, chatting happily about a nebulous future. After dinner, I write a letter to Mr. Maybeck. If anyone knows about possible commissions for the Exposition, it will be him. When a letter arrives in the mail from an unknown sender in Chicago, addressed to me, I tear it open immediately.

Dear Miss Williams,

I received your name from the esteemed architect Bernard Maybeck. As you may know, he will design the Palace of Fine Arts for the Pan Pacific International Exhibition next year. He recommended you as a skilled architect working in San Francisco.

Please let me introduce myself. I am Mrs. Minnie Towler, vice-president of the Alaska Garnet Mining and Manufacturing Company. We are a group of women, based in Minnesota, who mine garnets at the Wrangell Garnet Ledge in Alaska. We are to have a pavilion at the Exposition, and since it has become our policy to hire women when we can, we would like you to design it for us. If this meets with your approval, we can discuss it further on my next trip west.

Sincerely,

Minnie Towler

Vice-president

Alaska Garnet Mining and Manufacturing Company

When Lil gets home that evening, I cannot even wait for her to read the letter. "I have an exciting commission!" I exclaim. I'm sure my eyes shine, and my grin is as wide as the San Francisco Bay. Telling her it is exciting is most likely redundant. But Lil understands.

Taking me in her arms, she swings me in a giddy circle before I can even explain. Once I do, we dance another giddy circle and collapse with delighted gasps.

"You will do the lighting, won't you?" I plead.

"Of course! And we can attend the exhibition and watch people so overcome by the beauty of our designs that the garnets themselves pale in comparison!"

I dash off a note to Mr. Maybeck thanking him for this phenomenal referral, and another letter to Mrs. Towler. I make Lil read the letter three times to make sure I don't sound too desperate or too aloof.

> *Dear Mrs. Towler,*
>
> *I would be delighted to design your pavilion for the Pan Pacific International Exposition in San Francisco next year. My partner, coppersmith Lillian Palmer, will be available to design the lighting. We would be pleased to meet with you to discuss your ideas for the look of the structure on your visit.*
>
> *Sincerely,*
>
> *Emily Williams*
>
> *Architect*

"You know," Lil says as we wait for Mrs. Towler's reply, "I am so frustrated that most of the women in our own town see no need to support women's rights any more. Now that we have the vote in California, they believe the struggle ended. It's wonderful that women elsewhere in the country are continuing the effort. In Minnesota, women can only vote on school board elections."

I shake my head. "As if that's the limit of a woman's interest in politics."

Actually, school boards don't interest me since I have no children. Eva remains the youngest person in my life, and she is now twenty-five years old. When I was her age, I hated English at Stanford. I hope my niece wields more strength of character at twenty-five than I did. If I had stood up to my father, I may have been able to pursue a full course of study in architecture and gotten my license. Of course, he would never have paid for it. Ironic, since the money he left me finally allowed me to pursue my dream. I can only wish better for Eva.

"This exposition showcases the marvel of human innovation exclusive of women's struggle," Lil says.

"That makes this commission an even more wonderful surprise," I respond.

Talk of war in Europe fades entirely from my conscious mind as I work on the design of Mrs. Towler's pavilion. I meet Mrs. Towler and her mother, Mrs. Anna Rose, president of the company. From them I learn their pavilion will be inside the Varied Industries Palace, at the opposite end of the Avenue of Palms from Mr. Maybeck's Palace of Fine Arts. From Mr. Maybeck himself I learn that the buildings for the Exposition are being designed to come apart easily. Immediately following the close of the event in November, all will be torn down. The buildings will be magnificently beautiful built to last only nine months.

The issue of lighting the Exposition at night intrigues Lil. She pores over the plans of General Electric's director of Illuminating Engineering, Walter D'Arcy Ryan. Mr. Ryan quickly becomes a lighting god, and Lil constantly praises his innovations.

"Strings of incandescent lights along the building edges are so archaic," she says loftily.

"Are they now?" I ask, amused. Incandescent lights are still relatively new.

"Mr. Ryan envisions floods of light on the buildings, and artfully created shadows to provide depth." The faraway look in her eyes means that she envisions this majesty, too. "Oh, and Em, the Tower of Jewels! It will be covered in Austrian crystals—130,000 of them! Imagine how it will sparkle!"

"And your own design, Lil? How will you light our pavilion?"

She sweeps into glowing description of the electroliers she plans. Electric lamps in copper pendants will hang from from the ceiling, the hammered copper reflecting the light. I assure her it will be spectacular.

The Pan Pacific International Exposition overshadows everything until the end of 1915. Every tidbit about its construction is shared with the world. It becomes more than a tribute to the Panama Canal. San Franciscans want to show the world that in nine short years we have overcome the rubble and ashes of the Great Quake and rebuilt a city of great beauty. Constructed mostly of staff, a plaster and burlap mixture, magnificent temporary buildings take shape along the waterfront. Even though war tears at Europe, every major nation builds something for the Expo, and so does every state. I am humbled and proud to be a part of such a grand undertaking.

When the Expo opens in February, Lil holds her breath as Mr. Ryan's much-maligned lighting illuminates the San Francisco skyline for the first time. The General Electric engineer even installs a locomotive, painted a cream color to blend in, that produces great clouds of steam. Lights are shone onto the steam to reflect a softly colored backdrop to the Exposition. It all seems the stuff of magic to me, and I hope it will all work as envisioned. But with the first gasp from the crowd, Mr. Ryan becomes legendary instead of insane.

All thoughts of new commissions are driven from my head by the wonder of the Exposition. How can Lil and I, who live in the same city as this marvel, even contemplate normal daily life? We visit the Expo many times, first with Mr. Maybeck himself. He proudly shows off his Palace of Fine Arts and admires my pavilion for the Alaska Garnet Mining and Manufacturing Company. Mr. Maybeck also shows us the whimsical House of Hoo-Hoo and the Livestock Building, both designed by him to lesser acclaim than the Palace of Fine Arts.

On a visit with just the two of us, the outside world is kept at bay as we explore the exhibits alongside ours in the Varied Industries Palace. Here the Singer Sewing Machine Company displays pictures, embroidered with their machines, of Yellowstone's Old Faithful geyser and Venice, among others. They also have national costumes from around the world, all sewn with Singer machines. In another area, the Waltham Watch Company displays its machines for making pocket watches. I make a mental note to bring Ed here when he visits. He always carries his Waltham pocket watch! I am amazed by watch screws so tiny they look like grains of sand. At the lavish booth for the Eaton, Crane & Pike Company, they show the paper-making process by which they produce their fine stationery. The painted backdrop shows their mill in the Berkshire hills. The miniaturized machinery, a beating machine, press, and dryer, turns the raw materials into sheets of paper that are given out to visitors. I use mine to write a glowing letter to Eva.

When my niece and her family visit the fair, Lil and I make sure they see our favorite exhibits. The Vanderbilt Cup auto races fascinate my nephew Carl, as does the C.P. Huntington steam locomotive, the first purchased by Southern Pacific Railroad. Eva seems fascinated by everything, taking picture after picture of the buildings and exhibits in all lighting.

"Someday those photos will be worth money," I tell her seriously. "This is the biggest event of your lifetime."

She snaps another picture. "Certainly the biggest to date, Aunt Emily, but the century's still new. Amazing things happen every day. It's an exciting time to be alive." Her face glows with pleasure, and I am thrilled that she still wants to spend time with her favorite aunt.

The Pan Pacific International Exposition finally closes, and the remarkable buildings are pulled down in a shower of plaster dust. I'm sure my friend Mr. Maybeck thrills with the news that only the Palace of Fine Arts will be preserved. With the end of the hoopla, the war creeps back into our consciousness.

We were aware, of course, of the sinking of the *Lusitania* in May, and the loss of 128 American lives, but Lil and I had been caught up in the false gaiety of the Expo. News from Europe now makes it clear that nothing as grand as our Exposition will ever occur again.

For a few months, Lil and I drift as our thrilling year of exotic experiences fades into the reality of faraway war coming closer to home. In 1916, an article appears in a San Francisco newspaper that firmly declares women unfit for business and Lil rouses from lethargy.

With fire in her eyes, she rages, "What ignorance! What foolishness! How can a reputable paper print such garbage?"

With anger stiffening her back as she paces, Lil is magnificent in her fury. "Lil, we have each run own businesses for years. We must do something."

"The men all have their professional organizations. Women are moving away from civic clubs and into politics. Maybe I should start an organization for businesswomen."

We do our research. According to city records, 6,000 women work in San Francisco industry. Lil founds the San Francisco Business and Professional Women's Club. She becomes president, and I am on the board of directors. The members socialize, but also communicate ideas, collaborate, express solidarity and empower each other. We meet weekly at various restaurants and listen to speakers on topics of interest, or transact business with each other.

By January, 1917, Lil has achieved a great deal of respect in San Francisco's business community. An item appears in the San Francisco Chronicle.

As president of The Palmer Copper Shop, Miss Palmer leads one of the most successful electric fixtures organizations in this vicinity. Organized in 1916 on the co-operative basis, The Palmer Copper Shop specializes in designing fixtures which not only attain the desired lighting effects in a given room, but also conform to the style and contour of the room and the usage to which it is to be put. Its substantial and widespread success is indicated by the fact that its electric fixtures are sought for and shipped to New York, Alaska and Mexico. Last year the exhibit maintained by The Palmer Copper Shop at the Varied Industries building of the Exposition was one of the stellar exhibits displayed.

In April the United States enters the war, and Lil must close the Palmer Shop as all metal is needed for the war effort. We are once more faced with no prospects.

Emily Williams

Chapter 27: Castro Valley 1918
Eva VanValkenburgh

When I toil in the garden, I miss the cooling breezes of Inverness the most. Quite adamantly Mama insisted that I assume household duties befitting my advanced age of twenty-nine and put me in charge of the vegetables. I enjoy watching plants I've nurtured produce food, and I'm proud of my little plot. Today, however, a sticky summer heat glues my bodice to my skin and melts away the pleasure of gardening. A wide-brimmed hat shades my face but dampens my head with perspiration. I sit back on my heels, move the thick dark braid off my neck, and look longingly at the cool shadows of the almond orchard that stretches on either side of the drive down to the lane.

Tomorrow the Castro Valley Improvement Club, where I am secretary, meets. Tomorrow I must also attend to my job as bookkeeper for the Journal. I took the job hoping the newspaper might publish some of my photographs. So far, although the managing editor describes me as conscientious, honest, and a real Christian character, apparently he has no use for my art. But tomorrow will keep. Today I garden, although not the most pleasant of days to do so.

My faithful black cocker spaniel, Suzanne, naps in the shade of a fence post. I got her as a pup four years ago and she hasn't left my side since. My father disdains her as useless, but that is the farmer's view, not the lonely young woman's. I have piles of photographs of Suzanne, but my membership in the International Photographic Association lapsed since our move to the farm.

Huge dairies, like Howard-Shafter's in Inverness, fell on hard times before the war. My father left at a good time and bought this little farm in Castro Valley where he raises chickens and almonds. Mama's asthma prefers the coastal breezes to the inland dust, but she must be where Papa is. At least Carl can attend the Castro Valley High School and be gone most of the day during the school year.

As if my thoughts summon him, Carl appears on the lane. The postman's truck tops the rise behind my brother and stops. They talk, and Carl takes our mail. My heart leaps, hoping for a letter. The postman drives off in a cloud of dust, and Carl turns off the lane onto the drive up to the house. He trudges between the rows of almond trees, and his feet stir up little puffs of dust. I stand and brush garden dirt off my hands and dress.

Carl waves a white envelope and sings out, "Oh, Eeeeeeva, look what I have."

He infuriates me, of course. "Give me my letter," I demand. Suzanne barks at him, reacting to my tone.

He laughs, drops his tin lunch pail and strapped books to the ground, and runs into the orchard. At sixteen his legs are long enough to outrun me, but I dare not let him have my letter. He wouldn't act this way if it was from Aunt Emily, or Grandma Van, or even Annie. It will be from my pen pal, Teddy, so I must get it from him.

I hike up my skirts and run after him. Still barking, Suzanne scampers after me, her little legs racing. Beneath my feet, the uneven ground, plowed for drainage and weed control, hampers my pace. With four legs, Suzanne runs better than I. Carl ducks between the almond trees, zig-zagging from row to row until I lose him.

Panting, but striving for deep breaths so my brother can't tell I'm winded, I peer around the tree trunks. Laughter directs my focus upward. He sits in a fork of a tree, about five feet off the ground, two rows over from me, and peeks around the main trunk. I calm my breathing as I walk over to him. Suzanne puts her two front paws on the trunk as if she's treed him, and I laugh.

"Terrible infestation of pests in these trees this year," I observe dryly, looking him up and down.

He just waves the letter and grins.

"Come on, Carl grow up. You're not a kid anymore."

"Hey, you're the one chasing me through the orchard," he objects. But he jumps down and hands me the letter before walking back toward the house.

It's from Teddy, as I knew it would be, and still sealed. I choose a different row to walk along as I scan the postmark. Still at Camp Lewis in Washington. That's a relief, although I know he is eager to be shipped out.

Near the house, a gnarled old almond tree blooms valiantly. It could very well be the father of the entire orchard. I sit with my back against the trunk and Suzanne climbs into my lap. When I open the letter, a photograph falls out. We've been corresponding for nine years, but I rarely get a picture. In this one, he stands outside a building that might be a barracks wearing his army uniform. He has a wonderful smile, and he looks handsome in his uniform. His cap covers his hair, which I know is brown. I can't tell from the photograph what color his eyes are, although he tells me they are blue. Behind his glasses it might be hard to tell in real life. I hold the picture in one hand and read the letter with the other.

Miss Eva VanValkenburgh

221 Redwood Road

Castro Valley, California

August 3, 1918

My dearest Eva,

I have been promoted to corporal of Company K. You can't see the rank patch in this picture, but I think it gives me a distinguished air. We expect to hear soon about being deployed to Russia to quell the Bolsheviks, and we are growing tired of waiting now that our basic training is complete. It seems President Wilson cannot make a decision about committing more troops to Russia. Yes, I know you didn't vote for him (I am very proud of you for voting), but it is hard to say if his Republican opponent would have done better. If the rest of the nation's women were allowed to vote, like California's can, do you think they would have voted Democrat or Republican?

In your last letter you spent a number of paragraphs complaining about your brother. I wish I had that luxury. Remember, my brother, Aubrey, died of tuberculosis in Glasgow. Although that was a horrible impact on my life, it resulted in my emigrating to California, which has been pleasurable. Do you believe that something good always comes of bad events if we look hard enough?

How is that 'worthless mutt' of yours? Your letters always cheer me. Please write soon.

Sincerely,

Cpl. Edward James Walters, your 'Teddy'

"Oh, Teddy," I breathe softly to the almond tree. A whisper of wind rustles the leaves. I cover my face with my hands, horrified that my careless remarks about Carl reminded

Teddy of his deceased brother.

Carefully I fold the letter around his photograph and slide it back into the envelope, already composing a reply in my head. Teddy landed in New York when he emigrated from Scotland in 1907, and took a train across the country. He's already picked oranges in Los Angeles, gone to Utah on an ill-fated oil adventure, and enlisted in the army. Now he is off to Russia. What exotic and wonderful things he will see there! But I will worry so. My life remains so routine, so boring, compared to his. I wonder why he keeps writing, why he finds it at all interesting. Yet for nine years now a letter arrives each month, and I reply. I can write to Teddy about anything: politics, family, farm life, dreams of the future. We both dream.

I tuck Teddy's letter into my skirt pocket and hasten to finish weeding the garden. If the second half is less meticulously groomed, no one will notice but me. As I dig amongst the herbs and vegetables, I refuse to think about Teddy and focus on the mint and sage and carrots and radishes so that I don't long for the only person in the world who understands my deepest soul.

Just as I finish, Suzanne pushes up next to me, wagging her tail and licking my face.

"Are you hungry, precious?" I coo, making her stumpy tail wag harder. I carry the dog into the house.

"Eva? Is that you? Can you find a couple of eggs for me, honey?" Mama calls from the kitchen.

"Sure, Mama," I call back, setting Suzanne on the floor.

The dog will scare the chickens, so I leave her in the house.

The long sheds on the back property house the white Leghorn chickens that partly supply our livelihood. These are the same chickens that are raised all over Castro Valley. I think a hundred times more chickens live in this town than people! They are pretty enough birds, but messy. Carl usually gathers eggs and milks the cow, but I am pressed into service whenever I am the most convenient. Even though eggs have already been gathered for the day, I manage to find two fairly quickly and head back to the kitchen to deliver them to my mother.

She stirs something that looks like cake batter when I hand her the eggs. I sneak a finger into the bowl for a taste while she pretends to frown at me. I wonder what kind of cake will be for dessert, but I am willing to be surprised.

"Carl tells me you got a letter from Edward," Mama says.

Teddy, my heart says, but only I use the nickname. Everyone else calls him Edward or Ed. "Yes, I did. I had to chase Carl before he gave it to me, though!"

Mama shakes her head. "Eva, you are twenty-nine years old. Time to get your head out of the clouds and focus on finding a husband."

"Most of the men are overseas, Mama."

"This war can't last forever. They'll come home wanting wives, that's for sure."

"Maybe I'll wait for Edward," I say, only half-teasing. Teddy says nothing about marriage, but I do think about it.

She frowns. "Your father won't like that idea. The young man is a foreigner, after all. He has no family background." She adds chopped chocolate to the cake batter and pours it into a pan. "So what did his letter say?"

"His unit waits to be sent to Russia to fight the Bolshevisks."

"Oh, dear," she turns to look at me, concern in her eyes. "Are you all right with that?"

"I have to be. It's what he wants, but it does frighten me."

She puts the cake into the oven and turns to me. "Eva..."

"Gotta go feed Suzanne, Mama," I say over my shoulder as I hurry from the room.

Warm days turn cool, and the leaves float gently from the trees to the ground. We harvest another crop of almonds and send it off to market. Mama makes almond butter and almond cake and almond cookies. I have eaten so many not-quite-ripe nuts directly off the tree that I pass on most of her efforts. The seasons change. I quit my job, since it's clear the paper will publish none of my photographs, and each month I write to Teddy.

Cpl. E. J. Walters

Camp Lewis, Washington

November 28, 1918

Dearest Teddy,

Happy Thanksgiving! I hope this letter finds you safely stateside and not headed to some Russian conflict. We have just finished our meal of turkey and all the fixings, and stuffed ourselves with pumpkin pie. Does the army provide a decent pumpkin pie?

The newspaper hints that the war may be ending soon, and I fervently hope it is so. I feel I am separated from all who are capable of understanding beauty and true empathy. Everyone around here is pulled down by daily routine. How dreary! With your letters, however, I transcend drudgery and share my ideas with another who envisions a better future.

If the war indeed ends soon, will you return to Utah or Los Angeles? It would please me greatly if you stopped in Castro Valley to visit. After all this time, we should meet face to face.

Sincerely,

Eva

How bold I am to put such an invitation in writing! If I were more like Mama I could hint better, but I am curious to meet Teddy and see if the man in person lives up to the man in letters. Truth be told, there is little enough excitement since California women won the vote. Then the war started and everyone's energy went toward willing our soldiers to return home safely.

December 18, 1918

My dearest Eva,

We are still at Fort Lewis. I know that news will please you. The armistice was signed in November, and the Bolsheviks are quiet. There is no talk yet of discharge, but know if I am discharged today I will be on a train to Castro Valley tomorrow. I must learn if you are as lovely and gracious in person as you are in your letters. You have sent many pictures of almond trees and Suzanne, but only one of you and that many years ago. You say my letters brighten your day, but yours do the same for me. I have met a lot of people since coming to the United States, but very few that I call friend. I have told you that I have a thick Scottish brogue. On that first train ride to Los Angeles, so many people made fun of the way I talked that I vowed never to make assumptions about a person's intelligence based on their demeanor. With you, it is different. It is as if I have gotten to know your soul before I set eyes on you. My soul knows yours and is content.

Before leaving Los Angeles, I completed that correspondence course I took. I am a certified electrical engineer, and I am certain job opportunities exist in the East Bay for such certified professionals. I would very much like to meet you, as every future I can think of includes you in some way. We are for the moment still at war, however, and I dare not dream of a peaceful future quite yet.

Yours sincerely,

Teddy

December 26, 1918

Dearest Teddy,

I hope you had a happy Christmas, knowing it will be your last as a military man. Where only a short time ago you were chafing at waiting to go to war, it seems now you long for private citizenship again. How proud I am that you were able to complete your correspondence course! I am sure you will be able to find electrical engineering work near here, and I will dream of the future for both of us. I promise to be at the train station to meet you. I am counting the days.

Yours truly,

Eva

VanValkenburgh's almond orchard, Castro Valley, California

Chapter 28: Castro Valley 1919
Eva VanValkenburgh

Late afternoon seemed like a good time to schedule a visit, but when the day arrives the hours drag. I sit primly in the parlor, clad in my best dress and new shoes, Suzanne in my lap. Petting her calms me, and maybe she will hide the thickness of my waist. Mama attempts to control my hair, finally cut into short curls, and begs me not to engage in strenuous activity that will set them free to bounce and frizz. I am not made for sitting idly in the parlor, nor can I concentrate on reading. Teddy is on his way to Castro Valley. I tug at my curls and try in vain to remember if the photograph I sent him had curls or braid.

My father sits in his big chair, hidden behind the newspaper. He insists on reading the *New York Sun*, even though Grandma Van's relatives no longer own it. The front page faces me with a story about a labor strike in Seattle. I wonder if Seattle is near Camp Lewis. Papa states that he will not like Teddy and does not approve of this visit. I clench my hands and force them to relax.

Mama sits in her chair next to my father, working at her ever-present mending. Part of me hopes I will never have a son since the majority of her pile seems to be Carl's and I am hopeless at needlework. I laugh inside at that thought. Both my parents would be horrified. Sons carry on the oh-so-important family name. Carl will do so with ours and I will need a son to do so for my husband's.

The mantel clock strikes three, loud in the silent room. Carl will be home from school soon. It will be better if Teddy arrives first. Mama rises, setting her mending on her chair.

"I'll check the cake," she says as she leaves the room.

A splendid odor escapes from the oven and wafts into the parlor. Even Papa puts his paper down for a moment to savor it.

"Vanilla almond cake," he says, then stares at me.

I shift my weight on the couch and cross my ankles. I don't want to meet his gaze.

"This boy…" Papa begins.

"He's not a boy," I interrupt. "He's thirty-two, a soldier returning from war."

He ignores me. "This boy expects what from you, exactly? He has no family to go home to so he comes here?"

"I told you, Papa. His family lives in Scotland where his

father is a Presbyterian minister. They're English, actually, not Scottish." As if that makes a difference. With no relations among people Papa knows and respects, Teddy sinks into unimportance. Religion doesn't matter. Papa doesn't attend his Unitarian church, and Mama leaves her Episcopalian religion within the walls of hers. We never discuss God at home. "The state of Utah gave him a medal for his service to the country."

"Why Utah?" Papa asks.

"Teddy left Los Angeles with a friend, the son of the family he stayed with. They had an opportunity to acquire some land with oil on it." I fidget, knowing in advance what he will say.

"Huh. That turned out well for him." Papa chuckles.

"He used his army pay to buy three lots in the town of Berkeley. And he has a job already. He's an electrical engineer at Mare Island in Vallejo."

"Hmph." Papa's paper rises to hide his face again.

I know I should subside quietly, but I cannot. "Why can't I meet him at the station, Papa? I told him I would."

"Well, that was foolish of you, Eva. It's not proper. If he wants to call on you, he should come all the way to the front door." He doesn't bother to lower his paper to respond.

My father is an honorable man, usually affectionate, always truthful. I think Teddy might be a similar sort. If I find that is true, I will marry him despite my father's misgivings and the fact Teddy hasn't asked.

Mama returns from the kitchen and resumes her mending. Silence stifles us once more. The clock ticks off the minutes. I have to trust it, but it seems an eternity since breakfast.

Discharged on the twenty-first of February, Teddy lives in a rented house in Berkeley right now but must find a place to live closer to his new job. I do worry about him living so near San Francisco, where the Spanish Flu rages. At least he didn't return to Los Angeles, where the flu has virtually shut down the movie industry and killed so many. Even so, he will be moving farther away from me. I suppose we can continue to write letters.

The heavy silence inside amplifies outside sounds. Shouts reach me, and I rush to the window, dropping Suzanne to the floor. A car I don't recognize drives away down the lane, pursued by twirling clouds of dust. Carl shakes hands with a stranger who must have gotten out of the car. My throat closes, and I swallow, rubbing my hands on my skirt. I want to run to the door, but I also want to run out back and hide among the almond trees.

Teddy wears crisply creased khaki pants, with shirtsleeves rolled to the elbows. He is shorter than I imagined, about five and a half feet tall. Brown hair sticks out from under his hat. Glasses hide his eyes. He is slender, which makes me self-conscious. He and Carl continue talking, and that worries me all the more.

The front door opens, and Carl leads him in. "Eva, Ed is here. He caught a ride in from the station."

He grins but doesn't make a smart remark. I am grateful. Teddy removes his hat. I am surprised that he is completely bald on top. Carl stifles a laugh, and I glare at him. Suzanne barks, then rushes to jump on the stranger, wagging her tail.

"Welcome to our home, Edward," my mother says.

My father has risen from his chair and shakes Teddy's hand. "Thank you for your service, young man."

"You're welcome, sir." Teddy speaks with a wonderful Scottish brogue. I am delighted. "And you must be Eva."

He turns to me, and I offer my hand to be shaken. Intelligent blue eyes regard me with affection. "So nice to meet you after all this time," I murmur. I know everything about this man's soul and have no idea how to begin conversation.

Mama expertly maneuvers us into the dining room and escapes to the kitchen. We settle around the table, Teddy next to me, and she returns with the vanilla almond cake and a pot of tea.

"Thank you, Mrs. VanValkenburgh," Teddy says. "I haven't had home cooking since I left Los Angeles."

"What did you do in Los Angeles, Ed?" my father asks.

I sip my tea, which is too hot to drink, and try not to stare at Teddy. I also try not to catch Carl's eye. He sits across the table from me, perfectly positioned to make faces or wink.

"I lived with the Irvine family, friends of my father's. I picked oranges, paved streets, and after I got my license worked for Southern California Edison as an electrical engineer." He laughs, revealing straight white teeth. "I had a beauty of a car, too. A 1914 Stutz Bearcat. Had to sell it when I went into the service."

"Great car," Carl says, eyes shining. If only Papa were so easy.

"This is wonderful cake, Mrs. VanValkenburgh. May I have another piece?" and with that, my mother is his.

"Eva tells me you have a job in Vallejo but are living in Berkeley." My father makes it sound like the height of idiocy.

Teddy just laughs. "I start the job March 24, sir. That gives me two weeks to find new lodgings in the Vallejo area."

Conversation becomes general then, centering on the East Bay and its communities. We speak briefly of Inverness, and longer of Castro Valley. My father speaks proudly of the land he owns that once belonged to the San Lorenzo rancho, property of Guillermo Castro, a Mexican soldier. I cannot see why he values a Mexican soldier's history more than Teddy's, but I know better than to comment.

By the time Teddy takes his leave, I have stopped dreaming of the white knight of his letters and fallen in love with the electrical engineer. He walks down the lane between the blooming almond trees, and I watch until I can no longer see him. At least my father could have offered to drive him to the train station.

Throughout the spring, Teddy visits often for Sunday dinner. Mama outdoes herself fixing a mammoth meal so that she can send leftovers home with him. The new job suits him well, and early in June Teddy arrives in a car.

"It's a 1918 Model T," my brother tells me, entranced.

"I wish I could have waited and gotten the new 1920 model. It will have an electric start. No more hand crank," Teddy says.

"At least this one has the magneto-powered lights," Carl says.

They engage in a conversation with words that put me to sleep: rear-wheel drive, planetary gear transmission, drop forged front axel. I laugh and tell them I will see them inside.

That night Teddy stays later than usual since he can drive straight home and not worry about catching a train. After dinner, we walk through the orchard holding hands and watch the sun set over the valley. We are surrounded by blossoms in the act of becoming almonds. I am truly happy.

"Carl tells me he plans to move to Santa Cruz when he graduates," Teddy says.

I nod. "Yes. Mama isn't pleased, but he wants to go into lumber like our grandfather. Of course, Grandpa died before Papa was born. Maybe Grandma Van's tales of running the mill have inspired Carl."

"Well, he's got another year. Maybe he will decide to become a rancher before then. That will probably please your father more."

"Probably." I wonder if my father's often obvious dislike

bothers Teddy.

"Eva."

His tone changes. With that one word we move from family pleasantries to something serious and private. I turn to face him.

"You are everything your letters promised," he tells me.

He's said this before. "As are you," I respond, as I always do.

He drops to one knee, still holding my hand. With his free hand, he fumbles in his pocket. His fist encloses something small when he looks up at me, his blue eyes bright. "Eva, will you marry me?" He holds out a silver ring, a diamond sparkling as soon as the setting sun tickles it.

I have known it was coming, have hoped for it, so why am I surprised? Nonetheless, I gasp and giggle like some woman I am not. "I would be honored, Teddy."

He kisses me for the first time, and my heart feels as it does in that moment before dusk when the sun lights the day with its most glorious rays.

Carl is ecstatic. Mama is thrilled. Papa is polite and congratulates us.

During the summer of our engagement I am transported to a new and wonderful world. I still care for the garden, play with Suzanne, and spend long hours reading and dreaming, but Mama redoubles her efforts to teach me to cook and care for a home. She has long ago given up on the delicate embroidery required of linens for my hope chest. I am so happy, nothing irritates me. I float on almond blossoms between Teddy's visits.

In July, we walk in the orchard and discuss politics. We both oppose the country entering the League of Nations, although President Wilson supports it.

"My father admires Henry Cabot Lodge," I tell Teddy, "and he is against the League."

"Cabot Lodge has good family connections. Of course your father supports him," Teddy says.

I listen for sarcasm or frustration in his tone, but do not find any. "I don't suppose it's the first time a president's wishes oppose those of the American people."

"Nor will it be the last," he assures me.

"At least you and I don't have to worry over such large issues." I snuggle close to him as we walk. "When do I get to see your house?"

"I cannot take you there, Eva," he reproves me. "It is most unseemly for us to be so alone together before the wedding."

"Oh, Teddy, don't be so stodgy!" But I cannot be angry with him when I am so content.

In August, he drives me to San Francisco for my birthday. We have dinner at the fabulous Cliff House, where I exclaim over the crashing waves and white seal rocks.

"Centuries of bird droppings have made those rocks white," Teddy tells me.

"I prefer to believe it is a creation of God." I laugh and

take a bite of the best fresh crab I have ever tasted.

"It's true God creates all manner of things. All manner of people, too. Do you believe in God, Eva?"

It's a topic we haven't really discussed, our own beliefs. I know his father ministers to a Scottish congregation. He knows my mother goes to church. "I think everyone should believe what they feel and not be coerced to believe what a certain doctrine dictates."

"Many of the older religions have good theology," he agrees. "I have not yet found one that suits me perfectly, though I believe man should treat others as he would be treated."

"The Golden Rule. It's a good one," I tell him with a smile, "but it applies to women, too."

"Of course it does!" he assures me.

In September, the coal strike in Indiana seems as sticky as the weather. I sympathize with the miners' families, and Teddy for the men themselves.

"It is not right for the company to ban the United Mine Workers," he fumes. "The union wants only to help the working men. Clearly the company doesn't care."

"They claim the miners are all radicals and Bolsheviks. Since when does wanting to eat regularly make you a Bolshevik? I feel sorry for the women and children who watch their men suffer in disgrace, and go hungry."

"The women chose the life when they married miners. They knew it would be hard. The men are the victims here. They don't get their pay or any respect. Hard for a man to live like that."

"The women aren't getting pay or respect either. Are you saying respect for the men is more important than respect for their wives?"

He looks confused. "Eva, no one who is starving puts women's rights before bread."

I subside, but his words trouble me. Later that night, I open the window of my bedroom to catch even a hint of cooling breeze and lay atop my bedding unable to sleep. In our letters, Teddy and I discussed all manner of things and usually agreed. It's possible his convictions don't run as deeply as mine in certain areas. I wonder if that will become a problem.

We marry in October. I am thirty by then, and Teddy thirty-two, turning thirty-three the day after Christmas. We are ancient for newlyweds, but still giddy with happiness. Mama's Episcopalian minister performs the ceremony at home. Flowers from my garden cover the house: purple asters, pink roses, yellow chrysanthemums.

My family and friends surround us. Aunt Marion brought Grandma Van, s now ninety-two but determined to see me wed. Aunt Ellie and Uncle James Henry have come, but my cousin Hal is too busy with his family, and his sister Florence too deeply immersed in the San Francisco art scene to attend a barely-known cousin's wedding.

My mother's family is well-represented, too. Aunt Emily

and Aunt Lil have come from San Francisco. Aunt Edith came, but Emily's twin brother Ed is not. Uncle Paul, six years younger than me, has brought his girlfriend, Phyllis, who delights me. She holds Suzanne through the ceremony so the pup doesn't get in the way.

Even Annie comes from Fruitvale with her husband. I was unable to attend their wedding three years ago, so he is a stranger who hangs back and tries to melt into the woodwork.

Teddy has no one. His parents are overseas, as are his two unmarried sisters. His only friends are in Los Angeles and out of touch, or from the army and scattered to their homes. I am giving him an entire family, not just me. I hope he knows what he is getting into.

After the vows, and the almond wedding cake, and the food and well-wishes, we drive off in Teddy's black Model T. Mama and I have packed trunks with my things and sent them ahead to the small house in Napa that will be our first home. She will care for Suzanne until I send for her.

I am nervous. Mama would call it newlywed jitters, I suppose, but suddenly I feel I don't know Teddy at all. I am driving away from my family to make a new life with him, but I don't know what he eats for breakfast, or what brand of toothpaste he uses, or a thousand other things. I know what type of book he likes to read, and how liberal his politics are, but that seems like a thin basis for an entire life together.

We spend two blissful weeks honeymooning in Inverness,

and he loves away my doubts. I see this beautiful wild peninsula as a tourist instead of one who lived here for years, and I enjoy sharing the sights of Tomales Bay with Teddy. All honeymoons must end, and Teddy becomes anxious to return to work. I am eager to begin our life together, so we pack up the car and leave Inverness behind.

Napa in October is all rolling hills of golden grassland dotted with groves of oak trees. Vineyards laden with grapes enhance the scenery. It is a beautiful place, like others I have called home. Teddy's tiny house consists of just two bedrooms, a bathroom, a kitchen and living room. A small service porch contains a large metal tub with ugly serviceable faucets and an antiquated laundry contraption I shall never master. It is small, bare of furniture, and ugly, but it's ours.

"Welcome home, my love," Teddy tells me.

I bask in the warmth of those blue eyes and the soft brogue. I truly am home in heart and body.

Eva VanValkenburgh with Suzanne

Chapter 29: Napa 1920-1922
Eva Walters

January brings true disaster for our community. I knew of the 18th Amendment, passed last year, but had no idea how widespread its impact would be in Napa. The locals have grown used to the annual flooding of the town, but Prohibition yanks the rug out from under their proverbial feet. I suppose I should have been aware, but my mind clouded with newlywed bliss and so was taken aback when the local wineries began to shut their doors. A few decide to produce medicinal wines and so remain in business, and others will sell wine grapes to the East Coast. With the prohibition of manufacture, sales, and distribution of alcohol, I am thankful that Teddy's business is not in wine. Even so, when disaster threatens a community's livelihood, all manner of businesses in the area suffer, too. Taxes rise, and we are forced to sell our property in Berkeley. Letters keep my spirits high.

Dear Eva,

I am sorry to hear that you had to sell the property Ed purchased in Berkeley. I wish I could make this first year of your marriage easy for you, but if you struggle together it makes the relationship stronger. I know you and Ed will make it, sweetheart. Lil and I have had our struggles, as you know. I am barely in business as an architect any more, and Lil has had to close The Palmer Shop. Yet we live summers at Wake Robin and rent our other properties to survive.

Now Lil is president of the San Francisco Business and Professional Women's Club. The membership has grown so that we now have our own clubhouse on Kearney Street where we hold weekly luncheons. So don't despair, dear Eva, if you push on, you will come to a brighter day.

Love,

Emily Williams

Prohibition seems to affect Teddy's demeanor also. He begins to find fault with everything. I admit I am not the best housekeeper, but I can cook. Since I have not yet joined local society clubs, I spend my days cooking and cleaning, which are tedious, and playing with Suzanne. The cocker spaniel settles into her new home easily, and clearly believes she owns it. Books also are a great distraction and we have many of them, some purchased, some borrowed from the library in town, and some passed on from family. Today I have been tired and distracted all day, very low on energy.

On the table in the kitchen, *Dangerous Days*, the newest

mystery novel from Mary Roberts Rinehart, invites me to rest. Maybe a chapter before starting dinner? I slip into the chair and fall into the book's world.

The latch on the door brings me back to my world. Suzanne has been dozing under the table, but she lets out a bark. Dusk softens the light coming in the windows, turning it gray with impending night. Teddy comes into the kitchen, and the worry in his face clears, turning to anger.

"I thought something had happened to you when I saw no lights, yet here you are sitting at the table reading." He sees the dust cloth on the counter. "You let the dust pile up while you read?" He crosses to the table and flips the book closed, inspecting the title. "A novel?" The contempt in his voice lashes me even more strongly because I haven't experienced it before.

"Would it go easier if I was reading *Crowds*?" I try to make my tone conciliatory, even teasing, but it comes out a challenge. *Crowds: A Moving Picture of Democracy* is the tome on his nightstand. I often read nonfiction, but that one daunts even me.

He frowns. "It would go easier if my house was clean and my dinner ready when I get home."

I stand up and tuck the novel in a kitchen drawer. "Dinner will be on the table soon."

He leaves the room with a disparaging grunt and no welcome-home kiss from me. I hear him settle into his chair and open the newspaper. Suzanne hides on her blanket in the corner of the kitchen. I don't deliberately clang pans as I fry some ham and eggs, but the noise soothes my bruised heart. Mama says a wife must support her husband as he supports her. Teddy and I will learn.

In the weeks to come, I come to realize why I am so tired all the time and wish to sit. Once I confirm the pregnancy, I organize a special dinner for Teddy, planning to tell him the news so we can share the meal in delighted plans. The roast cooks perfectly, filling the house with the aroma of beef and onion. The mashed potatoes and peas keep warm in the oven. I light candles on the table and set out a plate of pickled beets and olives. Tomato cream soup simmers on the stove. I set out our last bottle of Napa red wine and go to change my dress.

Teddy comes in quietly, and I greet him at the door with a smile and a kiss. He seems distracted as he puts his hat on the rack and takes off his coat.

"Come on, Teddy, I have a lovely dinner ready."

His eyes sweep the room and narrow. "You didn't dust today?"

My lips tighten. I force myself to say lightly, "The dust will wait for tomorrow, but your dinner won't."

We enter the kitchen and he stops dead when he sees the wine. "Eva, it's illegal to serve that. I won't have it on my table."

"It's our last bottle, Teddy. I promise this is a special occasion." I wait until he sits at the table, then pour the wine and serve the soup. He nibbles on the olives and ignores the wine. I take my seat and inhale the aroma of the tomato soup, my favorite. If I'm pregnant and will be gaining more weight anyway, maybe I will have some mashed potatoes.

"What's the occasion?" he asks.

I pick up my wine glass and hold it up. "I'd like to propose a toast to our first child." My glass hangs there in air for a long moment.

"First child?" His face clears as he stops focusing on the wine and looks into my face. "Eva, are you with child?"

I nod. "As near as I can figure, our baby will be here a month before our first anniversary."

"Our first child. That truly *is* good news!" Now he does lift his glass to clink against mine, and we sip the wine.

My heart and soul sing as we enjoy the meal and plan our future, just as I pictured it would be.

I write letters to Aunt Emily, my parents, Grandma Van, and even Uncle Paul's sweetheart, Phyllis, with whom I feel a special bond. They write back with effusive congratulations. I always share my letters with Teddy and he appears to enjoy them.

He receives letters every so often from his sisters in Glasgow, multiple pages that make him smile or frown or read thoughtfully. He never shares them. When I ask what Ethelwyn and Gladys have written, he only says, "They would like to meet you."

My initial tiredness lasts only a few weeks, and I am healthy and strong so I feel wonderful. Teddy continues to come home with a storm on his face, and I know he worries about money. I walk into downtown Napa, intent on finding a way to help our financial situation.

Napa is the county seat of Napa County, home to a glove factory and the new Magnavox Company. It is also home to more than twenty brothels around Clinton Street. I stay away from that end of town and enter the office of the Napa Valley Register to see if the newspaper needs a photographer. They turn me away.

Not far away on Second Street an empty building beckons. An idea, just a hope really, sparks in my mind. I rub at the dirty windows and try to peer inside. Turning to face the street, I survey the small businesses that dot both sides of Second Street and watch people walk along the storefronts. A new business could do well here. I go back to the newspaper office to find out who owns the empty storefront.

That afternoon, I am deep in dreams and plans for my own photography studio. Just putting the idea into coherent thought makes me giddy. I can feel Aunt Emily's supportive thoughts across the miles that physically separate us. From her, I have the creativity to think of this idea and the confidence to pursue it. Still, my hands shake as I dial the number the newspaper office has given me. A man answers.

I try to project a businesslike tone. "I'm calling about your office space on Second. I'd like to know what the rent is, please."

"Who wants to know?" The man's voice is rough and rude.

I swallow. "Eva Van—Eva Walters. I plan to open a photography studio there." Fool! He doesn't care what you do with the space!

He makes an unpleasant growling noise that might be laughter. "Well then, the rent is $75 a month. Can't have a broad makin' more money than me." More growling laughter.

"Thank you for your time, sir." That is much more money than we can afford.

What was I thinking? Teddy and I barely scrape together enough money to pay for groceries. With coffee now at forty-seven cents a pound, I have begun watering it down each morning. What fantasy was I living in, to think I could afford $75 a month for rent?

Rubbing my belly thoughtfully, I walk through the house with Suzanne at my heels. The second bedroom still sits empty. Soon we will prepare it for the baby. Until then, could I use the space for my studio? I walk to the window and bask in the weak sunshine of early spring. I could set up my camera so that this window lit the subject. I could put a chair there, maybe a small table for a desk. The developing could be done in the service porch with its ugly wash basin. My mind is afire once more. Like Aunt Emily, I will find a way.

That night as I set dinner on the table before my tired husband, I think more of my dreams than of his exhausting day. "Teddy, I can bring in extra money if I open a photography studio. I can use the baby's bedroom until late summer, then we can fix it up for the baby."

He holds the paper in front of his face, but he hears me. "The Russian Civil War may be over, but there is terrible famine in the country."

"We'll need the extra money for the baby," I continue. "I can take family portraits and baby photos. Those are quite popular now."

"The League of Nations is meeting in Paris, but the U.S. Senate voted against joining. They must think another war is coming." He laughs at the absurdity. "Haven't we just had the war to end all wars?"

"Teddy." I take the newspaper from him and fold it. Taking his hand, I wait until he is looking at me. I say softly, "I want to do this. It will help, and I want to do it."

He smiles, but it's a quick, grim smile. "It will help." His tone makes it sound as if we are teetering on the brink of disaster.

"We are in this marriage together," I tell him. "You must let me help where I can. I won't continue once the baby is born."

He nods. "All right, Eva."

I give him back the paper and pass the peas.

I hang pictures of Suzanne in my new studio, but the wife of the newspaper editor becomes my first paying client. I appealed to him for leads since I was unable to pay for an advertisement in the paper. He told me if his wife was happy the whole town would know it. She brings their six month old daughter in for a portrait. The baby fusses and won't sit without her mother. I convince her that a portrait of both of his girls together would delight her husband. It does, and my business launches successfully.

In August, Congress finally ratifies the 19th Amendment. This fall I will be busy with a baby, but for the first time every woman in America will be able to vote. I write to Grandma Van, sharing my pleasure with her. I hum to myself as I ponder the impact of voting women on our country and move carefully around my studio. I am quite large now, packing away my photography supplies to prepare for the imminent birth of the baby. Teddy hopes for a son to carry on the family name. I hope to keep him happy.

My photography efforts have produced enough money to buy a lovely bassinet, an infant bed to use when the baby is a bit older, and some baby clothes. Teddy brings home a wooden rocking chair that I am sure will see many hours of use. On September 10, I enter Victory Memorial Hospital. Much later, I emerge with Teddy's daughter. We name her Sheila and take her home.

For the entire year of 1921, I focus on home and family. If the world falls to global pandemic I wouldn't notice. Sheila's smile lights my day, rewarding me for the fussy nights, the long days with colic, the panic when I don't know what she needs. Despite my inexpert mothering, watching her grow soothes my soul.

Suzanne sniffs the new baby gently, although Teddy urges caution. He thinks Suzanne may get jealous and nip. Sheila seems to trigger some mothering instinct in the dog, though, because Suzanne never gets impatient. I take picture after picture of dog and baby, individually and together.

Money remains tight, but Teddy smiles more often than not when he comes through the door at night. After dinner, I bathe the baby, and he holds her for awhile in his chair by the fire. I take father-daughter pictures that show faces glowing with firelight. While Sheila sleeps, Teddy and I play chess by the fire. He usually beats me, but it doesn't matter.

Then Teddy comes home one night without a smile. I greet him with Suzanne at my heels and Sheila in my arms, but it doesn't help. He sits in his big chair, and I perch on the couch, waiting.

"You like it here in Napa, don't you?" he asks.

"It's where my family is," I say, clutching Sheila tightly.

"I've been offered a job with Pacific Gas and Electric in Vacaville. It's more money, but it means moving the family."

"Oh, Teddy, that's wonderful!" How could he imagine that I, who moved from Cholame to Santa Cruz to Inverness to Napa would have qualms about relocating again?

Now his excitement bubbles over. "They are building a big substation there. It will be the world's largest."

"How exciting!"

We move to Vacaville early in 1922. The new house, little more than a shack, sits in the middle of five acres of land, two of which belong to us. On the hill a swamp full of frogs tempts Suzanne. Teddy and I dream of planting fruit trees, building a barn, buying a cow and chickens and rabbits. I can hardly wait for spring to plant a garden, and I must have an almond tree. PG&E's tremendous substation still awaits completion when we arrive, so Teddy works as a gardener while they finish it. We busy ourselves settling in and fixing up the property as much as we can.

On April 16, we get a call from Aunt Marion. Grandma Van has passed away in Santa Cruz.

Chapter 30: Santa Cruz 1922

Emily Williams

It seems a shame to bury an icon on such a beautiful day. Then again, it seems Santa Cruz itself pays tribute to one of its longtime residents. The sky is clear and blue, the sun shines brightly, and a faintly salty breeze tickles our faces. Lil and I stand slightly apart. This is more my sister's family than mine, but Ellen VanValkenburgh was a woman I admired.

Evergreen Cemetery covers a forested hillside. From the road below, we walk through the filigree iron arch proclaiming the name of the cemetery and up the steep main path to the gravesite where Mrs. VanValkenburgh will be laid to rest next to her

second husband, buried here sixty years ago. Graves of Civil War soldiers and Chinese workers who built the railroad to Los Gatos lie here along with pioneer families. Wild berries and flowers cover the ground. This beautiful setting will be her last resting place.

The asthma I've had my entire life worsens now that I'm in my forties. It clenches my lungs like a fist, and I gasp and wheeze even from the slight exertion of the walk up a slight hill. Lil lays her hand on my arm in silent comfort. Many doctors have told me the illness is psychosomatic, but I know the steel bands that constrict my airways are real. I carry a kit, as I have for years, with an atomizer from Parke Davis & Co. The blue glass bulb has a tube and a pump that pushes air into my poor excuse for lungs. As soon as the service ends, I can retrieve it from the carriage.

The most prominent members of Santa Cruz society attend the funeral service at the Unitarian Church, but only family arrives here at the gravesite—family, Lil, and I. Mrs. VanValkenburgh's daughter, Ellie, and her husband stand with their children and grandchildren. Ellen's unmarried daughter, Marion, stands with Henry and Nina. My sister holds a handkerchief to her eyes, but Henry remains staunchly dry eyed, his arm around his wife. They have always been one person, the two of them. Their son, Carl, is twenty now. When we arrived, he told me he remembers climbing on these brick walls as a child when they visited his grandfather's grave with his Grandma Van. Eva and Edward are here with baby Sheila. At nineteen months she fidgets in Eva's arms but cannot yet walk steadily on her own over this uneven ground.

Eva stands nearest me, and I can hear her murmuring to her daughter. "This is for your great-grandmother, baby. She was a wonderfully strong woman like you will someday be. Honor and respect her memory and the things she was able to accomplish because she would have loved you so much." She kisses the baby's head, and Sheila subsides, listening to the soothing cadence of her mother's words.

At the bottom of the hill, Mrs. VanValkenburgh's only living sibling sits on a bench. L'Amie is too frail to climb to the gravesite. Two young men stand with her. I believe they are her sons. Her husband remains at their home in Los Gatos, too ill to make the trip over the hill to Santa Cruz. Two husbands, four siblings, countless cousins on both sides, and this is all that's left. Families are smaller now. None of Ellen's children or grandchildren have families of seven or more children as was common in her youth.

The family women here are a cross section of society. All are strong, independent women who have chosen their own paths. Ellen VanValkenburgh herself chose politics. Marion followed her. She was her mother's shadow, not as prominent but no less committed.

Ellen's other daughter, Ellie, reminds me of Nina. They both chose family over politics or career. Nina and Henry have a happy marriage. To all onlookers they are two halves of the same person. Ellie and her husband, James Henry Manor, have a similar relationship. To them, the power of a woman shows in how well she raises her family and keeps her home. It's as foreign an idea to me as my drive to build a successful career is to Nina. As women gain strength in society, I'm sure more careers will open to them. I like to think Lil and I paved the way.

The Unitarian minister finishes his words of ceremony and the family begins to disperse. With no parent or spouse of the deceased, no one immediately steps forward to take the lead. Marion is the oldest child, but Henry the only son. He tucks Nina's arm in his and leads the way down the steep path. The rest of the family follows. This death is not unexpected, but it will leave a hole in this family, and in this community.

When we are on the train, returning to San Francisco, Lil pulls out a sheet of paper that I recognize as a rough copy of the newsletter of the San Francisco Business and Professional Women's Club. "I knew you'd be deep in melancholy over the passing of Mrs. VanValkenburgh," she says. "So I saved this for now." She hands me the newsletter, folded open to show the latest advertisement for my business.

Like a dress, ready-made buildings are seldom made to fit
Architecturally designed dwellings mean real homes
A well-planned structure, whether a
concrete building or a week-end cabin,
should to the smallest detail, suit your individual needs.
Before you build
Consult
Emily Williams
1039A Broadway Street   San Francisco   Prospect 1606

I exclaim in delight. "Oh, Lil, it looks magnificent! That should attract the women of the club and make 1912 a banner year!"

"The rest of the newsletter isn't finished yet, so I don't know exactly when it will run." She begins talking about deadlines and design issues. The tiny lines at the corner of her eyes distract me, and the glint of silver in the errant curl that has once again escaped her bun. Our forties have settled onto us well. Lil truly enjoys she working on club business. I think it distracts her from the closing of The Palmer Shop. She still designs lamps, but out of a home studio like she did long ago.

The advertisement doesn't run in the club newsletter until March. I fume a bit at the delay but hide it from Lil. Once the newsletter goes out, I wait by the phone for a flood of commissions that never come. I build three houses in 1922, all in San Francisco but none as a result of the ad. All three commissions came from Mr. Lester Stevenson, the builder for all three clients. I am quite sure he has never set eyes on a newsletter for the San Francisco Business and Professional Women's Club.

Although I never speak of it, Lil senses my disappointment. We continue spending our summers in Santa Cruz at Wake Robin. Lil and I invite Club members for the weekend, and Lil places an advertisement in *The Business Woman* newsletter that touts the Santa Cruz mountains as a vacation place with "good climate and food, old clothes and easy hikes."

I don't discuss my health with Lil, although I'm sure she knows. I cannot abide how weak the asthmas attacks leave me, and Lil is gracious. She accepts I don't want to talk about it, and she cares for me without my asking.

Lil also assures me commissions for my work will pick up, but we both know my ill health won't allow me to do much. Architecture changes, too. Mrs. Lucie Chase wants me to design a home for her, but she wants something more modern than what I usually do. She prefers the prairie-style stucco to the shingled Craftsman bungalow. I've never worked in stucco. Associates from the businesswomen's club say that even Julia Morgan's commissions suffer as people's tastes change. It is scant comfort.

It begins to be difficult to move between Santa Cruz and San Francisco each season. My body seems ready to retire, but my mind is not. I am restless, unable to settle on a course of action that agrees with my nature. Once again, Lil knows without my telling her.

One evening in late August we return to Wake Robin after dining in Santa Cruz. The steep dirt road winds its dusty way to the cabin, but the view through the stately redwood trees makes the drive worth it. We park Lil's little car in the garage built into the side of the hill and walk through the wooden gate as we've done a thousand times before. Lil's workshop, dug into the hillside next to the garage, is locked up tight for the night. She must not have any pressing orders as she doesn't even look longingly in that direction. I am content to be here in this moment, with this person, but I sense Lil has something to say as she is deep in thought.

We walk up the hill along the stone-lined path and cross the patio. Many summer evenings have been spent out here with our guests in front of the outdoor fireplace, swinging on the lawn swing and chatting. I follow Lil through our tiny kitchen into my favorite room of the house. A huge stone fireplace dominates the room, and Lil's old grandfather clock hugs the far wall. Two cushioned alcoves line one side of the room, and I long to sink into one of them with a book from the overstuffed bookshelves. Our shoes click on the green linoleum floor as I cross to the chairs in front of the fireplace. A bearskin lies on the floor. I constantly turn its head away from my chair as I cannot look at its glassy gaze. Near the clock the window-paned double doors lead out to a spacious balcony. From there, we can watch the mountains all the way to the valley floor.

Lil heads upstairs to the bedroom. I hear her moving around, probably changing her clothes. The bedroom opens onto a balcony above the first-floor balcony.

I know Lil will say what she needs to say when the time feels right. Content, I return to the kitchen and make coffee. One of the many doctors I've had over the years recommended coffee for my asthma. I can't say it's had any remarkable effect, but I've certainly discovered a taste for it. I pour two mugs and carry them into the living room. The sun sets, and orange light tints the silhouette of the trees that surround our retreat.

Lil joins me as I set her mug on the table near her chair. She has, indeed, changed into a more comfortable gown. "Em, we've been together a long time," she begins.

Suddenly I don't want to discuss matters of great import. My eye fastens onto the Revolutionary War cannon ball that we use as a door stop. "You know, Lil, I love that story you tell about the cannon ball."

She frowns, but she knows me well and humors me. "My ancestors in Stonington, Connecticut had that ball shot through the wall of their house during the Revolutionary War. It stopped just short of damaging the grandfather clock."

The clock obliges by striking the hour, and we laugh. Our eyes meet and the laughs die away.

"We've been together a long time," I prompt her softly.

"Almost twenty-five wonderful years." Love fills her smile. "We should think about retirement."

My thoughts have run in this direction, too. "Yes, where should we retire?" I look around this lovely room and cannot imagine living anywhere else.

At the same time, we say, "Why not here?" and laugh. We love Wake Robin, but winters in the mountains are difficult.

"Los Gatos is closer to the cabin than San Francisco. How about there?" I suggest.

"Los Gatos is lovely, and an artistic community. Remember the copper fireplace hood I did for the fireplace at the

Los Gatos History Club?"

I nod, recalling what a big job that was. "Los Gatos would be a lovely place to retire. It's like Santa Cruz but not in the mountains.'

"Well, you'd better get busy on a design," she says with a lofty wave of her hand that makes us both laugh.

For each stage of my adult life, Lil has been there. As a student, a struggling architect, a traveler, she kept me company. She supports me when I need her, and I support her when she needs me. I cannot imagine spending my life with anyone else. As we head into this new phase, this retirement, the certainty that we will be together soothes any anxiety over how and where we live.

Chapter 31: Vacaville 1926
Eva Walters

The days are always sunny in Vacaville. Teddy loves his job at the Vaca-Dixon substation, and I enjoy bringing the children to pick him up after work every day. Sheila runs ahead, singing the alphabet. She will be six years old in September, and will begin school in the Vaca Valley Union School District.

Those six years have flown by. I understand why women are still not prevalent in politics. They are much too busy raising the children. With laundry, cooking, playing, and refereeing squabbles, I have little time for photography, and I'm too busy to miss it. I know I can pick it up again once my children grow a bit. My focus has, of necessity, been on Sheila and her sister, Rosemary, now three years old. When Eddie was born almost two years ago, he completed our family. Edward Lowell Walters may be the apple of my eye, but he represents the future of his father's family.

Sheila skips up the steps, still singing, "...L-m-n-o-p...q-r-s..."

Rosemary runs after her sister, chubby legs struggling with the painted steps to the PG&E building. "Mo," I call, "be careful of the steps. They are quite slippery." They all know this. Teddy and I tell them every day.

Eddie struggles in my arms and I put him down, balancing him carefully and holding onto both of his hands. I allow him to walk a few steps forward on his unsteady legs before I scoop him back up and hurry after the girls.

Inside, Teddy sits at a desk in front of a whole panel of dials. The display fascinates the girls, but as usual he only has eyes for Eddie. I purse my lips to avoid chastising him because he doesn't understand why it's just as important to talk to his daughters. Taking his son from my arms, Teddy bounces the boy on his lap and finishes the daily log of readings from the dials. Even at this young age, I see resemblance. Teddy's brown hair thins and his son's grows in. Both have the piercing blue eyes that see deep into a person's soul.

"These dials help me keep the electrical load up to a certain number of kilovolts," Teddy tells the children. "I prevent blackouts as far away as Oakland."

"They're pretty, Daddy," Sheila says, her eyes bright and curious as she looks at the dials.

Teddy puts down his pencil and tickles Eddie. "How's my boy today?"

He completely ignores Sheila, and I frown. Rosemary stands forgotten on the far side of her father's chair. "Mo, come here, sweetheart," I say. She obliges, her eyes big and somber.

Teddy sees nothing wrong with his indulgence of Eddie. A man's son links him to future generations. A man's son carries on the family name. Every other family member must dote on the son and raise him up to be a fine man. In our household, we also have two fine daughters. I must make sure they are not totally pushed aside. Aunt Emily and Aunt Lil will help me, and even Mama favors my daughters.

When we arrive home, I send Sheila to wash her hands for dinner and help Rosemary wash hers. Teddy sits at the kitchen table with Eddie on his lap. I show him a letter that came from Phyllis. I suppose I should call her Aunt Phyllis since she marries my Uncle Paul this month, but the notion causes hysteria to bubble forth. Uncle Paul may be my youngest uncle, only six years older than me, but his new wife is younger than me, and we have become as close as distance will allow.

Dear Eva,

August is simply sweltering in New York, but Mama insists I be married at her home. Paul has been wonderful, of course, but I wish you and Ed could be here. I know it is a terrible journey with three small children, but you are in my thoughts. I laugh to think after tomorrow I will have a niece who is older than I! You must address me as 'Aunt Phyllis' when we next meet. Oh, that has made me laugh so hard I spilled my tea! I hope you are laughing also and know that I will never allow you to address me so. I should feel so old!

When we return to San Jose, Paul and I shall take up residence with his mother at the family home on Third Street. He will continue his banking there and his civic duties in the city. While here in New York, he has joined a new order that intends to move its headquarters to San Jose next year. Well, I shouldn't call it new — it is merely new to me. It has a long Latin name but is most commonly call the Rosicrucian Order and is a worldwide organization. It's not a religious order, more academic. It sounds like it would appeal to Teddy. Paul can tell you more about it when we see you.

Love,

Phyllis

I cannot answer Phyllis's letter before she returns to San Jose, but I am intrigued by this Rosicrucian Order she says will appeal to Teddy. I tie my apron over my dress and begin dinner as he reads. When he looks up from the letter, his face is thoughtful.

"Have you heard of the Rosicrucians, Teddy?"

"I have, actually. I read an article about them not long ago. Some very prominent people throughout history have been members, like Leonardo da Vinci and Francis Bacon."

"Art and science? Quite intellectual then."

Something in my tone makes him smile. "Women can be members, too, Eva. The Rosicrucians do not discriminate on religion or race, either. All members are equal."

I remember back to the time he told me about being teased for his brogue. He vowed to treat all people fairly after that. I wonder if he doesn't see his daughters as people. Maybe he will when they are grown. "It sounds like an organization we should check into."

The girls enter the kitchen, scrubbed and sweet and ready for dinner. Their hands may not be as clean as I like them, but I'd rather give Sheila self-confidence. A normal family dinner soon follows, with Teddy talking to Eddie as I feed him, Rosemary and Sheila piping in.

In November, Teddy and I take the children to Castro Valley to visit my parents. As with any such trip, we stop first at the Nut Tree in Vacaville for frosted honey cookies. It is a treat for special occasions, and the girls are thrilled. At barely three, Eddie shows interest in whatever his sisters like. Even so, his fierce independence means he makes his own decisions. They dote on him, but they draw the line at sharing their cookies with him after he gobbles down his own.

We intend to spend Thanksgiving on the farm. My parents enjoy visits from their grandchildren, and Teddy wants to talk to my father about the Rosicrucian Order. There will be a huge traditional meal and lots of family. Carl will be there with the woman he married, Alice. A great deal older than my brother, older even than I, she has three sons from a previous marriage, all older than my children. It makes holidays awkward to be around them. Since my three are closer in age than Carl and I, I hope they will fare better. In her letters, Aunt Emily assures me they will. She remains close to her sisters and her brother Ed, less so to Paul, who is so much younger.

The three older boys lead my children on wild adventures that cause my heart to take up residence in my throat. They climb on farm wagons and race through the almond trees, Sheila and Rosemary screaming and racing after them and little Eddie valiantly trying to keep up on his chubby legs.

"They're fine," my brother says. "They won't hurt the little ones."

"I worry for Eddie. He's too little to follow them everywhere."

"Sheila will watch him," Teddy says.

I am not convinced, but I defer to Teddy as has become my habit. I can give in with as much grace as I can muster, or I can create a battleground within the walls of our house. I believe that Teddy gives in too, sometimes, and that keeps the balance in our marriage.

Alice and I help Mama with the turkey and stuffing, the mashed potatoes and cranberry sauce, the rolls and green beans. The smell of the turkey, the best part of the holiday, permeates the house, the spicy fresh pumpkin pie with it. I am impressed that Alice helps despite being dressed in a fine new flapper-style dress and fancy cloche hat. I cannot afford the latest fashion, or even the ones just past. My dress comes from the first years of our marriage, and I feel fat and outdated next to her slim silhouette.

After the meal, the adults sit on the porch unable to move and the children restrict their activity to a small area of yard near the house. Alice's boys have cast iron cars to play with, and real glass marbles. I worry that Eddie will put the marbles in his mouth, but he seems more fascinated by the cars. One of the boys tries to teach Sheila and Rosemary to shoot marbles.

The adult conversation skims over the opening of the Holland Tunnel from New York to New Jersey, last May's flight across the Atlantic by Charles Lindbergh, and the beginning of a project called Mt. Rushmore. They plan to carve four presidents' heads out of granite. Teddy seems very well versed in the events of the day, much more so than Carl or my father, but he seems distracted. Finally he broaches the subject of the Rosicrucian Order.

"Eva and I plan to join a new organization," he says. Mama and Papa look mildly interested. I smile, knowing they are expecting something like a civic club. "The Rosicrucian Order has been around for centuries and teaches philosophical concepts from Egypt, Greece, India, and the Arab world."

Carl laughs, dismissing it. "Nothing from northern Europe is important then?"

Papa looks confused but intrigued. "It's a religion?"

"No, sir, it's not a religion. Carl, the teachings include much from the Renaissance. It's an academic society, pledged to cull the best philosophies from the world's history."

Papa nods. Alice and Mama talk quietly about Alice's new Hoover Cleaner. I cannot sit and listen to her talk casually about things I will never be able to afford. Nor can I listen to my husband talk about us joining the Rosicrucians. Sometimes it seems that my mind is the only part of me that measures up to Teddy's expectations. I am certainly not the best cook or housekeeper. Suddenly the role of happy housewife chafes.

I excuse myself and fetch my camera from my luggage. Over the years I have taken thousands of pictures but not replaced the camera as often as I'd like to. The early evening light colors the yard, and I snap pictures of the old farm cart with Eddie perched on it. I try to take one of the kids playing marbles, but they won't hold still long enough. I revert to my favorite subject—the bare almond trees sleeping until spring. Leaning against the familiar friend of an almond tree, the sturdy trunk caressing my back, I realize that all my dreams have been overseen by almond trees. I used to sit here and wish for a knight in shining armor to ride up and sweep me away. Here I read novels of great adventure and wished for my own. I waited for letters from Teddy and read them with a rapidly beating heart. And here I try to convince myself that my life is full enough.

My heart no longer beats as rapidly for my husband. Still a fine man, my intellectual equal, we are compatible. I recently read *Without Dogma* by Henryk Sienkiewicz, a sort of a biography of a fictional character. A book written in that style makes the hero sound so conceited, but the book interests me because the hero is a sort like my husband. I don't believe Teddy devoid of moral principles, but he does seem to lack a lasting purpose in life. The hero in the book battles for his very soul but he lacks dogma, by which I believe the author means more than religious beliefs. Most importantly, the hero is a complex man with good and bad struggling inside him.

Does it sound conceited of me to say I can understand his nature since I am sensitive and sympathetic myself? Ever since my teens I have felt I would someday write a book. I have never read a great philosophical book by a woman — not novels but real stories of a soul. So far I have never had the good fortune to enjoy one, although I'm sure some exist. A woman's sphere of life is such, with the petty details to fret and worry them, that it is hard for them to think in a large way or even think at all. Their energy is consumed with daily life. I know few women who think and have fine souls. My friends are of that type — the people who see the real me are Without Dogma. They have to be or I would shock them.

I am thirty-seven years old, married to a fine man. My soul has grown more during my marriage than in all the preceding years. If girlish daydreams of Prince Charming and true passionate love must be dashed, it should be with a man like my Teddy. I remember thinking if I ever found a man as good as my father I would marry him. I am fortunate that Teddy possesses a far finer intellect and expresses a far finer soul. With maturity I can see many mistaken ideas my father clings to. I expect my children to see as many mental faults in their parents, though. Those who keep a young mind remain fortunate indeed!

The next generation's young minds begin clamoring over some hugely important affront to one of their egos. I am the closest adult, and I rush to rescue whoever is so maligned. Alice's boys disappear. Sheila holds one of Eddie's hands and Rosemary holds the other. Tears well in my son's blue eyes and stream down his face. I sink to my knees and gather him into my arms. "What happened?" I ask the girls.

"He was playing, Mommy," Rosemary offers.

"The other boys took their car back. He wasn't hurting it, really." Sheila's face shows outrage at her brother's treatment. "He was playing nice with it, and we were playing marbles and all of a sudden they *swooped* in and took the car away."

I hide a smile in Edward's brown hair. Her newest word, *swooped*, gets as much use as she can manage. "Well, no harm done, my darling. You come with Mommy now."

Much too grown up to want to stay in my arms, he struggles to be free. I firmly catch one of his hands and use the other to gather the girls. "Let's go on into the house now, all right?"

Once more my camera hangs around my neck, patiently waiting for my attention, as yet again my life intrudes on my dreams. I know that joining the Rosicrucian Order with Teddy will give us a joint interest, something we can be passionate about together. I know, too, that as the children grow they will need me less, and I will have more time for myself and my art. In the meantime, I must enjoy every precious moment.

Walters farm in Vacaville

Chapter 32: Vacaville 1936-1938

Eva Walters

The Great Depression tries to defeat us, but we rise above it. My family has helped each other through tough times before, spiritually, emotionally, and financially. We will band together and overcome this. Aunt Emily and Aunt Lil rent out their Los Gatos property and are living at Wake Robin full time with Uncle Ed. Teddy and I add on to our modest farmhouse, almost doubling it in size. I sell chickens to bring in a little money.

It hasn't all been gloom and doom. Teddy's sisters visit us from Glasgow. He was so worried about the heat in Vacaville that   we purchase a tiny cabin near Tomales Bay. It feels wonderful to be back in Inverness again, and to share it with my children. Ethelwyn and Gladys are quite the inspiration for my girls.

While neither ever married, they are both doctors. They travel to New York by ship and take a train to Dixon, California where we meet them with the car. Such a different journey than Grandma Van made so long ago!

Sheila's eyes light up as the older women tell tales of growing up in Scotland, and of choosing career over family.

"Not unlike my Aunt Emily," I remind them.

"Mom, Aunt Emily was an architect," Sheila says. "Aunt Ethelwyn and Aunt Gladys are *doctors*. They had to go to a lot of college in order to realize their dream."

"Emily went to Stanford and University of the Pacific as well as the California School for Mechanical Arts. She is very well educated."

"That couldn't have been easy if Grandpa Williams was anything like Daddy," she scoffs.

I don't know what to say. Teddy has steadfastly refused to consider college for either of his girls. Before I can respond, Rosemary does.

"Sheila, you only want what you can't have. If Daddy had forbidden you to have a family, you'd be dating every boy at school."

A storm crosses my elder daughter's face. "Mo, that is not true." She clenches her hands into fists, then forcibly relaxes them. "I have a passion to teach."

Gladys leans forward and takes Sheila's hand. Her eyes are locked on my daughter's. She is about to impart the wisdom of the ages, and I hope Sheila hears it through her anger at her sister. "My dear, you must follow your heart. Today you dream of teaching. That may be where you go, but it may also be a passing fancy. What's important is that your parents have raised you to be strong and independent. Use those traits to their fullest."

I see the anger drain from my daughter as her aunt's words sink in. Rosemary, on the other hand, remains agitated. "But Aunt Gladys, what if our only dream is to be the best wife and mother we can be?"

Gladys turns to her with a warm smile. "Then that's what you should do, Mo. Guiding a child to their independence is as difficult as being a doctor." She turns her smile on me.

Warmed by her regard, I look out over Tomales Bay. I don't see the calm water or tree-lined shore, nor do I see Eddie's little sailboat pulled up on the beach. In my mind's eye, I see all the women in my family and the choices they made: politics, career, family. They taught me that I have the right to choose the life I want to live. All of them have contributed to the future generations of our family and our country.

Rosemary and Sheila, once again friends, walk along the shore deep in conversation. Ethelwyn and Gladys sit in silence, watching the lake doze. In the distance, I hear my husband and my son preparing to launch the sailboat. I wish life like this could last forever.

Of course, it doesn't. Teddy's sisters return to Glasgow,

and we return to Vacaville. By scrimping and selling a few more chickens, we are able to keep the cabin and use it to escape the heat of a Vacaville summer. I enjoy seeing my family play in the water, run along the beach, and sail the boat. In Vacaville, their summer faces are red and listless, tendrils of sweaty hair clinging to their faces. At the cabin, we are happy.

I still think of them as children, but Sheila and Rosemary take the bus to the high school in town, and Eddie graduates from eighth grade in just a few months. With them almost completely independent, Teddy seems to think I should spend more time cleaning the house. After nineteen years of marriage he should know better. I'm more likely to be sitting under the almond tree reading a book than dusting. My dreams these days are for my children's futures and to spend more time with my photography.

The mail truck rumbles down the lane, raising dust to choke people and chickens alike. Even our cow, Bessie, moves away from the fence. I rise and take the packet of letters from the mailman and exchange pleasantries about the weather, always hot and dusty. I spot an envelope that will be of interest to Teddy, and as soon as I've waved the mailman on his way, I rush inside to place the letter on the mantel where he will see it tonight when he gets home.

Teddy and I are still active in the Rosicrucian Order, and we attend the annual international convention in San Jose every year. I enjoy meeting people from all over the world and attending the seminars. I relish challenging my brain at these events. Teddy helps to greet international guests, and he often corresponds with them long after they return home. This latest envelope comes from Jamaica. I can hardly wait to cut the colorful stamp off the envelope and add it to my collection.

That night after dinner, Teddy relaxes in his chair by the fireplace, which of course stays unlit most of the year. He opens the letter and reads it to himself. I know he will share bits if he is so inclined, and I am content to watch his face. He is almost completely bald now, and his glasses perch on a rounded nose. His blue eyes have paled, but they are no less striking than they were in his youth.

"He marvels that at home in Jamaica people treat him like dirt, but in San Jose he was an honored international guest," he offers.

"He doesn't think a black man can be treated with honor?" I ask.

"No, that's not it. I think he is thanking us for the hospitality and wishing there was more of it in his home country."

Through the open doorway, I can see that Eddie and Rosemary are studying at the kitchen table. Sheila's books remain closed. I am proud of Eddie's diligence. Both his sisters lost their focus for a while when they were close to eighth grade graduation. Sheila, too, will graduate this year, from high school. I assume she wants to talk to Teddy again about college and that's why her books are closed.

Teddy and I open our own books to read, but my mind doesn't see the words on the page. It listens for Sheila, still in the kitchen, to gather her nerve. Finally I hear the kitchen chair scrape the floor as she pushes it back, and she stands in the doorway.

She is tall for seventeen, although she says 'eighteen in the fall' when asked her age. Her curly brown hair and laughing eyes are reminiscent of my own, although I didn't cut my hair that short until I was wed. She clasps her hands behind her back, and her feet twitch. I wish she hadn't chosen to wear Eddie's work trousers for this encounter. She's taken to wearing the pants around the house almost exclusively, although she still wears a proper dress to school and town. I've probably been a poor role model for this, since I have discovered delight in wearing Teddy's overalls in the garden.

"Daddy, may I speak with you?"

He looks up at her and closes his book. "Of course."

She takes a deep breath and charges ahead like a locomotive. "I would like to be a teacher. San Jose State College offers the courses, and I could live with Aunt Phyllis and Uncle Paul."

"You've already discussed this with the Williams family?" He responds to her, but his eyes are on me.

She resolutely keeps her eyes on her father and her chin up. "No, I haven't."

"We've already had this conversation. Why are you bringing it up again?" His eyes return to his daughter, his eldest child, whom he refuses to send to college. Money must be saved for Eddie when his time comes to go.

Teddy has assimilated the mulishness of a Scot. My family came from England also, hundreds of years ago, so tough pioneer stock runs in my veins. Sheila, therefore, is doubly determined.

"It doesn't matter to me how you feel about women's rights, Daddy. What matters to me is my education. In this day and age, I cannot sit by and embroider pillowcases when I want to teach."

I admire the certainty in her tone. For the first time as she discusses this, she remains calm. I close my book. "She comes from a family of well-educated women, Teddy. It would be strange if she did not go to college." Sheila darts a grateful glance at me.

"And how are we to pay for this whim?" His tone chills the room.

I have never heard anyone describe an education as a whim. Determined to help Sheila before, now I will move mountains to do so. "We have been discussing moving in to town," I remind him.

"Yes," he nods, "it will be easier for Eddie to attend the high school."

I try not to grit my teeth. Sheila took the bus for four

years, and Rosemary has just finished her first year of riding the bus into town for school. "So why not move this summer as planned? I will open a photography studio to pay for Sheila's college." I hold my breath and pray for Teddy's reasonable streak to assert itself.

He looks at me long and hard, his eyes suspicious. Finally he throws up his hands and shakes his head. "It's a poor thing indeed when a man loses control of his household, but fine. Send her to school. I'll not pay a penny of it."

I slowly exhale. I can count on the fingers of one hand the times Teddy lets me win on big arguments.

Sheila runs to him and kisses him on the cheek. "Thank you, Daddy! I will work hard, I promise!"

She runs back into the kitchen, where Eddie and Rosemary's ears must have grown large so they could listen. Now excited but hushed chatter breaks out.

"I will make an offer tomorrow on that house in town," Teddy says without looking at me.

I marvel that this intelligent man can be so foolish when it comes to education for women. I nod and don't say any more. Women won in our household tonight, and there's no use rubbing his nose in it.

One thing about Teddy, when he decides on something he moves forward. Before the month ends we are the proud owners of 307 West Street, just a block or so off Main Street, in Vacaville. Without being asked, Teddy moves my photography equipment into the detached garage at the back of the property. By the time the children and I arrive for inspection of the premises, my darling husband has hung a sign in the yard that says 'Photography Studio.' It's plain, but painted with love. My heart runs over as I hug him.

Eddie will have his own room, and Sheila will share with Rosemary until she moves to San Jose in the fall. She immediately sends off her acceptance in case her father changes his mind, and she's already a college student in her head. I am content, living in town. Eddie gets a summer job at the Nut Tree Restaurant. He is proud as a peacock of the money he earns, and we insist that it is his money, not to be used to assist us with household expenses. Frugally he stashes it away for the future as his father looks on approvingly.

I arrange my photograph albums and chemicals, hang my sample portraits, and open my studio. Once more I take pictures of families and sweethearts and babies. The darkroom becomes more than my workplace. It's where my art sings. When I'm developing film, I understand how Aunt Emily feels when she sees a house being built from her design. It's not unlike Mama watching her children grow. I'm somewhere between the two. I don't feel complete when my life lacks photography, but I cannot be without my children, either.

In early September, Teddy drives Sheila to San Jose with her trunk packed. I accompany them. Our daughter will live with Phyllis and Paul for the first year, at least. They great her with open arms and smiles.

"Oh, Sheila, it will be wonderful to have another woman in the house!" Phyllis cries as she leads us inside.

Teddy stays outside to talk with Uncle Paul, and the three Williams sons stay, too. Phyllis's eldest son is called Paul for his father. He's eighteen like Sheila, but headed to Berkeley. The middle son, Edwin, and the youngest, Waldo, are still in school. I'm sure Phyllis will appreciate Sheila's help with them.

"I'm excited to be here, Aunt Phyllis," Sheila responds. Technically, she should say great aunt. I never dared have Sheila call her that any more than I would dare call her Aunt.

"Thank you, Phyllis, for making this possible for her," I say.

She turns to look at me. "Sheila, darling, why don't you go on in to the kitchen? I baked some cookies and want to make sure you get some before those boys get at them."

Sheila's smart enough to know Phyllis has something private to say, but she nods and leaves the room. Phyllis lays a hand on my arm. "Eva, are you certain Edward hasn't changed his mind about paying for her college?"

"No, he won't. He's a stubborn Scotsman on this one."

"I never liked him," Phyllis says. "His arrogance knows no bounds."

He *is* arrogant. What am I to say to that? "He has agreed to let her go," I murmur.

"You would have enrolled her if you had to hitchhike the

entire distance to San Jose," Phyllis hisses. "You are just as stubborn as Edward, and you know it."

"True," I admit with a grin. Then suddenly we are both laughing and Sheila returns with extra cookies for us.

The ride home in the car is silent. I refuse to speak of our daughter and her college education, and he refuses to admit her happiness pleases him. I watch the miles of golden farmland pass by and dream of the photographs I will sell in my studio over the next four years.

At Putah Creek, Vacaville: Aunt Gladys, Sheila, Aunt Ethelwyn, family friend John Hukkalah, Eddie, Teddy, Rosemary. Eva, of course, took the picture.

Chapter 33: Vacaville 1938-1941

Eva Walters

The detached garage has been customized for its new purpose. It is part studio where clients can feel comfortable while I adjust the light and catch their likeness forever in film; part shop where images of Vacaville, Putah Creek and the Nut Tree can be had for a small price as postcards or framed prints; and part darkroom, where the magic really happens. I have made up business cards with my name in Gothic lettering right in the middle 'Mrs. E. J. Walters' and just below in bold capitals, 'Portraits.' I have the address on the lower right in a more discreet size, and 'phone 352 for appointments' on the lower left. I feel quite the professional, with babies and brides as my subjects. Business remains steady, and a year passes much too quickly.

Eddie settles in at the high school where Rosemary

ignores him. Phyllis pens glowing reports of Sheila, who stays too busy to write. Teddy still works at the Vaca-Dixon substation, but he drives himself to work. The children and I are too busy with our own lives to run up the painted steps to collect him.

In September of 1939, Germany invades Poland and overnight Europe is at war. I want to hold Eddie close and never let him out of the house, but that is not a mother's patriotic duty.

"All my correspondents through the Rosicrucians say the U.S. will be in the war by the end of 1940," Teddy says one evening.

Outside, November cold chills the air. Inside the fire cheers me more than his words. "I continue to pray that is not so," I say.

"Eddie will serve proudly as I did."

"I can only pray he sees the same amount of action."

A grunt follows that statement, and Teddy returns to his newspaper.

By the first of the year, Sheila finds a roommate in San Jose and moves out of Phyllis and Paul's house. She lives close enough to visit, and for them to watch over her as needed. Rosemary meets a fine young man, a walnut rancher near Woodland. Eddie talks of becoming a teacher. The war stays in Europe and doesn't intrude upon my family.

As parents, we make plans for our children then help them with their own plans as they become adults. No one ever plans for war. I hold my breath well into 1941, going about the business of ignoring a threat I cannot shoo away on my own. I take pictures of idyllic scenery and cooing babies and try not to think of war. Eddie and his school friends, though, boast about the damage they will do to Krauts and Japs when they graduate, and I shudder, shouting at them to watch what they say.

In June, Rosemary graduates from Vacaville High School. She has no desire to go to college, and her graduation becomes just another day in her life, just another school year ending for summer break. I try to make it special with an almond cake and words of pride, but she only has eyes for her walnut rancher.

When you wait two years with bated breath, it is almost a relief to be confronted with the demon you prayed to hold off. On December 7, 1941, every son's mother in America has her world shattered. The Japanese attack Pearl Harbor and our sons beg to enlist. Rosemary's young man manages to be among the first from Vacaville to do so.

"A lot of my friends are enlisting," Eddie says. His eyes are bright. Why can't he see how my heart breaks?

"You aren't eighteen," Teddy tells him. He sits in his chair in the parlor, newspaper obscuring his face.

"But you can sign for me. Please?"

He puts the paper down for a moment. "Son, I admire your wish to serve, and I am proud of you. Best to get your high school diploma first. You're in your senior year. We'll have this conversation again when you graduate in June. Fair enough?"

"Yes, sir." His lip quivers like it did when he was six.

For the moment, we push war out of our home, and I sigh with relief. We cannot escape it entirely, though. War talk overshadows everything we do and say. Mamas bring their sons in to my studio to take portraits before they ship out. I also take pictures of sweethearts for the fresh new soldiers to take with them. I am so proud of these young men coming forward to serve our country in its hour of need. I am proud, too, that Eddie wants to be one of them, but I am so worried. I have never been the sort of mother who holds her children back from potentially dangerous situations. All three of them waded in the creek, climbed trees, played in the orchards, and worked with all sorts of animals. This is just another danger Eddie will overcome but a much bigger threat. A brick settles in my stomach.

In January, the Japanese capture Manila, and President Roosevelt promises more aid to Britain, including planes and troops. Eddie reads nothing but the newspapers and his textbooks. Rosemary spends every waking moment talking to or thinking about her young rancher, Michael Chicconi. She cooks and cares for the house, keeping herself busy as she waits. I have no idea where her inspiration comes from, but she is a much better cook and housekeeper than I am, and I am proud of her.

Sheila begins her final semester of college and starts thinking about her fifth year, planning to get a credential to teach Physical Education to high school students. She is athletic, so teaching P.E. seems a fit. She has the solid square build she inherited from me and short curly locks like my own. She even has her own pair of overalls while I still borrow Teddy's. A lot of friends surround her in San Jose, young men and women alike. I don't know if her future plans include marriage, but I know it's not important.

In March a particularly cold and windy storm buffets Vacaville, even more brutal because it echoes the dread in our souls. Eddie receives passing marks on his exams, and Rosemary bakes Grandma Van's vanilla almond cake recipe for the first time by herself. It tastes better even than my own attempts. Sheila seems to be in her own world, motoring toward graduation with nary a care. Maybe it's because she doesn't have a young man to worry over, but maybe she's focused and determined like her ancestors. Britain now rations coal, and I worry for Teddy's sisters, now retired and living on the Isle of Man.

In June, amidst Eddie's graduation from Vacaville High School and Sheila's graduation from San Jose State College, Aunt Emily passes away. leaving Aunt Lil bereft. They have long since retired to a house on Whitney Avenue in Los Gatos, after a fire burned Wake Robin to the ground with all their papers and possessions inside. At the funeral, I am surprised when Aunt Lil tells me I was to be my aunt's beneficiary if Lil passed first. It warms my heart to realize I was so important to my favorite aunt. Her person will be missed, but what she has taught me will be passed on to my children and their children.

I am unable to offer Aunt Lil much in the way of condolence, caught up as I am in the midst of our own celebration and pending tragedy. Sheila will begin her fifth year at the college in the fall, and Eddie still insists on enlisting. The papers are full of news that that Jews are being arrested in Europe, but my mind cannot even take it in. I watch Eddie closely as he reads the paper, helps his father in the yard, or listens to the radio. I am consciously storing up memories.

I am very proud of the adults all my children are becoming. Sheila is tough and independent. Rosemary is sweet and determined to wait for Michael, or Chic as she calls him. Eddie struggles with school but talks about some day becoming a teacher like his sister. After graduation, he approaches his father again about enlisting.

We sit once more before the unlit fireplace. Echoes of Sheila's determination to go to college ring in the room as Eddie stands before his father.

"You are not yet eighteen," Teddy says, but he doesn't sound as firm as he did in December.

"I must serve my country." Eddie stands tall, as if already a soldier at attention.

I remember this need in Teddy. I remember this mixture of pride and terror in my heart. With deep dread, I accept what I know comes next.

Teddy nods. "I know, son, and I am proud of you. Have you considered which branch?"

"Navy, sir."

Navy. A boy from the landlocked town of Vacaville wants to sail the ocean blue. I admire his courage and determination.

Teddy nods. "Your mother and I give our permission for you to enlist."

My heart drops into my stomach as Eddie's face lights up. It is the right thing to do. I smile at my son and hug him back when he thanks me. Deep inside, the selfish part of a mother's soul, the one you never speak of to anyone, wants someone's else's son to fight the wars.

Eddie enlists and wears his new uniform to his sister's college graduation only two weeks later. Sheila beams with delight, and I'm sure my expression mirrors hers. Presented with a *fait accompli,* Teddy graciously congratulates his daughter and tells her he is proud of her. Her eyes, though, thank me. The music and the procession and the smiles of the graduates are all full of hope and new beginnings, but most of these young men will leave for boot camp as soon as the caps and gowns come off. These smiling girls will be left home to wring their hands over boyfriends and brothers, wondering if they will come home at all. Today, however, we push the world away and celebrate their accomplishment. I cheer and clap, my heart full of joy.

The summer passes in a haze of days at Putah Creek, where my young children used to play and my adult children still like to congregate in summer. They hold long conversations while sitting on a rock and dangling their feet in the water. The shade trees above them make dancing shadows on the water. I take roll after roll of pictures as Teddy and I watch and wait. For once, words are not needed between us, and we spend hours sitting next to each other on the porch swing, holding hands. I am very conscious of the new generation taking over. As a member of the older generation it is time for my husband and me to step aside and provide more of a supportive role as our children set forth into the world. I suppose all mothers faced with this stage of their children's lives wish the world was a more welcoming place.

Sheila's fifth year credential program starts in September and she strides into the midst of the would-be teachers like a conquering hero, never looking back. I know she will be the best high school P.E. teacher San Jose State College has ever turned out. She may well be the only one whose education was financed by her mother's photography.

Rosemary masters embroidery and starts filling her hope chest. She tucks into the top of the chest the letters she receives weekly from Chic. She hums happily as she plays house in my home, and I pray Chic comes home to her.

On October 8, 1942, Eddie turns eighteen and ships out from San Francisco that very day. Teddy and I see him off. I watch his ship sail toward the Golden Gate with tears streaming down my face.

Edward 'Eddie' Walters and his father, Edward 'Teddy' Walters

Eddie with his mother, Eva Walters

Chapter 34: Saratoga 1971

Eva Walters

Thanksgiving always means more than giving thanks. It's a time to reflect on what your life has become and how it arrived at this place. From the window of my apartment at Casa Del Rey retirement home in Santa Cruz, I watch the seagulls soar over the ocean, screaming at another generation of sunbathers on the beach.

This morning my friend, Marvin, has joined me for a quick game of cards. He likes to play Old Maid and tease me, but I assert seventy-seven is old only in body, not in mind. "Now eighty-two," I tell him, "is ancient." He shakes his head and laughs. He is, of course, eighty-two.

A knock sounds on the door and I freeze. Our eyes meet. I am not allowed to have a gentleman caller in my room. "Hurry,"

I whisper, "into the bathroom."

Marvin groans as he stands and grasps his walker firmly. At his first step, the walker scrapes across the floor and his knee creaks loud enough to wake Maisie next door, napping without her hearing aids. Silence from the other side of my door, then another knock. I motion urgently to Marvin. He takes two quick steps that are about as big as the slow one he took initially.

"Old man," I mutter, trying to temper it with a grin. Maisie had a man in her room last week and management fined her $100. That's a lot of money on my Social Security. Management seems determined there will be no shenanigans at this retirement hotel. It's cheap, or I would move. Not that I approve of shenanigans, but I've never considered a game of cards to be in that category.

Marvin reaches the bathroom door before the knocking increases to a staccato demand. Leaving my friend to deal with getting himself hidden, I cross the small spartan room to open it.

"Mom! I was getting worried." It's Eddie, quick to greet me with a kiss to my cheek. I wonder if he can hear my thumping heartbeat.

Eddie's fourteen year old daughter, Linda, carries a book. She waves at me, endures my hug, and plops down in the nearest chair to read. Her dark hair drops in waves to her shoulders, and her blue eyes are Teddy's. Her twelve-year-old brother, Scott, fulfills Teddy's desire for the family name to continue. His hair is curlier and reddish, but his eyes are green like his mother's. Freckles dance across his face, giving him an impish air. Since I lost Teddy four years ago, all the fondness I felt for him manifests itself in my youngest grandson.

"Hi, Grandma," he says. I am clearly not a twelve-year-old's favorite person.

"Happy Thanksgiving, Scott." I kiss him anyway. I have that right. I glance from my son to the bathroom. "Is it that time already, Eddie?" He is here to pick me up for a Thanksgiving dinner at his house, but it's surely too early.

"Mom?" His gaze follows mine, and he frowns. "You wanted to eat early. Gerry says it will be done at 4:00."

"Marvin, you can come out. It's just my son," I call toward the bathroom. "Oh, yes," I say to my son. I remember now. I dislike returning over the hill to Santa Cruz after dark, even if Eddie is driving.

Marvin shuffles out, nodding as I introduce him to my son. My granddaughter's attention has strayed from her book. I hear her mutter, "Great. My grandmother has a boyfriend and I don't."

"Better be going," Marvin says. He actually hasn't stopped moving toward the door since he left the bathroom. I am proud when my grandson opens the door to let Marvin hobble out.

"Come on, Mom. Turkey's in the oven and we don't want to be late for dinner." He takes my arm and motions for the kids to precede us.

"She'll serve on time even if we aren't there," I mutter,

making him look even more uncomfortable. "Let me get my purse."

Before long I am seated next to Eddie in his fancy Dodge Dart Swinger. The kids slump in the back. "Sit up straight," I tell them, then bite my tongue. It's not my place any more to correct children.

"You've got seat belts on, right kids?" Eddie says, checking the rearview mirror.

"Yes, Dad," they say in bored unison.

Eddie's eyes are still as blue as his father's. He is mostly bald on top now even though he is not yet fifty. I marvel often that my youngest child is in his forties. I creak a bit, but I do not feel ancient enough for him to be that old.

He concentrates on his driving and I let my mind wander through the soaring redwoods into the past. Sheila married, had a daughter, and divorced. She lives in the mountains, still in Santa Cruz but halfway to Los Gatos. She was a P.E. teacher, as she dreamed, for many years. Now she house sits and does errands. She's even been offered a sailboat ride around the world from some Santa Cruz hippie.

Rosemary and Chic married after the war and had two sons, nearly grown now. I rarely see any of them, busy as they are with the walnut ranch in Woodland.

Eddie married a sorority girl he met at San Jose State College. He's an elementary school teacher now, and I spend every Thanksgiving with them.

"Linda's a Girl Scout now, Mom," Eddie says, to break the silence. "And Scott plays Little League."

"Dad, I quit Scouts last year," Linda says. I can hear the roll of her eyes in her voice.

"Have you hit any home runs lately?" I ask the boy.

"Not baseball season."

Eddie gives me a pained look. "Sorry, Mom, they were excited for the ride over the hill from San Jose."

"They probably equate Santa Cruz with the beach, not a retirement home."

He rubs his neck like his father used to do. Eddie went bald early and resembles his father even more.

"Both hands on the wheel," I say automatically, then laugh.

He laughs, too.

Quiet reigns as we ride over Highway 17 to the Santa Clara Valley. I remember making this journey by train when we came from Castro Valley to visit Grandma Van. The locomotive huffed and puffed crossing the Santa Cruz Mountains which locals refer to as 'the hill.' When we cross Summit Road, I look off through the redwoods as if I can see the Williams Reservoir, named for my grandfather. I don't remember if I ever told Eddie how my Grandfather Williams developed the reservoir system for the San Jose Water Works. He's concentrating on the twists and turns of the mountain road, so I hold my tongue.

Forty-five minutes later, we pull up to Eddie's house in

Saratoga. It's a pricey neighborhood, the house financed by my father's legacy to his grandchildren after his death in 1950. Mama predeceased him by seven years. Teddy's parents died in Scotland without ever visiting. With Teddy's death I am the family matriarch. Every time I realize this, it's a shock.

"Mom, are you all right?" Eddie has sensed my pensive mood.

"It's just Thanksgiving," I tell him, but there's so much more than the word, the holiday.

"Thinking about Dad?" His tone sympathizes.

Actually, seeing my granddaughter makes me think of the women in my family. "Thinking more about my Grandma Van, and about Aunt Emily."

"Oh?"

"Do you remember the stories of Grandma Van? How she came west, and how she sued for the vote?"

"Yes, Mom, I do. Your grandmother died two years before I was born, but I know her through your stories. I do remember visiting Aunt Emily at Wake Robin. It was a great place for a boy."

I smile at him, recalling how he used to explore the forest around Emily and Lillian's cottage. His memories are different than mine, of course. If asked, he will tell of creatures hiding under logs, and oddly shaped rocks, and the possum skull he found and prized for years. Ask me, and I will tell of the strength of women who lived their lives as they chose. I cannot explain, even to a well-intentioned son, what these women mean to me.

Silence falls once more, except for the car radio and its ceaseless impersonal noise. I think the children have fallen asleep in the back seat, or maybe Linda reads. I hope the motion of the car doesn't give her motion sickness.

Once we get to the house, Gerry comes out to greet us with smiles and kind words, but her eyes are grim. Scott disappears into his room and Linda opens her book.

"What are you reading, dear?" I ask her.

She looks up as if surprised to be addressed. *"The Password to Larkspur Lane.* It's a Nancy Drew book."

I know about Nancy Drew. Both Sheila and Rosemary read them when they were girls. In the book, Nancy and her father are very close, but the book has no strong female role models other than Nancy herself. Maybe Linda will learn to be resilient. "Larkspur is a beautiful plant, but quite poisonous. Did you know that?" She shrugs. "Do you try to figure out the mystery as you read?"

"Of course. That's what makes it interesting." Now she smiles.

I smile at her. "You need a keen mind to figure out a mystery. You come from a family of women with keen minds. Has your father told you about Grandma Van?"

I see a flicker of interest in her eyes, but her mother intervenes. "Linda, put that book away and go set the table. Ed, can you get that turkey out of the oven?"

She bustles about and has no time for family discussions. I sigh. Talking with Linda will have to wait for another day. I sit and play the visiting grandmother, a role that chafes. I smile and nod when I would rather discuss Grandma Van's politics or Aunt Emily's career, or even my role as wife and mother. Instead I discuss how arthritis prevents me from gardening. I want to talk about the oil paintings Teddy created after he retired, and how he sold them at sidewalk artist's fairs, but all they can talk about is my health.

I want to tell them about Teddy's chess games that he played by mail. He sometimes had a dozen games going at once. He had an uncanny ability to discern the personality of an opponent from the messages they sent with their moves. He played with a prisoner outside Boston, and with a man in South Africa who wrote of the political struggles there. I find it all interesting, but it's not Nancy Drew or Little League baseball.

Gerry cooks better than I do. The turkey smells amazing and is almost moist. The gravy and mashed potatoes only have a few lumps, and the stuffing is delicious. She tells me she uses her mother's recipe in a tone you take with a child or a simple minded idiot, and I know it's because I compliment her stuffing every year. Does she think I forget?

Eddie is immersed in his family and his life, as he should be. He never asked about the trip Teddy and I took to Australia shortly after retirement. We went to open a new chapter of the

Rosicrucian Order, and it was a grand adventure. Eddie also never asks about my photographs, or my grief over the sale of our home in Soquel where Teddy's roses were so well loved. Living in a retirement hotel ages a person faster than the years do, but I don't expect anyone in this room to understand that. Teddy did.

The disconnect between what lives in my head and the conversation at the table makes me want to scream. I love these people, but I can only take so much. When we've swallowed the last bite of pumpkin pie, I begin to take my leave. Eddie looks uncomfortable because Gerry wears a storm on her face. Truly they want me to stay? It can't be any easier for them than it is for me to think of superficial conversational topics. Aren't they afraid that if I stay they will be required to think and respond in a real conversation about real issues?

Scott disappears into his room after dinner, and Linda goes outside. As I wait for Eddie to fetch my coat and purse, I walk to the picture window that faces the back yard. In one corner of the yard I see a sandbox, slide, and swing set that my grandchildren have outgrown. Opposite that a darling playhouse sits similarly abandoned. In the corner, one almond tree catapults me into memories of my childhood and of my home in Vacaville. Eddie has built a platform in the tree, and Linda lies there on her stomach, reading her Nancy Drew book. I remember lying in the same position to read in my father's almond orchard. Past and present fuse in my head.

My mother guided my daily life, teaching me not to touch a hot stove and not to cry over every scraped knee, but my character was molded by my aunt and grandmother. They lived lives I could admire and emulate. I grew up knowing I could enter politics like Grandma Van or work at any career I desired like Aunt Emily. I chose a husband and family as my mother did, but I was independent enough to use a career to enable my daughters to follow their dreams.

And that's the crux of it all. Children must be allowed to have dreams, and family must support them in following those dreams. Children need parents for daily guidance and other family for keeping dreams alive. Carl never had any children, so I was never an aunt, but I am a grandmother five times over.

Placing my fingertips lightly on Eddie's picture window, I seek to connect with my youngest granddaughter. "Keep hold of your dreams. Never let life deter you," I whisper to the girl in the almond tree.

The forty-five minute ride home through the gathering dusk is a time to be alone with my son. "Thank you, dear, for a lovely holiday," I tell him.

"Gerry did all the work."

"Oh, I know, and I told her the meal was wonderful. But I appreciate you coming to get me. I can't get around like I used to."

"I'm happy to do it, Mom."

The headlights of the other cars on Highway 17 make

flashing stripes inside Dodge Dart Swinger. We sit encased in a warm cocoon. "Your father would be proud of you, Eddie."

He flashes a surprised glance at me. "He would? I mean, proud of what at this moment? I know Papa loved me."

"Oh, I'm just getting melancholy, I suppose." But I smile widely.

"You don't look melancholy," he teases.

I chuckle. "Your children are smart. They have wonderful futures, don't they?"

He shakes his head. "Sometimes they are alive with promise, and other times they are caught up in the moment. Right now Scott is all about baseball, but he's too slow to make a career of it. He has to hit a home run just to make it to first base."

We laugh together. "And Linda?" I ask.

He looks at me longer than he probably should as we speed along this winding road. "She's a dreamer, Mom. Sound familiar?"

"Yes, it does. Dreamers run in the family, don't they?"

We are silent for a moment, the sound of the softly playing music on the radio filling the dark.

"Dreamers aren't a bad thing," I tell him. "The women in our family have done very well with their dreams. You give her strength, and I will help her dream."

He nods. "Gerry and I can do that."

The big meal takes its toll, and I drowse contentedly until we arrive at the Casa Del Rey. Eddie helps me up to my room and leaves me with a kiss on my cheek.

The nap in the car has left me too awake to sleep. Turning on the light at my correspondence desk, I pull out a fresh piece of stationery and uncap a pen.

Dear Linda,

I very much enjoyed sharing Thanksgiving with you again this year. When I was about your age, I wrote letters to my grandmother. She, too, lived in Santa Cruz, although at the time I lived in Inverness. I thought you might like to begin the tradition with me. Has your father told you any of the stories about my Grandmother VanValkenburgh?

I look up from the letter and stare into my memories, searching for a place to start.

Her first act of rebellion was to insist on marrying her cousin, Jacob Perkins.

Author's Note & Acknowledgements

I would like to thank my Auntie Sheila for getting me interested in the family history. Also, thanks to all my writer friends at TheNextBigWriter.com who convinced me this was a story worth telling and encouraged me to tell it well.

By the time I knew my grandmother, Eva Walters, she was an older relative who came for Thanksgiving with my Auntie Sheila. I was too young to appreciate stories of her life. At the end of my novel, I created the scene where Eva begins to pass on the rich legacy of her family's strong women to her granddaughter. I only wish she'd lived long enough to provide real details to fill the holes I had to fictionalize!

My goal in writing this novelized account of my grandmother, her aunt and her grandmother is to set my ancestors and family members against the greater events of the world at large. Some of these events they directly influenced and some influenced them. I have tried to remain true to their life events well as to the times.

About the Author

Linda (Walters) Ulleseit was born and raised in Saratoga, California and has taught elementary school in San Jose since 1996. When not writing, she enjoys cooking, genealogy, reading, and spending time with her family, which includes two young yellow Labradors. Her favorite subject is writing, and her students get a lot of practice scribbling stories and essays. Someday Linda hopes to see books written by former students alongside hers on Amazon bestseller lists!

Follow Flying Horse Books on Facebook!

http://ulleseit.wordpress.com

Also by Linda Ulleseit:

Wings Over Tremeirchson (a flying horse novella)

On a Wing and a Dare

In the Winds of Danger

Under a Wild and Darkening Sky

Made in the USA
Middletown, DE
20 May 2017